THE COMMUTER

Emma Curtis was born in Brighton and now lives in London with her husband. After raising two children and working various jobs, her fascination with the darker side of domestic life inspired her to start writing psychological suspense thrillers. She has published six previous novels: *One Little Mistake*, *When I Find You*, *The Night You Left*, *Keep Her Quiet*, *Invite Me In* and *The Babysitter*.

Also by Emma Curtis

One Little Mistake
When I Find You
The Night You Left
Keep Her Quiet
Invite Me In
The Babysitter

THE
COMMUTER

EMMA CURTIS

CORVUS

Published in paperback in Great Britain in 2024 by Corvus,
an imprint of Atlantic Books Ltd.

1 3 5 7 9 10 8 6 4 2

A CIP catalogue record for this book is
available from the British Library.

Paperback ISBN: 978 1 83895 975 3
E-book ISBN: 978 1 83895 977 7

Printed and bound by CPI Group (UK) Ltd, Croydon CR0 4YY

Corvus
An imprint of Atlantic Books Ltd
Ormond House
26–27 Boswell Street
London
WC1N 3JZ

www.atlantic-books.co.uk

Prologue

My windscreen wipers are on their fastest setting. I grip the steering wheel as if my life depends on it, straining forward, squinting through the rain. Lauren was right. I should not be driving. There's enough sense left that I'm aware my actions are unsound, but the thoughts drop in, cutting through the brain fog, urging me on.

I need to get home.

I need to stop all this before it goes too far.

You wouldn't have hurt Anthony, would you? You are gentle and thoughtful, funny and wise, and you've been through so much. Why would you attack my husband? Did he insult you, treat you with contempt?

Headlights flare out of the darkness, and I shield my eyes with my arm as a car swoops by. I swerve, skidding on the wet road, wresting back control of the car. I mustn't draw attention to myself. I shouldn't be doing this. I wouldn't be if it wasn't an emergency.

I need to get home. That is non-negotiable. I can't call the police until I know what's happened, because I sent you. I held Anthony to his promise. When I left the house, I thought, *You owe me now, Anthony*. I was so angry and confused.

What was I thinking? I should have found some way

of getting a message to you, even if it meant pinning a note to my front door.

Was Anthony hostile from the moment you stepped over the threshold?

The windscreen blurs, flashes of light distorted by rain. Focus.

Surely I should be at the motorway by now. The slick of water on the road ahead makes it move and shimmer like the sequins on Hazel's dress. I think I may have taken a wrong turn, but it's hard to know when it's pitch dark and belting down, when occasionally my vision blurs. There's a sign to East Horsley. I have a horrible feeling that's the wrong way. Or is it? I saw it on Google Maps earlier when I was working out my route. It's to the west, I think. I should have switched the sat nav to home before I left, but with Hazel and Lauren banging on my windscreen, shrieking at me to stop, I was in a blind panic and pumped with adrenaline.

I pull over and clumsily stab at the screen, then try my home number again, but the landline rings out and Anthony's phone goes straight to voicemail. I don't know if I want you to be there when I arrive, or if I want you to have fled, but please let Anthony be safe.

Why doesn't he answer?

I wish we'd never said goodbye. I wish it was Monday morning and we were together, back in our bubble. If I had the time again, I would get off the train with you, follow you anywhere. We could have been together. Whatever has happened tonight would not have happened.

I check the wing mirror as studiously as if I was about to join a race track, then veer onto the road, water sluicing in my path from a swelling ditch, windscreen wipers whumping. Occasional lights from oncoming cars splinter through the raindrops on my windscreen. I hate driving in the countryside. I feel safer on urban roads with their clear landmarks and frequent signage. In places like this, even though Surrey is hardly the depths of the country, one tree looks very much like another. I wish I hadn't come. I hated that party and really didn't like Hazel's friends. Zandra was horrible.

Focus, Rachel.

I need to get back on the right road, find the M25 and cross it. I take my speed up to sixty, concentrating hard. This is wrong; I know it is, but I can do it. I can save you and Anthony from the consequences of whatever's happened.

Or is it myself I want to save?

I think of you kissing me and walking away. Unless you're a consummate liar, you didn't have bad intentions. Whatever's happened isn't your fault. It's more likely to be mine.

As a car speeds towards me, a flash of lightning clarifies the landscape with a suddenness that takes me by surprise, and I'm momentarily blinded. My reflexes have been decimated by Zandra's lethal cocktails, and I put my foot down instead of taking it off. The car takes on a life of its own. It won't stop and I don't understand why, and a tree seems to surge towards me. I slam my foot down, crashing at an angle and pitching, my head ricocheting off the side window even as the airbag inflates. Oh . . .

The whiteness could be footage of a nuclear bomb going off, leaching the black out of the night and blinding me. The sudden silence is deafening. It expands, stretching my world like a balloon. I expect screams, the crunch of metal, cries for help and prayers, but nothing fills the void.

TEN WEEKS EARLIER

March 2023

Chapter 1

RACHEL

'Thank you so much for being here, my friends,' my husband says as he steps onto the temporary staging set up in the orangery of one of the most exclusive members' clubs in the world. He's a handsome man, a silver fox. Watching people mesmerised by him, people who very likely know all about his recent problems and admire him regardless, I have a lump in my throat.

'I am immensely grateful to you for lending your support to the men and women who have come through the Begin Again programme. We are extremely proud of our clients and those who work tirelessly to help them attain their dreams. Our success rate in changing the lives of ex-offenders is high, at eighty-nine per cent. But it isn't about numbers, it's about the men and women who are sent to us, their extended families, their community and their dignity as human beings. Above all it is about hope. As Ted told us just now, without hope he would never have achieved all he has, because hope made him aspire to be a better man. And that hope came from the Begin Again programme, and ultimately from you, the individuals and corporations who give so generously of their time and money.'

He goes on to explain how Stir, the company catering the evening, was set up by the charity to provide training and jobs for ex-offenders, and after summoning the staff onto the stage, he raises a hearty cheer. I get to my feet, clapping madly, and others follow my lead. Anthony nods at me, then smiles broadly. My grin in response stretches from ear to ear. What he does for these men and women is remarkable.

'Those are the lucky ones,' he says, after the staff have filed back into the kitchen. 'When I was a child . . .'

I've heard this speech a dozen times over the past week and even helped write some of it. Anthony's talking about his brother. Such a terrible tragedy. It happened many years before we met.

'. . . By the time he was fifteen, he had been to young offender institutions twice. He had no support and no hope. Society had washed its hands of him. He ended up in prison, where he took his own life. My childhood memories of Harry are of a funny, cheeky and optimistic boy. He became a gaunt, drug-addicted criminal.'

It's almost impossible to imagine Anthony coming from a background like that. He's silky smooth with steel beneath the surface, well-spoken, erudite. Self-made. I would have added mischievous, but sadly the mischief has ebbed away. To me that's more of a tragedy than his brother's untimely death. He is sparkling this evening, but in reality he's lost much of his potency since the heart attack that almost killed him last September. In the new year, his board of directors, who had clearly been plotting over Christmas, attempted to oust him. And to cap it all, his investment in cryptocurrency is currently valued at one third what he paid for it. The loss has had a damaging effect on his pride and the result is that he isn't always kind, and it's me who bears the brunt of that. It's upsetting, but I meant it when I took my vows. Whether or not he pulls himself out of this difficult patch, I'm here for him just as he was for me when I needed his strength.

The possibility that he knows I feel pity for him has been consuming me lately, although he hasn't said anything. It would account for the uptick in criticism levelled at me in recent months, and the outbursts of anger. At sixty-three and thirty-eight, the difference in our ages has never felt starker.

I find myself wondering if anyone else here has noticed that the lines on his face have deepened, especially the ones between his eyebrows; those quizzically arched eyebrows I fell in love with the first time we met.

'. . . As an adult, I realised that a perfect storm of circumstances and a dearth of aspiration, expectation and trust were the determining factors in my brother's short and brutal life. His fate might so easily have been mine, but I was able to learn from his mistakes.'

I dart a quick glance at my stepdaughter. Caroline has been scathing about this fundraiser, dismissing the guests as a bunch of fat cats and trophy wives. Nonetheless, she worked hard helping to put the event together, and it all looks so glamorous and beautiful. She rolled her eyes when I tried to congratulate her. Even thirteen years later, it's almost impossible for me to say the right thing in the right tone of voice. Ironically, despite never forgiving me for stealing her father from her mother, she's happy to live under the same roof as me for zero rent or contributions.

At twenty-six, she is, as the Americans would say, a piece of work. She knows very little about her father's troubles. He's adamant that's the way he wants it.

'. . . With your help,' Anthony is wrapping it up, 'Begin Again can create many more outcomes like those you've heard about tonight. There are some fantastic auction items, generously donated, so let's see those hands go up. Without further ado, I'd like to introduce Jimmy Lloyd, your auctioneer for this evening.'

I tip my wine glass to my lips to hide an involuntary sigh of relief. The speech has gone down well. At my shoulder, a waiter stretches to take away my dessert plate. He's young and good-looking, with black curly hair tied back, and long lashes shadowing dark brown eyes. I murmur an apology, because I haven't touched my semifreddo al cioccolato. I'm well above my calorie limit. The wine's seen to that. There's a top note of tension just below my ribcage.

I push that thought out of my head. Instead, I think about the fact that the waiter has done time, that he may have noticed the jewellery the guests are wearing, the designer handbags carelessly left where they can be rifled, and the wallets in the pockets of jackets taken off and slung over the backs of chairs. But as Anthony says, there needs to be trust, because without it the entire project fails. As the waiter moves to the next setting, I look up at him. He's extremely good-looking, fine-featured, with the cheekbones of a catwalk model. I can't help wondering what he did to land himself in this situation. Drugs? He's so young.

'Thank you.' I read his name badge. 'Kam.'

'You're welcome,' he replies.

There is something in his eyes I don't quite like. Scorn.

I turn my attention to the stage, burst out laughing at something Lloyd says and forget all about the waiter.

Chapter 2

I stand as Anthony reaches our table, but Caroline gets there first.

'Wow, Daddy. You had everyone eating out of the palm of your hand.'

He hugs her. 'It was all right, wasn't it?'

'More than all right.'

'You were amazing, darling,' I say, reaching to kiss him. His arm remains around Caroline's waist.

'I couldn't have done it without this one. What a daughter. I'm a very lucky man.'

Caroline is a resting actor for what seems like seventy per cent of any given year. Begin Again paid her to organise the event. She didn't do it out of the kindness of her heart. I mustn't be mean-spirited, though. I muster a smile.

'Getting Jimmy Lloyd was a real coup. How did you manage it?'

Caroline follows my gaze to the stage, where Lloyd, a comedian well used to the cut and thrust of prime-time television, already has his audience weeping with laughter.

'Oh, I've bumped into him once or twice. I must have made an impression, because he literally bit my hand off to do this gig.'

'Well, good on you.' I run out of things to say and take my seat.

Our friends Naz and Jennifer are deluging Anthony with whispered praise. He's enjoying the attention, but there's a sheen of sweat on his forehead that concerns me. He mustn't overdo it. I check my watch. One more hour.

Anthony flops back in the cab with a sigh. As we drive through the extensive grounds, I wait for judgement. I think I did all right; I laughed and smiled and sparkled, and I didn't show him up. As far as I know.

'I can't wait to find out how much you've raised,' I say.

He sighs. 'IFR will ditch the charity the moment I go.' International Financial Recruitment is the company Anthony set up twenty-eight years ago. It's made him a wealthy man and a mover and shaker in the city and across the world.

'What do you mean?'

'Exactly what I said. If they'd managed to turf me out in January, they were going to review the various charities the company's foundation supports and redistribute the funds. On top of what we raise from this event each year, Begin Again currently benefits from the interest on seven million, of which twenty per cent is earmarked for Stir, but the arrangement has to be renewed every three years. They could support several smaller charities with the same money.'

'I'm sorry.'

Anthony smiles. 'It's another incentive for me to stay on.'

'You can't work for ever. Your health—'

'My health is fine. Don't fuss. Did you enjoy yourself?'

'I had a wonderful time.'

'You weren't bored?'

'No. Why would I be?'

'Tim can be a bore. But you did well tonight. I was proud of you.'

I reach over the space between us and hold his hand.

The following morning, Anthony takes a call in his study. When he comes back, he looks thunderous.

'There were thefts last night,' he says. 'Credit cards and cash mainly. You'd better check your bag.'

It's on the kitchen dresser, a small diamanté clutch that holds my phone, debit card, lipstick and powder compact.

'Nothing's been taken.' I clip the bag shut.

'After all I've done for them.'

'One bad apple, in all these years. It doesn't matter, Anthony.'

'For Christ's sake, Rachel,' he snaps. 'Don't be so stupid. Of course it matters.'

My stomach flips. 'I'm sorry. I didn't mean to down-play it.'

'Just think before you speak.' He cups my face with his hands. 'Try, my darling.'

I nod and he lets me go. The old Anthony would never have spoken to me like that.

'Do they know who it was?' I remember the waiter, and the dirty look he gave me, but dismiss the idea. You can't point the finger at someone simply because you don't like the way they look at you.

'Not yet, but Robert will find out.' He grimaces. 'It's not so much the act itself, it's the sheer stupidity. We've given

these people a chance. Whoever it is has blown theirs.'
He sighs. 'Never mind. These things happen. We move
on.'

Chapter 3

A couple of weeks later, Anthony and I pour out of the theatre with the chattering crowd. We've been to see *The Lehman Trilogy* and are feeling emotionally wrenched. I was twenty-three when the financial crash of 2008 happened, fresh to the city and already redundant. It took me a year to land my next job. I'll never forget that time; never take anything I have for granted. My ability to be financially independent if there's a disaster is vital to me. That's why I work full-time when I don't need to. That and not having children. Anthony was forty-eight at the time, his reputation as a canny operator well established. He had men and women literally begging him to put them forward for anything, however humble. It shook him and changed his business for ever; made him more empathetic, less inclined to see the people he needed to place as units of currency.

We let ourselves in quietly. Voices drift from behind the closed door of the kitchen, where Caroline is entertaining a friend. A male one. It feels wrong to be sneaking around in our own house, but we agreed to be as silent as mice because she doesn't want her guest being reminded that she lives at home at the age of twenty-six, even though it's hardly unusual these days. The house smells of steak and chips. We head straight up to bed, where Anthony falls asleep almost immediately. I lie awake, still thinking. I am loved, and it isn't many years since I believed I didn't deserve to be, and that is down to Anthony.

It has been a lovely evening, apart from one incident. We had supper before the performance, and the waiter referred to Anthony as my father. I've overheard plenty of sneering remarks over the years, including 'child bride', 'young enough to be his daughter', 'meal ticket', 'gold-digger' and the classic 'She must have been looking for a father figure.' Everyone's a psychiatrist these days. I have to be honest, though: that last one has a grain of truth to it.

I've been accused of having abandonment issues, and I suppose that's accurate. My mother treated me as an irritation; my father ignored what was going on, in his benign way. Anything for a quiet life. Mum told me she loved me if there were witnesses. It was a long time before I noticed that, but when I did, it really stung. I don't know whether my father actively noticed, because I don't know when the withdrawal began. They are still together, but while I was a child and a teenager he left and came back three times. I liked to imagine that he returned because of me, but it was more likely because Mum was the one with the money. We lived in Surrey back then, in a spacious house. I remember Dad moving into one girlfriend's poky bedsit on the Clapham Road.

The way we three lived together – my father terrified of setting my mother off, my mother despising him and indifferent to me, apart from when I attracted male approval, at which point she flipped – was one of the reasons I so easily acquiesced when Anthony said he didn't want more

17

children. What if I couldn't bond with my child because of the way I'd been treated? You read about that kind of thing all the time. The abused going on to abuse.

I first realised my mother actively hated me when I was seventeen.

Mum didn't have female friends; she surrounded herself with men, tolerating their wives as a necessary evil. The third time Dad left, the morning after I'd sat my final A-level exam, she threw herself into dating. There was one particular man, about ten years younger than her, who was round a lot. His name was Keith.

One weekend she threw a garden party, inviting her friends and their despised wives, and Keith, who wasn't married. He was an artist, had fine features, long hair, buckets of charm and not much money. I'm not even sure where she met him; he just appeared. Anyway, over the course of that sunny afternoon, I talked to him quite a bit. I'd been working in a busy West End pub earning money for university and bantering with the punters had boosted my confidence and honed my social skills. Keith was flirting with me, and I was flattered and flirted back. At the end, when the final guests had rolled out of the garden, I started picking up glasses and cigarette stubs, but Mum called me inside. She shut the doors, presumably so the neighbours wouldn't hear, and went ballistic, calling me an attention-seeking little slut and hitting me so hard when I didn't react the way she wanted me to that I fell over and fractured my wrist.

Mum is a narcissist. It took me a long time to realise that, but once I had, it made so much sense. The love-bombing, the sulking, the withdrawal. The punishments, and God, the attention-seeking, the non-stop talking, the lack of interest in anything I might have to say. My words would dry up along with the achievements I worked so hard for, because what is the point if the people who are meant to love you most don't give a shit?

So yes, Anthony has been everything to me, including father. That's why I won't let the barbs get to me: because he doesn't really mean it. He's just scared of aging.

Something has woken me. I force my eyes open. Anthony is quietly snoring. I push back the covers, set my feet down on the floor, where they sink into the carpet. For ten seconds or so there is absolute silence, then what sounds like a muffled sob. My oyster silk dressing gown is draped over the chaise longue in the corner of the bedroom. I scoop it up, grope my way to the door and step out onto the landing. The glow from downstairs throws the slanted shadow of the banisters across the walls.

Raised voices send me scuttling back to pull the door to. Anthony used to sleep heavily, but the beta blockers have changed that. Now he suffers from bouts of insomnia. He would not appreciate being woken. Caroline should know better.

Caroline is losing it. Whoever's with her is making calming noises while her voice rises. I slide my arms into the dressing gown and tie the sash. I hope I don't need to interfere. I can predict the look of derision Caroline will give me if I appear in my nightclothes and ask her to keep it down.

There's a crash as something breaks. Glass, I think, gritting my teeth. The man shouts and I start downstairs, sinking into the shadows when he appears in the hall. Caroline darts out of the kitchen, screaming at him.

'How dare you! What is wrong with you?'

'You're the one with the screw loose. You fucking stabbed me.' His voice is muffled, like he has a bad cold, and he's clutching a wad of kitchen towels against his arm.

'Baby, I'm sorry. I'm sorry. Let me see.' In an instant she has gone from hissing and spitting wildcat to kitten.

'Get off me.'

'Please don't go like this. Let's talk about it. Please.'

I'm horrified, but fascinated too. How low will Caroline sink? I edge forward, peeking over the banister as she grapples with her companion. She never could bear to be thwarted. He pushes her, and she stumbles backwards with a sound that's somewhere between a mewl and a sob.

'Hey. Leave her alone.'

'Go back to bed, Rachel,' Caroline hisses. 'This has nothing to do with you.'

The man spins on his heel and lets himself out. Caroline slumps against the wall, quietly sobbing. When she doesn't pick herself up, I pad downstairs and check her over. She doesn't appear to have been hurt.

She shifts and pulls her knees up to her chest, glaring at me. She's wearing a sleeveless top sewn with gold sequins that overlap like fish scales and shimmer in the light from the kitchen. 'Why can't you mind your own business?'

'I only wanted to check you were okay.'

'Well I am.' Her eyes are teary and red-rimmed, her mouth petulant. She looks all of fifteen, doe-eyed and vulnerable. That's the trouble. She is able to play on soft hearts. Even mine.

'Who was he?'

'No one you'd know.'

I sigh. 'Okay. Fine. Try not to wake your father when you come up.'

I take myself back to bed. I've done my duty. Caroline is alive and well and can put the kitchen to rights herself.

Chapter 4

Waking the next morning, I feel across our super-king-size bed for Anthony, but he's already up. The room is dim, and beyond the closed curtains rain patters against the window pane. I allow myself a moment to wallow while the threads of my dreams dissipate. And then I remember what happened last night.

I sit up abruptly and swing my legs out of bed, reach for the gown I discarded in a pool on the carpet and run downstairs. Anthony is in the kitchen, sweeping the floor in his paisley dressing gown, his feet in garden clogs. It's an incongruous sight. His calves are splayed with blue varicose veins like an aerial picture of a river delta.

There were three rooms I wasn't allowed to touch when I moved here: Anthony's office, Caroline's bedroom and the kitchen. Anthony's ex-wife, Mia, designed the kitchen. To be honest, I wouldn't have ripped it out even if Anthony had given permission. It is effortlessly beautiful, with its clotted-cream cabinets, vast brushed-steel range, butler sink and York stone floor.

'Put something on your feet before you come in,' he says, seeing me standing there. 'There's broken glass.'

I lean in. 'I think my slippers are under the sofa.'

Anthony chucks them over. I slide my feet into them and pick my way across the floor.

'Why are you clearing up Caroline's mess? She should do it herself.'

'I told her to go back to bed. It'll only take me a minute. I'd rather she slept it off. I gather the evening got a little out of hand.' He sweeps the shards into a dustpan, tips them into an open newspaper, parcels them up and stuffs it all into the bin.

'You do know she attacked some poor guy last night?'

'You saw it happen?' Anthony's mouth has tightened. I know that look. Caroline is his little princess and thus beyond criticism.

'I didn't actually see her attack him,' I admit. 'I woke up when the row was in full swing.'

'There's no blood, so she can only have nicked him. She says it was an accident.'

'She was accusing him of something, Anthony. She lost her temper.'

He harrumphs. 'Do we know who the man was?'

'No idea. I didn't see his face. You need to talk to her. She can't go on like this, she's abusing our hospitality.'

'She isn't abusing our hospitality, she lives here. This is her home.'

I experience a wave of tiredness. I was awake for over two hours last night, thanks to Caroline's antics, and I don't have the patience for Anthony's blinkered pandering. 'No it isn't. It's *our* home. She's an adult. Can't you see that persuading her to leave would be the kindest thing you could do for her?'

You'd think Caroline was the only child to witness her parents' divorce, the only child asked to tolerate, if not to love, her father's new partner. With maturity comes

23

understanding. The trouble is, Caroline shows no sign of reaching that heady state. Early on in my marriage I was optimistic. I would sit it out. She didn't need a new mother but I would do my best to be a companion and mentor. Caroline would go to university, get a job, move in with friends or a partner and grow up. It was doomed to failure from the start. I was far too young to be put in that position, too wrapped up in Anthony, too selfish. Anthony should have known better, but that doesn't let Caroline off the hook. She's still entitled, spoiled and malicious.

'I told you when we got together that Caroline would always come first,' he says.

Anthony sees supporting Caroline's acting career by making it unnecessary for her to find a proper job as simply paying his dues.

'Yes, you did. But she's no longer your little girl. She's too old to let a date get out of hand. She could have done serious damage.'

'According to you, he walked away, so don't exaggerate.'

I'm so exasperated that the words explode from me. 'Your daughter doesn't understand how the world works. She doesn't care who she hurts or what she breaks. She goes too far and expects you to forgive her every single time. The trouble with Caroline is she cannot understand her own failure, or learn from it. She is never going to succeed in acting. She is mediocre at best. She needs to get a grip, get a job and get out of here. And away from you. For God's sake, Anthony, not only did you spoil her as a child, you risk ruining her as an adult. You need to stop funding her delusions. If you don't, then you're as deluded as she is.'

And suddenly it's there, so entirely unexpected that I don't have time to react. His arm pulls back, and as I recoil, the palm of his hand catches my jaw. I stagger, my hip colliding with the table. I grab the back of a chair and bring it down with me.

Anthony yells, his voice cracking over me like a whip. 'You will respect me. Do you understand?'

I've never seen him like this. The force of his fury is terrifying. I push away the chair and get up off the floor, trembling violently but determined not to cry.

We stand and stare at each other, and after a minute or two he coughs and mumbles something. At that moment, Caroline walks in. She's dressed in a pair of ripped jeans and a T-shirt with a hole where the seam is coming apart at the shoulder, raven hair bunched up. Caroline makes scruffy look enticing.

'Bit of an atmosphere in here,' she says, going to the sink and rinsing out a cloth. 'Have I interrupted something?'

She starts to wipe the surfaces. Anthony looks at me beseechingly, but I ignore him. He can explain himself to his daughter.

'We were discussing last night,' he says.

'I am so sorry, Daddy.' Caroline glances at me from beneath her lashes. I look away.

'You don't need to apologise,' Anthony says. 'Did he hurt you?'

'No. He just wound me up. He ... um ... we aren't exclusive, and I didn't know that. He's been hooking up with women he meets online. He said it didn't matter, but it does.'

Anthony heaves a sigh. 'Christ. Your bloody generation.'

I leave them and go upstairs to shut myself in the bathroom, rinse a flannel in cold water and press it against my cheek. Did Caroline notice the red welt? I sit on the side of the bath and wait for the anger and shock to abate. My mother hit me because I wouldn't grovel and apologise, my husband because I made him face himself.

No one's marriage is perfect; you compromise and bargain and cut each other slack, but you do not get physical. The received wisdom is that if a partner hits you, there are no second chances, but as I calm down, I take a mental step back. This is familiar territory after all. I left my parents, walked out into an unknown landscape, so I can do it again. But do I want to? I don't think I do. For one thing, I would be miserable; for another, Caroline would win.

He is my husband and I will deal with this. I'm not that child cowering in front of her mother like a frightened dog. But if there is a next time, I will leave.

I check my appearance in the mirror, pull the scrunchie out of my hair and brush it so that it falls forward, then go back downstairs and find Anthony on his own. I look straight at him. There is no shame in his eyes. Anthony doesn't do shame or guilt. It took me a long time to realise that. It isn't something he even thinks about; it just is.

Caroline has a cupboard in the kitchen in which she keeps her snacks, and later, when she's out meeting a friend and Anthony has gone to the gym, I steal chocolate chip cookies and Lion bars, crisps and marshmallows, and wolf them down, in my head the sight of myself in the mirror as a child, pudgy and pasty.

I'm so sorry about my daughter. She's greedy.

When I can't eat any more, my teeth aching from the sweetness, I go upstairs to lie down. I will not throw up. I will not start that again. It's been years since the last time. I smooth my hand over the tight mound of my belly, then moan and run into the bathroom, sinking to my knees by the loo, retching, eyes weeping, fingers probing, until it's all gone.

By Monday, we're pretending nothing happened. It's caused a weird kind of separation, like a chemical reaction, his swiftly raised hand flicking me out of the well-worn groove of my life. Amongst all the other emotions swirling around me, weirdly, I feel embarrassed for both of us.

The beautiful morning doesn't suit my mood. I'd rather have unbroken grey and drizzle, but the air is fresh and cool, the sun already warming the approach to the station. The manager of the deli unfolds his chalkboard, kneeling to make an adjustment with a stub of yellow chalk. I usually like the brisk tapping sound it makes – like Morse code – but now it scratches at my nerves. The florist brings out buckets of white roses tinged with green, bluish-pink hydrangeas, fragrant stocks and branches of pussy willow. She wishes me a good morning, and I nod and attempt a cheery smile even though I feel sad. Anthony has often bought me flowers here.

I've left Anthony at home, working in his study. He cut down his days in the office after the pandemic, and since his heart attack barely goes in at all. It's one of the reasons I've continued to go in every day. For my sanity.

I step through the entrance to the station, grabbing a copy of the *Metro* from the stack as I pass. The train pulls in, I get on and manoeuvre myself into a gap close to the door. I tend to ignore the pleas to move further down into the carriage, because I don't like feeling trapped, and at least this way I get a blast of air when the doors open.

Yesterday my husband hit me. I glance at the other passengers, half expecting shocked expressions, but no one is looking at me. I'm feeling antsy and crushed as the train slows on its approach to Gunnersbury station – if it's possible to feel both at the same time – like there's a heavy weight on my chest but my limbs are twitching.

And then everything changes, because you walk into my life.

Chapter 5

A dozen people at least squeeze on, contorting themselves to avoid the closing doors, irritated when I refuse to move. You apologise as you edge by, catching my eye briefly. I swiftly take in short brown hair with flecks of grey, brown eyes, clean-shaven jaw. Even in that awkward situation your glance sends a jolt of electricity through my body. It is the most extraordinary moment, and I can't account for it. I realise I'm staring and remove my gaze.

You can't get much further in; there simply isn't the space. It's awkward, so I open my copy of the *Metro*, folding it back on itself, and skim-read the news. Stop after stop, I anticipate you leaving. The crush eases after Hammersmith and then Earls Court, but you stay on.

Midway between South Kensington and Sloane Square, the train stops in the tunnel. I feel my skin begin to crawl as time passes and we don't move. Tension spikes amongst the other passengers. After what seems hours, but is probably only three minutes or so, we hear a crackle before the driver addresses us:

'Good morning, ladies and gentlemen. Apologies for the delay. There's a signal failure at Embankment. We'll be on our way as soon as possible and I'll be keeping you informed at regular intervals.'

The lights go out and flicker back on. I attempt to

regulate my breathing, to keep it silent, so self-conscious about the noise I barely breathe at all.

'You okay?'

It's a casual enquiry, or you've tried to make it so because you can see I'm doing my best not to advertise my suppressed panic.

'I'm fine.'

I return to the newspaper, my eyes glued to the words, but they swim in and out of focus. It's hot. So many bodies. The sweat on my back makes my skin prickle. I envy the people sitting down. None of them look up. It's as if they're frightened of catching the eye of someone who needs their seat more than they do.

Another crackle of static. 'A quick update, ladies and gentlemen. I've been advised that it will be about thirty minutes before we can continue our journey. Once again, I apologise for the delay.'

He actually does sound sorry. This time more people vocalise their displeasure. Down the train there's a shout. Someone has fainted. A woman calls out that she's a nurse, and the wave of anxiety subsides.

I'm only semi-aware of you sliding your phone into your pocket. You tap my shoulder and indicate the floor.

'I'm fine,' I repeat.

You shrug and lower yourself, pulling up the knees of your trousers as you sit, leaning back against the side of a seat. Seconds later, I follow suit. I grip my bag between my thighs and stomach. I feel I should say something, but I can't.

The lights go off again and this time they stay off. Around me phones glimmer in the darkness. I grip my hands together, digging my thumbnails into my flesh. The lights go back on.

'Anything interesting in the paper?'

I look round in surprise. 'Um. The usual. Cost of living, house prices, Ukraine.'

You take it out of my hands. I've folded it open on the Rush Hour Crush page.

'Do you think anyone ever responds to these?' you ask.

'Don't know.'

'I hope they do. They can be quite poetic. Like a haiku.'

'A what?' I stare at the legs in front of me. A woman's legs in suit trousers, with white trainers. I'm trying not to go into meltdown, and you're on about poetry.

'Didn't your English teacher ever get you to make them up?'

'No.' I close my eyes. Maybe if I imagine I'm somewhere else, I'll feel better. I visualise a beach.

'Mine did. He loved them. They're three-line poems with seventeen syllables. Five in the first line, then seven, then five. Think of them as a snapshot of a moment.'

I open my eyes and look round, and you smile. I know what you're doing, and it won't work. My breath is uneven. I know you can hear it.

'My teacher used to get us to make them up on the spot,' you say, ignoring my frosty reception. 'It felt like a game, but it made us think quickly. See the woman standing to my left.'

She's wearing a belted red coat and her fingernails are bright red. She has earbuds in and is watching something on her phone, lips pulled down.

'So this is a haiku,' you say. '*You were wearing red*. Your turn.'

31

'Sorry?'

'It's your go. Make up the next line. Seven syllables. *You were wearing red.* Go on.'

This is really annoying. '*I complimented your hair.*' I repeat it silently, counting.

'*Your smile tripped me up.*' You wrinkle your brow. 'Is smile two syllables or one?'

'One, I think.'

'Do you think they get together?'

'I don't know.'

'What woman could resist compliments from a random bloke on the Tube.'

I turn away. The train feels smaller and hotter. People are fanning themselves. I close my eyes again, try to find that sandy beach, that clear blue sky, but all I see is Anthony's face as his hand flies towards me. I try to make myself smaller. My lungs won't fill.

'Do one on your own.'

Anthony vanishes. 'What?'

'The guy with the green and blue scarf.'

You win. I give you my full attention. 'The whole thing?' I locate him. He has earbuds in too and looks unconcerned as he scrolls through his phone.

'Give it a try.'

I think for a moment, and then smile. '*I was trench-coat girl. You wore a green and blue scarf. You looked cool. Coffee?* Argh. I can't do this.'

'You can. That was superb.'

I bask for a millisecond in your praise, even though you're laughing at me. 'Your turn.'

You grin. '*I thought you would faint.*'

'Is this a haiku or a statement of fact?'

'Haiku. Be quiet. I'm doing you. *I thought you would faint. I wanted to be a hero. And catch you . . .* um . . . *today.*'

'One too many syllables in the second line,' I say.

'Huh. Okay. *I thought you would faint. I wanted to be your prince. And catch you today.*'

'That's not great, to be honest.'

'Picky! *I thought you would faint. I wanted to be your prince. I would have caught you.*'

'This is silly.'

'Fun, though. Now you do me.'

Your voice is comforting, soft with a faint accent. Northern, I think. Not Newcastle or Liverpool. Maybe Manchester. Your shoulder is barely a finger's width from mine. I pinch my lips together, force my mind away from our predicament, onto the task you've set me. Now that I've been given permission to look at you properly, I can see that your brown eyes are beautiful, your lashes unfeasibly long.

'*You were wearing black.*'

'An inspired start.'

'Shh. I'm concentrating. *You appeared out of nowhere. You made me forget.*'

'Forget what?'

That my husband hit me, I almost say. 'You made me forget that we're stuck in a tunnel.'

'Have you done the crossword yet?'

I shake my head.

'We can do it together. It's more fun with someone to bounce suggestions off.'

You take a pencil out of your inside pocket and hand it to me. I twist it round and read the name printed on it.

'Blake Jackson? Is that you?'

'Ah. No. It belongs to a friend's kid. I stole it.'

I laugh. 'Well, I hope he doesn't need it. Okay. One across. Though a learner, Mr Yates is skilled. Seven letters.'

'Masterly. Next?'

Chapter 6

'So what's your story?' you ask.

'What do you mean?'

'Everyone has a story. I don't need your deepest secrets, just something about you. Something you wouldn't mind telling a total stranger because you know you'll never see them again.'

'That's deep. Well, I work—'

'No jobs. Let's skip the dull part. Give me something more interesting.'

Shoulder to shoulder now, thigh to thigh, we've given up trying to keep our bodies from touching because the guy sitting on the floor on the other side of me is man-spreading and I'd rather touch you than him. I can't deny that it's thrilling to feel the warmth of your body through my clothes.

'I'm an only child.'

'Tell me about that.'

A minefield, but there's no reason why I have to tell the unvarnished truth. 'They had expectations that I suspect I disappointed. My parents didn't get on very well, so I was piggy in the middle. You?'

'I'm the second of four children. I have an older brother, a younger sister and a younger brother. I wasn't the oldest, or the youngest, or the only girl, so I always felt like the boring one.'

'You don't seem boring to me.'

'That's because I've deliberately cultivated an air of mystery. I've found it makes up for many deficiencies.'

'So what do you do?'

'I said no jobs. We've only got a few minutes together. Let's not waste them. Tell me something you've never told anyone else.'

I shake my head. 'You have nowhere near earned the right to ask me that.'

You grin, unapologetic. 'You can ask me anything.'

'Apart from what you do for a living.'

'Apart from that.' Your hands are draped over your knees. Bony hands with long fingers. Your shirt is slightly too short in the arm.

'Okay. What's your biggest regret?'

A cloud darkens your face, but then you smile. 'Not meeting you earlier.'

'Bollocks.'

'All right. Since I'm never going to see you again, my biggest regret is not thinking before I reacted, in a volatile situation. It changed my life.'

'I'm sorry.'

You shrug. 'A long time ago.'

I shuffle to get more comfortable on the floor. 'I'll tell you one thing I've not told anyone else. Since I'm never going to see *you* again.' What can I tell you? What do I want you to know? 'I shoplifted as a teenager.'

You burst out laughing. 'What was it?'

I blush. 'It didn't really matter what it was. I did it for the buzz. But usually small items of make-up. And don't laugh. I'm ashamed.'

I stole from under the nose of shop assistants and CCTV because it released something trapped inside me. It was like cutting myself, but without the pain. I don't tell you that, though. There is such a thing as too much information.

You give me a rueful look. 'We've all done things we're not proud of.'

There's something about you. We met half an hour ago and I already feel closer to you than I do to anyone else, even Anthony. It's an illusion, but a strong one. Once I get on with my day, you'll fade, just as I will. But I don't think I'll forget. In fact, I know I won't.

'Ladies and gentlemen.'

'Here we go,' you say.

'We're waiting for the station up ahead to clear, then we'll be on our way. Once again, I apologise for the disruption to your journeys. Thank you for your patience and enjoy the rest of your day.'

'Thank God.' My relief is tinged with disappointment.

At the first jerk, applause fills the length of the train, then everyone goes quiet. People who have struck up conversations with strangers scrutinise their phones as if it never happened. You help me to my feet. I mumble an inadequate thank you, and quickly bury my head in my newspaper. We pull into Sloane Square, then you do up your jacket and I know you're getting off at the next stop.

You heft the strap of your weathered leather bag onto your shoulder and move towards the doors. We arrive at Victoria. I should say something, touch your arm, anything, but the doors open, you step out and raise your hand in salute. I raise mine, and the smile you give me is so warm that it creates a chain reaction, beginning in the pit of my stomach and radiating into my fingers and toes. As the train moves away, I watch you until you disappear into the rush-hour crowd heading for the exit.

Chapter 7

Despite it only being April, London is experiencing a mini heatwave and I'm hot and bothered by the time I get home. I hang my coat in the cupboard and stand at the bottom of the stairs trying to get a feel for the atmosphere. Nine times out of ten I'll sense if Caroline is in. I'm fairly certain she's out.

I find Anthony in the garden, smoking under the blossoming apple tree. He sees me and hides the cigarette behind his back like a small boy. He 'gave up' years ago, but he's always had the odd one. I've never begrudged him the occasional indulgence, but the heart attack was a wake-up call.

'You shouldn't be doing that.' I say it kindly, determined to put what happened behind us. That fleeting contact with the man on the train, that last smile, has improved my mood. Normally I'd tell him about my day. I'd describe being stuck in the tunnel. But I don't want to talk about it. It's precious.

He stubs the cigarette out against the tree's pewter bark and kisses my cheek. I wrinkle my nose at the smell of his breath.

'I apologise for yesterday.' He says it like it's something to be got over, with a dismissive lift of his eyebrows. 'In my defence, I lashed out because you went too far. I'm well aware of Caroline's deficiencies, but to hear such vitriolic criticism from you was a shock. When you insult her, you insult me.'

'So it was my fault?'

'I didn't say that.'

'I think you did.'

'Don't be like that, darling. We've been married a long time; we're in this together. I've apologised, and if you do the same, we can put this behind us and move on.'

He yawns and goes inside, and comes back out with a bottle of zero beer and a bag of nigella seeds. I sit on the wooden bench, unable to move, watching him fill the bird feeder. He's the only one who ever remembers. He fastens the bag, then goes back inside to wash his hands. When he comes out again, he takes a long slug from the condensation-speckled bottle and sighs with satisfaction. I'm riled now. He really doesn't think he's done anything wrong.

This morning I met you.

I blink to get rid of the image of your smile, your brown eyes.

'You hit me, Anthony. It's a little hard to put it behind me, but I'm willing to if you listen to what I say and admit that Caroline has a problem.'

'All right.' He raises his hands. 'I concede that the situation is far from ideal, and that I've failed to be a good father by spoiling her, but what did you expect? She's my only child.'

'That's part of the problem,' I say.

'I don't wish to talk about this any more.'

'It's not going to go away just because you want it to.'

He watches two goldfinches vying for position on the feeder. Mesmerising though they are, it's an excuse not to look at me.

'Anthony?'

'What?' he says impatiently.

'Your daughter attacked someone in our house. He could press charges. He may have forgiven her in the short term, but you can bet he's slept on it. He may well think differently now.'

'Caroline assures me she's smoothed it over. She's apologised and he's admitted he provoked her.'

'To stab him?' I'm incredulous. 'A tongue-lashing from Caroline is usually enough to scare any man off.'

'Don't exaggerate. And from what I understand, he was as much to blame as her.'

'What you understand is what your daughter is telling you.'

Anthony sits down. I shift so we aren't touching.

'Did you pay him off?'

He sighs, as if I've said something utterly stupid. 'As you say, he could have pressed charges. It seemed more sensible in the long run to give him a small sum. There won't be any repercussions.'

'Did you meet him?'

'Certainly not. I transferred the money to Caroline to give him.'

I run my fingers through my hair. 'I think you were wrong. I think Caroline should have been made to deal with this herself. You're taking power out of her hands by making it all go away so easily. There needs to be consequences. She's only living here because of your money. Turn off the tap and she might just make something of herself.'

'I'll thank you not to tell me how to manage my daughter. You've been getting very assertive lately, Rachel. It doesn't suit you. It's those friends you've made at work, I expect.' He slides an arm around my shoulders and I try not to shrink away. 'Let's not ruin a beautiful evening by arguing.'

I haven't made friends at work, except Hazel, and she isn't a proper friend, she's a colleague I talk to more than the others. The sun is in my eyes. I close them and think of you. I think of the warmth of your shoulder against mine when we were sitting on the floor, the faded knees of your black jeans, your hands draped over them. Your voice pulling me out of my panic.

Caroline wanders outside. So she was home after all. Perhaps she's been eavesdropping. I wouldn't put it past her. She's wearing a white maxi dress with puffed sleeves down to her wrists, and espadrilles. Her thick hair has been curled and cascades around her shoulders. She looks exquisite, delicate, vulnerable, and I feel a pang for complaining about her to her father. I'll make an effort, show Anthony I'm not against her.

'How did it go?' Anthony asks,

'Great, but I'm knackered. We spent the entire day in a field. I think I may have sunstroke. The first assistant was running around like a maniac spraying us all with suntan lotion.'

'Did you have any lines?' I ask.

Something flickers in Caroline's eyes, and I wish I hadn't asked the question.

'No lines, but I was a featured artist. I was one of a group of friends round Sally Corr.'

'Oh wow. I love Sally Corr. She's brilliant. Would you like to have supper with us? You can tell us all about it.'

Caroline looks down her nose, and I realise too late how patronising that sounded. 'No thank you. I'm meeting a friend. We'll eat at the pub. I wouldn't want to put you to any trouble.'

'What friend?' Anthony says.

'Are you policing me now, Daddy?' she asks.

To my surprise, he doesn't quip back. He examines the base of his bottle, then tips the dregs down his throat. When he gets up and walks inside, his gait is heavier than normal.

'He worries,' I say, once he's out of earshot. 'You'll understand when you have your own children.'

'What? Like you do?'

'Okay. Fine.' I'm not putting up with any more of my stepdaughter's shit. 'I've had a long day. I'm shattered, and I want a quiet evening with my husband.'

Caroline rolls her eyes and flounces off.

By Thursday morning, the unseasonably hot weather has turned and April feels more like April should. I elbow my way onto the train, settling my bag between my feet. I glance discreetly at the faces. I am not looking for you. Really I'm not. I wasn't on Tuesday or Wednesday either. And no one here is looking for me.

I open my copy of the *Metro*. By the time I get to the Rush Hour Crush segment, we've reached Hammersmith and I'm able to grab a seat. I smile as I read.

To the man I saw on the Upminster train. You were wearing a black beanie, brown jacket and black trousers. You picked my

43

scarf up off the floor and asked me where I was from. You smiled when I said London. I wish I'd given you my number.

The next one makes me sit up straighter.

I'm the man in black. You're the claustrophobic blonde. I taught you haiku.

This is you, isn't it? I glance at my hand. Surely you noticed my wedding ring. Perhaps you don't care. But then again, you haven't asked for anything. There's no sign-off with *Let's chat*, or *Fancy a coffee?* So perhaps it's simply a wave hello, a friendly acknowledgement of the time we spent together. Or perhaps you're trying to be mysterious.

I should be cross, but I reread your message with a smile so wide my fellow passengers must think I've won the lottery. I fold the newspaper and place it carefully in my bag, controlling my mad grin as best I can. I won't do anything about it. How can I? I am Anthony Gordon's wife.

Chapter 8

'You look different,' Anthony says.

'I look exactly the same as I always do.' I finger the collar of my cream silk shirt, a guilty conscience making me too warm. Not that I've done anything wrong, just cut out the message from the *Metro* and concealed it under the drawer organiser in my desk at work. I can't help wondering if you'll be on my train, and imagining what I'll do if you are. 'Perhaps the light's more flattering this morning.'

'You always look beautiful whatever the light.' He pauses. 'Rachel?'

I drop my hand and turn. 'Yes.'

'When you wanted to talk, I brushed it under the carpet. That must have felt like I was threatening you all over again. It was unforgivable. I am so very sorry, and ashamed of myself. You must hate me.'

I understand the effort this must have taken and nod an acceptance.

'Could we start again? I hate that there's a distance between us now, and I hate myself for causing it by my own pride and arrogance. I love you. I'm not perfect, and I know I'm pushing my luck, but please don't leave me.'

'I'm not going to leave you.'

'You'll give me another chance?'

He looks older, his skin finer, his eyes pink around the

rims. It twists my heart. Perhaps we can put this behind us.

'Yes, of course I will.'

Caroline comes into the room and heads straight for the larder cupboard. I send Anthony a questioning look, but he shakes his head. She pulls out a box of my organic muesli, which I can't complain about, having recently raided her snacks, pours a generous helping into a bowl, adds milk and stands leaning against the counter spooning it into her mouth.

Anthony picks up his keys, kisses me, tweaks Caroline's hair and leaves for one of his rare days in the office. I take my coffee upstairs. When I come back down again, she's nowhere to be seen.

The moment I'm in the street, I allow a guilty smile to break across my face. The gloom is lifting as the wind blows away the clouds, there is dew on the grass, ducks floating on the pond; everything is brighter and sharper.

I step onto the train and take a position within sight of the doors. As we approach Gunnersbury, where you got on, I stand taller, become more aware of my body, more alert as energy flows swiftly. Gunnersbury comes and goes, then Turnham Green, with no sign of you. I plug in my earphones, deflated, and find a podcast Hazel recommended.

A few minutes later, I become aware of someone watching me. I catch my breath.

You raise an eyebrow in query, and I acknowledge you with an embarrassed smile. You make your way over to me, squeezing between passengers, earning frowns of irritation as people move to make room.

'How long have you been there?' I ask.

'Not long. I got stuck further up, so I've been jumping on and off again, switching carriages each time we stop, looking for you. Do you mind me saying hello? You can tell me to sod off if you like. I can take it.'

'You're fine.'

The train lurches and you steady me. I'm so startled by your touch, I almost lose the power of speech.

'What you did.' I try to sound stern. 'The message in the *Metro*. Have you done it before? Is that how you pick up women?'

'Oh yeah. I wait until the train gets stuck in a tunnel, then I seek out women having anxiety attacks and pounce. Then I solidify my position with a message in a free sheet.'

'And does it work?'

'Every time.' There's a light in your eyes. You look elated, not predatory. You hesitate before you speak. 'Don't you find it strange when you connect with someone without knowing the first thing about them? It's kind of pure.'

I'm tempted to retort that it depends on what was going through your mind at the time, but I don't in case you perceive it as a come-on. 'It's good to have a chance to thank you for what you did.'

'It was nothing. It helped distract me as well.'

The train pulls into Hammersmith; a few people get off and more get on.

'So, what do you do?' you ask after a pause that feels deliciously awkward.

'That question's allowed now, is it?'

'Yes. I think we've reached the dull stage of our relationship.'

47

You're funny. 'SCR. Social corporate responsibility. I manage my employer's societal obligations.' I try not to be cynical about it, to convince myself that the people high up in my organisation actually care about the stuff I put in front of them, but sometimes it's hard to believe it means more than any other transaction. 'What about you?'

'I work in advertising.'

In the pause that follows, I notice you glance at my left hand with its gold band. I curl my fingers into my palm.

'Married.' You say it with an air of finality.

'I thought you would have noticed that.'

'I'm sorry. I didn't. This is so embarrassing. I'll back off.' The skin across his cheekbones flushes.

'Don't worry. I don't mind chatting.'

We talk in the way new acquaintances do, searching for points where our tastes overlap. You don't read fiction, you haven't been to the cinema for years, but you enjoy films staring Jean-Claude Van Damme or Liam Neeson and anything to do with foreign espionage. I begin to despair, but we find common ground in our love for this city. You walk its streets, mapping it with your feet. You enjoy exploring houses once owned by famous figures. Darwin's house, Charles Dickens Museum, Dr Johnson's House, the home Ernö Goldfinger designed at 2 Willow Road. We happily talk about those, but as we pull out of Sloane Square station, you go quiet.

'So this is it?' you say after a moment.

'Yes.'

'Can we at least say hello if we bump into each other again?'

A bubble of happiness disperses my qualms. 'If we meet

by accident, it would be rude not to.' Your answering smile is reward enough.

The train slows; you twist round and peer through the window as we arrive at Victoria. 'This is me.' You give me a rueful smile. 'Am I allowed to know your name?'

'Rachel.'

'Hello, Rachel.' The train shrieks as it stops, almost drowning out your voice. 'I'm Sean.'

You hesitate as the doors open, as though you're considering accompanying me for a few more stops, but then you're gone, nipping sideways through the doors as they close. Once again I watch hungrily until you disappear from view.

'You're looking perky,' Hazel says, wheeling her chair round. 'Are you having an affair?'

'No.' I can feel myself going bright red. 'Don't be ridiculous.'

'I'm only joking.' She goes back to her monitor. 'You do look pretty, though,' she mutters.

I shrug it off, but I'm unnerved. If Hazel's noticed something, if Anthony did this morning, then I'm far too transparent.

Chapter 9

A week and a half goes by, and it feels like I've known you for a lifetime. The last time a man had the same effect on me, he was the married one. Anthony. The thought doesn't sit well, but despite my conscience, we bump into each other regularly. I would not condone my behaviour in another woman, so I won't condone it in myself, but when you get on the train and we jostle through commuters and schoolchildren to get to each other, my smile is so wide my face aches and the joyful adrenaline coursing through my body feels like a flock of birds soaring towards the sun.

Even though we never leave the train, there is all the feverish wanting, just without the messy physical side of betrayal. The sight of your blokeish grin, the sound of your voice, the rasp of your cheek against my skin, the press of your body against mine in the overcrowded train has switched me back on. It feels uncannily, ridiculously like first love. I used to dread rush hour, now I live for it. Abstinence is exquisite. I'm too stupidly euphoric to question myself. That will come later.

Although I'm curious about your life, I quickly learn not to probe too deeply. We don't exchange contact details or arrange to meet in the real world. Those are the rules. My rules. We are rush-hour friends and I've promised myself I won't attempt to take this precious thing beyond the train. Nor will I bring to it my unhappiness or neurosis. I don't moan about Anthony, and if I talk about Caroline, I make it amusing not whingy. If this seems dishonest, it's self-defence. I know little about you except that our minds fit, and our hands feel made to clasp. Being with you wakens and sharpens my senses, makes me euphoric to the point where the oxygen inside me feels as though it's bubbling.

These moments of happiness are fragile and could easily be broken if either of us steps over the line. I don't want to have to leave for work earlier or later to avoid you.

So this is enough. It has to be.

Only it isn't.

Six weeks from when we first met, you elbow your way through the crush to where I'm standing in the central aisle. Apologising good-naturedly to people as they reluctantly give you space, you grab hold of a bar and swing against me as the train moves off.

'Hello,' you say.

'Hello.'

Needing to go from *hello* to something more meaningful in as short a time as possible, there is an imperative to get the social niceties over with. Sometimes we dispense with them altogether and gaze at each other until one of us laughs. There is nothing quite like these mornings. I just want to be close to you, to feel your arms around me, to see you smile.

Things have settled down lately. Anthony is preoccupied, but we've been kinder to each other. I've reminded myself he's had a difficult time of it, and he's obviously dealing with what happened between us. To hit your wife is a big deal, and he knows it.

I haven't told you about that, and I'm not sure why. I think it may be fear that you'll make me talk about it, pick the incident to pieces, point out my hypocrisy. You won't understand why I haven't left and you'll push me into a corner. It can't really be love, can it, if I'm unwilling to let down my defences? My happiness dissolves. I'm not sure I like myself very much at the moment. I'm lying to both of you.

'Shit.' I'm brought back to reality with a jolt.

'What?'

'Don't turn around.'

I grab your arm, ducking so that my face is lower than your shoulder. I resist the urge to drop to the floor like someone's pointing a gun at me.

'Caroline is on the train.'

Chapter 10

'Has she seen you?' you ask.

'No. Well, I don't think she has. She's facing the other way. What am I going to do?'

'Stand behind me. It's Victoria next. You can get off with me.'

'What if she gets off too? She might be changing lines.'

'Then we'll wait and see.'

You are perfectly calm; even, I suspect, amused.

'This isn't funny.'

'Your face is. You look like you've been caught fare-dodging.'

We nudge our way through the packed train, muttering 'excuse me' and 'sorry'. The doors slide open and I lean out. No sign of Caroline. We both step off. I breathe a sigh of relief.

'I wonder where she's going? She must have an audition. Bloody hell, that was close.' I glance up at the display. 'Three minutes.'

You lightly stroke the nape of my neck, making me shiver. 'Three minutes with you on a platform. Thank you, Caroline. Do you want to sit down?'

I look back at the board. Two minutes. I shrug and follow you to a bench.

'We could pretend we're on a date,' you say.

53

'We could.'

'I'd be thinking about how to make my first move.'

'And what would that be?'

You're relaxed, but the stakes aren't as high for you. I'm so physically aware of you it hurts.

'We're about twenty minutes into the movie. It's a scary film, so you wouldn't necessarily notice anything.'

'Oh, I've noticed.' Caroline has gone. Caroline saw nothing. We are off the train, which is against the rules, but it isn't my fault so it doesn't count. 'What's happening now?'

'She's opening the door to the cellar. Something dark and skeletal scuttles across the floor at the bottom of the stairs.'

I laugh. 'You have a vivid imagination.'

'Look at me.'

I do as I'm told.

'I want to kiss you.'

'I'm in my late thirties. I don't kiss strange men in public places.' I actually can't think of anything I'd rather do, but there are a lot of people around. Tourists with wheelie cases, just off the Gatwick Express, make up a large proportion.

'I'm not a strange man.'

'We can't,' I mumble, attempting to get to my feet.

You pull me back down. 'You can miss this one.'

There's no reason why not. No one will question it if I'm ten, or even twenty minutes late. Hazel might raise an eyebrow, but not because I've done anything wrong, simply because it would be out of character. All my good resolutions vanish with the train.

'Is this making you uncomfortable?' you ask.

'A little.'

'Why?'

'When I saw Caroline, I felt like everything was about to fall apart.'

'Would that be so bad?'

'Yes, it would. I chose Anthony and made promises.'

'You can fall in love more than once, Rachel. It's not unknown. Anthony left his wife for you.'

I shake my head. 'It isn't comparable. I'm sure I'd have got over him and met someone else, but instead I allowed it to happen.'

'He pursued you,' you point out. 'You were inexperienced.'

'That's very kind of you, but I wasn't exactly a vestal virgin.'

You touch my cheek and my skin burns.

A train pulls in, disgorges its passengers, absorbs some of the crowd and moves off without either of us noticing. You take my hand, and we get to our feet and walk down the platform to the mouth of the tunnel. I lean against the wall. My heart is going like a drum.

'Is this okay?' you ask.

'Yes.' It comes out as a croak.

I wrap my arms around your waist. You want to kiss me. I want to kiss you, but it feels impossible to cross that level of static. Your eyes fix mine, your smile catches at the corners of your lips, and I ache for you. It's you who turns all that intensity into a kiss, you who dips your head and touches your lips to mine, our smiles clashing, before the kiss deepens. I feel all of sixteen, tasting coffee and toothpaste, breathing in the scent of soap and shaving cream. My body is on fire, my knees like jelly.

'We have to do something about this,' you say. 'I don't care about your bloody principles. If you wanted me as badly as I want you, you wouldn't care about them either.'

'Let me think about it. It's harder for me.'

Your face shuts down. 'How do you know? I have a life as well. I may not be married, but I have things going on, things that will be affected if I get involved with you.'

'Like what?'

'Like where I plan to be. I have a job opportunity in Manchester. They need an answer soon.'

This is a nasty shock. 'You could have said something.'

'I didn't want to put pressure on you. But please do not assume I'm free to do what I like while you're the one with the ties.'

The lights from an oncoming train illuminate the tunnel. I know this is the one I'll get, that I've spoiled the moment. You've shut down and I don't know how to get back to where we were. This is a different side of you; a darker side. You've only ever given me an edited version of yourself. I'm guilty of the same thing, although I've shared more. There's an edge to your character, a degree of wariness I should have sensed weeks ago. Or perhaps I did and ignored it until now, because things have changed. We've kissed and we've quarrelled. This relationship has been turbocharged, and I'm ignoring the alarm bells because I want to be with you so badly.

Our goodbyes are strained. You give me a crooked smile as the doors close and the train moves off. You're right. I am being unfair on you. The idea of you going to Manchester is at once a relief and a catastrophe. How would I bear it?

56

Underneath the misery and indecision, something else niggles. I sensed Caroline's presence down the train before I saw her. Or maybe my brain recognised the tilt of my stepdaughter's head, or something in the way she carried herself. What if it was the same for her? What if she was pretending not to have seen us? I feel like this is the day everything changes, and I'm not ready for it. Not nearly ready.

Chapter 11

I cross my fingers as I walk through the front door, hoping Caroline won't be home. She's out most nights, either having a drink with friends or at a show.

Unfortunately, I'm out of luck. She is in the kitchen with Anthony, a glass of white wine in her hand. Is the atmosphere strange, or is it just me? Has Caroline told him she saw us together? I glance at Anthony, sitting at the kitchen table. I don't think so, but then she catches my eye and smiles.

Anthony doesn't accuse me of anything. I bend and kiss him on the lips and he strokes my back. I turn away and go to the fridge. I haven't thought about what we're eating tonight. Anthony is old-fashioned and never questions his wife holding down a full-time job while also keeping him fed and watered. Caroline's too unreliable, so I don't take her into account. There's the makings of sausage and mash. I take out a handful of potatoes, find a chopping board and a peeler. I watch the pair covertly as I work. At one point Anthony gets up and leaves the room, and there is something in Caroline's expression that causes me to lose my rhythm and almost slice into the top of my thumb.

'How was work?' she asks.

'Okay,' I answer carefully.

'You seem different.'

'In what way?' I dump the peeled potatoes in the sink and rinse any dirt off them. I can feel Caroline's eyes on my back.

'I don't know. Brighter somehow.'

Is she goading me? I fill a saucepan with cold water and put it on the hob. 'Thanks.'

She comes over and leans against the worktop, so she can see my face. 'I'm worried about Dad. He seems down.'

'He has a lot on his mind.'

'Like what? He can't still be worrying about the aborted coup. That was months ago.'

Caroline is so self-absorbed, it astonishes me. 'He won't get over that. You know what he's like. He's proud.'

If she's going to say something, I wish she'd hurry up.

'Well, I'm off out. Would you mind leaving the hall light on?'

I nod, not reassured. It's possible she didn't spot us this morning, but it's equally possible she's dangling me on a string.

I go in search of Anthony. He's sitting in the gloom of his office, his face lit by his computer screen. He looks ten years older than his sixty-three years. I feel a mixture of compassion and resentment. I can love two people at once, can't I? It happens all the time. I don't like myself for it, but it's life.

'Supper's ready.'

'Have I disappointed you?' he asks.

The question is so unexpected and out of character that

it takes me a moment to respond, long enough for him to read the worst into my silence.

'I . . . No, of course not.'

'Don't lie. You've changed since my heart attack. Everyone's changed. Even Caroline.'

No, I want to say. I've changed since you struck me. I can't face that conversation, so I poke it back into its box and close the lid. I've never seen him like this. Angry and sad at the same time. A line from a Dylan Thomas poem pops into my brain. *Rage, rage against the dying of the light.* He's afraid and he needs reassurance. I see that now. Oh God, have I been as selfish as my stepdaughter?

I crouch by his chair, my hands on his thigh. 'I'm not disappointed in you, Anthony. You're a wonderful husband and I depend on you for my happiness. You mustn't let it get to you. You'll soon feel more yourself.'

I glance at his monitor, but he's minimised whatever he was looking at. I wonder what it was that depressed him. Correspondence? A bank statement? Or has Caroline said something?

When we first met, I was too naïve to realise that behind Anthony's crackling energy, charm and drive lurked a black dog. All I saw was his light, his aura. Having grown up in a house dark with my mother's distrust, jealousy and spite, I saw him as someone who would light up my life and bring me out of myself. But men like him, with huge ambition and much to prove, often have inner demons. He kept them at bay for thirteen years, but they're barging their way out now. It isn't his fault. I am not going to leave him.

I can make Anthony happy, or happier, and still allow

myself to fall crazily in love with someone else. It is possible to have both, isn't it? Am I really such a bad person? This is not a new story. Other people have done it, so why can't I? But perhaps it's over. We parted company on a jarring note today.

Chapter 12

I don't know what to do about you. The last thing I want is for you to leave London. I didn't sleep well last night, unable to satisfactorily balance sticking by Anthony and spending illicit moments with you. Moments that I won't allow to go anywhere. I'm aware of my hypocrisy, but I can't help it. I'm obsessed with you.

You're still bristling after yesterday. That's the problem with our time limit; our conversations are abruptly curtailed. It meant that we both went to sleep on a quarrel. Allowed it to straddle the night into the next day.

'I don't want to put pressure on you,' you say. 'But I don't want to wreck your life either, or mess up mine for all the wrong reasons. You're unhappy at home, fine. But if all I am is a distraction, that isn't fair.'

'Sean, you're not. It's just that I don't really know who you are.'

'Your rules. Not mine.'

'Ask me something then.'

You lift your eyebrows. 'Fair enough. Why did you marry a man so much older than you?'

'I fell in love with him.'

'Not enough.'

'All right. He was there at the right time, when I needed someone like him.'

'Someone rich and powerful?'

'Someone who understood me and accepted me. I was a mess. Anthony felt like the answer. He was the answer . . . at the time. And now he needs me. There isn't time to go into it now, but I will, one day.'

'So there will be a one day?'

I smile. 'I'm trying my best to do the right thing. I can't just let go and see what happens, even though I'd like to.'

'Why don't you have children?'

Be brave, I think. 'I would have liked them, but I've accepted it won't happen. I've made my peace with that. Anthony was fifty-two when I married him. Naturally he wasn't keen to start over.'

'Surely when an older man marries a younger woman, it's part of the deal that he gives her children if it's what she wants, whether he likes the prospect or not.'

'Well, yes, but not in this case. I was only twenty-six, and children were the last thing on my mind; I was only interested in my career. And then I was in my thirties. Maybe if I'd really pushed, he would have said yes, but I didn't feel that strongly.'

You consider my words. 'Didn't you?'

I stammer. 'No . . . I mean, well, I don't think I did anyway. I don't know. Our life is good if you factor out Caroline. And she doesn't affect me that much. She's often out either auditioning or she'll have a small part in something, and when she's resting, she works with one of the charities my husband supports. A few years ago she even got a gig on a cruise for six months.' I smile at the memory. 'Shakespeare on the *Queen Mary*. The pandemic scuppered that.' I fold my arms. 'A baby would have been lovely, but not having one is not the defining event of my life.'

'Rachel, if you want a baby, you can have a baby. We can make it happen.'

'It doesn't work like that, Sean. It's probably too late anyway.'

'I've always wanted a family.'

I wasn't expecting you to be so honest, and it makes me want to cry. 'How do I know this will last? What if I walked out on Anthony and it all fell apart?'

'There are no certainties in life. It doesn't mean you don't take risks.'

'What are your circumstances? Do you own your own place? Do you rent alone, flat-share or what?'

Your jaw tightens. 'I flat-share. Not ideal, I know.'

I nod. It's what I suspected. 'I signed a prenup when I married Anthony.'

The suggestion of a prenup was unexpected. Anthony made the request when we were out for dinner the day after he proposed. By that time, I had moved in with him, after Mia had been generously paid off and moved with Caroline to a rented cottage in Putney. It was before she met Dave Poole, her current husband.

I was upset, but we were in a public place so I had to swallow it and have the conversation, and in the end, Anthony talked me round. If he was unfaithful, or demonstrably cruel, or left me, he would give me three million pounds. If I left him without provocation, I would get nothing. I was so in love with him, so naïve, that I couldn't conceive of either of those scenarios happening. He talked about the age difference, but I simply assumed that one day I would lose him, and it would be devastating, but I would be young enough to rebuild my life. I wanted to be with him – despite friends counselling against it, despite my mother's nasty insinuations, despite Anthony's qualms that he was asking too much of me and running the risk of making a fool of himself. We were soulmates. The twenty-five years between us meant nothing. So I signed the agreement, in front of his lawyer and one of his colleagues.

I explain the terms to you, adding, 'So we wouldn't have much money.'

'I don't care about the money,' you say, surprised.

'It matters, though. What if I was lucky enough to get pregnant? What if I wanted to stay home with the baby? Or we needed money for IVF?'

'Why are you doing this? Why are you looking for the negatives?'

'Because one of us needs to be practical.'

'When both of us could be happy.'

At that, I well up. It's embarrassing. Even those who seemed locked into their screens are eyeing us.

'So why aren't you married?' I ask.

'I've only ever had one long-term relationship, but that ended when . . .' You grimace. 'I thought we were for life, but let's just say I disappointed her. And then you come along, and suddenly there's hope.' You stroke my cheek with a lazy finger. 'Even though I don't know you, you're part of my life. If you didn't turn up one morning, I'd be gutted. I get off the train at Victoria and I feel like something's been interrupted, that there are opportunities to know you that I won't get back. You could stop all that by meeting me outside, but you won't.'

'Sean—'

'No, let me finish.' Your voice takes on a note of urgency. We're through Sloane Square, our time almost up. 'I'm ready for something new. And this – whatever it is – is making it very difficult.'

'I'm sorry. To tell you the truth, there are problems at home. Anthony's changed. He's become more critical; he can . . . Oh God.'

'Tell me.'

I pull myself together. I am not revealing that Anthony hit me. Maybe sometime, but not now. 'I love him, but it isn't working. I don't blame him, but I dread going home these days.' The words are wrenched out of me. 'Sometimes I wish the heart attack had killed him. Does that shock you?'

'No. I just wish you'd told me before.' You hold me against you and kiss the top of my head. 'It'll be okay. I promise.'

The dark tunnel gives way to the bright lights of the platform. We're at Victoria. You have to go. I don't beg you to stay and you don't ask me to get off with you. Perhaps I have shocked you after all. You reach into your pocket and take out your leather card holder, and something hits the toe of my shoe. I look down. You've dropped a packet of chewing gum. I pick it up and hand it to you.

'Keep it.' You wrap my fingers around it. 'I'd like to think part of me is with you above ground.' You give me a smile that is pure cheese.

'Chewing gum?' I raise my eyebrows.

'Stops me craving cigarettes. Obviously I'd have preferred to give you a single red rose, but I forgot to put one in my lapel this morning.' He's blocking passengers trying to exit the train, so he steps out with a wave to me, and then he's lost in the crowd.

I don't know what urge propels me out of the doors before they close. The hard rubber seal knocks my shoulder. I drop the chewing gum packet into my bag and rub the pain away as I follow you. There's quite a crowd between us, a surge of people on the move. I tail you up the escalators, across the concourse and out of the station, where the snap of morning air brings me to my senses. And yet I keep going.

It isn't long before you stop in a doorway and pull your phone out of your pocket. I slide into a queue of people waiting at a bus stop and watch. You're angry with whoever you're talking to, your forehead bunched into a frown. At one point you thump the wall with the side of your fist. It sends a shudder through me. Yet another reminder that I barely know you. This is you above ground, a very different man, a man with concerns you won't share with me.

It might be my overactive imagination, but I sensed something roll through you when I told you about the prenup. Is it possible you expected me to divorce my husband and finance our life together with whatever settlement I could get? Did you assume it would be half of Anthony's wealth? Is that why you want me? My shoulders slump. Why do I think I don't deserve to be loved? Escape from this life feels impossible. You are not the solution to my dissatisfaction. You are a symptom.

The phone call has ended. You hang your head, and then to my surprise you turn and plod back the way you came, not in such a tearing hurry now. You go back down into the station and head for the westbound platform. Are you going home? What's happened? Have you been fired?

There are different shades of you, as there are of me. If the boot had been on the other foot, if you'd followed me home, somehow witnessed my interactions with Anthony and Caroline, you might have been just as bewildered. We are different things to different people, and I shouldn't have done it.

If someone has the power to make you so angry, you're either very close, or you hate each other. Either way, I can't help feeling jealous. For the rest of the day I'm distracted and unhappy, and barely achieve anything. All I can think of is you, standing in that doorway, convulsed with anger and frustration. You are as much a mystery to me as you were the day we met. Not your fault, as you've pointed out. But this has shifted things; knocked my trust. Trust and love do not necessarily go hand in hand, whatever the romance novels tell you.

'I've booked karaoke,' Hazel says, breaking into my thoughts.

'What?'

'For my party. I tell you what, Rach, It's going to be a blast. I can't wait for you to meet my friends. You'll love them. They're all nuts.'

I cannot, at that moment, think of anything I'd less like to do than hang out with a bunch of strangers at a karaoke club. 'I can't wait,' I say.

'Only three more sleeps!'

ONE WEEK LATER

Chapter 13

'Rachel?'

Cool fingers encircle my wrist. My eyelids are heavy, I crack one open and iridescent light silhouettes the blur of my lashes. I try to raise a hand to block the light, but it barely feels part of me, let alone something I have any power over. Slowly, my senses awaken, the smell of antiseptic tickling my nostrils, the taste of dry saliva in my mouth, the open weave of a blanket nubbly against my fingertips. There are sounds too: murmurs and beeps, footsteps. The beat of my heart.

'You're in hospital, Mrs Gordon.'

'Uh.'

My mouth is bone dry. When I run my tongue across my lips I feel the knobbiness of a scab; it's like licking bark. I also notice, gradually, that my entire body hurts. Not a sharp pain but a dull, insistent ache. The skin on my face feels tight and stings when I touch it.

'Don't try to speak, lovey. You're in the critical care unit at Kingston Hospital. You've been in an induced coma, but you're going to be all right. You'll feel groggy from the drugs, but don't worry, take it slow. You've fractured your skull, broken several ribs and your collarbone, so you'll be on painkillers for a while. I'll be right here if you need anything.'

'Water,' I rasp.

The nurse raises the bed, making me wince, and eases a straw into my mouth. 'Little sips.'

'Ow.'

'We had to intubate, I'm afraid. That's why it hurts to swallow.'

A blur of powdery greens, pinks and blues catches my eye. The nurse follows my gaze.

'Aren't they lovely?'

'Who brought them? Is there a card?'

'Yes. Here.' She tweaks a card off the windowsill. It has a picture of a teddy bear holding a heart. I squint to focus on the words: *Get Well Soon, from everyone at Asset Plus*. There are loads of signatures and Xs.

'Oh, and there's this,' the nurse says. From behind my colleagues' gorgeous bouquet, she picks up a slender glass vase containing a single red rose. 'There's no card. Perhaps you have a secret admirer.'

'I don't think so. I expect it's from my husband.'

Anthony isn't really the single red rose type, but I can't think who else would have sent me something like that. Naz?

The nurse turns her back on me as she rearranges the cards and flowers on the windowsill.

'What happened?'

'The doctor will explain. I'll let him know you're awake. He'll be so pleased. You've done well, Mrs Gordon. We thought we might lose you at one point.'

Lose me. I have difficulty processing the concept, have no idea of context and remember nothing at all that might explain any of this. Tiredness swoops. I allow thick sleep

72

to overwhelm me. It's a blissed-out feeling, to let go, to sink ...

While I sleep, someone lightly touches my hand. I open my eyes with a sharp intake of breath. No one's there, and I drift off again, then wake when the nurse pulls aside the curtain.

'Was someone just here?'

'I don't think so, lovey.'

'I felt them touch my hand.'

'I expect you were dreaming.'

I don't know how much time has passed. I exist in a drug-fuelled limbo, registering time passing by the changes in the light outside my window and the progress of the three other patients in the ICU. It's busy here, with lots of machinery and people in and out, checking vital signs, feeding, washing. There's a young woman the other side of my blue curtain who cries whenever she wakes. I dread to think what happened to her. At some point in those heavily edited hours, I've managed a few spoonfuls of ice cream with a bite of banana and a cup of lukewarm tea.

I feel disassociated from the pain. Maybe it's because I'm stuck in a hospital bed and once I'm home it'll feel real. When I try to think about it, and about what happened to me, it feels as though my world has flipped over and tipped me off.

'My name is Mr Wilson. I operated on you.' The man places his fingers into the palm of my hand. 'Can you try to grip my fingers? Good. That's good.'

He lays my hand back on the covers, then helps me drink. I swallow, and the cool water sharpens my mind.

'What happened to me?'

'You were in a car crash.' His voice is measured and calm. Like a seasoned teacher explaining a knotty maths problem. 'You suffered a head trauma, and there was some swelling. You've been unconscious for three days. We had to put you in a coma to give your brain a chance to recover. The drugs we gave you; there are withdrawal symptoms associated with them, but most of that your body will have experienced coming out. That's why we've taken it slowly. I'll explain which drugs you've been given when you're able to take the information in. For the time being, rest and try not to worry. You're on the mend.' He pauses. 'The police are hoping to speak to you at some point today. They've been informed you're awake. Maybe this afternoon if you feel up to it.'

'The police?'

'You were driving. There was alcohol in your system.'

'Oh my God. But I wouldn't...I would never...Was anyone else hurt?'

'There was no other vehicle involved.'

I release a sigh. 'I don't remember any of it.'

'It's normal for your memory to be impaired,' he says so kindly I almost believe he isn't judging me. 'Every experience is different. It may take days or weeks, and some memories may never return. But some will. Be patient.'

I can't remember getting into my car, let alone where I was going. I work my way through my mental database. I am Rachel Gordon, married to Anthony Gordon, and we live in a three-storey double-fronted Georgian house overlooking Kew Green. As far as I know, I've never drunk more than one small glass of wine if I'm driving.

Anthony will be able to answer my questions. I wonder where he is. Someone would have informed him they were bringing me round, surely.

'Has my husband been in?'

Mr Wilson sits down and covers my hand with his. 'I'm very sorry to have to tell you this, Mrs Gordon, but your husband is dead.'

On the windowsill, the flowers swim in and out of focus. I try to breathe, but my lungs have constricted. I don't understand. 'You said I was alone in the car.'

'You were. It was an accident in the home.'

I experience a weird sensation then, almost as though I'm dreaming, or hypnotised. I have no control over what comes out of my mouth. 'It wasn't an accident,' I say. 'I killed him.'

Chapter 14

I'm wheeled, bed, vital signs machinery and all, into an empty room, where I'm told to wait. I can't exactly go anywhere, so I lie there staring at the ceiling, still in a state of disbelief and denial. I can't even cry. There is a void in my head. Anthony is dead and I've just told the surgeon I killed him. It must have been a dream, because there is no way on earth I could or would have done anything so evil. I love . . . I loved him, and the idea that he isn't here any more is too staggering to process. I don't remember arguing with him or having any reason for wanting him gone. Yes, we had problems – doesn't any couple – but nothing we couldn't resolve. He'd had a bad year, but we would have got through it. I supported him in the same way he supported me when I needed him.

When I try to recall our last conversation, I find that I can't. I remember things that seem far off, odd things like that waiter at the auction and his contemptuous stare. I remember the huge round of applause Anthony got when he walked off stage. But much of what floats around my mind has a dreamlike quality. Anthony was angry about something. What was it? I can feel his ill humour. Was it something I'd done? That can't have been our last exchange, can it? There must have been something better, some kinder moment. Some better version I've forgotten.

The door opens and a uniformed officer walks in. He's a big guy, flabby, in his mid thirties.

'Mrs Gordon? My name is Police Constable Richards. I'm here to interview you about your accident. Are you up to answering questions?' He looks at me dubiously.

I haven't seen myself in a mirror yet, but some parts of my face feel as though the skin and muscle have been stretched tight, and every bone feels bruised. I wriggle my toes, still amazed they work. It could have been much worse. Apparently my car collided with a tree and flipped on its side. The fire service had to cut me out. As well as the broken ribs and collarbone, there are stitches in my right thigh and left arm. Under the bandage round my head I've been warned I have a bald patch where the surgeon sawed into my skull to relieve the pressure. Thinking about my brain tissue being exposed makes me nauseous, so I try not to, but at least the physical damage distracts me from the emotional. I don't cry.

'I'm a bit foggy, but I'll do my best. Could you tell me what happened to Anthony first?'

'I'm afraid I can't discuss that. It's a separate case.'

'Oh. But surely—'

'I'm sorry. Someone will come and talk to you about your husband soon. Full name?'

'Rachel Constance Gordon.'

'Age and date of birth.'

'Thirty-nine. Twenty-third of February 1985.'

'Address?'

'112 Kew Green, TW9 8NH.'

Once we start, he is surprisingly empathetic. I guess what he sees is a fragile woman who has done something extremely stupid and paid for it. A car was written off, a tree badly damaged, but no one was killed. I have no recollection of any of this. All I can do is sit there in agony, apologising and hoping he'll charge me and leave so that I can go back to sleep. I don't want to think about any of it. I wish Anthony was here. He would know what to do. For the first time, tears well and run down my cheeks. I smear them away with my hand, and PC Richards reaches for a box of tissues he finds on a shelf.

'What will happen to me?' The charge has been read: drink driving and causing an accident while under the influence.

'A DUI carries a maximum sentence of six months in custody.' When I gasp, he adds reassuringly, 'But you're more likely to be given a fine and a suspension from driving. Either way, I'm afraid you'll have a criminal record.'

'Do I need a lawyer?'

'If you retain one, then by all means use him. But you're not arguing the charge and I can't imagine any judge sending you to prison for this. No one was killed. Accept responsibility, show remorse and move on with your life. I hope you recover soon.'

When he leaves, I wonder how long it's going to be before anyone remembers I'm in here, but the porter appears moments later and I'm wheeled back into the ward, officially a criminal.

I wake in the night, alert to danger. A figure in a baseball cap is standing at the foot of my bed, silhouetted by the light coming through the panel of glass in the door. There is something about the quality of his silence that persuades me he isn't staff. Sedated by painkillers and groggy from sleep, I don't feel fear. The figure turns and leaves the room. I heft myself up and out of bed, stumbling after him.

The reception desk is unmanned; there's no sign of anyone. I follow the corridor to the lifts, pressing my hand against the wall to steady myself, feeling as though I've just stepped ashore after a day on a boat.

None of the indicator lights above the lifts are moving. I let myself into the cold stairwell. Someone is running, the soles of their shoes tapping. I lean over, see a hand sliding down the banister and follow, concentrating on staying upright, my fractured ribs screaming at me to stop. I shout at him, then slump against the wall, woozy with pain, almost blacking out.

'Mrs Gordon. Mrs Gordon! What are you doing?' The nurse has an arm around my waist, a hand on my wrist. 'Now, now. We can't have you wandering about the hospital in the middle of the night.'

'Did you see him?'

'No, dear, I haven't seen anyone. Come along. Back to bed.'

'There was no one at the desk,' I mumble.

The nurse holds the door open for me. 'I nipped to the toilet.'

Chapter 15

Detective Sergeant Helen Jones has small, regular features and a blonde bob with a knife-edge fringe. Everything about her is neat, from her pressed shirt to the plain gold studs in her ear lobes. With minimal make-up – no foundation, just mascara, eyeliner and blusher – she also looks very young, and I can't help wondering if she's new to the job. There's something about her posture, a pent-up excitement like the anticipation of an animal waiting to pounce on its prey, which makes me think of how Caroline would play her if DS Jones was a role.

Once again I've been transferred to the private room.

'Good morning,' she says. 'How are you feeling?'

I eye her warily. Why have they sent a detective? I've accepted the charge. 'Better than yesterday.'

'Good. That's good. I'm sorry for your loss. I've just spoken to the nurse. Apparently last night you reported seeing a man at your bedside?'

Is that what this is about? The intruder. It's a relief. 'The nurse said there was no one there.'

DS Jones nods. 'She was wrong. I've checked the footage. I'm very sorry this has happened, Mrs Gordon. Perhaps you can tell me if you recognise him.' She hands me a grainy printout and I study it carefully. The baseball cap means I can't see his face.

I hand it back. 'I've no idea who it is.'

'Can you think of any reason a man would have approached you like that?'

'Maybe he was looking for someone else.' It gives me the shivers to think of him standing there watching me when I was at my most vulnerable.

Jones slips the picture into her briefcase. 'It's possible. I'm sorry that you've been made to feel unsafe. There'll be a constable in the corridor tonight. Oh, and I've brought this for you.' Only then do I notice that she's holding a bag. My bag. 'It was under the passenger seat of your car, so it didn't go in the ambulance with you.' She puts it on the bedside cabinet and sits down.

I reach for it, relieved. 'Thanks.' I'm still not sure what she's here for. Surely Constable Richards could have dealt with the intruder issue. 'I've been charged,' I say tentatively.

She smiles. 'I know. But this isn't about your DUI. The results have come in from your husband's post-mortem, and I'm very sorry to have to inform you that there's sufficient evidence to suggest he was deliberately killed.'

For a moment I can't speak. I'm caught between deep shock and the uncomfortable awareness that I'm under scrutiny.

'Who found him?'

'His daughter.'

'Oh, poor Caroline. Are they positive it wasn't a heart attack? He had one last year.'

'I'm afraid not.' The detective glances down at her notes. 'Bruising was found around his neck that indicates an attempt to choke him, although that isn't what killed

81

him. That was the impact when Mr Gordon's head hit the floor. It means, I'm afraid, that I'm going to be interviewing you under caution. Do you understand?'

I nod, and she places a digital recorder on the side of the bed. The moment the little red light goes on, I feel guilty.

'Can you think of anyone who might have wanted to hurt your husband?'

'No. Anthony didn't have enemies.'

'How long had you been married?'

'Twelve years.'

'And Caroline was his daughter from a previous marriage?'

'That's right.'

'You don't have children?'

'No.'

'How would you describe your marriage?'

'It was happy.'

'No problems?'

I find if I press the flat of my hand against my ribcage, the pain abates a fraction.

'Not really,' I say firmly. 'I'm not saying things were perfect, but we loved each other.'

'Mr Wilson mentioned that you said something strange when he told you Mr Gordon had died.' She glances down at her notes. 'You said, "I killed him.". What exactly did you mean?'

'I don't know,' I stammer. 'I was still heavily drugged. I expect I was dreaming. I often have gory nightmares.'

'Those are the worst, aren't they?' DS Jones pauses, flicking back through her notes. 'Can you talk me through that night?'

'I'm sorry. I don't remember anything.'

'Nothing at all?'

'No.' I'm growing weary, the pain nudging towards unbearable. I want to take a pill and curl myself round it.

'I should warn you, just so it doesn't come as a shock, forensics officers have searched your house.'

'Okay,' I say slowly, unsure what to make of this, but knowing it can't be good.

'Do you drink whisky?'

'No. Never.'

'And Mr Gordon?'

'Anthony doesn't . . . didn't drink.'

'Forensics didn't find the bottle or a glass, but there was a small spillage on the kitchen table that hadn't been wiped up properly. Do you know who might have been drinking with your husband that evening?'

'I've no idea. Possibly Caroline.'

'Miss Gordon says not. She was driving to Oxford, so she wouldn't have had a drink before she left, and she doesn't like whisky. Why did you have it in the house, if your husband was teetotal and neither you nor Miss Gordon liked it?'

'Because Anthony was a good host. He kept all sorts of spirits. He's never drunk alcohol, so it isn't as if he's an alcoholic. It was a choice he made when he was much younger. I agree it looks very odd, though.'

'It confirms that someone else was there that evening. And since the bottle was removed, it's clear they didn't want it known. The DS rests her notepad on her knee and leans forward. 'Your husband was a wealthy man, so you'll understand why we're taking this extremely seriously.

83

There are people who will have gained substantially from his death. Yourself, for instance.'

'Anthony made a lot of money, but I have a job and I didn't rely on him financially.' I can hear a nip of defensiveness in my tone.

'What do you do?'

'I'm head of corporate social responsibility at Asset Plus. They're a wealth management company in the City.'

'Ah. A job with a conscience.' DS Jones tilts her head, giving me a look that is both arch and sceptical. It feels like barbed wire to my nerves. 'But you don't need to work.'

'I don't see what that has to do with anything.'

'Everything is relevant. Do you remember attending a party at the home of Hazel Gifford?'

'No. I don't remember anything about that.'

Jones looks at me strangely. 'What is the last thing you remember?'

I think hard. Where was I? Home? Yes. At home. The scene unravels like a film, surprisingly clear. 'There was a problem with my stepdaughter. Anthony and I had arranged to go to the theatre, so Caroline invited a male friend round for supper. Something happened – a row maybe. It woke me up, so I went downstairs. The guy was just leaving. He was angry because she'd assaulted him. She was begging him not to go. It was pretty awful. Anyway, the following day Anthony and I argued about it. I said I thought it was time she moved out.' I frown. 'Sorry, I can't remember anything after that.' My head is itching round the scar. I rub the bandage.

'When was this?'

I have no trouble remembering the date of the performance. 'The fifteenth of April. It was a Saturday.'

'Are you saying you don't remember a thing between mid April and now?'

'No,' I breathe. 'I don't.'

'Really?' There's the slightest lift of her perfect brows. 'Going back to Ms Gifford's birthday celebrations. According to her statement, you were originally intending to stay the night.'

Was I? It seems unlikely. 'If that's what she says.'

'She only lives forty minutes away,' DS Jones says. 'Probably less at that time of night. You could have gone home.'

I frown. 'I imagine the plan was for an all-nighter.' Again, unlikely. But maybe she steamrollered me into it.

'Do you like Hazel?'

'She isn't a close friend, but yes, I like her.'

'How often do you see her out of office hours?'

'We go for a drink sometimes.'

'After work?'

'Yes.'

'Have you ever made other plans, say to meet up at the weekend?'

'No.' The truth is that Hazel suggests it from time to time, but I always have an excuse. I feel bad about that, but although she's friendly and fun and really wants to be friends, she can also be snippy and judgemental. I don't like it when I don't know from one day to the next which version of her I'll get.

'So Hazel isn't really a friend, she's a colleague you enjoy the occasional after-work drink with, presumably in the company of other colleagues, but never take the trouble to see socially otherwise. Until this party.'

'To be honest, I didn't particularly want to go.'

DS Jones waits, an inscrutable smile playing on her lips, as if she knows something I don't. That's probably true given I can't remember a thing about that night or the days preceding it. 'Ms Gifford said something else. She told me that from hints you've let drop, Mr Gordon could be quite controlling.'

'I've never said anything like that to anyone.'

'But you were drunk, so isn't it possible you might have confided in your friend?'

'If she said that, I expect it's because she wanted more out of our friendship. She rationalised me not letting her into my life outside work as Anthony telling me who I could and couldn't see. But it wasn't like that.'

'What was it like?'

I chew my lip while I consider how to put it. 'It was that best friend thing. Like school. I enjoy her company at work, but I don't want more. I know that makes me sound horrible, but you can't manufacture a liking for someone. I don't hate her, I just don't want a closer friendship.'

'She also said that you told her you weren't sure why you were still in the marriage.'

This gets worse and worse. 'I mean, there's no reason she'd lie. But I don't normally share stuff like that with her. Maybe Anthony and I had had a row and I needed to get it off my chest. It doesn't sound like me, but then I don't usually get blind drunk, so I suppose . . .' My voice trails off. 'I honestly don't know.'

DS Jones hooks one side of her blonde bob behind her

ear. 'If we could go over a couple more things about that night. Caroline Gordon says that only you and she knew your husband would be on his own on Saturday evening. Do you think you might have told anyone else?'

'I have no idea. I don't remember. Maybe Hazel when I got to her house? I might have mentioned it.'

DS Jones is looking at my hands. I didn't realise I was fidgeting with the blanket. I stop.

'Did you love your husband, Mrs Gordon?'

I hold her gaze. I'm telling the truth when I say, 'Yes, I did.'

'Were you having an affair?'

'No.' I say it with conviction.

'Are you sure? There are seven weeks you say you don't remember. That's time unaccounted for.'

'I wasn't unfaithful to Anthony. I would never have done that. There would be something on my phone if I was seeing someone, wouldn't there? Messages between us. His number would be in my contacts.' I swallow, my eyes watering from the pain. 'I don't understand why I would have decided to drive home. What did Hazel tell you?'

'That you'd been drinking cocktails. She doesn't know why you left the house when you did, except that it was likely to do with a voicemail you received. According to the records, it was from your husband, and was left around the estimated time of his death.'

'If he was losing consciousness, he might have called me instead of 999.'

'It's possible, but we can't know that for sure.'

'But that's what it looks like, isn't it?'

'If you'd suspected a medical emergency, you would have called an ambulance, don't you think?'

'Yes, I definitely would have.'

Why didn't I? I can only think of one reason, and it's insane. Because for some reason, I needed to get there first. I wonder if the detective sergeant is thinking the same. I said *I killed him*. That can't be true. I refuse to believe it.

I need my phone. I unzip my bag and feel around inside. I can't find it. Jones watches as I tip everything out on my lap. Pens, a tortoiseshell claw clip, a small hairbrush, battered powder compact and lipstick, loyalty cards, debit cards, a notebook, business cards, both mine and associates', a packet of tissues. All the clutter of my former life. 'My phone's not here.'

'No. I have it.' She reaches into her own bag and takes it out. 'I had it couriered over from Forensics this morning. Perhaps you could open it and have a look. I'll have to take it away again, I'm afraid, but it's all charged up for you.'

Irritated, I throw everything back into my bag, then tap in the passcode. I ignore the voicemail, even though I'm curious, because I don't want DS Jones listening in, and scroll through my recent WhatsApp messages. There's one from Hazel from the day of the party, making sure I had the correct postcode and explaining how not to miss the entrance to the narrow lane into the development where she lives; and then a later one wanting to know I got home okay. I check my emails, but they're all work-related until people hear the news, and then there's a flurry of good wishes, and one from HR asking me to get in touch as soon as I'm able. Nothing to suggest I was having an affair. I allow myself a moment of relief. I have nothing to be ashamed of.

'The voicemail?' DS Jones prompts.

Resignedly I open Anthony's voicemail. There's a scraping noise, then he says in a hiss that he normally reserves for the local cats who dare to prowl the garden, 'What have you done?' After that, there's another noise, like a double thud, before the message cuts off.

Chapter 16

I first met Anthony after my second interview at his company, for what was supposed to be a brief chat, a courtesy really.

At school I'd taken maths because my father said mathematicians were like hens' teeth, so I'd always be employable; French because I enjoyed languages; and history of art. I'd wanted to study history of art at university, but by the time I was ready to apply, I'd already banished that dream. I needed to get the qualification that would see me fastest into employment in a sector of the economy where I would not have to rely on either my parents or a man. I was determined to look after myself, whether I married or not. So I obtained a BSc in mathematics and business and got a place on a graduate scheme for a Square Mile accountancy firm, which I hated but endured for two years because it meant I could move away from home. Until it almost killed my soul.

I still loved art, still went to galleries in my spare time, but I was pragmatic. The girls I knew who went on from history of art degrees to work in auction houses and galleries invariably had rich and loving parents. I wasn't going to ask for handouts, even if it killed me. I'd rather have slept rough.

I had no idea there was such a thing as a corporate social

responsibility coordinator until I met one at my firm, but it sounded like the compromise I needed. I started to look around for a route in and applied for the role of sustainability manager at IFR, and was called back for a second interview.

I wore a light grey tailored trouser suit that day, with a cream silk shirt and high heels. There were only two other candidates. A man in his thirties who sat with one leg crossed over the other, looking so nonchalant it had to be an act; and a woman who was constantly scrolling and clicking on her phone, her attention never caught for long. Once or twice she looked up, glanced at me, then looked down again. After our interviews, we were taken to the top floor to meet the CEO, and led into a glass-walled conference room to wait. The man was the first to be called. He strolled in and came back out ten minutes later looking pleased with himself, nodded in our general direction and left. Then it was the woman's turn. She was in the room for slightly longer, or perhaps it just seemed longer because my nerves were kicking in. I was also hungry, my mind in a food groove. She left with a lift in her step and a smile. She even murmured good luck, which was more than I'd done for her.

I had googled Anthony Gordon. I knew his career history and that he was married with a daughter about to hit her teens. My first impression, on pushing open the door, was of a tall, slim man with satanic eyebrows and a wicked smile. I remember an instant attraction on my side, an uncurling deep in my belly, and the awareness of a spark of interest on his.

Behind him, the city looked staggering, the sun glinting off glass, blue sky crossed with aeroplane contrails. The wall to my left was floor-to-ceiling bookshelves painted in the same shade as the walls, a dark pencil-grey. The wall to my right was dominated by a huge picture. Gloomy and chaotic, it was painted with broad, violent brushstrokes and scratches in a dour colour palette. I stared at it for a moment, distracted.

'Prometheus,' I said at last. I had made out the figure of a prostrated man, a crow on his abdomen, picking at his entrails.

'Bravo. I take it you know the story?' Anthony Gordon's voice was attractive. Rich, with a touch of east London. I remembered what else I'd read in his Wikipedia entry. Grew up on a council estate, attended state school. From there to Cambridge.

'Prometheus was doomed to be chained to a rock for all eternity, his innards gnawed at by crows, for bringing fire to humans when he'd been told not to. He knew it was wrong and against Zeus's express wishes, but he felt strongly enough to do it anyway. It was worth the punishment.'

Anthony's eyes narrowed. 'But what is the story really about?'

The atmosphere was strange, expectant. I wondered if the others were given this test. What would the myth mean to a powerful man like Anthony Gordon? And then I knew. 'Betrayal.'

'That's right.' He sounded pleased, and I felt an inner glow. 'Prometheus betrayed Zeus, and Zeus never forgave him. No matter that Zeus himself was a great betrayer of friends and family; he was the boss. So you're Rachel Elliott.' He stood up, leaned over his desk and held out his hand. 'Good to meet you.'

Our ten minutes turned into half an hour, at the end of which we sat in silence and contemplated each other, our smiles growing.

'Well . . .' Anthony said.

'I know I haven't been offered it yet,' I blurted out, 'but I can't take the job.'

He raised his eyebrows. 'Was it something I said?'

I stifled the urge to giggle. 'I'm so sorry, but I find you too attractive.' Horribly flustered, I leapt up and headed for the door. I still can't believe I said those words. I was so young.

'Hang on.' Anthony rose from his chair. 'I apologise if I gave you the wrong impression.'

'You didn't. You absolutely didn't. I'm . . . Oh God, this is so embarrassing. I'll just say goodbye and thank you for the opportunity.'

'Go on, then.'

'What?'

'Say goodbye and thank you for the opportunity.'

I spluttered with laughter and fled the room.

'You were in there a long time,' his PA said. 'That's a good sign.'

When I left the building, I went into the first newsagent's I passed and stood by the rows of chocolate. The bright packaging, the sugary smell that pervaded the place made my heart race. Extremes of emotion make me want to eat junk food: euphoria, misery, rage. Something about those endorphins and stress hormones let loose in my system brings on cravings for sugar, salt and bad fat. I turned myself around and walked out of the shop. Outside in the fresh air, I did my breathing exercises, my eyes locked onto the offices on the other side of the road. I'd learned the hard way to navigate the urge to binge until I'd brought myself under control, even while the tension was building to a peak, even with all the agitation. The times I failed, self-disgust would throw me into turmoil. I'd hear my mother's voice – *Is that a spare tyre I see, darling? Careful, or you're going to get dumpy* – and I'd stick my fingers down my throat.

I wasn't offered the job, and I can't deny that it hurt, even though I was offered another, with better pay, within a fortnight. But that wasn't the end of it. Despite how it looked to those who wanted to slag me off, I did my best, turning Anthony down when he rang a week later, and the following week, and the week after that. But then I found him waiting for me in the foyer of my new place of work – I'd added it to my LinkedIn profile – and that was that.

I'd spent my teenage years wolfing down romance along with the food as an antidote to unhappiness, and here was this self-assured, successful alpha male, straight out of a Mills & Boon novel, and he wanted me and I was perfection to him. Anthony was experienced, funny, indefatigable and passionate, and I let myself be drawn in. Two months later, he left his wife. I hadn't expected that. Of course it was wrong, of course I felt bad; I'd been brought up to feel bad. But part of me exulted in my triumph over another woman. And we loved each other; that is indisputable.

How sad that only thirteen years later, things had started falling apart. I'd changed, grown up, and maybe Anthony found that hard to deal with. It wasn't what either of us had envisaged, but it could have been predicted. My mother said something, but I didn't listen; I never listened to either of my parents. They didn't deserve it.

Chapter 17

DS Jones and I sit in stunned silence, then she takes the phone off me and puts it in her bag. She takes a small notepad out of her pocket and a pen.

'Passcode?'

I reel it off.

'What *had* you done, Mrs Gordon?'

'I don't remember. But I know I'd never have hurt Anthony.'

'Are you certain about that? His death leaves you free. No messy divorce, no squabbles over goods and chattels. Perhaps there was a man. Sex and money are powerful inducements.'

'Absolutely not. We were happy together.' Anthony's face, nostrils flared, flashes up behind my eyes. Then it's gone as quickly as it came, leaving me stiff with shock.

'It doesn't necessarily follow that you wouldn't see someone else,' DS Jones says. Her steady gaze hasn't left my face. 'Plenty of happily married couples do.'

'There's no evidence of that on my phone.'

'Perhaps you have another one.'

'If I did, where is it? You obviously didn't find one in the house, so if it exists it would have been with me that night. And you would have found it in the wreckage. I'm sorry, but I'm very tired. Could we start again tomorrow?'

It's true. My eyelids are growing heavy, my body wilting.

'Of course. This has been a difficult conversation for you. There is just one more thing, though. We've spoken to your husband's GP. You haven't mentioned it, and neither has his daughter, so I'm wondering if either of you knew he had recently been diagnosed with terminal cancer.'

My muscles go lax. 'No. I didn't know that.'

'I'm very sorry. It must be a shock. It seems he had less than a year to live.'

It takes a moment to acknowledge this new horror. 'When did he find out?'

'Three months ago.' Her voice softens. 'I'm sure he meant to tell you before it became obvious. I imagine people need to get used to their diagnosis before they share it with loved ones. Or perhaps he did, and you've forgotten.'

I recall little things: Anthony coughing and blaming COVID long after the pandemic petered out or ascribing his breathlessness to the heart attack. Oh, Anthony. He made regular trips to his doctor in Harley Street. I offered to go with him, but he always turned me down. What if he was actually going to hospital for treatment? Then there was the not wanting to go for long walks and the more frequent early nights. Again, behaviour easily explained by a heart issue. I never asked for details, because he was ultra-sensitive to people speculating on whether his physical and cognitive powers were compromised.

'Is there any way forensics could be wrong about him being pushed? Could the cancer have had something to do with his fall? He must have been on strong drugs.'

'His consultant oncologist says it's possible, but that doesn't explain the bruising on his neck.'

I have to be satisfied with that. A few minutes later DS Jones leaves, and I sink down into the pillows and close my eyes. I feel weak with regret. I hope he did tell me about the cancer, and that the conversations we subsequently had helped both of us come to terms with his diagnosis. Above all, I hope he wasn't angry and disappointed in the final weeks of his life, but I know in my heart he would have been.

I don't want to believe I was unfaithful, and yet I have a sensation of wanting to be somewhere else, with someone else, a sense of something unfinished, something intense enough to leave an ember where memory should be, an absence that has nothing to do with Anthony.

Chapter 18

Tim Vaughan, Anthony's lawyer, arrives the next day with a crumpled copy of the *Metro*. He drops the paper beside my thigh. I've known Tim for almost as long as I've known Anthony. He's a thoroughly decent man, one of the few to give me a chance after Anthony left Mia. Large and ungainly, his face as rumpled as a towel dropped on the floor, he makes up for his physical shortcomings with charm and infinite patience. And woe betide anyone who underestimates him. He is also Caroline's godfather, a conflict I'm especially conscious of today.

'I'm so sorry,' he says glumly. 'I can't believe what's happened.'

'Neither can I.' My voice wobbles. 'Did you know Anthony had cancer?'

'Yes, I did. I'm sorry. He told me he'd tell you when the time was right.'

'Was he scared?'

Tim takes a seat. 'I think he was more angry than scared, to be honest. He felt robbed.'

It's what I've been thinking. 'Poor Anthony. Maybe he did tell me.'

'I expect you'll remember eventually.'

'What's going to happen next?'

'I've spoken to Detective Sergeant Jones. We can knock

the DUI on the head if you plead guilty to driving under the influence, pay the fine and accept the ban. You won't go to prison for that, so don't be anxious. Thank God no one else was hurt.'

'Yes, thank God.' The knowledge that I could have killed someone is never far from my mind. It's horrific how close I came to ruining lives other than my own. 'DS Jones thinks Anthony's death was suspicious. Who would want to hurt him? It's as unbelievable as me getting into a car when I'd been drinking heavily.'

'That doesn't sound like you at all,' Tim agrees.

'He left a voicemail. Probably just before he died. I listened to it for the first time when I was with the detective.' Aware of others in the ward, I drop my voice to a whisper. 'He said, "What have you done?"'

Tim frowns. 'What do you think he meant?'

'I don't know, but when the doctor broke the news to me, I told him I'd killed Anthony. I just blurted it out. I don't know why, except that I hadn't been conscious for long.' I sigh heavily. 'But I said it and the doctor told the police.'

'Have you repeated it?' Tim is no longer leaning forward. He's sitting up, shoulders straight, lawyer's brain sharpening.

'The detective brought it up, but otherwise, no.'

'Right, well do yourself a favour and don't say it again. If you're asked about it, say you were groggy from the drugs – which you were – and you have no idea what you meant.'

'What's going to happen now?'

'There'll be a full-scale investigation. The main thing is, you weren't there.'

'Then who was?'

99

'That's the question, isn't it? Forensics may turn something up.'

I close my eyes, start to sink into sleep. Beside me, Tim scrapes his chair back and lumbers to his feet. His broad hand covers mine.

'It's a lot to take in. Get some rest and I'll drop by tomorrow. You'll want to know what's in Anthony's will. I'll bring it.'

Does he believe me? I sink into darkness with a sense of relief. I wish everything could be blotted out until this whole mess goes away.

When I wake again, I'm alone. I pick up the newspaper Tim left. At the feel of it, its faint petrol smell, a memory cuts through the fog, so swift and sharp it takes my breath away. A man on the train. He's holding the overhead handle with one hand, the other curled around my shoulder. We gaze into each other's eyes as the train rocks, and I fall against him.

I push the paper away, so that it falls to the floor. My hands feel stained by it. The image has gone, leaving only shock.

Chapter 19

Beyond the curtains surrounding my hospital bed, voices murmur. Everyone speaks in low tones here. I wonder if it's out of respect, or if they're simply overwhelmed by their situation. Catastrophe catches you unawares.

Someone coughs. I open my eyes. Caroline is standing at the foot of my bed. It's the first time I've seen her since before my accident. She's wearing dark jeans, an outsized cream jumper, the sleeves of which almost entirely cover her hands, and a mouse-coloured scarf draped around her neck. My hair is untidy and snags when I try to comb my fingers through it. Lying flat on my back, I feel at such a disadvantage I'm almost frightened.

'Is Tim here yet?' I croak, fumbling for the hand control to raise the bed back.

'Not yet.' Caroline sits down. She isn't wearing make-up, and she looks tired. I feel a pang of guilt for thinking badly of her. She's lost her adored father, after all. 'I just don't understand what's happened,' she says. 'You should have been with him, not getting out of your head and totalling your car. What the hell were you thinking?'

'I wasn't to know he would be attacked.'

'Unless you had something to do with it.'

Her words jolt me like a jab in the chest. 'That's a horrible thing to say.'

'Well what do you expect?' Caroline says. She runs her fingers through her hair, then says, 'I've been thinking. We don't get on, and now that Dad isn't here, we don't need to live together.'

My heart lifts a little. The thought of sharing the house with her, without the buffer of Anthony's presence, is not one I relish. 'If I can help—'

She interrupts. 'I'm sure you can afford to rent somewhere nice.'

My eyebrows fly up. 'What do you mean?'

'Dad always said he'd leave me the house. You're just the second wife. He understood his responsibilities. Don't look so shocked. I won't begrudge anything Dad's left you, but you'll have no further claim on the family.'

'Caroline. I . . .'

'Of course you can't manage it yourself. I'll have a look round if you like. I've got some time. A flat in Richmond or Putney would suit you.'

'That is not realistic, and you know it.'

'I know you drove my father to his death.'

'That isn't true. He loved me.'

'And that was his mistake. He deserved better. I know things about you.'

'What?' I'm not ready for the guilt that floods me. Then, to my relief, Tim arrives. Caroline scowls – clearly she has more to say – and the moment passes.

I don't want a wheelchair, but the nurse insists, and a porter pushes me into a small private room that looks as though it's used by staff to snatch sleep when they get an opportunity. He removes a pillow and folded blanket from the sofa and leaves. DS Jones slides in and stands by the door. Tim perches his bulk on the edge of a table pushed up against the wall, and I transfer onto the sofa, where I feel at less of a disadvantage. Caroline parks herself at the other end of the sofa. It's small; there's barely six inches between us.

'Are you recording the meeting?' she asks DS Jones.

'Not this time. I'm here to observe.'

Tim swaps his glasses over and opens a yellow manila folder.

'Thank you for coming here today. I thought it best to read Anthony's will with both of you present, because it won't be what either of you are anticipating and I expect you to have questions that require immediate answers.' He pauses. 'The first thing I need to explain is that Anthony made a new will on the twenty-first of April.'

I glance at DS Jones, but the detective's face is inscrutable.

'There are various disbursements,' Tim goes on. 'A hundred thousand pounds to be divided between Anthony's nieces, nephews and godchildren, a hundred and fifty thousand to the Begin Again programme, and fifty thousand to Stir.' He clears his throat, then reads, 'I hereby leave the balance of my estate to my wife, Rachel Constance Gordon.'

'What have you done?' Caroline gasps, glaring at me.

The same words Anthony used. I can't keep the shock from my face. 'I didn't know anything about it.'

'I don't believe you, you conniving bitch. Dad hadn't been well and you got to him.'

The barrage of words makes me shrink. 'That isn't true.'

103

Tim lifts his hand. 'There are conditions attached to the legacy. I'll give it to you in writing, of course, but you should know the essentials. Apart from Anthony's share of IFR, which Rachel is entitled to spend during her lifetime and to bequeath where she likes – I gather that package is worth in the region of seven million pounds – the family house and all other investments are bound up in a trust that reverts to Caroline and her future children upon Rachel's death. These assets can't be liquidated during Rachel's lifetime.' He glances at me. 'You would only be entitled to the interest on the capital.'

'I don't believe this,' Caroline interrupts.

Tim waits for more, and when there's silence, he continues. 'This arrangement remains in place if Rachel remarries and has children. Anthony's financial advisers will be able to tell you both how much the pension and investments are worth, but even taking into account the recent losses incurred by his investment in cryptocurrency, it's a considerable sum. And of course, crypto may rally.'

Caroline lifts her head at this, but she doesn't comment. Anthony didn't tell her about that investment, and I wasn't going to. Tim takes a slim envelope out of the folder and passes it to her. 'This is for you. Anthony hoped it would explain his decision.'

Caroline wipes her eyes and blows her nose. 'Have you read it?'

'Yes. He wrote and signed it in my presence and that of another witness. He wanted to make sure there was no ambiguity about his intentions or his state of mind.'

'What witness? Do you mean her?' She flicks a hand in my direction.

'No. A colleague. Perhaps you'd like some privacy?'

'Nope.' She slides her thumb under the envelope flap and tears it open. She reads the letter inside, then shoves it over. 'This has you written all over it.'

My darling Caroline,

By now you will know I've had a diagnosis of cancer and won't see you grow into the fine woman you have the chance to become. I want to explain why I've made what must seem like a grossly unfair decision.

When I left your mother, I felt desperately guilty about the way you suffered, and because of that, I over-compensated. I was so anxious not to let you down again, so anxious for you to be happy and to feel loved, that I never challenged you. Not only that, I smoothed every bump in your path. As a result, I fear you are not discovering your potential as a human being. You have never struggled, never had the chance to prove your mettle. If I made you wealthy at this crucial juncture in your life, I truly believe I would ruin what is left of it. Hungry people fight for what they want. Wanting for nothing at your age is a dangerous state to find yourself in. I appreciate that this will come as a dreadful shock, and that you will feel betrayed by your father all over again, but I hope one day you will understand that it's for the best. I hope you will thank me.

Please wake up, Caroline. I know the idea of acting is one that you don't want to give up on, and neither do I wish you to discard your dreams, but now you have the added incentive of keeping a roof over your head, like I did as a young man. Perhaps you will use your imagination and find a way to prevail. It could be the making of you.

I love you very much.
Dad

I've barely finished reading when Caroline snatches the letter out of my hand, screws it up into a ball and flings it across the room. DS Jones picks it up and smooths it out as Caroline lets rip.

'I refuse to accept this. She's got to him. How the fuck could you let this happen, Tim? Why didn't you persuade him out of it?'

'My dear, you knew your father better than anyone. Do you think I could have done that?'

'He would have listened to you.' She glares at him mutinously. 'What kind of cancer was it anyway?'

'Small-cell lung cancer.' Tim is on surer ground. 'He knew he didn't have long. He was going to tell you, but . . . well . . .' He leaves the rest of the sentence hanging.

Caroline turns to me, her eyes filled with loathing. 'You knew he was dying and said nothing because you wanted to persuade him to change his will.'

'I'd never have done anything like that even if I had known. And Anthony wouldn't have been influenced by me if I had attempted something so horrible.' I could stop all this, could offer to split everything down the middle, even though it would go against Anthony's dying wishes. I'm not sure I can live with it otherwise. The disappointment and betrayal Caroline is feeling must be acute. I open my mouth to speak, but she forestalls me.

'Wasn't half enough for you, you greedy, gold-digging slut? You'd better watch your back, because you are not getting away with this.'

'Come now, Caroline,' Tim says. 'That's uncalled for.'

'Don't you dare side with her. She was having an affair.'

'I . . . That's just not true.' I'm thrown off balance by this. I wasn't having an affair. I wouldn't.

'I saw you.'

She pulls her phone out of her bag and begins frantically scrolling. When she finds what she's looking for, she holds the phone up and moves the screen from me to Tim to DS Jones. It's a photograph. In it, you can clearly see my face, even though it's taken from a distance. I'm on the train; it's rush hour and it's packed. In front of me, his back to the camera, is a brown-haired man. I appear to be gazing raptly into his face. I'm completely gobsmacked. I hold out my hand and Caroline gives me the phone. I expand the picture with my thumb and forefinger. There is no denying it's me. All I can see of him is the collar of his dark coat, his hair, the edge of his ear.

'That isn't proof of anything. He could be a complete stranger.' I know as I say it that this isn't true. I feel it in my gut.

Jones is holding out her hand. I pass her the phone as casually as I can.

'How many strangers do you look at like that?' Caroline asks, eyebrows raised.

'Maybe he spoke to me. I don't know. It could be anything.'

'What date was this photo taken?' DS Jones asks.

'The thirtieth of May.'

107

'Did you take any more?'

'No,' Caroline replies. 'I got jolted, and then they were gone. I assume Rachel realised she'd been seen and they got off at the next station. I couldn't follow them because I was on my way to an audition. I didn't want to be late.'

'Can you forward it to me, please. I'll get you to make a statement later. It would have been helpful if you'd mentioned this before.'

'Sorry. I forgot about it.'

I protest at that. 'I don't believe you. You've been saving it. Were you going to show it to Anthony?'

'At some point,' Caroline says. 'I took it on impulse, but I wasn't sure what I was going to do with it, so I decided to wait until I needed it.' She turns her attention to Tim, whose face is a poker player's mask. 'I'll contest the will. I'll prove she manipulated him. This changes things, doesn't it? She wanted rid of my father, and she wanted his money. If she'd left, she would have been bound by the prenup.'

'It doesn't work like that, I'm afraid. Regardless of Rachel's behaviour, contesting the will is unlikely to result in the judge overturning it. You'd be better off coming to a private arrangement with Rachel than going to court.'

Caroline jumps up and shoulders her bag. 'It's obvious whose side you're on.' She catches a glance between me and Tim and laughs. 'Oh, it's like that, is it? How lovely.'

Tim looks utterly horrified. 'I beg your pardon.'

'Well, I don't beg yours. I know what this is about. The two of you have been plotting. I hope you're noting this, Detective.'

DS Jones doesn't so much as twitch. I suspect she's

reading the situation, taking mental notes. Neither of us is going to come off well.

'You need to calm down.' It's the first time I've seen Tim betray a streak of anger.

Caroline scowls and turns to DS Jones. 'Give me that letter back.'

Jones hands it to her, and she storms out, slamming the door.

'Oh dear,' Tim says with a sigh. He shuffles his papers together, indicating that the meeting is over.

'I'd like a chat with Mrs Gordon,' DS Jones says, adding, 'If you have time,' as she pushes herself away from the wall and takes the seat Caroline has vacated.

Tim sits down again. He looks up at me, and his face is desperately sad.

'I don't understand,' I say. My eyes fill with tears, and I wipe them away with the back of my hand. 'I wish I could remember.'

A flicker in Jones's eyes tells me she's hard put not to roll them. I feel sick, fearful and angry at myself, at Anthony and Caroline. There is no arguing with that photograph. It seems there was somebody, however much I want to deny it, and that somebody has not come forward. There must be a reason, and it can't be good.

Chapter 20

Everything I've thought about myself is a lie, everything I've said is a lie or hypocrisy. I've insisted I wouldn't have betrayed Anthony, and yet there's photographic evidence that says something very different. It isn't conclusive proof, but it isn't nothing either.

'We'll get to the bottom of this,' Tim says. 'Don't worry. Just answer the detective's questions, then you can rest.'

DS Jones sits forward, placing a digital recorder on the table, and takes a folder out of her black leather work bag. 'Are you ready?'

I compose myself and nod. Then remember to speak. 'Yes.'

She opens the folder and shows Tim and me a printed-out spreadsheet. 'This is a record of your movements during the seven weeks prior to your husband's murder. The period of time you've forgotten.' She doesn't add *allegedly*, for which I'm grateful. 'We've collated your phone records, emails, work diary, social engagements, et cetera, and created a timeline. You were late for work several times during those weeks. Mostly it was no more than fifteen minutes here and there, but it marked a change to your normal habits. There were two occasions when you were considerably later. The first was Monday the seventeenth of April. Your train was stuck in a tunnel. Signal failure. The second was Tuesday the thirtieth of May. I was wondering about that, but now we know it's the date on the photograph Caroline has just shown us. It seems likely that, as Miss Gordon said, you did get off the train with this man.'

'She said she assumed that,' Tim puts in. 'That isn't even circumstantial evidence. I've surprised you've suggested it.'

DS Jones gives a haughty shake of her head. She doesn't much care what Tim thinks, or she'd like us to believe that. 'Rachel?'

'I have no idea.'

'Let's just park that, then. I've been going through the notes and recordings from our previous chats, and I've found a couple of inconsistencies.'

Somehow that doesn't surprise me. 'Like what?'

'You say you have total memory loss for the seven weeks preceding Mr Gordon's death. And yet Hazel maintains she didn't mention her plans for a party to you until around three weeks before. So how could you know you didn't want to go?'

'If she said that, then she's forgotten. She started talking about it much earlier.' I actually remember Hazel skidding her chair over to my desk with her heels. *I'm going to be thirty in June! Party time!* But I have no idea when that was.

'And you can say that because . . .' Jones raises her eyebrows.

'Sorry. I don't know.'

'Mrs Gordon, I simply do not believe in your memory loss. Your consultant thinks it likely that you don't remember the crash happening, maybe even what led you to get in the car, but not the weeks preceding it. The only messages

111

about the party were sent within that time. If there was an unrecorded conversation—'

'I'm sure there was.'

'Unfortunately, that can't be proved.' Her voice softens. 'Must have been nice to have a chance to let your hair down. I expect it was difficult to do that, being married to a man so much older than you. I imagine that became a little wearing after a while. Not to mention being treated like a trophy wife when you're a perfectly intelligent woman.'

'Detective,' Tim says, a warning in his voice. 'If you have a question, ask it.'

'Of course. Was the age difference between you and your husband becoming a strain?'

'Not particularly, no.'

'Really? Powerful men tend to go for younger women as they get older. They don't always realise those women have minds of their own. Perhaps you found someone who treated you as an equal. The man Caroline saw you with.'

There is nothing I can say to that. I simply don't know.

'If you were unfaithful to your husband, you're going to be feeling ashamed, worried that it'll reflect badly on you given the way he died, but it's always better to tell the truth.' Jones smiles. 'You can't be arrested for infidelity. I'd advise you to think very carefully, Rachel. Presumably you had to communicate with this man. Let's meet him, find out where he was on the night Mr Gordon died and see if we can build a clearer picture of what happened.'

I glance at Tim. He doesn't meet my eye. Does he not believe me either? It occurs to me that this is the first time DS Jones has called me by my first name. Her attitude towards me has become a little less respectful.

'I can't very well set up a meeting when I have no idea who he is.'

'Well, no, but let's be positive. The consensus amongst the doctors is that your memory will return. It's just a matter of time.'

'I hope so.' I put my hand on my thigh, covering the dressing. Underneath it, the stitches throb.

'Did Mr Gordon give you any hint that he was planning on changing his will?'

'I don't know.'

'If you can't remember, can you at least account for his decision?'

I think about it. 'I told you about the row we had over Caroline. That's the last thing I am absolutely certain I remember clearly.'

'The supper you told me about?'

'Yes.'

'You said Caroline assaulted her guest.'

'That's right. With a kitchen knife.'

DS Jones sits up straighter. 'Did he report it?'

'If I was told, I don't remember.'

'I can find out.'

'I don't think the wound was bad. Although if he didn't report it, it's highly probable Anthony paid him off or gave Caroline the money to do so. That would have been in character. He was always throwing money at her problems.'

'So you persuaded Mr Gordon to punish her?'

I frown. 'No. We had a frank discussion.'

'Which resulted in him cutting his daughter out of his will and leaving everything to you?'

'I have no idea, but it seems likely the two things are

related. I'm not convinced he would have told me he planned to change his will, though.'

'You were his wife. Didn't you talk to each other?'

I glance over at Tim. He's listening carefully.

'We didn't really talk about money, because it was never an issue. I knew very little about his finances before he lost money on crypto. I hadn't even known he'd invested in it. It hit him hard and I noticed, despite him trying to hide his anxiety, so he had to talk to me. But the day-to-day financial stuff . . .' I wrinkle my nose, feeling a little ashamed. We had so much it never came up. 'No.'

'He was diagnosed with cancer around the same time and doesn't appear to have told you that either. I thought the point of marriage was to have someone on your side. Your relationship doesn't sound very convincing.'

I feel wretched and ashamed.

'I've never thought about it like that. Finances aside, I thought we did tell each other everything.'

Jones gives me a long look. Cancer and a possible lover are significant conversations not to have had.

'He might have told me about the cancer,' I mutter.

'Can we go back to what you said on learning of your husband's death?'

'Mrs Gordon has already explained that she was drugged and disoriented,' Tim says. 'She has retracted the statement and I see no reason to go over that ground again.'

'Things have changed. There is now a clear incentive for her to have wanted her husband dead.' Jones's voice is clipped.

'There is not,' I say. 'I was happily married to Anthony. I had everything I wanted.'

'Except the possibility of benefiting financially from a divorce.' DS Jones glances at Tim. 'Mr Vaughan?'

He nods. 'The police know about the prenup, Rachel.'

'If there was someone else involved,' DS Jones says, 'you would leave the marriage with nothing. Unless, of course, you were widowed. The man Caroline saw you with? Did you ask him to kill Mr Gordon?'

'No!' I turn in desperation to Tim.

'Detective,' he says, 'Mrs Gordon is tired. The painkillers are very strong and affect her ability to think or articulate clearly what she wants to say. This is simply not a level playing field. We've established she doesn't remember any exchanges between her and her husband. She may do so in the fullness of time, but for the moment there is little to be gained in badgering her.'

'Of course. My apologies, Rachel.' There's the hint of a sneer in Jones's voice.

Pulling myself together, I manage a question. 'Have you talked to the charity Anthony supported? The Begin Again programme? It worked with former prisoners to rehabilitate them. Maybe he did something to upset one of them.'

DS Jones nods. 'We've spoken to Stir as well. There was a guy they needed to let go. Alexander Stratton.'

I feel the brush of a feather against my neck, and frown. The name rings a bell. But then it's gone.

'He stole items from guests at a charity function. But we've interviewed him, and his alibi checks out. He was babysitting for a friend on the night Anthony died.'

I remember the waiter who seemed so contemptuous of me at the fundraiser. 'What did he look like?'

'White. Late thirties. Brown hair, brown eyes. Why?'

115

'Oh, nothing.' That guy was younger, maybe as young as twenty, and he was mixed race.

'If there isn't anything else . . .' Tim says.

'Thank you, Tim.' I say after DS Jones has left the room. 'You were wonderful.'

'I feel like I'm shoring up a dam.'

'Don't you believe me either?'

'Of course I do.' His eyes tell me different. 'But I'm beginning to wonder if there might not be a lot more to what happened that night.'

'Please don't stop representing me. I couldn't bear it.'

He looks uncomfortable. 'I told Anthony I'd look after you, and I will. But you have to understand, as her godfather, I have a duty to Caroline as well. I can't take sides. I have to be scrupulously fair.'

Chapter 21

Two weeks later, I'm driven home in a taxi. It's a lonely feeling, like arriving at Heathrow after a long absence and finding there's no one to greet you. The last time I remember being here, Kew Green was a lush emerald. Now the heatwave has turned the grass pale and crisp, the sky is an unrelenting blue, and beady-eyed crows stalk overflowing bins. The horse chestnuts, hazels and plane trees provide shade while children play, there are people sitting outside pubs and on benches, teenagers in huddled groups, and the late-afternoon sun beats off the bonnets and roofs of cars. Passengers getting off the bus in front of us wilt.

We turn off the main road and approach the house, where there are journalists waiting. Half a dozen of them. They see the taxi and raise their cameras. How did they know I'd be coming home today? One of the hospital staff must have told them. I avert my face as they rush me, a barrage of clicks and flashes, calling out their ridiculous questions. *What happened, Rachel? Did you kill your husband?* I grasp my keys and shove them clumsily at the lock, let myself in and slam the door in their faces.

Inside the hallway it's cool and dim after the bright sunlight. I place my bag at my feet and gasp in a breath. The house is silent.

Anthony isn't here.

The door on the right, which leads into his study, is closed. I open it and go in. It's the same room it's always been, but it feels different, a looking-glass version. The desk hasn't been cleared, so it seems as though he's just popped out, but the Edwardian mantel clock isn't ticking because only Anthony is ... was allowed to touch it. Dust has settled on the surfaces. I'm grateful that Kath hasn't been in to clean it, so I can keep the scent of Anthony a while longer. I step back and pull the door shut, drag myself upstairs and fall into bed. I am a widow.

I don't know how long I sleep, but it's twilight when I wake. I slip into my dressing gown and start the painful journey downstairs.

There's a clang, and I stop, one foot on the floor, the other on the bottom step. My instinct is to retreat to my bedroom, but it feels like too much effort. I have to face Caroline sometime.

I hold my breath and open the kitchen door, then stand stock still on the threshold. A man is rummaging through the drawers in the dresser. I take in the open patio doors. I wouldn't put it past Caroline to have forgotten to lock up when she went out. There have been occasions when someone has strayed down the alleyway leading from the river path, past the row of cottages, to the door in the wall at the end of our garden, and attempted to climb over, so security is important. He hasn't noticed me, and as he closes one drawer and opens another, I quietly prise a kitchen knife from the magnetic strip on the wall.

'I have a knife,' I say. I'm weak and it's heavy, and I need both hands to hold it steady.

The man wheels around, his hands held up. 'Jesus, Rachel, you gave me a fright!'

I release my breath. It's Dave, Mia's husband.

He lowers his hands. 'Sorry, I was looking for a bottle opener.' He indicates the bottled beer on the counter near his elbow. 'Mia and Caro should be back any minute. I hope you don't mind. We've been here since last week. The poor girl's in a terrible state.'

When I don't say anything, he adds, 'We're going home tomorrow. I can't leave the dogs with my brother for too long.' They have two Border collies, Paddy and Katie, whom they dote on. Mike looks after them whenever Dave and Mia are away. 'We'll be back for the funeral.'

I've always liked Dave. Scruffy and rarely clean-shaven, on the attractive side of beta, he is the antithesis of Anthony with his 'don't give a shit' attitude about material possessions and air of benign goodwill to all men. It isn't hard to understand how Mia, hurt by the end of her marriage to an inflated ego, would have fallen for him and the more tranquil life he offered.

After a silence, he touches his head. 'Looks painful. Is it painful?'

'It's bearable.'

'Make you a brew?'

'Just a glass of water. I'll get it.' I notice the basket of vegetables on the counter and pick up a potato. It smells earthy. 'Thanks for bringing food. Are these from your garden?'

'Yes. We didn't know what you might need. There are eggs as well.'

I look around. The kitchen is messy, but I don't mind. Life's too short. I cut a slice of bread, cut it in half, put half back, scrape a thread of butter on it, then fill a glass with water and go outside. The bread is incredible, soft and crusty with a sprinkling of sea salt.

'Did you make this?' I ask as he follows me out.

'I did.' He joins me on the old wooden bench, crossing his long legs at the ankle. His skin is bronzed, heavily lined and leathery. He isn't wearing any socks, and there are holes in his shorts and in the hem of his faded Glastonbury 1990 T-shirt. He lays his arms along the back of the bench and contemplates me.

'I'm very sorry about Anthony. It must have been a terrible shock for you.'

Aeroplane noise floods the air, something I'm so used to I rarely look up. I can tell just by the sound it makes whether a plane is coming in to land at Heathrow or on its way out.

'I assume Caroline's told you about the will,' I say.

'Yeah. She's not a happy bunny.'

'Did she show you Anthony's letter?' I shade my eyes to see his face better. Dave is an intelligent, self-sufficient man; someone you'd want on your side in a crisis. I remind myself he is going to be on Caroline's side, not mine. Just like Tim.

'He knew he was dying. He had time to think about things, to make decisions. I understand where he was coming from, but it wasn't fair, you know, to pull the rug out from under Caro like that.' He pauses. 'What are you going to do about it? Are you going to kick her out?'

'I don't know. I want to get through the funeral before I make any decisions.'

'You'll do the right thing.' He says it like there's no question.

120

I refrain from telling him it might have been helpful if she hadn't called me a gold-digging slut in front of Tim and Detectives Jones. I'm determined not to be petty or vindictive. Fortunately, we're stopped from pursuing the conversation when the door to the street closes with a thud.

'Darling,' Mia calls.

'Out here.'

The two women walk into the garden. Mia is visibly taken aback when she sees me.

Behind her mother, Caroline rolls her eyes. 'I didn't realise you were coming home today.'

'I was discharged.' I respond, feeling like an unwelcome guest. 'I wasn't getting much sleep in the hospital.' In my mind's eye, I see the shadowy figure standing at the end of my bed.

'Do you know when they'll release Anthony's body?' Mia asks.

It's an irrational response, but the sound of his name on Mia's lips jars. He is *my* husband. Was my husband. Nevertheless, I respond politely.

'Very soon. Monday or Tuesday next week. They'll let me know.' Detective Jones gave me the news earlier this morning. 'I'll look at dates for the funeral and make the arrangements.'

'Why don't you let us do that?' Mia says. 'There's such a lot to organise. You just concentrate on getting better.'

'I'd rather do it myself.'

'Really?' Caroline says. 'I'm not sure that's appropriate.'

'What do you mean?'

'I heard that the first thing you said when you were told Dad had died was that you killed him.'

'Caroline,' Dave says.

To my horror, heat climbs through my body. 'Who told you that?'

'The nurses like to gossip, and I'm good at listening. I hope it was worth it.'

I press my cold tumbler against my wrist in a desperate effort to cool down. 'I had just come out of a coma. I didn't know what I was saying.'

'Nonetheless, you said it.'

'Caro, perhaps leave this until tomorrow,' Dave says. 'Rachel is exhausted.'

'So am I,' Caroline retorts. 'I've barely slept.' She whips her head, snake-like, back to me. 'I found his body. How do you think I feel?'

'It must have been horrible, but I had nothing to do with it.' My mouth is bone dry. I take a glug of water. 'I don't know what happened to him that night.'

'Don't you think it's odd that he cut me out of his will just a few weeks before he died? He would never have done that without being coerced.'

'Did you know about his diagnosis before Tim told us?'

'No,' Caroline says. 'But I'm assuming you did. You must have been desperate when you realised you might lose your luxury lifestyle. You should be ashamed of yourself, manipulating a dying man.'

'Caro,' Mia says. 'Don't get angry, darling. Rachel understands.' She leans forward and fixes me with her eyes. 'Anthony must have knee-jerked. If he'd given himself time to think about it, I'm sure he'd have been fairer. We don't begrudge you your share, but honestly, for him to leave Caro high and dry, it's dreadfully hurtful.'

Caroline does an excellent job of looking dreadfully hurt, but there is hatred in the gaze she aims at me. 'Give up, Stepmother dear. You're not a good enough actor. You've been out for what you can get all along. You never loved my father; you just spent his money.'

This is so patently untrue that I'm left with my mouth hanging open.

Dave puts a quelling hand on her shoulder. 'Enough, Caro.'

Later I carry out a fingertip search of my bedroom, reasoning that if I was having an affair, there would be evidence, because that's the kind of person I am. In my teens it would have been a train ticket or a biro, but these days I don't know what kind of trivial souvenir I'd have taken to pore over later. Without a digital trail, I'm certain I would've kept something solid and real.

There's nothing in my dressing table, nothing slipped between the layers of clothes in my chest of drawers. It's only when I check my bedside cabinet that I find something. And even this could be nothing.

Amongst miscellany is a pack of chewing gum. I lay it in the palm of my hand. Once upon a time I used gum to quell the urge to binge-eat, but I haven't resorted to it in years. Anthony hated the sight of me chewing, and because I wanted him, I stopped. The habit was hard to kick.

I suppose I could have lapsed.

I wrap my fingers around it, close my eyes and an image swims behind my lids. I'm on the Tube, staring out of the window at the crowd moving towards the exit. Amongst them is a man. I can't see his face, but I know it's him, because he's central to the picture and he's the figure my gaze is drawn to. I open my eyes and carefully put the packet back in the drawer. My stomach feels tight. Confirmation that Caroline was correct in her assumption is not the kind of information I'm looking for.

Chapter 22

On Monday morning, I shower and cut off what remains of my hair, careful to avoid the stitches. The semi-knitted wound makes me queasy and I don't do a very good job. Perhaps it will grow back thicker. That would be nice. I rifle through the drawer where I keep my holiday clothes, fish out a silk scarf I bought in Athens a few years ago and wrap it around my head. Knotted at the base of my skull, it turns me into a stranger. I have dark circles under my eyes, bruises in shades of yellow and purple, and I look as though I've been having chemo. I wait until 9.30 and then I FaceTime Hazel from my bed.

'You remember nothing about coming to my house?' she says. 'Oh wow. Tell me everything.'

I was ready to see shock on her face at the sight of me, but still touch my face when her eyes inevitably widen. I nervously adjust the edge of the scarf. She says, 'Oh,' and I say, 'It's fine.'

She's sitting against the backdrop of the open-plan office. I scan the familiar space around her. It's not that I'm in a hurry to get back to work, but I miss the normality of it.

'Rachel?'

I pull my focus back to her face. 'I only know what the police told me, and that's the bare bones. They said I drove away from your house minutes after I missed a call from Anthony. He left a message on my voicemail.'

'That's right. You went as white as a sheet. What did he say?'

I pause.

'Sorry. I shouldn't ask.'

'No, it's all right. I . . . um. He said, "What have you done?"'

'God, that is weird. Does it mean anything to you?'

'No. Absolutely nothing.'

'You poor thing. Well, I can definitely help.' She sounds a little too pleased to be the one tasked with fleshing it out for me. 'Okay,' she says, then nibbles her bottom lip. 'Well, there were five of us: us two and three friends of mine, Zandra, Lauren and Cynthia. We got pissed on Zandra's cocktails.'

'How much did I drink?'

'Dunno. I stopped counting.' She grimaces when she sees my expression. 'Sorry, I didn't mean to joke about it.'

'Doesn't matter. What happened next?'

'We were talking about people you didn't know, and I was worried you were bored. You didn't make much effort to join in the conversation, even though I kept trying to include you, so in the end I gave up. I don't think you were upset; just not in the present, if you know what I mean.'

'The perfect guest.' I smile ruefully. 'I'm sorry.'

'You're forgiven.'

'And the phone call?'

'We were dancing. It was about twenty minutes before the limo was meant to arrive to take us to the club. You grabbed your bag and ran outside. You didn't even go upstairs to fetch your stuff. I must get it back to you. Anyway, we did our best. I'm sorry we didn't try harder, but you wouldn't see reason. You lashed out when I tried to take your keys off you. The rain was horrendous, but you got in your car. Lauren and I came after you and banged on the window, but you just screeched off. It was awful.'

I can picture their horrified faces, the rain spoiling their make-up, wreaking havoc on their blow-dried hair, but I have no sense of having actually been there, no sense of the extreme anxiety I must have been experiencing to have done what I did.

'I should have called the police,' Hazel goes on. 'I should have sent everyone home, but Lauren and the others kept saying, "Why should she spoil your party?" They were really angry with you and convinced me we should go ahead. It wasn't much fun.'

'I'm so sorry I ruined the evening.'

'It's given my friends something to talk about.'

I let this go. A bit of grim humour never goes amiss.

'You're not in a good place, are you?' Hazel says.

My eyes prick. 'I miss Anthony.'

'Of course you do. You have to give yourself time. The police will find out who's responsible. That'll help.'

'I'm not so sure.' I lean back into my pillows. 'They think I had something to do with it.'

'Oh my God. Why?'

'Anthony cut Caroline out of his will in the weeks before he died. They're saying I knew about it, but I didn't.'

'But they know you were with me. You have an alibi.'

'They think I may have had an accomplice.'

Hazel laughs. 'I mean, you are a highly organised

individual, but hiring a hitman? I can't see that. Did you withdraw a large amount of cash that week? Or buy yourself a burner phone?'

My mouth twitches. When she puts it like that, it does seem farcical. 'Not as far as I know.' I don't want to ask the next question, but I have to. 'Did I ever talk about a man?'

'What kind of man? Do you mean were you having an affair?'

'I'm not sure. I don't think so, but there's some stuff going on; stuff I don't understand. Caroline saw me on the Tube with a stranger and took a picture. We looked like we were having a meaningful conversation.'

'Ah.' Hazel pauses. 'Actually, you did go beetroot once when I suggested you had a lover. But you denied it.'

'When was this?'

'Can't remember, but not that long ago.'

I draw a ragged breath. 'And when I was in hospital, I chased a guy down the stairs after I woke up and caught him watching me.'

'Really? Wow. This is seriously weird. I think you would have told me if you were seeing someone. If you hadn't said anything at work, you'd have mentioned it at my party. You were hammered.'

'I still don't understand that. It's not like me.'

'It wasn't like you at all. You scared me.'

'I'm sorry.' I genuinely am. I might be ambivalent about Hazel, but she has a good heart.

'You don't have to apologise,' she says. 'Why don't you come back to my house? It might help.'

'I can't drive. I lost my licence.'

'I can pick you up from the station. It's no trouble.'

I don't want to go back there yet. Maybe in a few weeks, but now feels too soon. 'I'll let you know,' I say. 'But thank you.'

I end the call as quickly as I can. My head is so full of contradictions and confusion it's hard to get to grips with what really matters. I have no sense of direction, just a desire to put this part of my life behind me, and no one is going to let me do that. I crush my fist against my mouth to stop the moan of despair. Enough of the self-pity. As a child, if I cried, my mother would just roll her eyes.

Chapter 23

The doorbell rings. I go out onto the landing and listen while either Mia or Caroline answers it. I detect DS Jones's voice and battle with the instinct to slip silently back into my bedroom. At some point, the detective will catch up with me. I might as well get it over with, whatever 'it' is.

'Rachel.' Dave pushes back his chair when I walk into the kitchen, adding unnecessarily, 'The detective's here to see you.'

I glance at DS Jones. There is something in the way she looks directly into my eyes. Something self-satisfied, triumphant. I recently learned from Tim that my gut feeling was right: this is Jones's first case as senior investigating officer. This is career-defining; this is her proving she isn't just a pretty face. At my expense.

'You can use the front room,' Mia says, as though this is still her house. The way she's behaving is strange, almost as though I never happened. Perhaps she never got over Anthony after all. Or perhaps she never got over the loss of this house. 'You can be private there. We'll probably be gone by the time you're finished. We'll see you on the thirteenth.'

When I look blank, she adds, 'For the funeral. We're coming the day before to help Caroline get the house ready.'

'Oh. Okay.' So they just went ahead and did it without checking with me. I deserve it.

*

Jones closes the door, indicates the armchair and props her small backside on the arm of the sofa, immediately giving herself the advantage. 'I spoke to Gail Kelsey this morning.'

When I look blank, she adds, 'Ms Kelsey is one of the nurses who looked after you in the ICU. Late forties? Highlighted blonde hair? Do you remember her?'

'Oh. Yes. I think so, anyway.'

'Let me read her witness statement.' She gets out her phone, swipes it and reads from the screen. '"It was about eleven o'clock. I'd nipped to the toilet, so I put my head round the ward door to check everyone was asleep. I noticed Mrs Gordon's curtains had been opened a few centimetres, and she wasn't in her bed, so I had a look for her. I couldn't find her on the floor, so I went to the lifts, but before I pressed the button, I heard someone on the stairs. I ran down and caught her."' She looks up from her phone. 'That all ties in with what you said.'

I nod in agreement.

'Kelsey goes on to say, "That's when Mrs Gordon shouted a name. Sean."' Jones then asks, with deceptive gentleness, 'Do you have any idea who Sean is?'

'No, I don't.'

'But you called out to him. And there's the photograph Caroline took. Even you must admit to the possibility that you were seeing another man.'

'There's no concrete proof, though, is there?'

DS Jones looks at me shrewdly, and an awkward silence stretches between us.

'I think you've been lying since the beginning. I think you met someone, fell in love with him and plotted to kill

131

Anthony because you knew you wouldn't benefit from a divorce. Did this man coerce you, Rachel, or was it the other way round? Did you deliberately ensnare him so you could get rid of your husband without getting your hands dirty?'

I stare at her in disbelief. 'You know that's not true.'

There's a packet of chewing gum in the drawer next to my bed that I'm sure I didn't buy. If it belonged to this man, his fingerprints will be on it. If he has a criminal record, the police will have physical evidence to connect us. There is a vice round my head. Do I fetch the chewing gum now and ask DS Jones to test it just in case? That would be the honest thing to do. That would show I have integrity. But it could also condemn me.

'How do I know it, Rachel? Explain it to me.'

'I can't.'

'Let me help you. I'll go through the facts, shall I?' She lifts her hand and counts on her fingers, gripping the tips before letting each spring away. 'One. When you first met Anthony, you told him you found him extremely attractive. If that isn't predatory behaviour, I don't know what is. Two. You ousted the wife he loved and moved in, signed a prenup and got your man to the altar. Three. Twelve years later, Caroline is cut out of her father's will. Shortly after that, he is brutally killed while you're at the house of a friend, leaving you in line to inherit the bulk of his fortune. Do you agree with all that?'

'Not the accusation of being predatory, but yes, broadly, that is what happened.'

I wonder who told DS Jones how me and Anthony got together. Few people know about it. Would I have told Hazel? It's the kind of thing she would have been curious about. She's always asking people where they met their partners. I doubt it, though . . . My stomach drops. I remember one boozy night, the work Christmas drinks.

'Did Hazel tell you how Anthony and I met?'

'It doesn't matter who told me.' DS Jones shakes her head, her expression almost sympathetic. 'It doesn't show you in a very good light, does it?'

'I tried to walk away.'

'But you were in love. I know. I'm sure the attraction was genuine; a bolt of lightning.'

I glare at her. 'It was.'

'Was it like that with Sean too?'

It's as if a curtain is suddenly pulled back. A man turns. I'm momentarily dazzled by his smile, and then he's gone, and I'm looking into DS Jones's pale blue eyes.

'What is it?' Jones says, frowning. 'What have you remembered?'

'I haven't remembered anything. I had a twinge.' I touch my ribs. 'Why not Caroline?'

'I beg your pardon.'

'Caroline didn't know her father's will had been changed or that he'd sustained huge losses in cryptocurrency. Anthony made me swear not to tell her. And she found the body. She was in the same situation as me that evening, out of town, but close enough to be able to drive home, and she could equally have paid someone to do it. So why focus on me? Unless you're biased.'

'I'll pretend I didn't hear that,' DS Jones says curtly. 'If you have a complaint to make about the way the investigation is being carried out, you should do so through the official channels.'

I shrug.

'You've been tying yourself in knots trying to make us believe you've lost your memory, but you've slipped up on numerous occasions. That's why the focus is on you. I went to see your mother yesterday, and the picture she painted was pretty telling. She said you lied all the time. Even about the smallest things. She was worried when you were a teenager that you were sleeping around.'

Good old Mum. She always did know where to drizzle the lemon juice. Of course I was a liar. It's what comes of growing up on edge, too terrified of having my deficiencies pointed out to my friends to want to invite anyone home, having to make excuses; having to lie. That's what eating disorders teach you, the shame so intense you'll do anything not to get found out. I only asked for help once I was at uni, and that was because I wasn't the only one with severe problems in my student accommodation. As for sleeping around, that's a gross exaggeration. I did have sex before I should have done – that's low self-esteem for you – but it has nothing to do with what's happening today.

'We've been estranged for a long time, Detective.'

'So she said. She's very unhappy about that. She still worries about you.'

'No she doesn't. It wouldn't occur to her. Don't you think it's strange that she said something so nasty? I don't know about yours, but mothers tend not to do that. So, is that your case against me? That my mother has accused me of being a liar and a slut?'

'Is that why you don't have children? Because you think you might be like her?'

I'm so shocked by the question, I'm almost lost for words. 'Is that what you really think of me?'

Jones sighs. 'It doesn't matter what I think of you.'

'Then why ask a question like that?'

'It helps to build a picture.' She's becoming irritable. I suspect she knows she's crossed a line. 'Do you want me to tell you what I think happened that night?'

I shrug but don't say anything. I can't help but be interested in her version of events.

'You came to an agreement with this man, either financial or romantic, to deal with your inconvenient husband, accepted Hazel Gifford's invitation in order to give yourself an alibi, then had an abrupt change of heart after listening to Anthony's voice message. You couldn't get in touch with your accomplice because you'd agreed not to exchange details that could link you, so you panicked and got into your car, hoping to stop what was already a fait accompli.'

I think about this. I hope it's not true. 'Are you going to arrest me?'

'Not at this present time, no.' Her gaze flickers, and I see something vulnerable. What she has is flimsy. She needs more and she's going to keep digging until she gets it.

'In that case, perhaps you can give me advance notice next time you want to interview me, so I can make sure my lawyer is present. I'm not talking to you again alone.'

When she's left, I sit for a while, thinking. She went all the way to York to interview my parents. She must be desperate. I feel pretty desperate myself. For a mother to say such horrible things about her own daughter is petty and vindictive beyond belief. I've never thought about it in that way, but perhaps DS Jones is right and one of the reasons

I didn't put up a battle over children with Anthony was because I *was* worried I might turn out like her. That makes me very sad. It's been ten years since I've seen her. I think it's time we had a conversation.

Chapter 24

After lunch, eaten alone in my bedroom, I write a long and careful email to Tim outlining what was said between me and the detective, trying to remember everything and knowing I'm bound to have said something I shouldn't. I pack what I need for the night and get ready to leave.

'I'm going to Mum's,' I tell Caroline. 'I'll be back tomorrow.'

'Your mother's? I thought you weren't on speaking terms.'

'We aren't,' I say shortly. I turn on my heel, put on my sunglasses and leave the house.

On my way through King's Cross station, I pick up a copy of the *Metro*, and open it once I'm settled in my seat. There's a picture of me on page two from the day I came home from the hospital, and an article outlining the case. It seems clear the journalist found a willing interviewee in Caroline, because they mention the way I deliberately went about wrecking Anthony's first marriage, my shopping habits – that bit is rubbish – and my convenient amnesia. All very salacious and wonderful tabloid fodder. At least the scarf and glasses give me some anonymity. I push the paper away from me in disgust, but it shakes me. If they want me to be perceived as the evil second wife – and why not when it makes a good story? – then what hope do I have of turning public opinion? I type my name into the internet. Big mistake. The comments under various online articles are vile. Mostly different iterations of *murdering bitch*, along with various unsavoury and violent acts the trolls think are my just deserts.

By the time I get out of the minicab outside my parents' house, it's early evening. I ring the doorbell and watch my mother's now stout figure darken the wobbly glass door. I didn't let her know I was coming until I was past Grantham, worried she'd find some reason to put me off. I tweak the scarf, then irritably take it off and stuff it in my pocket.

She is seventy. I haven't seen her since her sixtieth birthday party, which Anthony insisted I attend. My mother was cool, my father trying desperately to make everything friendly. It was held at their golf club and I was seated at the back of the room alongside a collection of relatives I hadn't seen since I was a teenager. It was painfully awkward. They obviously thought I'd deserted my parents. My devoted mother. I sat through the dinner, through the speeches, and then left. I haven't spoken to either of them since. If I do feel guilt, it's about my father. But keeping in touch with him has been impossible. I didn't want to make him choose, because there was no way he'd have chosen me.

After the initial shock at my appearance, Mum smiles. Possibly that remark to DS Jones was designed to galvanise me into doing precisely this. Visiting.

'Rachel,' she says. 'How are you, darling? What a dreadful time you've had.'

She air-kisses my cheek. The smell of lipstick, powder

and perfume is overwhelming. She never used to load it on like this. She's clinging to a beauty that has already deserted her. I feel a moment's pity, but I quash it. She neither wants nor deserves my compassion. 'You don't look too bad. But perhaps you should cover up that head with a nice scarf. I could lend you one.'

'I'm fine, thanks. If I can't show my stitches in my parents' house, where can I?'

She frowns. 'Well, as you long as you're happy. Take your shoes off and come in. Your father's walking Toby. They should be back soon. He's going to pick up some supper from the local Tesco. Frozen fish pies. That's all right, isn't it? You didn't give me time to go to Waitrose. I can always phone him if you'd rather have something else.'

'Fish pie is fine.'

The kitchen is untidy and smells. The floor is dirty and the surfaces are cluttered. Mum was always slovenly, but we had help when I was small, so it was under control. The window above the sink looks out onto a small garden bright with flowers in the twilight. Dad's work, I assume. I pretend not to notice the lipstick mark on the glass she hands me.

'I'm so sorry about what happened to Anthony.'

She hasn't sent a condolence card, and none of the flowers that came to the hospital were from her.

She's given me a gin and tonic, which I don't like purely because the smell reminds me of her. I take a sip and put the glass down.

'Why did you say those things to the detective?'

Her gaze is theatrically innocent. 'What things, darling?'

'About me being a liar.'

139

'I'd have thought that was obvious. It's important to tell the truth.'

Exhausted, and a little unnerved, I swallow another mouthful of the G&T, and then another. 'DS Jones asked if I didn't have children because I was afraid I might be like you. That I'd treat my children the way you treated me.'

My mother raises over-plucked eyebrows. 'What on earth are you talking about? You were very much loved as a child. You were never mistreated. I really don't know what I've done to deserve this.'

'I'm not like you, but I was raised by you, so what worries me is that there are bound to be things I picked up by osmosis. You know, nurture versus nature. When you're cruel to a child, you're planting a seed.'

'For heaven's sake.' My mother peers at me like she's studying a particularly interesting beetle. Before she squishes it. 'Rachel, darling. I have no idea what you're talking about. I adored you. I may have been strict, but that was only because I don't like spoilt brats. I lavished you with love, but I made sure you understood the consequences of disobedience. Your father was always too soft with you. A child's behaviour ultimately reflects on her mother. You do see that, don't you? It was no fault of mine that you were difficult, that you lied when you were caught out. I've heard people say I'm the most honest person they know.'

'They weren't necessarily being complimentary,' I respond. 'You harped on about my weight in front of my friends. You made me feel ashamed. You can say you were simply being honest, but it was only your opinion, and I was a child. I believed it all.'

'I don't like vain little girls either. You were very attention-seeking.' She wrinkles up her face and does a passable imitation of an unspeakable brat. 'Look at me, look at me!'

I see myself, a small, chubby child standing behind my mother in the school office. We're not the only ones there. Mum makes some laughing comment about my weight. I see the dismay on the face of the school secretary, her pity, and my eyes prick.

Mum sighs and reaches for me. I step away and she huffs.

'You can't blame your problems on me, Rachel. I certainly didn't bring you up to commit acts of violence against your husband.'

She turns away, opens the dishwasher and starts unloading it. I automatically go to help her, pulling out the basket of cutlery.

'I have not committed any acts of violence.'

'That's not what the journalists think.'

I laugh. 'Jesus, Mother.'

'Don't swear in this house. And there's no smoke without fire. Are you in therapy, by any chance?'

I groan under my breath. 'No, I'm not.'

'Because that's where this stuff comes from. Young people don't take responsibility for anything these days. They blame their failures on anyone but themselves. Mostly their parents.'

Why did I come here? She will never understand.

'Charming detective,' she says.

'She must have been,' I retort, 'for you to have told her so much about me.'

'What do you want me to do? Shall I phone her and tell her it's not true, or that I exaggerated? I was only trying to do the right thing.'

'That would be nice, but I doubt it would do much good. No, I came because I'd like you to hear me out. You damaged me as a child, and you're still trying to damage me now. You couldn't bear it when I married Anthony. You couldn't countenance that I was loved despite your best efforts.'

'Please don't raise your voice. You're giving me a headache. I'm sorry you feel that life is a competition between us. It couldn't be further from the truth. I was happy for you and I feel your grief now.' She presses her hand to her heart and then says quietly, as my father's key turns in the lock, 'If you were in any way responsible for Anthony's death, you will have my support. He made me unwelcome in his house and drove a wedge between us.'

'Mum—'

'And you should be profoundly grateful that I didn't mention your selective memory to the detective. I was tempted.'

I freeze. 'What are you talking about?'

'You know exactly, Rachel. If you were in trouble for anything, it was *I don't remember*. And the nasty things you've said about me. It's all rubbish. False memories. I did not draw attention to your puppy fat. I did not shame you in front of your friends. It hurts that you continue to push that narrative. I did my best, as a mother to a difficult child. I gave you love, and what did you give back? The moment you had your rich man, you dropped me and your father. Not good enough for you.'

142

'Mum. If you'd let me get a word in—'

'You're my only child, and contrary to what you might think, I do love you. Hugh, darling. Look who's here!'

My father enters on the tail of their cocker spaniel and blinks twice when he sees me, then places his shopping on the counter and pulls me into a hug. He smells of beer. I imagine he enjoyed a quiet half-hour in the local pub before coming home. Did Mum tell him to prolong the walk? I wouldn't put it past her.

My eyes start itching within five minutes of getting into bed. I'm in my childhood bedroom and I strongly suspect Toby curls up on this bed at night. Fair enough. I didn't give my mother any notice, so she's not going to have changed the sheets. No problem. I have a packet of antihistamines in an unfastened pocket inside my bag. When I pull it out, a business card comes with it. Curious, I read the smart embossed print: *Dr Dominic Parrish MRCPsych, Clinical Psychologist.*

It lists his number and email address, and disturbingly, there's a scrawled note on the back.

Get in touch if it would help to talk.

Weird. I have no memory of being given this. Perhaps someone at work thought I might need a shrink and happened to have it to hand. Was I visibly struggling during those seven forgotten weeks? They hold so many frustrating secrets, and this is simply another of them. Something is nagging at me, but I can't pin it down. I put the card back where I found it, wash a pill down with water and drift off to sleep.

*

I'm out of bed and ready for the minicab at 6.30. I don't leave a note, but I know my mother is awake and listening. I imagine her lying in bed, ears pricked, eyes wide. The visit hasn't done me any good. My demons are still with me. She won that round, like she's won most rounds. I expect she's delighted that I no longer have my perfect life. DS Jones was right in a way. I would have screwed up motherhood: over-compensated, overthought every decision, overwhelmed my poor child with an excess of love.

My phone rings as I'm walking up to the front door. I drop my keys back into my bag and check the caller display. It's Tim. My stomach tenses unpleasantly.

'I've got some good news for you,' he says.

The tension eases. 'What is it?'

'The CPS have refused the police permission to take their case against you to court on the grounds that the evidence is flimsy and circumstantial. Basically, they're not prepared to waste taxpayers' money on it and the case is closed.'

'Oh my God. That's wonderful news! Thank you so much.'

'Don't get too excited. It can be reopened if stronger evidence comes to light in the meantime.'

'Thank you. Thank you so much. For everything you've done.'

'There is some bad news as well, I'm afraid. I had a letter from IFR's community engagement officer. They won't be renewing the trust next year. The Begin Again programme and Stir are going have find new sponsors.

'Oh no.' I should have seen this coming. Didn't Anthony

144

say they would stop supporting the charities once he'd gone? Only he meant retired, not dead. 'Would it be worth me talking to them?'

'I don't think so. Not in the present circumstances. I'm so sorry. I know how much the charities meant to Anthony. Take care of yourself, Rachel.'

He sounds sad, and I want to say something about Anthony, something about friendship, but I can't. The words won't come because I'm sensing a lack of trust in his voice. I don't want to open that can of worms, so I tell him to give my love to Jennifer, his wife, who has been notice-ably absent from my life since Anthony's death, and hang up.

It occurs to me that Naz hasn't been anywhere near me either. She was Mia's friend really. She's been friendly since I married Anthony, but I suspect that now he's gone, she's distancing herself. She talks to Jennifer, who no doubt talks to Tim. Maybe they all think I'm guilty.

Chapter 25

As promised, Mia and Dave arrive back on 12 July, the day before the funeral. The house takes on an air of hyper-activity, but I'm pointedly excluded from the preparations. A stress tic has developed under my right eye. I don't know how much longer I can go on like this.

It's just over a month since Anthony's death. Sometimes it feels like it happened yesterday, sometimes years ago. Time is doing funny things, and without work I barely know what day it is.

When Asset Plus 'regretfully' let me go after I hit the headlines and the company was name-checked, I read the email and wept. They didn't give me the opportunity to tell my side of the story, simply informed me it would best for all concerned if I handed in my resignation. They did not want to have to sack me. I didn't want it either, so I wrote a formal resignation letter and emailed it, then called Hazel to tell her the news.

'Yes, I know.' Hazel sighed. 'They've promoted me.'

The words slammed into me, but I held it together. 'I'm pleased for you. At least some good has come of it.' Then I realised how bad that sounded. 'I mean, not out of Anthony's death, out of losing my job. I hope we can still be friends.'

There was a pause. I had never been that good a friend to Hazel, and now the boot was on the other foot.

'Of course,' she replied. 'I'm here for you. Just call me. We can meet up.'

When hunger gets the better of me and I go downstairs, I realise halfway down that I'm gripping the back of my neck so hard I'm going to leave marks. I stuff my hand into the pocket of my long cashmere cardigan.

I find Mia, Dave and Caroline sitting around the kitchen table with lists in front of them and cups of steaming coffee. Dave jumps up and meets me halfway, his expression even more doleful than usual. Watching Mia turn and smile warmly at her daughter makes me feel bereft. I would have loved a mother like her.

'Would you like something to eat?' Dave asks. 'There's fresh bread and cheese and my pear and chilli chutney.'

'Thank you.'

I look from Mia to Caroline as I cut myself a slice of bread. Mia won't catch my eye and instead is ticking things off on her list that I can clearly see have already been ticked. Caroline has her hard gaze fixed on me and a slight sneer on her lips.

'We're busy,' she says. 'What did you want?'

I'm not going to explain myself in my own house. I cut slivers of Cheddar with a cheese shaver and add a smear of chutney. No butter. Ever since DS Jones mentioned talking to my mother, I've been back to feeling like she's watching every bite I take. *Greedy guts*.

'Um . . . Rachel?' Caroline says.

I put down my knife. 'Yes?'

'About tomorrow. You will make yourself scarce, won't you?'

147

'No,' I say, taken aback. 'Why should I do that?'

'Because tomorrow is for Dad. I don't want it to be all about you.'

'It isn't going to be,' I say through my teeth. 'I can sit at the back. No one will notice me. But I have as much right as you to be there. He was my husband. You can't keep me away.'

'No,' Mia says. 'But we can ask you not to come. You can mourn Anthony any way you like, but you simply cannot be part of the congregation. Caroline's right. Whether you intend it or not, the focus will shift to you. You may not have been charged, but people still think you were involved in what happened. If you have any compassion for my daughter, you'll respect her wishes.'

I look at Dave. He's the one person who might be fair, but he says nothing. Presumably he has no intention of disagreeing with his wife or her daughter. I'm simply not worth the aggro. Caroline has set her lips so hard there's a white line around them. The three of them wait for me to speak.

'I can be out,' I say at last.

'Good,' Caroline says, picking up her phone in a dismissive manner. 'It's what people will expect.'

Chapter 26

I genuinely intend to stay away. I grab an early lunch while Mia and Caroline are upstairs getting ready, and leave, taking the Tube as far as Gloucester Road before I realise the futility of it and turn back. Anthony's funeral is at two o'clock. By the time I get back to Kew, it's already ten to. I give myself a stitch half jogging, half speed walking, the pain in my ribcage sickening, the healing scar on my thigh stinging. Every so often a muted wail escapes me. My head is sweaty and itching under the scarf. I pull it off. On the green, I steady myself against the gnarly trunk of a plane tree while I catch my breath and reluctantly retie it. It's inappropriately brightly coloured, but going home to get the fedora Anthony bought me for walks in the country, and which I've rarely worn because I feel like I'm ineptly aping a lady of the manor, would lose me another fifteen minutes.

I reach the path leading to the church entrance, push open the doors and feel the relief of cooler air. People are shuffling to their feet and picking up their copies of the order of service. As the organ plays the first bars of 'The Lord's My Shepherd', I'm able to slide discreetly into a pew at the back. No one turns round. I can see a corner of the casket from where I'm sitting, and the huge spray of white roses laid on top. It's hard to believe it contains Anthony.

I'm so busy trying to work out who's there, looking for

clues in the backs of heads, that I don't realise the music has stopped. I drop onto my seat so hard the impact jars my bruised bones. I yelp in pain, and heads turn. Fortunately, Mia, Dave and Caroline are at the front, so there is no way they can see me, but I'm spotted by my housekeeper, Kath, who gives me a small nod before turning away.

Caroline walks elegantly up to the lectern, opening a book and gazing out at the assembled mourners. She is magnificent, if a little gothic, in a short black dress, vertiginous heels, and a black hat with a wide brim and a drift of black netting. She has chosen to read John Keats's poem 'To Sleep'. After his heart attack, Anthony insisted on writing down what he wanted for his funeral, but he was never one for poetry, or in fact literature of any kind. It was me who put this one in front of him.

Caroline is reading well, clearly but with a hint of a catch in her throat, as though she's bravely holding back tears. I have no doubt she loved her father, but this is a performance.

When she closes the book, she directs her gaze at me, giving me a look that should have frozen me but has the opposite effect. I feel a small triumph. I haven't done what I was told. Anthony was my husband. I have as much right to be present at his funeral as anyone else in this church.

Anthony's cousin reads the eulogy and has everyone in stitches with tales of his misspent youth. I'm grateful to him for focusing on the positive, rather than rolling out the story of Harry, the tragic brother. At the end, the choir sings an 'Ave Maria' and people begin to ready themselves to exit, locating bags from beneath the pews. I should leave too, quickly and inconspicuously, but I remain defiantly seated as the congregation is played out to *The Lark Ascending*. I'm not prepared to slink away as though I'm ashamed to be seen in public.

Amongst the friends, neighbours and relatives I recognise are representatives from Begin Again and Stir, and several of Anthony's ex-colleagues. I wonder if the entire board of directors is here, and whether they feel at all guilty for the way they treated him after his heart attack. I doubt it. Men like that rarely do. They are sharks. I hope they won't have the front to come back to the house.

As I walk up the aisle, Caroline draws Mia's attention to me. Dave says something to Caroline before putting his arm around her and steering her towards the door. Sensible man, reminding her that she's the hostess and should be outside the church with the vicar, not getting involved in an unseemly altercation with her wicked stepmother.

I sense someone watching me as I make my way to the central aisle, and to my surprise I realise it's Hazel. I've never been more grateful to see a friendly face.

'You came. Thank you,' I say, kissing her on the cheek.

She goes pink with pleasure. 'I thought you might not be able to. I thought I'd come for you.'

'That was kind.'

'Solidarity.' She smiles, tucking her arm through mine. 'It's brave of you to come.'

'I don't feel particularly brave. They hate me being here.'

'He was your husband.'

'Yes,' I say with a slight smile. 'He was.'

'How're you holding up?'

'Oh, you know, life is pretty shit. Home is horrible. Caroline can barely bring herself to speak to me, and when she does, she's abusive.'

'Ignore her. Her outfit's a little attention-seeking, don't you think? Who does she think she is? Audrey Hepburn?'

I laugh. 'Probably.'

'Are you going back to the house?'

We've exited the church. There's a crowd walking across the green, groups and couples, elderly and young. My neighbours are walking together. I shouldn't go with them; it'll only create unnecessary tension. But then where do I go? To the pub? I feel lonely and deflated. I sigh, turning to Hazel.

'I've been politely requested to stay away.'

'Oh, that's awful. Do you want me to go in and report back?'

I recoil in horror. 'God, no.'

Hazel looks mortified. 'Silly idea.'

I feel a tight knot of hatred in my stomach. How dare Caroline read that poem? How dare she steal Anthony's limelight with her eye-catching outfit? How dare she tell me to stay away from my own house?

'Come with me.' I am not going to be swept under the carpet.

We follow the stragglers. Hazel, who is considerably shorter than me, practically has to jog to keep up.

'Are you sure about this?' she asks.

'Absolutely.'

I grab the front door just before it closes. There's a bottleneck in the hall, where Caroline is greeting her guests. Our hall is reasonably large, but a crowd taking off coats, talking, hugging and air-kissing makes it feel like a cattle pen. Caroline has removed her hat; her glossy hair is teased up into a tight bun and she looks exquisitely beautiful. One more reason the crush hasn't eased.

Someone jostles me; someone else recognises me and their eyes burn into my face, before their eyebrows lift. There are mutterings. Appalling bad taste! How does she have the nerve? I can't go back and I can't go forward. Sweat prickles beneath my arms.

Caroline sees me and her smooth forehead bunches into a frown. 'I thought we'd agreed,' she hisses. 'What the hell are you doing here?'

'I changed my mind.'

'You were at the funeral. Wasn't that enough for you? Why do you have to make everything unpleasant?'

'Steal your thunder, you mean? Why do you always have to be the centre of attention?'

'You're pathetic. Just leave, Rachel. Even you must be able to see you're not welcome here. It's upsetting for my father's friends.'

Hazel is behind me, her hand pressed to the small of my back. It's such a major irritant I have to resist the urge to elbow her in the ribs. I need to get out, but she's pushing me forward. I close my eyes to block out the accusing faces, and claustrophobia descends. I don't know what to do except to pull everything in; every breath, every muscle, every pulse; to close my eyes and disappear.

Anything interesting in the paper?

You. I gasp. I know that voice. I open my eyes, but it's the same people staring at me. I'm causing a scene.

'Get out.' Caroline says, and there's a stark warning in her voice.

I can't move. My feet are glued to the ground, my thighs as heavy as lead. My heart is flinging itself against my rib-cage like a trapped bird.

153

'Come on,' Hazel whispers. 'We should go.' She tugs at my arm, and I wrench it away and scream at her.

'Don't fucking touch me!'

She flushes and her eyes well, but I don't care. I don't want to be clung to.

'Nice,' Caroline sneers.

It rises inside me, something as black and tacky as treacle collecting in my throat, until without warning I'm opening my mouth and spewing bile.

'You always had to have your daddy's undivided attention, didn't you? You couldn't bear it that he wanted me, so you did your best to make life shit for us. You couldn't let him be happy. I wouldn't be surprised if it was you who killed him.'

'You hateful cow,' Caroline spits. 'You're about as welcome here as a kids' party entertainer. Can't you read the room?'

'I don't need to read the room. This is my house.'

I lash out, clawing at her face, and suddenly hands are pulling me away, then my knees give out and I'm on the floor, struggling and scratching like a cat. I call her a bitch and worse, and I don't know myself because I'm howling with laughter too, tears spilling over, nose running, and I cannot stop and the room is spinning.

Someone slaps my face and the shock stills me into silence. I look up. I'm surrounded by legs, then they step back and Dave grasps me by the arm, hauls me to my feet.

'I'm so sorry you had to witness that. My stepmother isn't herself,' Caroline says with great dignity as he supports me through the gawpers.

*

154

I'm sitting on a chair in the kitchen, Dave crouched beside me holding a glass of water.

'I'm sorry,' I mumble.

There's a movement at the door. Caroline is standing there, arms crossed, face like thunder. 'I can't believe you had the gall to show up. Everyone's talking about you, when they should be talking about Dad. It's exactly what I told you I wanted to avoid. What the fuck is wrong with you?'

'What the fuck is wrong with *you*?' Hazel snaps. 'Can't you see she's not well? She's been through a lot.'

'This is none of your business. Who are you anyway? You're not one of Dad's friends.'

'I'm Hazel. And I'm a friend of Rachel's.'

'Oh, you're Hazel. The clingy one.'

Hazel's mouth drops open. She looks at me. I shake my head, mortified. I've never said anything like that. It's how Anthony described her.

'Caroline,' Dave says. There's a warning in his tone.

'Whose side are you on? Has she got you wrapped round her little finger too? You do know you're not nearly wealthy enough for her, don't you?'

Dave flinches, but he doesn't rise to the bait. 'You're upset, love. You don't know what you're saying. Go back to your guests. I'll deal with this.'

'What do I tell them?'

Dave glances at me. 'That your stepmother is exhausted and not herself. They'll understand.'

'More like she's a fucking lunatic,' Caroline throws at him over her shoulder as she opens the door. 'She needs to talk to a professional.' She pauses in the doorway. 'For everyone's sake.'

'She's right,' Dave says as soon as she's gone. 'You really ought to get professional help.' He turns to Hazel, who has been hovering in the background, feverishly interested. 'Thank you for your support,' he says gently. 'Why don't you go and join the other guests.'

Hazel leaves us with obvious reluctance. I feel sorry for her; she so badly wants to be part of the drama.

Dave places a hand on my shoulder as he lifts himself up with a grunt and rather sweetly rearranges the scarf on my head that had come so askew it was half-covering my right eye. 'I don't know what to say to you.'

'You don't have to say anything. You've been very kind. I'm going up to my room.'

He nods, relieved. 'Get some sleep. You look like you need it. We're off early tomorrow morning. I might not see you, so take care of yourself.'

I give him a shaky smile and go out into the hall, trying not to glance through the open sitting room door as I pass, but unable to help it. Hazel is still here, which doesn't really surprise me, but what is surprising is that she appears to be having a civilised conversation with Caroline. Can Caroline have apologised? If so, it's a first. People shoot me curious glances. All I can think about is what I saw in that moment of pure panic, and the thoughts accompanying the images. The almost tangible quality of them. In that moment, I was *there*.

In that moment, I thought of that man as *you*.

Chapter 27

The following Tuesday, I'm standing outside the private practice of Dr Dominic Parrish MRCPsych. It's a little disconcerting being seen at what appears to be his home, but it's here that he has his consulting room. He greets me wearing faded black jeans and a white shirt with the top button open and the sleeves rolled up. He is clean-shaven, his mid-length brown hair is attractively tousled, and my first impression is that he looks like the kind of man who strolls through life without putting a foot wrong. Those are the ones you have to worry about.

I didn't want to see my GP because of the awkwardness of my situation, but I remembered the card and made the call. I told Dr Parrish, when I was explaining myself, that I'd found it in my bag but wasn't sure how it'd got there. According to him, we met in the Pavilion, a pub I used to frequent with colleagues after work. He was there with his girlfriend and we got talking. I'm reassured by that piece of information. At least he wasn't trying to pick me up. Apparently I was in a bit of a state. I can't imagine why, unless I was already cracking up during those forgotten weeks. It's possible, especially if I was in the throes of an illicit love affair with a fellow commuter. Put like that, it sounds faintly farcical. I wrinkle my nose, feeling cheap. Apparently I didn't divulge any secrets, but he sensed I was troubled and pressed his card on me before I left. I can easily believe I didn't tell him anything. I grew up in a house full of secrets.

I do have to start talking, though. I absolutely accept that. What happened at the funeral took me dangerously close to the edge, and it was public and embarrassing.

'Rachel, come in,' he says.

The use of my first name without asking permission puts my back up, partly because it reminds me of DS Jones, but I step inside. The 1950s flat is low-ceilinged, painted white, and has kilim rugs on the parquet floors and splashy artwork in autumnal colours on the walls. Through the open sitting room door I notice more art, a large sofa draped with exotic blankets, a Middle Eastern coffee table. Dr Parrish has good taste. Or his girlfriend does. He reaches across and closes the door.

He shows me into his consulting room and indicates which of the two mustard-coloured upright armchairs I should sit on. A sunscreen blind has been pulled down, giving the room a gentle light. The floor is carpeted; the only things on the wall are framed certificates. No distractions.

He takes my medical history and notes down my answers on his PC. Then he moves over to the other upright chair and places a pad on his knees. I wonder what's going through his mind. I assume he knows all about me. Unless he makes a point of not googling new clients. Coming to them clean.

'There's no pressure.' He smiles encouragingly. 'I'm here to listen and to help you understand what's going on and move forward, not to tell you what to do or how to do it. Shall we start from the beginning?'

My fingers automatically go to the healing scar on my head. 'I wouldn't know where that is.'

'What feels like a beginning to you?'

I ponder this. 'Waking from the coma.'

'Then we'll start there.'

'Do you know about me?'

'There's no judgement here, Rachel.'

So he has done his research. I give him a rough sketch of my life since the accident. He watches, not staring, not scrutinising. He seems perfectly at ease. Which is more than can be said for me.

'I'm finding it really difficult,' I finish lamely. My words seem to dissolve as they leave my mouth.

'I can imagine you would. You've had a tough time. Tell me what it is that you're finding most difficult. Is it the loss of your husband? Or your physical injuries? The opinion of others?'

'Um . . . no. Though that's a part of it. It's the feeling that somewhere along the line I've messed up. Even if I had nothing to do with Anthony's death, I somehow triggered it. That this is all my fault and could have been avoided if I'd only been stronger and refused Hazel's invitation like I wanted to.'

'Those are *what ifs*. Best to ignore them.'

'Easier said than done.'

'Could you be conflating several things? The attack on your husband with past events? Things we suppress from a long time ago can eat away at us.'

I dart a look at him. 'It has nothing to do with the past.'

'You sound very sure. Why don't you tell me something about your upbringing.'

159

'It was tough,' I admit. I give him an edited version and add, 'I'm estranged from my parents these days.' I pause, but he doesn't comment, just waits. 'I had to do it, or I would never have had a life of my own. I don't think I should feel bad about them, but I do. If I allow myself to go there, I feel physically sick with guilt, particularly about my father. My mother is a narcissist, but she's lonely. She's brought it on herself, but that doesn't make it any easier to bear.'

'That's perceptive of you.'

He glances down and I follow his gaze. My thumb is scratching at the back of my other hand. There's a welt. I stop, but then I don't know what to do with my hands, so I pull a tissue out of the box and dab my nose.

'Tell me about your relationship with them.'

This is something I've explained to the numerous psychiatrists and therapists I saw in my late teens and early twenties, and when I start to speak, I hear my voice echoing through those earlier consultations. My mouth is bone dry. I pull a bottle of water out of my bag, unscrew the lid and take a long drink.

'Are you an only child?'

'Yes. Do you think I'd have had it easier if I'd had siblings?'

'Possibly. It would have been different.'

'I ate to please my mother, because if I left anything she'd snarl at me. And later on, when I was a teenager, I started throwing up to please her, but the thinner I got, the more sarcastic and mocking she became.'

'How is the bulimia?'

'Under control,' I say without a quiver in my voice. Because it is, just, despite the building pressure.

An image gatecrashes my mind, and I frown. I'm hanging over the toilet, retching. When was that? It must have happened during the lost weeks.

'Did your husband know?'

I look up, startled. For a moment I'd forgotten where I was. 'Yes. He knew everything about me. But he's the only one. It's not something I talk about. It has nothing to do with my meltdown after the funeral.' I told him about that in our initial phone call.

He smiles. 'Noted.'

Dr Parrish begins a process of subtle prodding to drill down into my negative thoughts, into my relationships with myself, my body and other people. I allow it to flow, answering his questions and noting the changes in his physiognomy like he notes mine. When he touches on the subject of children, I start to cry, then blow my nose and shut the conversation down.

When my fifty minutes are up, I feel a deep sense of shame. I've revealed more than I ever meant to. What if he says something? What if the press have followed me here and they offer him money for my story? How can I even think that? He's a professional psychiatrist. Of course he wouldn't talk to the press. I stand up so abruptly that my head swims and I sway and grab for the back of the chair.

Parrish moves fast, steadying me with a hand under my elbow. 'Are you okay? Would you like to lie down for a few minutes. You can use the sofa in my living room.'

'I'll be fine.' I force a smile. 'That was very helpful. Thank you.'

He looks concerned, but he shows me out of the consulting room nonetheless. 'Do you have your diary? I encourage patients to stick to the same time each week if at all possible. I find routine and consistency helps build trust.'

'I'm sorry. I don't think I want to do this again.' I hurriedly precede him down the long, narrow corridor. I try to open his front door, but the latch sticks.

'Here, let me.' He reaches past me and I press myself against the corridor wall. He opens the front door and stands back. Heat pours in from the walkway. 'Are you sure? I think we made progress today. If something we've touched on has upset you . . .'

'It's nothing to do with that. I just don't like feeling I've exposed myself. It's like . . .' Why am I babbling like this? I'm exposing myself even more. 'It's the focus on me. It's like I'm attention-seeking.'

'That's your mother again,' he says, with such a kind smile I can't be cross. 'You know where I am if you change your mind.'

I swear under my breath when the door closes behind me. It's hotter outside than in. Instead of summoning a cab, I walk out of the estate and into Richmond Park, where I slowly calm down, my jangling nerves soothed by the sight of a herd of grazing deer.

Something else is bugging me, something that has nothing to do with my problems. Meeting Dominic Parrish for the first time felt a little like meeting Anthony. Oh my God. That's awful! At least this time I didn't embarrass myself by mentioning it. *I can't follow up with more appointments because I'm attracted to you, Dr Parrish.* After all that soul-searching, all that unpeeling of layers, I'm thinking about his forearms. I wrinkle my nose. Is that what my brain does in all this mess and muddle? Christ alive. I am definitely not going back.

And then it occurs to me. Is this what happened with the man on the train?

Chapter 28

About ten days later, the weather turns. It's miserable out, pouring with rain and so dark it feels like twilight rather than morning. Kath has arrived to clean and has studiously avoided me, which makes for an awkward atmosphere. Anthony was always the one she liked, not me. I should let her go, but I don't know how to start the conversation.

I glance out of the window at a resigned-looking pigeon perched on the uppermost branch of next door's battered cherry tree and decide I can't sit in the gloom a moment longer. I put on my stout walking shoes and the raincoat I bought to replace the one left at Hazel's house and leave through the back because Kath's vacuuming the stairs and I don't feel like walking past her.

Before his heart attack, Anthony and I would often walk along the river, either west to Richmond and beyond, or east as far as Hammersmith, and have lunch as a reward.

I reach Richmond and the terraces. Incredibly, despite the rain, the ice cream van has customers: hardy American tourists in voluminous waterproof ponchos. There's a couple with a dog, long raincoats on, hoods up, holding hands. Watching them makes me realise how lonely and isolated I've become.

I turn away and gaze out at the rain-lashed water. The ducks and swans that normally hang out near the riverbank hoping for scraps are nowhere to be seen. A man is jogging past the boatyard near the bridge, dark tee soaked, feet slapping as they hit the rain-sheeted surface. He seems familiar, and as he gets closer, I recognise Dr Parrish. I'm so overwhelmed at seeing a familiar face that I step forward, and before I know it, I'm calling his name.

He stops and bends over, gripping his knees, peering up at me through dark strands of wet hair.

'Rachel?' he pants. 'Sorry. I didn't recognise you. You look like a garden gnome in that thing.'

I laugh, loneliness momentarily forgotten.

'What are you doing out in this?' he asks.

'I needed the fresh air. Bad night. But I've interrupted your run.'

'Doesn't matter.'

'Perhaps I should take it up.'

'I've heard it's good for mental health.'

I smile. The weather is so bad, our efforts to exchange pleasantries while rain streams down our faces begin to feel a bit nuts.

'Well . . .' I say.

'Shall we get out of this?'

I only hesitate for a moment. 'That would be good.'

'And it's Dominic, by the way.'

We walk up to George Street and duck into Ole and Steen. The café is busy, the atmosphere fuggy and wet. There is a sense of camaraderie amongst the customers as they burst through the doors, brushing raindrops from their hair. Dominic and I queue for coffee and cinnamon rolls and find a table upstairs. I take off my coat. He sits drenched in sweat and rainwater. Steam isn't quite rising off him, but it feels like it should be. Fortunately the seats are made of leather.

I pull a nub of sweet dough from the bun and pop it in my mouth. It's delicious, but my stomach tightens in protest. We chat about this and that. He asks if I've seen the latest streaming sensation; I ask what kind of books he reads. Mostly non-fiction, or American thrillers by the likes of John Grisham, Tom Clancy and Michael Crichton. We talk about the pleasures and benefits of being out in all weathers, but there's something nagging at me and I can't hold it back.

'Do you mind if I ask you a work question?'

He looks as though this is what he's been waiting for all along. 'Not at all. Go ahead.'

'Do you think it's possible to hide your thoughts and memories from yourself?'

Unlike me, Dominic has had no trouble demolishing his bun. He brushes crumbs from his fingers and wipes his mouth on his napkin. 'Entirely possible. It's about protecting oneself from emotional pain. It's common amongst people who've suffered abuse as children or gone through a trauma.'

'Like I have,' I say.

'Yes, absolutely. Your memories are still there, you just don't access them. Unfortunately, there's a flip side. Suppressing distressing memories can cause problems down the line.'

'Trauma isn't just about what's done to you, though, is it? It can also be to do with what you do to others.'

'That's true.' He gives me an odd look. 'Torturers have been known to suffer from PTSD.'

I wince. That's an uncomfortable thought to get my

head round. 'So I could be suppressing the memories of the weeks leading up to Anthony's death and my accident because of something I did?'

'It's possible. Do you think that's what happened?'

'I don't know. Sorry. I shouldn't have burdened you with that.'

'It's fine. In your circumstances it's natural to question everything.'

'It's all so ridiculous, but what if the detective is right? What if I made some terrible pact? Just because they can't prove it doesn't mean it didn't happen.'

'What's their theory?'

I outline DS Jones's hypothesis about the events of that night and my motivation and thought processes, then tell him about Caroline's photograph and the name Nurse Kelsey heard me shout. I shift my gaze over his shoulder so I don't have to meet his eyes as I go on. 'When I woke up from the coma and was told Anthony had died in an accident, I blurted out that I'd killed him. It isn't true. I was nowhere near him, but . . . well, it's freaking me out that I don't remember. Surely when I said it I would have had some kind of image in my head. But I didn't, and I still don't. I don't know where the words came from.'

He leans back, his hands linked behind his head. 'I don't know you, but I'm not a bad judge of character, and I honestly don't think you would have killed your husband or done any of the things the detective is accusing you of. For one thing, why not simply ask for a divorce?'

I look down at my plate, then push it away and say firmly, 'Because of the terms of the prenup. If I left Anthony, I would get nothing.'

167

'Did you want to leave Anthony?'

'I don't think so.' I feel heat in my face and cup my cheeks with my hands. 'But I don't know.'

'In your wildest dreams, can you see yourself doing something like that? Even thinking it?'

'No.'

'There you are then.' He sits forward, takes hold of my hands and clasps them between his. The sensation of warmth and reassurance is extraordinary. 'Rachel Gordon, you are not a scheming murderess. The man your step-daughter photographed you with could have been anyone. It was simply her interpretation.'

'I'm pretty sure he wasn't just anyone.' I watch his face to see how he's taking this, but it's hard to tell. He has a psychiatrist's ability to be blank while still somehow exuding empathy and understanding. 'You must think I'm a horrible person.'

'Far from it.' He smiles, and I cannot but be aware of how attractively his brown eyes crinkle. 'You can talk to me any time you want. It might help.'

'But we've established I'm not your client.'

'No. But as a disinterested friend, I could be useful.'

Can we be friends? There is no one else I can talk to about this. It's an alluring proposition. It's also, given my inappropriate thoughts at the end of our session, terrifying.

I wrinkle my nose and pick up my mug of coffee. 'I don't want to talk about myself any more.'

'No problem. We can talk about something else. Shall I tell you a little about me?'

I nod, relieved to have the focus shift. I learn that Dominic Parrish grew up in the countryside near Leeds, that his mother was a nurse, his father a surgeon; that he wanted to go into medicine but the idea of opening up bodies grossed him out, so he decided to open up minds instead. That makes me smile.

'I'm sorry I behaved badly last time we met.'

'Don't worry about it. Patients are often resistant at first.' He pushes his chair back. 'Sorry, I need to get on. I have a patient at eleven. I'm so glad we bumped into each other. I hope I've helped.'

I reach for my raincoat, looking up into his handsome, smiling face. 'You have. Enormously.'

'Good.' He really seems to mean it. I like him. He's a nice man.

Chapter 29

It's been quiet here for the past few days. Caroline has had a speaking role in one of those history documentaries where they dramatise parts of the narrative, so she's been out early and back late, and on occasion not back at all. Her scenes are finished now, sadly. In the meantime I've been rattling round the empty house like the last penny in the piggy bank. Fortunately, there's a lot to do, a lot of forms to fill in. I've obtained the required death certificates – thirty copies – because everyone I've been dealing with, from the utilities companies to the tax man, needs one. On it Anthony's death has been recorded as a cerebral haematoma caused by blunt-force trauma. This piece of paper at least means I can get the practicalities sorted out. Every time I look at the certificate, I find it hard to breathe, but I apply myself to each task, ticking them off on my spreadsheet one by one.

Dominic Parrish calls when I'm battling with an online request to cancel Anthony's American Express card. I probably sound too pleased to hear from him, with my squeaked hello.

'Your situation's been playing on my mind,' he says. 'I know you don't want to have any more sessions, but perhaps we could meet? There's no charge. I'd like to help you.'

I hesitate, questioning my motive for saying yes, genuinely worried it might be because I want an excuse to spend time with him. So I shouldn't. On the other hand, I cannot afford to turn down an offer of friendship. I'll go mad if I spend much more time on my own.

'A conversation would be nice. Thank you.'

It might be foolish – in fact it probably is – but perhaps he can help. I'll be careful.

The following evening, we're sitting outside a busy pub in Putney. I chose this spot because it's unlikely we'll be seen by anyone I know, and even though there's absolutely nothing in it, I don't want to be judged by my neighbours. It's hot, and Dominic is wearing dark glasses. His white shirt is open at the neck, sleeves rolled up, jacket loosely folded over a third chair. His watch is one of those chunky diver's ones. Last time I saw him, he was soaked to the skin, his wet T-shirt plastered against his chest. I've tried not to let that image haunt me.

'After I saw you,' he says, 'I did some research into coma dreams.'

I take a sip of cola. 'That was thorough of you.'

His eyes shift across my face as though he's mapping it. 'Knowledge is never wasted. Anyway, I found myself falling down a rabbit hole. There's a lot of chat about it, but essentially there are people who report dreams in which they've lived a whole other life, where they've met people, formed relationships. Even the geography works on a logical level. Streets and houses, landmarks, et cetera, are unchanging. And there's none of the out-there stuff: no giant frogs.'

'Giant frogs?' I raise my eyebrows.

'Whatever. You get the drift.'

'I do. So I wake up claiming to have killed my husband. Does that mean I murdered Anthony in a realistic dream set in a realistic parallel world? It's hardly comforting.'

'Doing something in a dream does not make it something you want to do. It's more likely to be because you've watched a violent film or seen some catastrophe play out in the media.'

'Or been in a car accident trying to get to the husband I've arranged to have murdered.'

He straightens up and leans forward, elbows on the table, knuckles under his chin. 'Is that what you really believe, Rachel?'

I shake my head. 'I just need to know what happened, even if it's not what I want to hear. Why didn't I tell Hazel the reason I was so anxious to go home? If I was that worried about Anthony and I was innocent, surely I'd have said? But if something I'd planned had gone horribly wrong, I'd have kept my mouth shut. I keep saying I wouldn't have done something like that, but what if I did? What if I'm not a good person?'

'For what it's worth, I believe you are.'

'You're very sweet.'

His smile is rueful. No man wants to be called sweet, but I'm not going to apologise.

'Let's hope your memory comes back. Have you heard the term "dissociative fugue"?'

'Something to do with memory?'

'Exactly. It can last hours, or months. People have been known to live their whole life not realising they're missing

172

chunks of it, particularly if they've suffered through wars and climactic events. It's rare, though.'

'Do you think that's what's happened to me?'

'It's possible. It comes without warning and often after a trauma, recent or historic, or some kind of major stress factor like divorce. So you fit the profile. I could ask around and find someone to diagnose you if you like.'

'Thank you,' I say, surprised. 'That's so kind of you, but I don't think it's necessary. The case is closed.'

'Have you been back to see your friend?'

'Hazel? No. I keep meaning to, and she's suggested it, but I haven't found a time. The police have been, and everything seems to check out.'

'That's not the same as going there yourself. Why do you think you haven't gone?'

'Is this the psychiatrist asking?'

His chuckle is a low rumble. 'Sorry. Occupational hazard. You don't have to answer.'

'No, it's okay.' I give the question serious thought. 'Because it scares me.'

'Thought so. Look, why don't I come with you?'

'I can't ask you to do that,' I protest. 'It would take up half your day.'

He smiles. 'We'll go in the evening, just the same as you did that night. Be brave. Contact her and arrange it.'

I'm not ready to roll over. 'You hardly know me.'

'Does the idea of getting to know me better scare you?'

'No.' There's a sullen tone to my voice, but the corners of my lips twitch.

Somewhere, so distant I can choose to ignore them,

alarm bells are ringing. I barely know the man. He appeared when I badly needed a friend. That's all it is.

'Well then.' He signals a passing waiter for the bill. 'Shall we go for a walk?'

I nod my agreement. Caroline might be at home, and the prospect of her resting bitch face is hardly enticing.

'Yes. Sure. But you have to promise you won't psycho-analyse me.'

'Ah, fuck no,' he says. 'You've had your freebie.'

Dominic has long legs, but he adjusts his pace to mine. The ambivalence I felt when we first met has gone. It's a long time since I took a walk with an attractive man who wasn't my husband. As far as I can remember, at least. Every so often I steal a glance at his profile, and once he turns his head and catches my eye.

As we walk, the light becomes hazier. It's beautiful, the air balmy, the moon a pale sliver. Dominic suggests we get a bite to eat, and I don't argue because I don't want the evening to end.

'I didn't realise how much I needed to get out,' I say. 'That sounds selfish, doesn't it? I only buried Anthony a month ago.'

'Don't be so hard on yourself.'

We find a table on the veranda of a place by the river and watch the sun go down over the houses and houseboats on the far side of the water. I don't know what makes me do it after almost two months of abstinence – maybe I'm nervous, maybe I simply want to let go of everything for a couple of hours – but when Dominic orders himself a mai tai, so do I. They are served by a good-looking waiter with a lilting Irish accent and are the colour of the sunset: ruby red turning to warm gold. The first hit is fiercer than I expect.

'Are you still with your girlfriend?' I feel myself blushing. That was such a clunkingly obvious question. 'I mean ... I don't mean ...'

'What girlfriend?'

'The woman you were with when you first met me.'

'Oh, sorry. Yeah. We're not together now.'

'Ah. Did you break it off, or did she?'

Dominic hesitates.

'You don't have to tell me.'

'I don't mind. I did. She's thirty-five. I was acutely aware I should ask her to marry me or end it. It would have been selfish to string her along.'

'Why not marry her?'

'Because I wasn't head over heels in love.'

'Wake up. You're home.'

I crack open an eye. 'What time is it?'

'Just gone ten. You've been drooling.'

'Thanks.' I wipe my mouth on my sleeve, embarrassed to be so much more the worse for wear than him. 'Coffee?'

'Tempting, but not this time.' Dominic grins and leans over me to open the door of the taxi. 'I'll wait until you're safe inside.'

Unoffended, I slide out, totter up the path and let myself in, turning to wave before closing the door, grimacing when I bang it. Oops. The kitchen is untidy, meaning Caroline has been in. I decide it can wait until morning and pour myself a pint glass of water to take up to bed. Dominic is lovely. Arrogant perhaps, but so empathetic. It's a good thing I'm

175

not his patient, because transference would definitely be on the cards. I lurch and laugh at myself. I am never getting this pissed again. It's too dangerous.

On the way to the stairs, I see something I missed when I first came in. The sitting room door is ajar, and there's a light on. One of the reading lights probably. I walk in, skirting the sofa to get to the switch, and yelp in shock, dropping the glass. It spills its contents over my feet as it tips and bounces.

Caroline is lying inert on the sofa. Her eyes are closed, her hair fanned out across the maroon and olive cushions, one arm draped over the edge, her fingertips grazing the carpet. Beside her on the coffee table is a tumbler with the dregs of a clear liquid in it, a half-empty bottle of vodka and several packets of pills. Suddenly stone-cold sober, I call the emergency services and then Dominic. He'd just arrived back at his flat, but he redirects the cab and is with us before the ambulance arrives.

Chapter 30

Dave is asleep in Caroline's room. He and Mia arrived at the hospital at four in the morning. Mia is still there. My head is banging, my stomach churning. I shouldn't have drunk. I'd vowed not to after the accident, which makes me feel doubly awful. I make myself coffee and two slices of toast and marmalade and wolf them down. My phone pings with a message from Dominic.

How is she?
Still in hospital but doing OK.
And you?
Can barely string a sentence together.

He signs off with a grimacing emoji and a message to call him when I'm up to it.

Caroline is discharged into Mia's care later that day. She is a mess, an unkempt, bruised-eyed version of herself. She looks genuinely sorry, and she keeps hugging Mia and apologising for scaring her. She doesn't thank me for saving her life; doesn't even mention my part in it. I don't want her gratitude. I'm just glad I didn't let her down. It goes a little way towards making up for past failures.

Something good has come out of this latest catastrophe. I can now call Dominic a friend and not wonder if it's true, because only a friend would have supported me through last night in the way he did, with kindness, compassion and practicality.

'The man who helped me with Caroline last night, he's actually a psychiatrist,' I tell Mia. 'He's offered to come over and see her. He'd like to help.'

Mia had regarded us with some suspicion when she found us in the hospital. I introduced Dominic as a friend but I suppose she was justified.

'It's up to you,' I go on, 'but he's good. I had a session with him after . . . after what happened at Anthony's funeral.'

'Just the one?'

'Yes.'

She raises her eyebrows. 'It's hardly a recommendation if you haven't been back.'

'He gave me strategies. I'll go back if I need to.'

'Why was he with you last night?'

'Because I called him.'

'I don't understand. Why would you call someone you barely know in a situation like that?'

'Because I don't barely know him.' My voice has risen. 'He's become a friend. Recently.'

'I see.'

'Mia,' I say, pulling myself together. 'It isn't like that. I literally have no one else I can talk to.'

She gives me a long, hard stare, then relaxes. It's obvious to anyone who knows me that I've been abandoned by my friends since Anthony's death.

'So you'll phone him?' I ask.

She nods, and then her eyes fill with tears. 'I wish Caroline had talked to me. She's been badly hurt. It isn't so much the money, it's the betrayal. She and her father had such a close bond. To cut her out like that – his only child – is upsetting on such a personal level, not to mention devastating for her sense of self-worth. I simply do not understand why he did it. Caroline is a hard-working young woman. She may have chosen an insecure career path, but she's put her heart and soul into it. This is her father telling her he doesn't trust her, that he thinks she's wasting her time. If you influenced him, I hope you're ashamed of yourself. It's in your gift to help her financially, but you can never undo the emotional damage.'

'I'm sorry.'

She's tired and understandably upset, so I don't argue. I don't remember whether I did influence him, that's the trouble. I only hope I didn't. I would hate to have been the cause of so much distress.

'All I know is he did it out of love. He knew he was running out of time, and he could see Caroline was too. He wanted her to find her feet before it was too late, especially after ...' I clamp my mouth shut. I didn't mean to say anything.

'After what?' Mia asks.

'It's nothing. Dave, this coffee is delicious.'

'Rachel,' Mia snaps. 'After what?'

I put my mug down. 'There was an incident. Caroline attacked someone after a row. Anthony paid the man off.'

Chapter 31

CAROLINE

Rachel is reading the Sunday papers at the kitchen table, and looks up as Caroline comes in. 'How're you feeling?'

'I'm fine.' Caroline gets a bowl and spoon out of the cupboard. She slops milk over honey oat clusters.

Rachel folds the paper and pushes back her chair. 'I'll walk round to the shops and get a few groceries. Message me if you think of anything you need.'

And then she's gone, leaving Caroline alone with her parents. Dave says he's going to call his brother about the dogs and leaves the room.

'Caroline, darling,' her mother says. 'Would you talk to someone?'

Caroline raises her eyebrows. 'In what sense?'

'A professional.' Her mother's voice is breathy. Anxious. It's unnerving to think she's scared of her. She doesn't want to be that kind of daughter. 'His name is Dr Parrish and he's a clinical psychiatrist. He came to the hospital with Rachel on Friday night. He's been so helpful. He's offered to come over for an informal chat. Then, if you're willing, Dave and I will take you home with us. You can recover in the countryside.'

'Oh my God. You've got it all planned out.'

'We're worried about you, so of course we've thought it through. What did you expect when you chose to take those pills and wash them down with vodka?'

'Mum!'

'Sorry. I didn't mean it. I'm still a little tired.'

'Don't be silly. I'm the one who should apologise.' Caroline has no trouble looking pitiful. She has never felt this bad before. 'I worried you and dragged you all the way from Shropshire in the middle of the night. You don't need to take me home with you, though. I'll be fine.'

'At least think about it, darling. It'll do you good to be away from the pressures of London. You'll have space to think.'

'And leave Rachel here? What if she changes the locks while I'm away? I wouldn't put it past her.'

'She won't. Rachel feels terrible about what's happened.'

Caroline leaps in. 'What has she said?'

'That she understands.'

'And takes responsibility?'

'Some, yes. But in the end it was your father's decision, not hers.'

'You're talking about her like she's a reasonable person. She's turned you against me.'

'You know that isn't true. Rachel knows what I think of the situation. But I don't think outright war is the way to go. Gentle persuasion . . .'

'Oh, Mum. Where has gentle persuasion ever got you? You're wearing charity shop clothes and you drive a heap of junk; you and Dave practically grow your own furniture. You don't even have Netflix. You should have taken Dad to the cleaner's.'

Her mother sighs. 'Your father was generous, and frankly, I have the kind of wealth that makes me happy. I don't need material possessions. Please, just see this man. It's up to you whether you come home with us or not, but I wish you would. You need a change of scene.'

Caroline twists back her damp hair. 'One thing. What was Rachel doing with this man in the middle of the night?'

'She said she just wanted some friendly company,' her mother says. She studies Caroline's face. 'You won't ask him questions, will you? It's none of our business who Rachel sees.'

'Of course not.'

'Good. I've made an appointment for tomorrow. He's coming here. I thought that would be easier for you.'

She still feels like death warmed up. The overdose-slash-cry-for-help seemed like a brilliant idea on Friday night when she came home from meeting yet another friend with a juicy role in a Netflix drama. These past few days, on the set of *The Stuarts: Plague, Fire and War*, have been great, but there's nothing but tumbleweed in the pipeline. Her agent says it's very slow out there, but she knows plenty of people who are busy. Why do her so-called friends never put in a word for her? She hates everyone. She drank vodka, and swallowed the pills. She never intended to kill herself, just make people realise she was there. She almost laughed when her mum suggested Rachel's psychiatrist.

'You won't mention this to anyone, will you?' she says, winding her arms around her mother's neck and placing her head on her shoulder.

'Of course not, sweetheart. I won't breathe a word.'

*

She feels much more human the next morning, but when she looks in the mirror, she's horrified by the dark circles and eye bags. She brushes her hair and cleans her teeth, then walks slowly downstairs, her hand on the banister. Her mother is standing in the hallway, looking up.

'This is Dr Parrish, darling,' she says, ushering him forward.

He smiles encouragingly. 'Good morning, Caroline.'

'Morning,' she says, without enthusiasm. 'Where're we doing this, then?'

'Perhaps the sitting room would be best,' her mother says.

Caroline stalks into the room ahead of Dr Parrish. He closes the door, then turns to face her.

Chapter 32

RACHEL

Caroline walks into the kitchen, the picture of repentant misery. She presses a balled-up handkerchief against her eyes. Dominic follows her and stands in the doorway, his hands deep in the pockets of his slim-fit black chinos. He catches my eye over her shoulder and smiles.

'Is everything okay?' Mia asks.

'We had a good talk,' Dominic says. 'We've agreed that some time away from this house and its memories would be a good thing.'

He turns to Caroline. 'I hope you find a way through this. I know it feels impossible right now, but with time you'll get stronger. The important thing to realise is that your father loved you. What he did came from the heart.'

'You've been very kind, Dr Parrish. I felt like I was in good hands. I'll be okay with Mum and Dave now. There are things I need to resolve. I feel very stupid. I'm sorry I worried everyone.'

'You have nothing to be sorry for,' Mia says.

I watch all this in silence. Something feels off. Caroline looks pleased with herself; I even catch a smirk. And then I realise what it is: she thinks she's wound Dominic around her little finger, like she does every man whose path she crosses. I can't help feeling jealous. I glance at him. He raises his eyebrows and I experience a rush of relief. He's immune. Caroline simply can't see that. She never can. She wanders upstairs, fingers trailing on the banister, and I show him to the door.

'Thank you.'

He doesn't seem to have heard me. I touch his arm and he turns too quickly, as though I've startled him.

'I just wanted to thank you,' I say. 'It was very kind of you to make the time.'

He gives me a sheepish smile. 'Do I get Brownie points?'

I laugh. 'Of course. And a gold star too.' I want to kiss his cheek, but I refrain. He hesitates, for the same reason I hope, then leaves.

Chapter 33

RACHEL

Dominic is true to his word and drives me down to Hazel's the following day. When he turns into her estate and parks outside her house, I make him swap places. Once in the driver's seat, I place my hands on the steering wheel, my foot on the brake pedal.

'Do you remember being here?' he asks.

'No.'

I get out and walk up to the door while Dominic watches from a few feet away, leaning against the car, his arms crossed. My breath shortens as I raise my finger to the doorbell. It feels ominous.

Hazel greets us in a bright blue sequinned shift dress that stretches over her curves, and a lot of make-up. Pale blue eyeshadow shimmers on lids fringed with thickly mascaraed lashes. Her skin has a layer of foundation, her cheeks are contoured, her lips a rusty red. I try to disguise my shock.

Hazel laughs. 'Don't look so horrified. It's what I was wearing at my birthday party. I thought it might help. I can change if you want.'

'No, don't. It's perfect.'

Hazel glances at Dominic. 'Thank you for bringing her. I appreciate it.'

It feels like she's giving him his cue to leave; like he's my chauffeur. Dominic doesn't take the hint. He pushes himself away from the car and joins us.

When we walk inside, I recognise my wheelie case sitting at the bottom of the stairs. The house smells of fragrant candles, and music is playing. The volume is low but there's a heavy beat that makes me tap my fingers against my thigh. Dance music. I wander into the sitting room, look around and frown. I have a flash of movement, hair swinging, hips swaying, mouths laughing. The air is infused with a sweet perfume. It's a confusing rush, but it brings home one thing: the memories aren't far beneath the surface. I'm scared now, although I try not to show it. It feels as though I've strayed too close to a flame. Dominic and Hazel watch from the doorway. This is what I'm here for, I remind myself: to be shaken and twisted and jerked until something is dislodged.

'Drink?' Hazel asks. 'I've made a virgin sex on the beach for you. I didn't think you'd want the real thing. What you're listening to, it's the same playlist. Same scented candle as well.'

She's laid out various nibbles: hummus and pitta bread, nuts, and smoked salmon rolls. We sit on stools and chat. It's awkward. There are so many things to slide over: Hazel taking my job, me ruining her birthday party.

Dominic lets me take the lead; he doesn't interrupt or attempt to steer the conversation, like Anthony would have. I don't think Hazel has warmed to him. I don't know why that should be, but it makes me feel protective. He's a thoughtful man. A man I'm becoming fond of.

'He doesn't like me,' Hazel says when he goes to the loo.

'Of course he does.'

'He's barely spoken a word.'

I smile. 'He probably doesn't want to impose himself. I'm here to try to remember.'

'Men often don't like their partner's best friends,' Hazel says, as if I hadn't spoken. 'It makes them feel threatened.'

'Hazel,' I splutter. 'We're not in a relationship.'

'Sorry. I thought from the way he acts with you that was what was going on.'

'I've only just lost Anthony. And how does he act with me?'

The look Hazel gives me is so knowing it feels intrusive. 'Like he's your shepherd or something. And you've been distant lately, so I may have jumped to conclusions. My mistake.'

'I've been splashed all over the media, suspected of being complicit in the murder of my husband. If I've been distant, it's only because I've been forced to withdraw from the world for my own sanity.'

'Oh, of course! I'm so sorry. I've been insensitive.'

I feel a rush of guilt. 'Please don't worry. I should have been honest with you, but I just feel like I'm drowning in it all at the moment. Dominic is a friend, and right now he's the one thing keeping me from losing my mind.'

When Dominic comes back in, he finds us poring over Hazel's laptop. On the screen is a photograph of three drunk and disorderly women dancing in the living room, arms raised, hair flying. Then there's one of me sitting next

188

to a woman in blue. We are deep in conversation. Hazel asked her friends to send over any photographs they had of the night. She's thought of everything.

'Look at this one,' she says.

I look. The photograph is of Hazel's friends, hands raised, heads dipped, hair falling forward, but at the side of the shot and out of focus, there's me. I'm crouched awkwardly, one hand on the sofa arm, the other reaching for something. I squint. I can just make out a bag under the side table.

'Your phone,' Hazel says. 'It was ringing.'

At precisely that moment, my phone rings. Startled, I look around, my memory of where I left my bag hazy.

'Your bag's right there,' Hazel says, pointing beyond the laptop. It's tucked away under the table at the end of the sofa. I didn't put it there, so Hazel must have. I'm not sure I like this game. I go to get it, crouching, hand on the arm of the sofa to steady myself, reach inside, take out my phone and answer. First I hear breathing. Then a voice.

'What have you done?'

I scream.

Chapter 34

Dominic grabs the phone off me. 'Who is this?' he barks, before turning to Hazel, who appears to shrink. 'They've hung up. I presume that was a friend of yours.'

'It was my brother. I was only trying to help. I thought it might jog Rachel's memory.'

'What the hell were you thinking?'

'Stop it, Dominic, please,' I say. 'You're making things worse.' I'm shaking like a leaf as I pull on my denim jacket.

Dominic is white with fury, his jaw taut, the veins in his neck standing out. He looks like he wants to do violence. The need to get him out of the small, stuffy house is suddenly more urgent than the need to convince Hazel I don't hate her.

The light is on in the front room, and from the car we can see Hazel standing where we left her.

'You were horrible back there,' I say.

'I'm so sorry. It was just your face. You were terrified.'

'I don't need you to fight my battles.'

'I know you don't, but honestly, Rachel, I know a toxic friendship when I see one. Hazel is too invested in you. She's trying to fudge your boundaries. When you don't reciprocate, a situation like that can turn nasty.'

'I don't think she's aware of what she's doing. I think she's just lonely.'

He grunts. 'Did it help?'

'Not really. I mean, there was a moment when we first went in that I felt something. It was the music, I think. The beat. I saw something; nothing cohesive, but movement in the room. Dancing.'

'Well, that's good. That's excellent. So it was worth doing.'

I'm not so sure, but I don't say it. I get the distinct feeling Dominic wouldn't appreciate being told his time has been wasted.

He starts the engine and does a three-point turn. I look back at the house. Hazel has moved to the window. When I catch her eye, she snaps the curtains closed. It's only then that I realise I forgot to take my suitcase. I don't say anything. I can't face going back in for it after such a messy exit.

Dominic drives to the spot where the crash happened. I feel nothing, remember nothing, but the blackened gash in a tree and tyre tracks veering off the road tell the story clearly enough.

He pulls over and we sit with the engine running. Then I say I don't want to be here, and he indicates and pulls out without asking me any questions, for which I'm grateful. We stop for petrol before the M25, and while Dominic is inside paying, I quickly message Hazel.

I'm so sorry about what happened today, you were only trying to help. Please forgive me and don't think too harshly of Dominic. He was trying to protect me. I know you're pissed off, but drop me a line next week, and maybe we could meet for a coffee. You can bring my belongings! Xx

Then I turn off the sound so Dominic won't be alerted

when Hazel replies. He'd be outraged if he knew I'd made excuses for him.

He gets back into the car. 'I'll apologise to Hazel.'

'You will?'

'It'll stick in my craw, but if it's what you want, of course I will.'

What if Hazel mentions I've messaged her? 'No, I think leave it. We all need time to cool off.'

He mumbles something.

'Sorry, what?'

'I said, I don't want to lose your friendship over this. You're important to me, Rachel. I'll never forgive myself if I've ruined things.'

I watch the night roll by, street-lights flaring. I'm not quite sure how to answer him, but I have to say something. 'Ruined what things?'

He doesn't speak. The effort he's putting in not to turn and look at me is rather sweet.

Later, I check my phone. Hazel hasn't responded to my apology. I reread it – it sounds genuine, because it is. It has two blue ticks beside it, meaning message received and read. Well, that's me told.

ONE YEAR LATER

July 2024

Chapter 35

I'm making coffee. Dominic comes up behind me and pulls me against him, nuzzling my neck, and I experience a moment of pure happiness. My hair has grown out and been cut into a stylish bob that I'm tempted to keep. It's so little trouble. The scar on my head has faded.

'Shall we go for a walk?'

I put the cafetière down. 'Now?'

'When you've had your shower. It's a beautiful morning.'

I glance out of the window. The side fence with its bowing trellis is thick with white roses. Fruit is ripening on the cherry tree. The sky is blue, it's Sunday morning, and best of all, I have this new relationship that has been allowed to blossom in Caroline's absence. Barely a month after she left to recover in rural Shropshire, she auditioned for the role of an English woman in a Canadian soap, *Meadowville*, and by some miracle, she got it. She's been in Toronto ever since.

'Okay.' I sip my coffee. 'Give me ten minutes.'

It's still early, so the car park isn't busy, and most of the people getting out of their cars and turning their faces up to the sun are dog-walkers. We head towards Pen Ponds. Dominic has been quiet in the car, but it's only now that it clicks. I don't think this is a random yearning for fresh air and nature; I think he's brought me here for a reason. My default position on surprises these days is to brace, so I do just that, becoming so tense I can barely speak. What does he want? I have a tendency to catastrophise, so obviously I'm thinking the worst. He's had enough. I have too much baggage, too many mood swings. I'm too needy, or even too distant. Yes, maybe that's it. I'm too preoccupied with my own troubles. I've been neglecting him. It's my fault.

High up in the trees, parakeets are screeching. When we reach the lakes, we watch a moorhen couple lazily paddling round the perimeter, occasionally darting their beaks into the shimmering water. Dominic heads towards the nearest bench and I follow him. The morning sun feels glorious on my back. I'm still feeling that strange tension, and for once it's not coming from me.

'What is it?' I ask.

'Does it have to be anything?' He places his hand on my thigh. I cover it with mine, pushing my fingers between his.

'You're making me nervous.'

'Sorry.' He takes a breath, extricates his hand, raises it to my jaw and turns my head so that I have to look at him. 'Do you love me?'

I have a thousand answers to that. He's gazing at me with such hope that I can't say the one true thing: that I simply don't know. I love being with him, making love with him, having him stay over at the house, watching TV, working. But is this for ever? I no longer trust myself.

'Now you're making *me* nervous,' he says.

'Sorry. It was just so unexpected.'

'Really? You must know how I feel about you. But if you don't feel the same way ...'

'Of course I do. But it's been such a strange year and I'm still in limbo. I can feel DS Jones breathing down my neck all the time.'

I'm grasping for reasons that won't hurt his feelings.

'She has nothing new. If she did, she would have arrested you months ago.'

'But it doesn't go away. It's like some kind of malignancy. I can't escape the thought that sometime in the future the doorbell is going to ring and she's going to be there with that self-satisfied smirk on her face.'

He strokes my hair back from my face. 'You're getting things out of proportion.' A curious pigeon alights beside me and he shoos it away with his foot. 'Have faith.'

I burst into tears. He pulls me into his arms and hugs me hard, kissing the top of my head.

'I want a baby,' I sob. 'And that won't happen, not with this hanging over me.'

I jump up and walk away. I can't bear to see the look in his eyes, to hear his excuses. We haven't talked about this at all, but he broke up with his last girlfriend because she was thirty-five and he didn't want to commit. And I'm even older than that.

'It might,' he calls after me. 'If it's what you really want.'

Time splits, and I hear a voice. *If you want a baby, you can have a baby.* I gasp.

The trouble with memory and its recovery, mine at least, is that the snippets that return are out of context. Sometimes they're wisps, hard to catch hold of; like trying to remove an escaped scrap of egg yolk from a bowl of whites. Sometimes they are clearly delineated, at others hot and fierce and frightening, like those that reassemble the incomplete and scattered fragments from the night of Anthony's death. I tell myself that it's because I don't know the answer that this nastiness is allowed to fill the vacuum. I'm nagged by the mystery of who was responsible and what part I played.

The fleeting glimpse I've just had feels true. Those words were spoken, by that man, to me. Over the past year, I've had enough memories of him to know that the friendship existed, and that we were close, but they're always set against the backdrop of the District Line train and its stations, never anywhere else, so that reassures me I wasn't sleeping with him.

Now I've remembered that we talked about having children. That implies we thought we had a future and what happened next was not simply a financial transaction. Is that even possible when we'd only known each other a handful of weeks? It might be if we were in the first throes of romance. It isn't inconceivable that we could have talked in those terms, created a fantasy life together.

'I've done this all wrong,' Dominic says. 'I was going to ask you to marry me.'

When Anthony asked me, joy bubbled up and overflowed. There are no bubbles now. What is blocking them? Dominic loves me. He's solid and reliable. He's extremely attractive. It would infuriate my mother to know I was loved by another alpha male. Christ. Why has everything become about Mum recently?

I've delayed my response for too long. A shadow crosses his face.

'I take it that's a no?'

'We're happy as we are, aren't we?'

198

'Is your objection to me or the institution?'

'To the institution. I want to be my own woman.'

'I'd never stop you being that. But you have just said you want children. That requires commitment.'

'I am committed.' I try to hug him, but his body is stiff. This is not a man used to getting a negative. All the more reason to stand my ground. 'We can share our lives in the same way. We don't have to be married to have kids. A ceremony and a certificate won't stop us if it's what you want too.' When he doesn't answer, I flush. 'I've hurt your feelings.'

He smiles at last and pats my arm. 'It's a lot to take in. I was expecting a yes. I'm an arrogant bastard. Let's pretend I never asked.'

'I'm not going to do that. It means a lot to me that you did.'

The next morning, I wake up alone. For a moment I think Dominic has left me, but then I smell coffee and breathe a sigh of relief. Yesterday was difficult and will have changed things, tested him. I put on my dressing gown and am halfway down the stairs when I see a denim jacket hanging over the newel post. Near it, a familiar pair of well-worn brown boots have been carelessly discarded. My stomach curls in on itself. Great. Hopefully this is a flying visit.

I find Caroline sitting at the kitchen table staring at her phone, dressed in faded jeans and a soft white shirt, unbuttoned enough to show a glimpse of the pale valley between her breasts. Dominic has his back to her and is washing up a pan left soaking overnight, looking adorably rumpled in checked pyjama shorts and a T-shirt. He turns, a scouring pad in his hand.

'I was going to give you a shout when breakfast was ready,' he says with a sheepish smile. 'There's coffee if you want some.'

My stepdaughter barely acknowledges my presence. Finding Dominic here must have been quite a shock for her. I wonder how the conversation went and grit my teeth. Time to be the bigger person.

'Hi, Caroline. When did you get in? It must have been late.'

She drags her eyes away from her phone. 'One.'

'How long are you staying?'

'I have a three-week break before they film my next episode.' Her voice is loaded with disapproval.

'I'm sure you don't want to stay here, but you're welcome to use the guest room for a night or two.'

Caroline finally puts her phone down. 'I'm not going anywhere. I don't have the money for a hotel.'

'Airbnb?'

'You haven't lived in the real world for a long time, have you? I pay rent in Toronto. I'm sorry if my being here disrupts your love life, but I'm staying.'

She turns to Dominic. 'Did you take a look round that day and think, this is nice, I'll have some of that? A big house on Kew Green, a grieving widow with more money than sense. Some psychiatrist you are, preying on vulnerable women.'

Dominic chucks the scouring pad into the sink bowl. He speaks calmly, but it's clear he's riled. 'It's none of your business what I do with my life, or what Rachel does with hers.'

'I cannot believe you're sleeping with the woman who

murdered my father. You've got to be warped to want that.'

'I did not murder Anthony,' I say. 'I . . . I know this is . . .'

Dominic rescues me before I can trip over my words. 'I have a suggestion. Caroline, there's a room in my flat you can use while you're in London. My consulting room is there, but we needn't disturb each other. You can take it or leave it, but if you decide to leave it, you are not staying here. Rachel is going through a lot, and the last thing she needs is your sniping.'

'Don't you think what happened to Dad affects me too?' Caroline's nostrils flare. 'And this is my house as much as hers.'

Dominic walks over and rests his fists on the kitchen table. 'No. It isn't. The house is Rachel's.'

'Until she's charged.' She wrinkles her nose. 'It'll happen eventually. You do know that, don't you?' She turns to Dominic. 'Perhaps I will take you up on your offer, Dr Parrish. It smells bad in here. Can you give me a lift?'

'What happened to your car?'

'It's at Mum's. I could hardly leave it at Heathrow for a year, could I?'

She stomps upstairs, and ten minutes later comes back down with her suitcase. Dominic dumps it in the boot of his car and Caroline gets into the passenger seat without a backward glance. I close the door and raise my eyes to heaven. Thank God for that. I owe Dominic big-time.

Chapter 36

CAROLINE

She still misses her father. She guessed it would be hard, but being back in the house is so painful. It smells different, the atmosphere is weird and it no longer feels welcoming. Dominic has taken over: moved things round, left his belongings all over the place like a wolf marking its territory.

Perhaps she shouldn't have stayed away so long, but she couldn't pass up the opportunity. Having been used to the insecurity of random bit parts here and there, it's been incredible being part of a series. She's now a name in Canada. Google Caroline Gordon and *Meadowville*, and there she is, Diana Porter, bitchy Brit friend of the main character. The director's already hinted that she's going to be offered a contract for a second year. Her agent says that with that behind her, she'll find it easier to get better roles in the UK. It honestly feels like her luck is changing, and about time. She wishes her father had lived to see it. It's Rachel's fault he didn't.

Dominic is driving one-handed, his left hand resting on his thigh. She covers it with her own hand, pushing her fingers down between his. He doesn't pull away, but his face is set. She knows that face; she knows all his faces. She knows when he's acting and when he isn't. Unfortunately, he isn't acting now. He doesn't want her around. She's interrupted his cosy idyll. She'll just have to remind him of what he's been missing. It won't take much, of that she's certain.

She didn't realise quite how painful it would be to see him in what appears to be a happy relationship with Rachel. She thought she'd be able to compartmentalise, but it isn't easy at all; she's jealous and suspicious.

'Can we stop this charade?' Dominic says. 'If you leave me alone, I'll see to it that she gives you a chunk of the inheritance.'

The shock is huge and silences her for a moment. He can't mean that. He loves her.

'You've changed your tune. I thought we were on the same page.'

'Oh, Caroline—'

'Don't you *oh, Caroline* me. You know perfectly well that everything that woman has she stole. My father would never have cut me out of his will without her interference.'

'The reason he did that, sweetheart,' there is a sneer in his voice when he uses the endearment, which excites her, 'is because you attacked me with a fucking cheese knife.'

She glares at his profile. 'The reason I did that, *sweetheart*, was because you'd shagged some woman you met on a dating app, and you were so fucking smug when you told me you couldn't promise to be faithful.'

'I was being honest. Monogamy doesn't come naturally to me. But I would have done my best.'

'Have you been unfaithful to your darling Rachel?'

'No.'

'Ooh. Treats in store then.'

'Shut up.' He turns into the Roehampton Estate and follows the road round until they reach his block. 'I've helped you enough. I've compromised myself. I've done things I'm ashamed of because you demanded it of me.'

'I needed your help. It wasn't my fault.'

'And I helped you without question. Now leave me alone. We're finished.'

'Is she as good in bed as I am?'

'I said, shut up.' He pushes the power button and opens his door.

She has more to say, but she can't step over the cliff edge. She doesn't want to take them to a point where they can't be together at all. Best to sweep it under the carpet and focus on the Rachel problem. She follows him up the staircase.

'You don't really love her. She's just made your life more comfortable. It's nice to have money washing around, isn't it? And we *will* get my money. Every penny of it. So you don't need her. Not like you need me.'

'I need you like I need a red-hot poker up my arse.'

He lets her in and she breathes in the familiar smell of the place. Being back here is like taking a drag from a cigarette after a long abstinence. She opens the bedroom door and flops down on the bed.

'If you hate me so much, why are you letting me stay here?'

'The lesser of two evils,' he mutters.

She smooths a hand over the grey velvet eiderdown. 'Brings back memories.'

Dominic puts her case on the floor. 'You know how everything works. If I have a patient, I'll warn you.'

'Don't worry. I won't be in much. You'll barely know I'm here.'

He stands there, not saying anything, jangling his keys. She can feel his nervous energy. She gets up and slowly closes the bedroom door. His eyes darken and she steps forward, takes his hand and presses it against her breast. He groans, grinds his mouth against hers, then pushes her away and leaves the flat, slamming the door after him. Caroline does up her buttons and laughs. He'll be back. Her lips wobbles and she braces herself, blinks, recalibrates. She's okay. Everything will be okay.

Chapter 37

RACHEL

'How are you, Rachel?' Peter Marlow says, somewhat stiffly.

I'm running a duster round the sitting room as I speak to Anthony's financial adviser. Peter is also Mia's brother, so not my biggest fan. Over the years, he's softened, partly due to the fact that his sister has happily remarried, but he's never warmed to me, or I to him. However, I don't have a choice. He's managed Anthony's money for thirty years. He is the man I need to speak to.

I deliberately waited until Dominic had left to make the call, not because I don't trust him, but simply because he wouldn't be able to stop himself from guiding me, and I had enough of that with Anthony. 'I'm okay.'

'What about money? I could sort something out in the interim. Anthony wouldn't have wanted you to go short.'

I rub the side of my neck. 'I'm fine. I was given a decent payout when I agreed to voluntary redundancy, and there's money in the joint account I can access. If all else fails, I'll sell my jewellery.' Anthony gave me several pieces over the years: always diamonds, always high-end. I don't wear most of them, just my favourite cluster earrings and my engagement ring. The rest are kept in a safety deposit box, to avoid paying the astronomical insurance fees.

'Good. Well, let me know if anything changes.' He's anxious to get me off the line.

'The reason I rang is because I'd like to sell my stake in IFR and set up a trust for the Begin Again programme.' I've spent wakeful nights considering how I can use the shares to honour Anthony. I tell myself that it isn't about Caroline, but in a way, it is. I have a childish need to prove to her that I loved her father, that I did not marry him for his money.

'Have you thought how that would play out?' Peter says. 'The investigation might have stopped focusing so hard on you, but it is still ongoing, and the perception of you in the media is a negative one. Your generosity might be perceived as you trying to spin the narrative. It might make people even more suspicious.'

'People will be suspicious whatever I do. Could you draw up some options for me?'

'If it's what you really want, but I'd advise you to hold off telling the charity what your intentions are.'

'I'll let them know when I see fit,' I say, sniffily. 'I'll be moving the money as soon as I have control of Anthony's estate.'

Later that morning, I strip Caroline's bed, not caring that she only slept in it for one night. I can smell her perfume on the sheets, and that's enough. I bundle up the bed linen and drop it in the corner. I pick up the framed photograph of Caroline, aged about ten, with her parents, then put it down. I don't need to feel guilty. Mia is far happier living in rural bliss with Dave than she ever was with Anthony in this house. She told me that the first time we met, at Anthony's father's funeral. She watched me closely, and I was careful not to react the way she evidently wanted me to.

'That makes me so happy,' I said, touching her arm. I enjoyed her irritation. God, I was smug and naïve then, feeling superior to the woman I'd ousted. I'm not proud of that. It's too late to apologise, though; that would make us both squirm.

I pull open the little drawers in the dressing table one by one. Those on either side of the mirror contain junk jewellery, bits of make-up and hair accessories. The drawer under the marble top contains more junk and a manila envelope. I've always respected Caroline's privacy. Always. But today I can't resist poking around in my stepdaughter's life.

Inside the envelope is a call sheet for a film that came out in 2018. *Any Day Now*. I didn't see it, missing the screening because of some work thing I could have got out of if I'd really wanted to. There was a row with Anthony. Looking back, I acknowledge he was right to be furious; it was an opportunity for me to build bridges with Caroline. Too late now. I've made a lot of mistakes over the years.

I put the call sheet back where I found it, wander over to the bookshelf and scan the DVDs. There aren't many. Caroline collects the roles she's had in ads, music videos and company promotional videos in folders on her computer, but she owns hard copies of the films. I imagine that's because it's nice to see them there, like books authors have written slid into their shelves amongst the greats.

There it is. I'm pulling it out when I hear Dominic's key

in the lock. I shove it back and tiptoe down to the next landing. Not that he would question my presence anywhere in the house, but I don't feel good about snooping.

'Rachel?' he calls up.

'Just making the bed. I'll be down in a minute.'

'How did it go?' I ask. 'Did she speak to you at all?'

He gives a wry grimace. 'She accused me of repeating what she said in confidence.'

'Which you didn't.'

'I assured her it wasn't the case, but she doesn't believe me. I get where she's coming from. Last time she saw me, I was listening to her tell me her problems. She trusted me. Then she comes back here only to find that I'm with you.'

'Even if we had told her, it would have been the wrong thing to do. She would have made life impossible for us.'

'True. I'm glad I thought of lending her the flat. Honestly, before you appeared it was dire. Talk about a frosty reception. I've never been so pleased to see anyone in my life as I was when you walked through the kitchen door.'

I laugh, kissing him. 'The atmosphere *was* strained. Did she say anything else?'

'Just more spiteful ranting about how I moved in on you, how as your psychiatrist it has to be against the rules.'

'But you're not my psychiatrist.'

'No, I most certainly am not. I got away as quickly as I could. She was unpleasant, but it's only three weeks, and if it keeps her out of your way, then it's worth it.'

'Thank you. I've made a mess of things, haven't I?'

Dominic looks at me strangely. 'It isn't your fault. You're doing exactly what Anthony asked you to do, because

209

that's the kind of person you are. No amount of sulking, aggression or emotional blackmail on Caroline's part should make you put aside your principles. Sooner or later she'll get the message.'

'She's doing what he said, though,' I point out, wanting to be reasonable. 'She's finally standing on her own two feet.'

'Let's wait and see, shall we?' There is a hint of impatience in his voice. 'By the way, she asked me to ask you if she can use her father's car. It'll only be for visiting her mum or friends outside London.'

'Yes, sure. It's just sitting there.' I'm no longer banned from driving, but I haven't used it yet. There's an emotional block there, though truthfully, I'd feel embarrassed driving a hundred-and-fifty-thousand-pound Bentley to the supermarket, while Caroline will carry it off with style. 'The more time she spends away, the better. I'll sort out the insurance if she gives me her details.' I move behind him, curl my hands around his broad shoulders and gently dig my fingers and thumbs into the muscle. 'I'm sorry you've been dragged into this. Caroline can be unspeakable when she feels like it. It's kind of you to put her up this time, but I don't think it's an offer you should repeat. She'll take advantage, and she'll drive you crazy.'

'Yeah,' he says, turning away from me to pour the cold dregs of his coffee into the sink. 'You're not wrong about that.' He turns back to me and smiles.

'Why are you looking at me like that?'

'Because you're so beautiful.'

Chapter 38

CAROLINE

When Dominic lets himself into the flat at 8.45 the following morning, Caroline is on her best behaviour. She has showered and dressed, had breakfast, cleared up and filled the dishwasher. She has cleaned the cloakroom that patients use, polishing the basin and hanging a fresh hand towel on the ring. In the sitting room, she's plumped up the cushions and tidied the wine glass off the coffee table so that, as Dominic requested, there is no sign of human habitation. Not the tidiest person, she is proud of her efforts.

'Did you have a nice evening?' he asks.

He's as stiff as a bar of chocolate that has been kept in the fridge. But Caroline likes her chocolate that way. It tastes all the better when it melts in her mouth.

'I went to see a friend's new play.'

He checks his watch and evidently decides there's time for another polite enquiry. 'Any good?'

'Yeah, not bad. The audience didn't fall asleep. Always a plus,' she adds with a smile. She's trying to read him, trying to gauge what went on between him and Rachel after he left her yesterday. She's shaken him out of his complacency, no question, but what that will mean in the long term she has no idea.

'Right, well, I need to get myself sorted. Are you going out?'

'Yes. I'm meeting a friend at the Tate Modern.'

He doesn't hide his relief. He doesn't even ask if it's a male or a female friend. That stings.

'I have patients till four thirty, so I probably won't see you.'

'Probably not, no.'

She waits for him to say something else. When he doesn't, she steps back and closes her bedroom door. She listens to his footsteps, then the sound of him opening the door to his consulting room. She stiffens her resolve. Dominic might think he's in love with Rachel, but he isn't. Not really. She doesn't sense passion, just compromise. And yeah, in life and love people compromise all the time and for all sorts of reasons, but she isn't going to. She wants her man and she wants her money and she intends to have both.

She wonders if Dominic telling her the time he was going to finish was an instruction to stay away, or a covert invitation. If it was the latter, it was pretty clunky: almost as though he'd winked at her at the same time as tapping his watch. Somehow she doesn't believe that. It would be too easy.

Returning to the flat in the afternoon, Caroline senses more than hears the mumble of voices through the door at the end of the corridor. She takes off her boots and moves around in her socked feet. In the bathroom, she brushes her

212

hair until it shines, curls a tendril round her finger and lets it bounce, then settles herself in the sitting room and flips through a copy of *BJPsych, The British Journal of Psychiatry*.

She doesn't have long to wait. After ten minutes, Dominic shows his client out. Caroline doesn't move from her position on the sofa, except to adjust her posture, imagining his greedy eyes lingering on her body, so much younger than Rachel's. With her legs curled on the cushions, jaw supported by her hand, hair draped through her fingers, hip raised, a slice of flat stomach visible between her untucked shirt and the top of her low-slung jeans, she imagines herself modelling for an artist: *Reclining Woman*. There is a tiny tattoo on her hip: the outline of a rose on its stem. She had it done on her eighteenth birthday. She never told her father, only her mother and Dave. She remembers Dominic trailing his fingertips around its curves, then kissing it, the first time they slept together, after the *Any Day Now* wrap party. He'll remember that too.

Five minutes later, he still hasn't come in, and her body is beginning to ache. She stretches and rearranges herself. When the door finally opens, Dominic is holding his case.

'I'm off. I expect I'll see you tomorrow.'

She sits up abruptly. 'Do you have to go right now?'

'You know I do.'

She gives him a cat-like smile. 'Are you sure you can't fit in one more patient, Dr Parrish?'

'I don't have time for this, Caroline.'

She rolls her eyes, drops the seductive tone and gets up. 'Stay for ten minutes and have a chat. I think you owe me that at least.'

She follows him into the kitchen. The room is small.

There's a row of units with white doors, and a beechwood table against the opposite wall with two matching chairs tidily pushed in. Above them there's a black and white photograph of a stag in the mist, and a large clock. Dominic undoes his cuffs, rolls up his sleeves and leans against the window, arms folded. Caroline props herself against the counter and copies his posture. She absorbs his tension, revels in it.

'You're not in love with her, you know.'

'It's none of your business.'

'Oh, it is. Because you still want me; you can't deny it.' She smiles. 'Ooh. And there you go: a micro-adjustment in your facial muscles. You're not the only one who can read body language. I did the same training as you. It's crucial to our craft, isn't it? You always said it's what makes you a good psychiatrist. Come on, don't pull that face. I'm winding you up.' She pauses. 'You're confusing love with apathy.'

'I have to go.' Dominic is brusque. She's rattled him.

'Do you really?' She fingers her shirt buttons.

'I told Rachel I'd be home by five.'

'Ah. You took preventative measures to guard against temptation. I'm flattered.'

'I never know whether you're acting or not.'

'You know me better than anyone else.' She steps towards him, makes her voice soft. 'I'm sorry for what I said. I'm only being like this because I'm scared too.'

'You've never been scared of anything. That's always been your problem. You push people too far.'

'By people, do you mean you?'

'Yes, but your father too. I want you to be happy,

214

Caroline. But I can't be responsible for your happiness. It has to come from you.'

She flips her head up. 'Don't tell me you're happy with her, because I won't believe you.'

'I was happy enough to ask her to marry me.'

She stops scowling abruptly. 'Was? And what did she say?'

'She said no.'

She underestimated her stepmother. 'Wow.'

He raises his eyebrows. 'I'm flattered you're surprised.'

She needs to think this through. The ticking of the clock is the only sound as she worries over the implications, chewing her bottom lip. If Rachel doesn't want to marry Dominic, that means she intends to retain control of all aspects of her life. A plan begins to form in her mind. It actually might be for the best. Caroline is no fool. She doesn't trust Dominic not to push her aside for a life of luxury with Rachel. That could be exactly what he's planning. As it is, things are clearer cut now that the merry widow has put her cards on the table.

'I've got to go.' he says.

'Do what you like.'

She marches into her bedroom, closes the door, drops onto her unmade bed and flops back, arms splayed. The front door closes and the flat falls silent. She stares up at the ceiling, from which a silvery scrap of spider's web hangs. Dominic will come round. He doesn't love Rachel; he is having all his needs met, and if left alone will be perfectly content with the status quo. She is not going to leave him alone.

Chapter 39

RACHEL

At my suggestion, we go out to supper, to the French restaurant on Station Parade. I'm planning to tell Dominic about my plan for the shares on neutral territory. I could have done it at home, but there are too many distractions there, and this way I feel more in control. We're greeted with excessive delight by the maître d'. He didn't bat an eyelid the first time I brought Dominic here, many months ago. I was nervous, and so grateful to him for treating it all as normal, I over-tipped. We are shown to a table and handed the wine list. Dominic deliberates and chooses a bottle of Pinot Gris.

I pick up the menu but barely read it, choosing the same thing I always have: the French onion soup and the fish. I'm a bundle of nerves. Since the proposal, things have been tense. Dominic hasn't mentioned it again, but I have a feeling his ego hasn't quite recovered. Telling him about my conversation with Peter Marlow might help. It'll prove I'm including him in my plans for the future.

His phone rings, and he swivels to get it out of the pocket of the jacket he's hung over the back of his chair. He checks the caller display, apologises and walks out into the street. I watch him for a moment. The conversation is heated. He sees me looking and turns his back. I shrug. Listlessly perusing the menu while I wait, a memory intrudes.

I'm standing in the doorway of a District Line train at Victoria, ignoring the other passengers jostling to get on and off, my eyes glued to the back of a man disappearing through an exit. I'm upset about something . . .

'Rachel?'

I blink, momentarily confused, then gather myself. 'Everything all right?'

He sits back down. 'Yes, just my brother.'

I know he's having trouble with Steven, the awkward brother who can't hold down a job, so I don't probe.

'I remembered something,' I say.

'Oh yes? What?'

'I . . . I'm not sure exactly. A man. I didn't see his face.'

'Okay. Same sort of thing as usual?'

'Kind of. I was on the train watching him walk down the platform towards the exit.'

'It's in your power to remember. It's only your mind that's stopping you. Whatever it is you're blocking, you're going to have to deal with it eventually . . . Rachel?'

'I want to run something by you.'

Dominic raises his eyebrows but accepts the change of subject. 'I'm all ears.'

I tell him about the shares, then pause, watching his face. He's gone still, his eyes holding mine. I feel a glimmer of unease. 'It's what Anthony would have wanted.'

He nods, breaking eye contact and looking down at his plate.

'What do you think?'

'I think you're knee-jerking. You will find a sponsor.'

'Dominic, I've been searching ever since Tim told me IFR were pulling out. I've used every single contact of Anthony's. I've tried his friends. Well, the CEO has at least.' I can't call them my friends any more. 'We've had nibbles but none of them have bitten.' I can feel myself getting worked up, my face reddening. 'The problem is, because Anthony was deliberately killed and I've been in the papers as a suspect, brands are worried about being tainted by association. They spout stuff about tightening their belts and looking at other good causes. Ex-cons and murder suspects are a hard sell.'

'It'll mean you have a lot less for your own needs than you anticipated.'

'I'm sorry you don't approve,' I say stiffly. 'But I haven't earned any of it. The charity meant so much to Anthony, and I intend to honour his legacy. And as for my needs, I'm not exactly high-maintenance.'

'Darling, I get it.' His tone is right, but somehow the words don't ring true. 'I just want to make sure you under-stand exactly what it means. Your stake in IFR will be your income.'

'Yes, I know, but I have the interest on Anthony's other investments too, and I'm keen to go back to work. I miss it.'

'I imagine that's no easier than finding a sponsor.'

'No,' I agree, downcast. 'People see my name and run a mile. I may start my own consultancy instead.'

Dominic's smile is thin. 'I can see you've already made your decision. It would have been nice if you'd included me.'

'I just did.'

'No, you told me what you'd decided. There's a big difference. Have you told the charity yet?'

'I'm waiting until probate's been granted.'

'Very wise.' Then he dexterously changes the subject.

That night we make love. Dominic is gentle at first, but as his urgency increases, I feel something change in him. There's an anger, a savagery, which confuses me. I'm aware of his brute strength and have to fight back to hold my own. When it's over and my head is on his shoulder, my body sweaty and pressed to his, I run my finger down his arm then lift myself up on my elbow. His eyes are curiously blank.

'What was that about?' I ask.

'What do you mean?'

'You were rough. It felt like you were angry with me.'

He rolls over and sits up. 'I'm not angry. Sometimes I like it like that. That's all it was.'

He spoons my body, his hand around my waist, and for the first time with him I am physically uncomfortable. When I close my eyes, I see myself being pushed up against a wall and kissed. Another tiny chink has opened. I want to grasp its edges and pull it wide, but I fear what I'll find if I do. I've accepted that there was a man. The mystery is why he vanished from my life on the night I crashed the car; the night Anthony died. The answer cannot be good. Is Dominic right? Do I have the power to unblock the memories if I really want to? I make myself small, hugging my arms around my body. It's too frightening to think about.

Chapter 40

CAROLINE

Caroline is in the bathroom cleaning her teeth when Dominic lets himself in the next morning, so she doesn't realise he's in the flat with her until she feels the soft *whump* of the front door closing. She pricks her ears for his footsteps along the wood-floored corridor and the sound of his keys dropping into the hand-painted bowl in the kitchen. She rinses her mouth out and considers her reflection, full on and in profile, lengthening her neck. She looks hot, her hair mussed from bed. She runs her fingers through it and leaves it as it is. She's wearing high-leg knickers and a vest through which the shape of her nipples can clearly be seen. He's put up a fight so far, but it's only a matter of time before he succumbs. She remembers with a clench of her insides what happened after he closed the door that day, when her parents and Rachel thought he was counselling her after her overdose. He slammed her up against the wall and kissed her so hard her lips felt bruised and swollen. She's amazed no one noticed. He was livid with her. She smiles. Maybe that's the answer. Make him angry.

He is going through his post in the kitchen. The way he stands, the way his shirt hangs on his broad shoulders, the shape of his shoulder blades, everything about him makes her go weak at the knees, even after six years of knowing him. It's even worse now that he's playing it cool, the feeling so strong she could rip his clothes off. He may hate her now, but everyone knows what that means. He hates himself for loving her. In his heart he knows they're destined to be together. That's been her touchstone since the day they met.

'I didn't hear you come in,' she says when he finally senses her presence and turns round. 'Do you have an early appointment? You should have let me know. I'll jump in the shower and get out of your way. I can get a coffee round the corner.' She meets his eyes with a challenge. *Keep your hands off me if you can.*

His gaze sweeps over her, taking everything in, but he looks more irritated than interested. She crosses her arms over her breasts.

'We need to talk,' he says. 'Put some clothes on.'

She stalks into the bedroom and gets dressed, but she's encouraged. He's fighting it. She can work with that.

'What's going on?'

'Rachel intends to liquidate her shares in IFR and use the proceeds to fund Begin Again and Stir.'

Caroline looks at him blankly. This she did not expect.

'Did you hear me?'

'Yes, I did. Surely it'll only be a portion of the money?'

'It's all of it.'

Hungry, she peels a banana and takes a bite. For her gold-digging stepmother to make a decision like this is incomprehensible. Rachel is going to give a huge chunk of the money away? Caroline could almost forgive her for the

221

first sin – she was only doing what women have done for millennia, after all – but not for this. Why is she reframing herself as a holier-than-thou philanthropist? The only thing Caroline can think is that Rachel is seeking to fix the damage done to her reputation. It's laughable.

'She can't be allowed to throw my father's hard-earned money away on a bunch of criminals. It's down to you to persuade her not to. She won't listen to me.'

'I'll do my best, but she's stubborn. When Rachel gets an idea into her head, she sticks to it like glue.'

Caroline chucks the remainder of her banana into the food caddy. 'I know that.'

'Your uncle is looking into it for her. She wants it to be ready to green-light the moment probate is granted.'

'Don't you have a say in any of this? Why didn't she discuss it with you?'

Dominic looks pissed off. 'She did. I told her I thought she was making a mistake, but that only made her shut down, so I had to back-pedal. I explained I was open to it, just wished she'd talked to me first.'

'You're a psychiatrist. Surely you know how to make her see things your way.'

'Because I'm a psychiatrist,' he says through his teeth, 'I understand how Rachel's mind works. The harder I push, the harder she'll dig her heels in.'

Caroline makes up her mind. 'You're going to have to deal with her before she gets control of the estate.'

'Deal with her?' Dominic frowns.

She stares straight into his eyes, sees understanding bloom.

'You have got to be fucking kidding me.'

'I'm serious, Dominic. We stand to lose everything, and all because you made a mess of things. This is on you, and if you want to benefit, you'll do what I say.'

'I've been with her for a year. She means something to me. I can't kill her.'

'Because you've fucked her?'

He just shakes his head.

'If you refuse, I'll tell her what we are to each other. Oh, and I'll also report you to the GMC. You had sex with an emotionally vulnerable patient who'd just attempted suicide. You'll be struck off.'

'You're threatening me?' He is incredulous.

'I'm prepared to do what it takes. Don't be angry,' she wheedles. 'You know it makes sense. You won't be a suspect because you don't stand to benefit from Dad's estate – it goes directly to me. I'll have an alibi. I'll go back to Canada. You'll play the grieving boyfriend for, say, six months. Then we meet by chance and fall in love. Who else knows what she wants to do with the money?'

'Only Peter. She hasn't mentioned it to the charity yet, but it's only a matter of time. What if he says something?'

'I don't think he will, and even if he did, there is no way of proving that Rachel told you her plans. Anyway, Peter's never liked Rachel. He was absolutely livid when she moved in on Dad. And he adores me. If we're careful, he won't smell anything off. He won't give a shit what happens to her. In fact, I suspect he'll think she's got her comeuppance. Look, I understand. This is difficult for you. Obviously it's not the outcome either of us would have wanted, but there is no choice. You can see that, can't you? All I'm asking is that you think about it.'

He works his jaw. 'All right. I'll think about it. But don't expect a different answer.'

Don't push it, she tells herself. Let him sleep on it.

Chapter 41

RACHEL

Unexpectedly, Tim rings the next morning. My heart does a little skip. I haven't seen him since the day of the will reading. A whole year.

'Tim!'

'Sorry to ring so early.'

'That's okay. It's good to hear your voice.'

He coughs, as aware as I am of the distance that's grown between us. 'We need to have a chat. It's sensitive, and I'd rather talk face to face, if you have time.'

If anything, I have too much time. 'Yes, of course. I'll come to your office.' I could do with a reason to get out of the house.

A small parcel arrives. I take it into the kitchen and read the carrier's label. It's from Asset Plus. My personal belongings from my desk. I had an email from HR yesterday, apologising for not sending it sooner – there was a mix-up apparently and the box had only just been found. I wonder if it was Hazel who packed it, when she inherited my job and my desk. It's been a year since I've heard from her as well.

I take the parcel into the kitchen, slice through the tape and sort through the contents. Hair accessories, hairbrush. A small velvet zip-up bag containing tampons, make-up, store-brand ibuprofen and antihistamines. A breakfast bar well past its sell-by date. A newspaper cutting.

Interesting. For some reason, I have cut out the Rush Hour Crush section of a *Metro* and circled one of the messages with a blue pen: *I'm the man in black. You're the claustrophobic blonde. I taught you haiku.*

I've made a note of the date of the issue in biro: Thursday 20 April 2023.

Haiku? I google it.

A Japanese poetic form that consists of three lines, with five syllables in the first line, seven in the second and five in the third.

Hearing Dominic, I push the cutting into my pocket; the implications are unsettling to say the least. Is this the point at which Sean came into my life? Or is that a huge leap?

I tell Dominic I'm going clothes shopping, and he doesn't question it. He seems distracted, giving me a quick kiss and almost running down the steps to his car. I clean up, do some admin, then head out.

I've used the District Line many times in the last year, and each time I've been alert, looking for clues, unsettled, nervous system spiking. I have stood in this train locking eyes with a man. He has held me and I've held him. We've laughed and talked and maybe even bickered. Why is my brain refusing to give up its final secrets? What is it I so dread knowing?

We cross a steel-coloured Thames, chug through the suburbs, past back gardens with smart extensions and roofs with jutting dormers. As the city becomes denser, looming terraces subdivided into flats with dirty window panes nudge surprisingly close to the tracks.

I tweak the crumpled cutting out of my pocket and read the message again. What if Sean wanted to make contact and chose this way? *I taught you haiku.* So something got us talking. And then I remember what DS Jones told me. One of the times I was late for work was because my train had been stopped in a tunnel. I message her and ask what date that happened.

She comes back to me as I'm exiting the station. *Monday 17 April*, she's typed. *Why?*

I don't respond. So it had nothing to do with Sean. Though . . . oh, wait. If the message was in the paper on the Thursday, it isn't unreasonable to assume we first met on the Monday.

Ought I to show the cutting to the detective? I fold it and slip it back into my bag. I'll think about it.

Chapter 42

I am unprepared for the surge of emotion that seeing Tim again after so long precipitates. He is synonymous with Anthony. He's also kind, and awkward, and familiar. We don't hug, as we might have done once. I get a pat on the arm, then he folds himself into his chair and clasps his hands on his desk, his brow furrowing.

I smile uncertainly as I take a seat. My own hands are restless, thumbs rubbing repetitively at knuckles, so I grip them together. 'It can't be that bad.'

'No. No, it isn't. But it's something I've been battling with ever since Anthony died. Whether to mention it or not. It isn't a legal requirement, but it may be a moral one.'

'Then say it.'

He slaps his meaty hands down on the edge of the desk, as if having my permission to speak has finally made up his mind, even though I know he's already decided, or I wouldn't be here. He's simply preparing me for what is evidently going to be yet another unwelcome surprise.

'When Anthony changed his will, it was only a couple of months after his diagnosis. He was dealing with that as well as worrying about you and Caroline. He knew he was leaving you both comfortable financially – more than comfortable; wealthy – but he'd become increasingly anxious about Caroline's inability to face up to the reality of her situation. He honestly believed she would never make a success out of acting. He could also see she was committed to such an extent that she wouldn't consider an alternative career, and he was enabling her to live with the delusion.' Tim sighs heavily. 'When she attacked her guest and didn't seem to understand why it was a problem, it was the final straw. Anthony realised he'd encouraged her to feel she had no responsibility for anything, and then of course, you had your say.'

I shift uncomfortably. Anthony must have told him everything. I often wondered if he talked to Tim more than he did to me. 'So he changed his will. I understand all that. I was worried you thought I pressured him into it. I still believe he was right – it could be the making of her – but I don't think he did it the right way.'

Tim nods thoughtfully, chins bulging. 'What this is all leading up to is that he had second thoughts. He felt he'd been too hasty and that to pull the rug out from under her with no safety net might actually break her.'

I'm alert now. I don't say anything, even though Tim's silence suggests he expects me to fill in the blanks.

'He called me to say he wanted to make some adjust-ments, so that the will was kinder to Caroline.'

'I see,' I say.

'We made a plan to meet and talk about it the following week, but he died in the meantime. I hadn't destroyed the other will, or his letter to Caroline, and there was nothing I could do. I wasn't legally obliged to disclose our conversa-tion, and I have no proof it actually occurred. I don't know what exactly the adjustments would have been, but I was given to understand they were fair.'

'Why are you telling me this now?'

'Because I thought . . . I hoped you would do something for Caroline, and now Peter tells me you're contemplating giving away a vast chunk of your inheritance.'

'He's told you? He had no right to discuss my business with you.' I can't believe it. Does he think I'm incapable of making decisions without input from a man?

'I understood he had your permission.'

'Well, he didn't,' I say crossly. 'I should have told him not to mention it. It never occurred to me he'd be indiscreet.'

'I apologise. It's an admirable plan, Rachel.'

'But?'

He smiles ruefully. 'But I felt it was important to let you know what was on Anthony's mind before you publicly announce that funding the two charities to the tune of several million pounds is what he would have wanted. And . . . well, I do feel that Caroline has a right to know her father understood the deep hurt he would cause her and that he wanted to retract. But of course, it's up to you.'

There's such concern in his eyes that I feel unable to maintain my angry stance. Instead, I say what he wants to hear. 'You did the right thing in telling me. Please don't feel bad.'

My thumbs are going again, working into the muscle between bones. I lurch between emotions these days, while the effort to hide what's going on inside me makes me breathless. It's similar to claustrophobia. That same panicky feeling that makes my limbs feel heavy, the sinews holding me together ache. All I can think about is getting back home and eating every sweet thing I can get my hands on. I could stop at a newsagent's on the way back.

'Rachel?'

'Sorry, I missed that?'

'I was just wishing you good luck, my dear.'

I'm being gently dismissed. I'd like to let him know that I don't bear him any ill will, but that would smack of begging for crumbs, so I just say goodbye and leave before I can start crying. When I get out of the building and the heat of the day hits me, I sniff back my tears and hold my head up. Life will happen, one day will segue into the next. People will begin to forget about me. Things will improve.

Chapter 43

I don't stop for chocolate. Instead I keep walking, first listening to my breath enter and leave my lungs and then, when that doesn't work, mentally detailing the things that catch my eye: red double-deckers and tourists, verdant trees, SUVs and cyclists, three drunk men having a friendly argument outside a pub, a child being picked up while her mother pushes its buggy one-handed off the kerb, a cyclist swerving to avoid her, yelling something obscene. I walk until I'm tired and my feet are aching.

What Tim disclosed has shaken me. Anthony was never one to vacillate. He was decisive. He must have been feeling so torn, knowing he didn't have long, wanting to do the best for everyone, worrying about his only child.

It occurs to me that Tim might be lying about Anthony's intention to change his will again. As Caroline's godfather, he could be trying to stop me from disposing of my shares outside the family. But I can't believe he would resort to such underhand measures. He doesn't have an agenda, simply a conscience. He was trying to do the right thing.

I will honour Anthony's final wishes. I'll give the shares to Caroline because I won't be able to live with myself otherwise. I'll raise the funds for the charities by some other means. Perhaps that could be my job. My purpose. That cheers me.

I don't want to give myself the opportunity to change my mind and then later be accused by Dominic of keeping another important decision from him. I've learned my lesson there. So I get an Uber from Kew station to his flat.

Luckily he's given me a key, which I keep on my ring. I let myself in. It'll be twenty minutes before his next fifteen-minute break, so I settle down at the kitchen table with a cup of tea and my phone. I open WhatsApp. My last message to Hazel, from a year ago, is still there, unanswered. On impulse I type a new one.

Hi. It would be lovely to hear from you. Please get in touch. R xx

I press send. There. It's done. Two blue ticks. I wait five minutes but there's no response. She must still hate me. I'm surprised how much this upsets me. Karma. She doesn't want my kind of friendship, and I don't blame her.

The loop of a brown leather strap is visible over the tabletop. It belongs to Caroline's shoulder bag. Its presence doesn't surprise me. She'll own more than one. I open the Kindle app on my phone and try and settle down to the book I've been reading, but after a few minutes curiosity gets the better of me and I lean over and pull the bag onto the table. Inside it is the little leather pouch Caroline keeps her various cards in, a pair of sunglasses, her phone, a packet of antihistamines and a lipstick.

I contemplate these items as their significance sinks in, then close the bag and creep silently down the corridor. Behind the consulting room door two people are speaking. One is Dominic, obviously. The other, I realise with a chill, is Caroline.

'I know it's difficult,' Dominic says.

'You don't know anything,' Caroline responds. She chokes on a sob.

I hear a shuffle and a step and imagine him going to her. Then a silence that seems to pulse with tension. What's happening? Are they holding each other? Are they kissing? I curl my fingers around the door handle, wait and wait, feeling the pulse of the silence. Then I turn it and burst in.

Dominic is on his feet, leaning over Caroline, his hand on the back of her head. He reacts first. He takes his hand away and straightens up. His eyes are cold with fury, his voice dripping with contempt.

'Get out, Rachel.'

Chapter 44

Caroline leaps up and pushes past me, red-faced. Dominic and I glare at each other. The front door closes with a bang, making the entire flat shudder. It's just him and me in the small consulting room, which smells of Caroline's perfume, and I have never felt so far removed from him. It's as if he's been pulled back until he's a pinpoint.

'What the hell did you think you were doing?' he demands.

I blink. 'Me? What were *you* doing?'

'My job.'

'Right.' I can't keep the scepticism out of my voice.

Dominic swears under his breath and tells me to sit down. I do, but to my discomfort, he remains on his feet. 'Caroline is my patient.'

I absorb this while I scan the room, unwilling to settle my gaze on his face. 'Since when?'

'Since last week.'

'And you didn't think to tell me?'

'I don't tell you anything about my patients. That would be highly unprofessional.'

I look at him now, my eyes narrowed. 'Physical contact between a psychiatrist and a patient is highly unprofessional, isn't it?'

He steps closer. There is an element of threat in the way his fists are clenched. 'How dare you question my methods. Caroline was in distress. I offered a modicum of comfort. If you're so jealous that you can't see that, if you don't trust me ...'

I rub my face. Tears prick behind my eyes, fury, misery and disappointment combining to leave me feeling as though I've walked through a bloody battle. I command myself not to lose control. 'I thought ... I thought ...'

Dominic's expression softens. 'I'm sorry you were upset by what you saw, but Caroline needs help.'

'Couldn't she have found another psychiatrist? Why choose you?'

'Because I was here. Because I saw her that time, when she was in a bad way. That was your suggestion, remember, so don't you dare hold it against me.'

I take a deep breath, trying to steady my emotions. 'I thought she hated you.'

'She did, but we've crossed paths regularly while she's been staying here, and I expect she finds my presence reassuring.' He sighs heavily. 'I shouldn't have yelled at you, but I was so angry that you thought you could just march into my consulting room. It was astonishingly disrespectful.'

'I wasn't thinking,' I mutter. 'I heard your voices.'

'And leapt to conclusions.' He forces a thin smile. 'What are you even doing here?'

He is clearly not interested in my answer, because when I hesitate, he keeps talking. Which is good, because I am no longer in the mood to share Tim's news.

'You're very stupid, but I do love you,' he says fondly.

'Why don't you go home? We'll talk later.' He steps forward and lifts my chin with his fingers, bends over and kisses my lips. 'But don't you ever do anything like that again.'

Chapter 45

He called me stupid. He meant it as an endearment, but it didn't feel like one. That settles it. I'm not telling him or Caroline anything, not until I'm sure he wasn't lying. Caroline wanting to see a therapist isn't surprising, but for her to choose Dominic Parrish, the partner of her hated stepmother, takes some swallowing.

I don't understand what's happened. I relive the moment, picturing Dominic with his hand on the back of her head, his fingers in her hair. I thought she despised him. Obviously not.

Shit. Dominic is absolutely right. I am stupid. How could I have condoned Caroline moving into the flat? What was I thinking?

Back home, I grab a roll of black bin bags from the drawer in the kitchen and take it up to Caroline's room. I've put up with her antics for far too long; a malicious attempt to steal Dominic is the final straw.

Her clothes fill five bags. Once I'm finished with them, I tackle her shelves. My eye is caught by a gap between two DVDs. It wasn't there last time I was in here. The shelf was tightly packed and *Any Day Now* was in its spot, and now it isn't. I remember putting it back, but I was in a hurry, so perhaps I left it askew. Did Caroline let herself in while I was out and saw that the film had been moved? Why would that bother her? Perhaps it didn't. Perhaps she simply wanted to watch it again, gloat over her moment. It bothers me that she might have been here, but I don't know why I'm surprised. As far as she's concerned, it's her home. Odd, though. Then it occurs to me that she could have taken it because she didn't want me to watch it.

I go downstairs, switch on the television and open Amazon Prime. It takes a minute or two to search for and find the film. For £3.99 I can rent it, so I do.

Once it begins, I fast forward until I spot her. I rewind to the end of the previous scene, then let it play, standing in front of the television with the remote control in my hand.

The scene opens with a woman walking into a grand ballroom with swagged brocade curtains and glittering chandeliers. She's wearing a shimmering gold dress and immediately becomes the object of general fascination. Men and women turn to watch her progress. Close by, Caroline, who must have been about twenty when it was filmed, is sitting at the bar, where she's in animated conversation with a man who has his back to the camera. Her hand strokes the stem of her champagne flute. The camera lingers on the woman as she's greeted by her date, who leads her to the bar. Her elbow knocks against Caroline's companion, and he turns round, eyebrows raised. I do a double take as Caroline reaches forward and touches his arm, bringing his attention back to her.

Dominic.

I rewind and press play again, pausing the film as he turns his head. I'm not mistaken. Dominic is an actor.

The sound of the front door opening startles me. I

frantically prod buttons on the remote control to exit Prime and switch the television off. I walk out of the room as Dominic empties his pockets onto the side table.

'You're home early,' I say.

'I cancelled my appointments.'

'You needn't have done that.'

'I'm concerned about you. You overreacted to a perfectly innocent situation. Thank God it was Caroline rather than another of my patients you were accusing.'

He is an actor and a liar. For him not to have told me he knew Caroline from before is hard to process. When I remember his story of how we met in the pub, I'd laugh if it didn't risk me bursting into tears. Caroline must have found some opportunity to slip his card into my bag. She could have done it at any time. At what point did she decide that a relationship between me and her former lover, because I'm sure that's what he was, would be of benefit to her? Was I being set up all along? To what end? Oh, for God's sake, Rachel. It's money. There's nothing subtle about it. When Caroline was young, it was jealousy and resentment, but these days it's about money and resentment. I wonder how far back her relationship with Dominic goes. Further than the making of this film?

She wanted me to meet him. Or maybe it was Dominic's idea. Maybe he suggested he get close to the wealthy widow after the will didn't go Caroline's way. They cooked up a plan between them.

That he could have lived with me, made love to me, asked me to marry him. He must be a psychopath to have hidden it so well.

'We need to talk,' I say. Such a cliché. He knew it was

240

coming, though, I can see that from his face. A sympathetic look so badly applied it's ludicrous.

'What can I say to reassure you that there's nothing going on between me and Caroline?' He smiles. 'I'm flattered that you were jealous.'

'I'm not jealous. I'm pissed off, because I've allowed you to make a fool of me.'

'No one's made a fool of you, darling. My relationship with Caroline is purely professional. You should be pleased that she's come round to me. She isn't as bad as you've painted her.'

'She can be charming when it suits her.'

'She isn't being charming. She's very unhappy.'

I shrug. 'I don't want to talk about Caroline. I want to talk about us.'

'I'm happy to do that. I love you. I only want to do what's best for you.'

'It's not working.'

'That's because you've got yourself into a pickle. It just goes to prove that you need someone to help you keep a sense of perspective. You need me, Rachel. You can't deny we're good together.'

I'm obviously not being clear enough. 'I don't need you. I don't trust you, and I don't believe you, and after today, it just doesn't feel like our relationship means anything.'

Dominic flinches. 'It means something to me. We can talk this through. You're knee-jerking because of what you think you saw.'

'You had your hand on her head.'

'She was in a bad way,' he says sharply. 'What you saw was out of context.'

241

'Was it?'

'I'm worried about you.'

'You needn't be.'

'Perhaps you need space,' he says, trying to claw back control of the conversation. 'I'm happy to give you that, but I hope when you've calmed down you'll realise I'm not the monster you've turned me into.'

'*Any Day Now*,' I blurt out, unable to hold it in any longer. 'You were in that film with Caroline. You've known her since 2018, possibly longer. So excuse me if I don't believe a word you say.' The penny drops. 'You hid the DVD, didn't you? To stop me connecting the dots. Only it had the opposite effect, because when I noticed it was gone, I wanted to know why, so I found it on Prime and watched it. If you'd just left it there, I never would have known.'

There's a deathly silence. 'All right. I knew Caroline before I met you.'

'No kidding.'

He shrugs.

'Are you even a real psychiatrist?'

'Yes. I caught the acting bug at university when I was doing my medical degree, then after I'd done my two years' general training, I left to go to drama school. I wanted to give it a go before I committed to a career as a doctor.' He wrinkles his nose self-deprecatingly, and for a nanosecond I find him attractive again, but it's gone as quickly as it came. 'It didn't pan out – I didn't like the lack of control – so I finished my training.'

'I want you out of my life.'

As I say the words, I don't feel anything but grief, but it isn't grief at losing him, because he was never really mine.

It's grief at the loss of the non-existent child we could have created together. I hadn't realised until this moment quite how much I wanted it. I push away from the abyss. I will not think about that now.

He leans forward, his brow knitted with concern. 'I frightened you. I'm sorry, but you just barged into my office. This one little thing shouldn't mean the end of us.'

'You're not listening.'

'I am. You can't do this. I won't let you. You love me.'

'I don't, and I'm not sure I ever did.'

He scowls. 'You gave a pretty convincing impression.'

'Perhaps I simply wanted it to be real. It was good while it lasted, but now it's over and I'd like you to leave.'

'You cold bitch.'

'You can come back for your things in the morning. I've already started packing up Caroline's belongings. You can take them away too. I don't want her coming back here. I don't ever want to see either of you again.'

And there it is, the whole teetering pack of cards tumbling down. The silence between us seems to stretch on and on. Eventually Dominic goes upstairs. While I wait for him, I prise the key to the house off his ring, and take the key to his flat off mine. He throws the bin bags down and they tumble down the stairs like falling bodies. I fling them one by one out into the street, then hold open the front door and wait.

On the threshold, he turns to me. 'You're going to regret this.'

I hand him his key. 'I've taken mine back. You can bring Caroline's when you come for the rest of the things. Or get her to post it through the letter box.'

243

In my fury, I go online and find the contact details for a female journalist whose work I admire. I email her asking if she'd be interested in a feature about me. I mention that I'll be announcing my plans for an eye-watering charitable donation, putting it in the public domain. It'll demonstrate to Dominic and Caroline that they cannot treat me like that and get away with it. The journalist jumps at the idea and, obviously terrified I'll change my mind, agrees to come in the morning.

I can breathe again. I've cut whatever flimsy tie bound Dominic and me together and I don't care. I'm only upset because I'm so humiliated by the whole sorry episode.

I need to remember more. My memories have been trickling back, but they're tantalisingly incomplete. They bring feelings. Happiness. Thinking my heart will break. Regret. I don't believe anything has been entirely lost. My problem is that I'm frightened of what I might find out about myself, about what I did. It's all there.

I get up and go into the kitchen. I make myself a cup of mint tea, sit down and try to relax. Start with one thing, see where it takes me.

Watching a man walking away from me down a station platform. Start there.

June 2023

Chapter 46

As I walk to the station, my mind works itself into an anxious knot. Yesterday I followed you up to the street. It wasn't part of the rules, but I can't be sorry. I've seen another side of you. I've seen you angry and frustrated. I now know you're keeping things back from me. We do not make any sense as a couple and it's time for me to accept that and let you get on with your life. It's idiotic. I don't know you well enough to be grieving your loss, but it feels as though my world is falling down.

I'm a grown-up. It's not love, it's lust. It's the lure of the forbidden. I feel the impact of my feet on the pavement as I walk faster. And then a small voice in my head says, *Like it was with Anthony*, and my shoulders sink. Is it love or is it itchy feet? Without giving us a chance, which would mean sneaking around and lying to my husband, I'll never be able to answer that question. I don't even know how you take your coffee, which side of the bed you sleep on, whether you have siblings or if your grandparents are still alive. What we know about each other isn't enough to sustain a relationship. I have to let you go. I will let you go.

I adjust what I'm going to say: *It's been wonderful, but I've thought about it and you're right: if we can't progress, then it's just a game. And I can't do it any more. It's making both of us*

247

unhappy. It's not you, it's me. I'm the one with the commitments. It's my fault for being selfish and greedy. I'm sorry.

I shuffle onto the train with the other commuters and peer out through the dirty windows as we speed past the backs of expensive houses and the National Archives, cross the glistening sweep of the river and dip under the Great West Road on the approach to Gunnersbury. It feels as though we've reached a critical point, but if I count the days I have seen you and multiply those by the thirty minutes it takes to get from Gunnersbury to Victoria, plus a handful of snatched moments on a station platform, it adds up to less than a day in each other's company. For you to suggest I leave my husband and move to Manchester on the back of a few, admittedly intense, hours together is madness.

And yet.

Being with you is incredible. You are irresistible. I love the feel of you, the smell of you. I love your low voice and your husky laughter. When you look at me, I turn to marshmallow. Could this really have happened? I think of my insulated life: the best food, a beautiful kitchen, a house overlooking Kew Green, the Thames with all its beauty on my doorstep. Luxurious holidays and first-class flights. A gilded cage, absolutely, but a cage I always thought of as my own choice. Until now.

Much as I've tried not to, I've lost respect for Anthony since he hit me. It's changed things. I can still see the savagery in his face; as though his mask had slipped. I've tried so hard, but I can't un-remember that blow. It's driven a seam of steel through my veins. My life is a sham. But that doesn't mean I should fall into the arms of the first good-looking and sympathetic stranger.

I replay our first kiss, the way you pressed me up against the wall, the cool of it against my back, the heat of your body moulded to mine. Tears prick the corners of my eyes. I will say it. I must, for both our sakes. You should find yourself a proper girlfriend, and I should make a considered decision about my marriage and either leave or stay and take control. The grass is rarely greener on the other side. I can do it. I'm older and considerably wiser than I was when I met Anthony Gordon.

The doors open. I pull my shoulders back, take a deep breath. I'll offer to catch an earlier train in future. I'm doing the right thing.

But you don't get on.

My disappointment is more acute than my relief at the reprieve. I feel embarrassed, as if the other commuters know what's going on, can see it written on my tense face. I keep my head down until the train reaches Victoria, then I jump up, leaning out of the doors as passengers surge from the train towards the exits. I see you. You're walking fast, head ducked, as though you know perfectly well I'll be watching for you. You don't want to look my way. And that is the unkindest cut of all.

Chapter 47

I spend the day trying to fathom what's going through your mind, and conclude that you think you've said all you can say and have decided the best way of getting the message across, that you find the whole thing impossible, is to ghost me. I wonder whether you are suffering as much as I am, then the next moment become convinced you don't care. I expect you're already composing another message to another stranger on the Tube. Despite your insistence that you've never done anything like this before, you could be a serial angler, chancing your luck in the fish-filled waters of the Underground system.

'What's up?' Hazel asks, planting her bum on the corner of my desk.

'Nothing. Just tired.'

'You are still coming on Saturday, aren't you?'

'Of course I am. I wouldn't miss it for the world.'

I've actually been wondering how I can wriggle out of it without causing offence, but one look at Hazel's face, so hopeful and tense, and I know it's not an option.

'And you'll stay over? It's going to be a late one.'

'Of course.' My heart sinks.

She grins, turning as she sashays back to her desk. 'You won't regret it. Dress up to the nines. I'm going to give you a night to remember.'

On Friday morning, once again you don't appear, but this time I'm ready.

At Victoria, I hang back until the last moment, then step off the train, and for the second time this week I follow you. I'm wearing my powder-pink jacket, so I don't make the most inconspicuous stalker. There are so many people that I briefly lose sight of you, then I spot you ahead of me, absorbed by the morning crowd. I'm in time to watch you tap through the barrier, but when I reach it, my card won't work. I tap it again and again, then run to a member of staff, who points out that I've been trying to get through with a supermarket loyalty card. Mortified, I dig in my bag for my debit card.

I take the steps two at a time, and stop to scan the crowd, but the concourse is busy and I can't see you anywhere. As I turn back, a hand clasps my wrist, and you're there. You pull me against you and hug me hard, and slowly my arms slip around your waist and I yield to the bliss of being held by you. I could stay like this for ever, but we're getting in the way of the commuters surging into the station.

'Come on,' you say. 'Let's go somewhere quieter.'

You take my hand and we head out in silence. I'm too scared to say anything in case I ruin the moment. We cross the busy main road and walk into Grosvenor Gardens, a small triangular oasis wedged between the station and Buckingham Palace Road.

'Why are you avoiding me?' I ask.

'Because I knew you wanted to say goodbye and I didn't know how to handle it. I should have been braver, but I was angry with you.'

'Because I brought it down to money?'

You rub the side of your neck. 'Yeah. It made it feel sordid. I'm ashamed of the way I live; like I've failed as an adult because I'm still flat-sharing at thirty-seven.'

'I'd be in the same boat if I wasn't married.'

You hold my hand tighter. 'I'm not angry any more. I understand where you're coming from. You made a vow to your husband and you don't want to break it, because that's the kind of person you are. I admire that.'

'I don't deserve your admiration. I was asking too much.' I smile ruefully. 'It's just that it's so hard to bear. Because we ... because we haven't ... it's almost worse than if we had.'

You kiss me. I allow myself only a few seconds to feel everything – your mouth, your hands and the deep longing that billows inside me – before I reluctantly pull away.

'We can do something about that,' you say.

'What ...'

'You can't move for hotels round here. Tell work you're dealing with a problem at home and you're going to be late.'

I frown, shifting away from you. 'Are you actually suggesting we have sex so that our unfinished business can be finished? Because that's horrible.'

'Sorry.' You stroke my hair away from my face. 'I want your body with every fibre of my being, because you are the sexiest woman I've ever met. But I also want to spend time with you and do the things normal people do when they fall in love.'

It's exactly what I wanted to hear.

A pigeon drops down beside us and starts pecking around our feet. You shoo it away and it flaps across to the next bench, where a woman is sitting with a book. I make a decision.

'I'm not having sex with you in a hotel in the middle of the day.'

You grin. 'Not that kind of girl?'

'No, I really am not.'

'And I totally respect that.'

'I'll meet you after work for a drink.' It's a mad promise. It means lying to Anthony. But this is important. Sean and I have to have a proper conversation, however it ends. Otherwise we're always going to be living this tantalising half-life.

'In the real world?' you ask, looking hopeful.

'In the real world. I'll meet you outside Mansion House Tube station at six thirty.'

'Done.' You check your phone and pocket it. 'I should get to work. I'm already late.'

We head back to the station, both of us loosened. You kiss my cheek at the entrance, then wait as I go in. You're still there when I reach the steps, only then turning to walk away, almost as though you're making sure I don't follow you again.

I wait until lunchtime, then I phone Anthony at work and tell him I'm going to the pub with Hazel and some of my other colleagues and not to expect me back before 9.30. That's as far as I can push it without raising suspicion.

I spend the rest of the day wondering if I've been an idiot. However this evening ends, there is a world of difference between conversations on a train and spending an evening together. I will be betraying Anthony. But God, I want it badly. I'm so used to having people crammed around us, having to whisper, that the prospect of time alone is intoxicating. I imagine us walking through the city holding hands, standing on the Millennium Bridge and watching the sunset. Kissing.

And then I cringe. I want to be with you, but I don't want the whole messy drama of it: not sneaking around; not sex in places we have to pay for or some grubby flat-share in Gunnersbury. Obviously we can't go on like this. It's been a temporary madness and we need to face it and say good-bye before we learn to hate each other. Tonight must be goodbye. A lump rises in my throat, but I squash it down. This is not real, not lasting love. It's an infatuation that will cause untold damage before it blows itself out. No wonder Sean is confused.

Chapter 48

You are waiting for me as I turn the corner and approach the station, but you don't attempt to embrace me. Instead you keep your hands tucked into your jacket pockets. I don't know whether I'm more relieved or disappointed, but definitely a mix of both. We fall into step and I lead you to the Festival Gardens at St Paul's Cathedral, where Hazel and I sometimes come to eat lunch. My physical awareness of you is acute: I can feel static electricity in the gap between our hands, feel the magnetic pull from your body, my feet moving in time with yours.

There are tourists wandering around, and a party of schoolchildren on a trip, all in hi-vis jackets. A Chinese couple are having their wedding photographs taken on the lawn. Her dress is exquisite: a sparkling beaded bodice and a froth of white netting that billows in the breeze. Her mother keeps darting over to adjust and fluff it out.

We spot an empty bench on the raised terrace behind the gardens and grab it.

'Can I go first?' you say.

I nod.

'I haven't been entirely honest.'

'I don't suppose I've been all that honest with you either.'

'Yes, you have. You've been clear about your feelings

from the beginning. It's been frustrating and exasperating and sometimes I've hated you for imposing rules, but you've refused to give me false hope. In return, I've lied to you. I've let you believe I'm something I'm not.'

'Which is?' I ask.

A crow alights a few feet from where we're sitting. He is a beautiful specimen, with the blue sheen on his wings, the lick of grey in his ruff. An elder statesman of crows. I let him be. The bride and groom kiss, holding hands.

'A man worth knowing.'

I drag my gaze from the couple. 'That's for me to decide.'

'You can't very well do that without the information. Christ.' You bang your head against your knuckles. 'I shouldn't have put that stupid message in the *Metro*. I should have left well alone. I don't know what the hell I was thinking. I don't work in advertising. I made that up. I currently work in a mobile phone repair shop, and I'm on borrowed time there. And I know we agreed not to give details about ourselves, but I already knew who you were when we met.'

You're frightening me. 'I don't understand. I think I'd have remembered.'

I see you as you were on that day, turning to grin at me before you left the train. A complete stranger who had understood I was struggling and stepped in to help.

'It's time I told you the truth. You'll probably hate me afterwards, but that's better than the alternative.'

'You really don't need to tell me anything.'

A dozen possibilities bolt through my mind, most of them unlikely, but three rise to the fore: you're married; you're a disgruntled employee of IFR; you were interviewed for a job by Anthony and fixated on him after you weren't offered it.

'I was at the charity gala.'

'Which one?' I go to so many, both with IFR as Anthony's wife and as part of my job.

'Your husband's. The Begin Again programme.'

'Oh? But I didn't see you. Whose table were you on?'

When you don't answer, the penny slowly drops. I lean back against the bench, close my eyes and listen to the traffic rumbling by. Then you say one word. It's as if you've read my mind.

'Yup.'

March 2023

Chapter 49

XAN

Xan makes his way to Table 6, stacks half the plates and comes back for the rest. He likes the constant movement of waiting tables at these big events: weaving round guests and pushed-back chairs, alert for bag straps and other trip hazards, jackets and scarves that have slipped to the floor. It's both mindless and mind-consuming. If he focuses on the task and doesn't drift, it's almost like meditation. He used to meditate in prison. He doesn't any more. No time. He doesn't make eye contact with the guests, but occasionally one will get in his way. Some will smile, some will even tell him he's doing a great job and add that they love what Stir does, the whole ethos of the charity. Some women will give him a look bordering on predatory.

Stir takes on a variety of contracts, from weddings and bar mitzvahs to charity galas and conferences, raising money for the Begin Again programme. Big companies love to use them, because it makes them look good, not to mention the tax incentive. But this event is all about people like him, the ex-cons – or prison leavers, as the politically correct call them these days.

'Right, clean yourselves up, team,' their supervisor

shouts as the doors close between them and the hubbub of the dining room. The man served time for slugging someone outside a pub eighteen years ago. The guy died. It's not so far off his own crime. 'On my word you will walk out, arm's length between you, and stand with your backs to the wall but not leaning against it. Questions?'

'Aprons on or off?' Kam asks.

'On.'

Kam Jackson is the youngest of tonight's cohort and the most recently released. He's only nineteen; it isn't too late for him. Whatever his current circumstances, he has youth and good looks on his side. In Xan's view, Kam's problem is he doesn't always think before he acts, and he can be a prat. If he stays the course, he could still make something of himself, but Xan worries about him. He has a sense that his relentless cheerfulness hides something deeper and darker. He met plenty like that inside: the jokers hiding their pain. When Kam isn't mucking around, when his face is at rest and he doesn't know he's being watched, the light leaves his eyes and he looks demoralised. Not Xan's problem, though. He has enough of his own.

At thirty-seven, Xan worries he is dangerously close to too late. A man should be in his chosen career and making his way up the ranks by the time he's thirty. He tries not to dwell on the odds of success. He *will* succeed. He owes it to those who tried to help him when he was growing up, the two kind and decent people he gave so much trouble to: the foster parents who took him in after his father kicked him out. He is making progress. There are businesses out there who employ men like him, though they aren't the type of thing he aspires to. His goal is the golden ticket, an apprenticeship with IFR, with the possibility of a permanent contract. They take on one ex-offender per year, if there is one who makes the grade. Working his way through past success stories online, there seems not to be a pattern: women, men; the youngest twenty-one, the oldest fifty-eight. It's what he is after, and it's what he intends to get.

He wants what most people want: a career, a spouse, a couple of kids. Self-respect. His old line of work, hospitality – what he's doing now essentially, except with responsibility – he wants nothing more to do with. He doesn't want to be back on the front line, dealing with drunk punters, splitting up fights, being nice to the idiots crowding his bar, scooping up men and women so plastered they can't get out of the door, let alone negotiate an app to call a cab. He wants a career that comes with respect, with a smart office. A job he can leave at 5.30 to return to a house in a quiet street with a pretty wife and a bunch of kids. He's had enough excitement to last him a lifetime.

They file out and make their way round the walls, standing with their hands clasped behind them, feet apart. It reminds him of the day he was arrested, the start of a protracted nightmare that even a year after leaving prison isn't over for him.

The tall, slender man with the silver hair and a certain louche elegance who walks onto the stage is Anthony Gordon, Begin Again's founder and indefatigable supporter. Xan is fascinated by Gordon and has read everything there is to read about him. He knows about his humble beginnings and how hard he's grafted to get where he is. He knows about the heart attack last year, and the aborted coup by his board of directors. He understands that behind the charm there is a steely determination. He likes that the man has altered himself from the inside out, that he speaks the right way, holds himself the right way, that to be with him you wouldn't guess he didn't go to public school. To him, Gordon is someone to emulate. Gordon doesn't know him, but Xan hopes that will change soon. He's heard he's getting an interview.

Gordon expects personal accountability from the programme's clients. That is rule number one, and even though many of the applicants for those precious places begin by chucking excuses around like they're confetti, their bravado is soon shed. Xan has never denied his responsibility, but there were mitigating circumstances and he clung to them like a life raft.

That wasn't good enough. If he wanted to progress, his counsellor said, he needed to take responsibility not only for the crime itself, but for all its twists and tangles, because blaming others, or fate, or coincidence, would hold him back. He changed his tune immediately and he's a better man for it. He's ready to live again, to find a route back into the world. He may have a criminal record, but he doesn't see himself as a criminal. He's a man who made a mistake on the spur of the moment. It should never have happened, and he will always deeply regret it and feel a guilt so profound it's become part of his mix, but he can and will move on and up.

The applause has started, and it's time to go back to work. He spots an empty bottle on Anthony Gordon's table and goes to get it. As he picks it up, he steals a glance at Rachel Gordon. He's seen photographs, but those don't capture her beauty. She's leaning across the table, gesticulating as she speaks with quick, nervy movements, diamonds refracting the light as her hands emphasise her words. She could be described, politely, as slender, but in his view she's too thin, her sleeveless dress drawing uncomfortable attention to her bony shoulders and sternum. Her fine blonde hair is parted at the side and tucked behind her ears, revealing a pair of diamond studs that flash in the light from the chandeliers.

He goes back into the kitchen and puts the bottle in the recycling box. Women like her live on a different planet; they do their charitable thing, but they don't have a clue about the people they're supporting. It's simply an exercise in whitewashing their own superficial lives. They all look alike to him. He doesn't have time for them.

By now, many of the guests are pissed, the buzz is good, people are ready to be entertained. The auctioneer gets funnier, aware he needs to up the ante to keep his audience engaged. A bored crowd won't bid, they'll be too busy discreetly checking round for their belongings, ready to make a quick exit. But this guy, a famous comedian, has them eating out of the palm of his hand with jokes, flashes of satire and moments of painful self-denigration. Hands shoot up, astronomical prices are scored. Holidays, cars, golfing trips, spa breaks, jewellery. It fascinates Xan how money can be spent so fast and so carelessly.

He's startled when a guest touches him lightly on the forearm. He looks down at her hand and clocks the diamonds on her fingers.

'So what have you done to get yourself into this situation?'

'That isn't something I discuss with strangers.' He tries to smile, to keep it light. Her perfume is heavy. The flirtatious way she's looking at him makes him want to run, but he's trained to be civil, to ignore provocation and act professionally. These things happen from time to time. People who wouldn't ask questions sober will ask them drunk. Frankly, the men are a lot worse. Patronising wankers. Moving away, he almost trips over her bag. It's gaping open at the corner of her chair and he can clearly see her purse.

'Bye-bye,' she calls, wiggling those beringed fingers. Then she winks.

Later, he sees Kam at Gordon's table. Rachel Gordon smiles up at the kid and says something as he clears her plate. Kam replies, then turns away. The next moment, he is standing beside the woman with the diamond rings. Xan watches in horror as Kam bends to scoop up a dropped silk scarf, distracting her while his other hand is busy extracting something from her bag. Shit. What an idiot. Xan can't believe his eyes. How could he be so stupid?

Should he say something?

What's the point? You can't stop people self-destructing by being reasonable. Kam will have to work that out for himself.

Chapter 50

On Monday, checking his notifications during his coffee break, Xan finds an email from Rob.Parker@stir.com.

Dear colleagues

I am disappointed to have to share with you that several items belonging to our guests were stolen on Friday evening. As you know, we have a zero-tolerance policy at Stir. If someone breaks the law while working for us, that person will be dismissed. Given that you are being helped to restart your lives by the Begin Again programme and employed by Stir in a position of trust, you will understand why we take this stand.

I only add, because I appreciate that the perpetrator might be tempted to take the easy option by simply saying nothing, that if I have not heard from them by nine o'clock tomorrow morning, every member of staff on duty on Friday will be dismissed. Please think about what you have done and do the right thing.

With kind regards
Rob

'Fuck,' Xan says under his breath.

He tries to call Kam, but he doesn't pick up. He tries again at intervals, but Kam must have switched his phone off, which strikes Xan as odd. For people Kam's age, their phone is their sixth vital organ. At the end of his shift at Fones4Less, Xan makes his way to Acton and Kam's fifth-floor flat.

When Kam comes to the door, he's in shorts and a T-shirt.

'I've been trying to get hold of you all day,' Xan says.

'Sorry, mate. I switched my phone off. I was sleeping. What's the big emergency?'

'Have you looked at your emails?'

'Nah.' Kam looks at him as though he thinks he's a sandwich short of a picnic, and Xan sees the rationale behind that. Gen Zs do not email. He feels old.

He follows Kam into the sitting room. It's neat and bright, furnished with a glass-topped table with four chairs round it and a white leather sofa opposite a huge television. Kam picks up his phone, swipes it into life and taps in his passcode. Xan waits impatiently.

'Ah, crap,' Kam says, reading Parker's email. 'What a twat.'

'I know it was you.'

'What you on about?'

'Kam, I saw you. You've got to tell Parker or the whole fucking lot of us are out. If you don't, I will.'

His gaze is drawn to Kam's hands. The lad has always struck him as nervy, but right now his hands are shaking like he's about to piss himself.

'Come on, mate. Please.'

268

'You don't understand.'

'I do. It's an urge. I get it. Have you used the cards?'

Kam nods miserably. 'Yeah, but they've been stopped now.'

'So what is it? Drugs?'

'What the fuck has it got to do with you?'

Xan resists the urge to grab him by the collar and shove him up against the wall. 'It has everything to do with me. I'm not losing my position because some little toerag can't keep his hands off other people's belongings. If I'm sacked, I lose my chance at the apprenticeship, and I'll lose my other job too. It's not happening.'

Kam's Adam's apple bobs as he swallows. 'You can't prove it was me. Could have been any one of us. Could have been you, for that matter.'

Xan is losing patience. 'But it wasn't, was it? It was you. If you're feeding a drug habit, then you need to get help, but think about the rest of us. None of us can afford to lose this. Begin Again is our chance, and you ... Oh, for Christ's sake.' He bangs his fist against the wall. 'You were given a chance too. Why would you throw it away? I don't understand.'

'Who are you?'

Xan spins round. There's a small boy standing in the doorway. He's holding a toy truck. His head is shaved at the sides.

'Hey. What did I tell you, Blake?' Kam says. 'Stay in your bedroom.'

'Who's that man?'

'He's a mate.'

'Can I have something to eat?'

'Sure, if you scarper.' Kam goes into the kitchen and

269

comes back with a pack of digestive biscuits. He untwists the end, takes one out and gives it to the child. Then he turns him round and gives him a gentle push. 'Go to your bedroom. I'll come and see you in a minute. Okay?'

'Your son?' Xan asks when the boy has gone. He frowns as he does the calculations in his head. No. Not son. 'Brother?'

'Half-brother.'

That makes more sense. 'Where's his mum?'

Kam shrugs. 'Fucked off the minute I got out of the nick, didn't she? Apparently it's my turn.'

'What about when you're working?'

'His sister takes care of him.'

'And how old is she?'

'Fourteen.' He adds hastily, 'But she looks way older. And she's mature. Like she's seventeen or something. She's good with him.'

Xan claws his fingers through his hair. 'The money you took,' he says weakly.

Kam motions him to follow. In the kitchen, he opens the cupboards. They are stuffed with tins and packets of food, the fridge as well. Then he takes three Primark bags off the stairs and dumps their contents on the floor. Small trainers, T-shirts, shorts, coats.

'They'd run out of all sorts,' he says. 'And my sister needs girls' stuff. Sanitary stuff, you know. She used to take Mum's but there're none left.'

'What about your mum? Can't you ask her to come home?'

'I don't know where she is, but she took her passport. I reckon she's gone away with some bloke. My sister said she had one. She's probably gone to Spain. She always liked it there.'

'And left her children?'

Kam's sigh says everything. 'She took Tessie and left me alone for two weeks when I was thirteen. Told me not to tell the school or I'd go into care and get raped. So, yeah. I ended up in care anyway. Didn't get raped, though.'

There's a flash of his cheeky smile when he says this. Xan's heart breaks. He wishes he'd never seen him steal the purse, but even if he hadn't, he'd still be in the shit. Christ. Either way, he loses.

'Have you talked to Social Services?'

'No way. I'm here now, aren't I? I'm well old enough to take care of them.' Kam slumps down on the leather sofa and rubs his face. 'What you going to do?'

Xan groans. 'The only thing I can do.'

'Shit, mate. Please. They need me.'

Xan's chest feels so tight he can barely breathe. 'I'll tell them it was me.'

June 2023

Chapter 51

RACHEL

I don't take my eyes off your face while you tell your story. I get the feeling it's a long time since anyone has listened to you like that.

'Did you try to explain to your manager at Stir?' I ask.

'How could I? I saw the situation Kam was in. I know it sounds stupid and short-sighted, sacrificing my chances for someone who'll probably fuck up again, but it was an impossible situation. I . . . um . . .'

'What?'

'I did try to see your husband. I emailed him and asked for a meeting. But he refused. We're not allowed to contact him directly and I didn't expect him to reply, but he did and it was humiliating. He said I'd been flagged up as a possibility for the apprenticeship. That I'd thrown it away.'

'Can I see the email?'

There's an infinitesimal hesitation before you respond. 'Sure.' You fumble with your phone, your fingers clumsy. I take the phone from you and read the words my husband wrote, and all I feel is shame. How could he?

To: Alexander Stratton
From: Anthony Gordon
Subject: Dismissal

Dear Mr Stratton

I am extremely surprised to hear from you and even more surprised to be asked to intervene in Robert Parker's handling of this situation. I am fully behind his decision to dismiss you, as I have been when this kind of thing has happened in the past. You are not the first of our beneficiaries to throw away what has been so generously given to them and no doubt you won't be the last. It's disappointing, and especially, I might add, coming from you. If someone is flagged up to me as a possibility for the apprenticeship here at IFR, I'm naturally interested in their progress. You were one of those, so it is a pity you were unable to resist such obvious temptations. I'm sure you possess the wit to understand why I can be of no further help to you.

Yours sincerely
Anthony Gordon

'Your name is Alexander?'

'People call me Xan. I'm sorry.'

'Why give me a false name?'

'I didn't. I said Xan, but it was noisy and you heard Sean. To pull you up on it would have spoiled the moment. I didn't expect to see you again.'

I decide not to pursue this. 'It's a horrible email. I'm sorry.'

276

'Not your fault.'

'Are you going to take the job in Manchester?'

'That's fallen through.' Your attempt at a cheery smile is the grimace of a scarecrow. 'I'm staring into the abyss.'

I try my best to keep my expression neutral for fear of causing more hurt. All you want is to put the past behind you and carve out a life for yourself, but because of what happened, you can't. Kam has wrecked your chances, Anthony has driven the final nail in.

I am outraged at what's happened to you – the injustice of it and the part Anthony played in crushing your spirit – but it isn't that simple. I am a professional, working indirectly in the charity sector, and I know perfectly well that if you react emotionally to situations, you only make matters worse. It's vital to step back and bring a rational approach to each problem. Anthony has to come down hard from time to time; he is the CEO of two charities dealing with clients who have committed crimes. If one of them abuses their position, particularly where the charity's precious donors are concerned, it doesn't matter who is managing who, ultimately the buck stops with him.

On the other hand, the Begin Again programme is all about second chances. If I could only get the two of you together, give you an opportunity to explain, Anthony might see that you're someone worth holding onto. I decide, with some qualms, that it's worth a shot.

I turn to you. 'I've got an idea.'

'Rachel, this is my problem. You don't have to fix it for me.'

'Just hear me out. Please.'

Your face has taken on a wooden aspect, but you nod.

I explain what I've decided to do; you argue against it, but I press my point and you cave in.

'So I can make the call?'

You shrug. 'Yeah. It can't make things any worse.'

I resist the impulse to respond with *famous last words*. This is not the time to be facetious. 'Great.'

It isn't great. My chest is tight and there is a rock in the pit of my stomach. I get up and walk away, too ashamed to allow you to overhear my conversation. I'm still in two minds when I'm out of earshot, but then I look back at you, watching forlornly from our bench. You're broken. If you hadn't been, you would not have allowed me to do this. And so I call my husband.

And I tell my lie.

Chapter 52

XAN

As Rachel turns back towards him, a young couple intercept her, their faces bright and eager.

'Would you mind?' The woman is holding out her phone, gesticulating at her companion. She wants a photograph taken of them in front of the statue, a bronze of entwined lovers. Sweet.

Rachel hesitates, then agrees with good grace. The woman swings her hair over one shoulder and gazes up at the man. Rachel snaps and snaps before handing the phone back.

'Thank you so much. Love the jacket. That pink really suits you.'

Rachel accepts the compliment and sits back down next to Xan. 'It's done,' she says breathlessly. 'The rest is up to you.'

He catches something in her gaze. She looks excited. They stare at each other for a long moment, then he breaks the silence. Someone has to say it. 'That will be it, won't it? We won't see each other again.'

'Xan . . .'

'You don't have to answer. I know this is goodbye.'

They hold hands and slowly she starts to smile. She has never seemed more beautiful to him. 'It'll be all right. You just have to be strong. You deserve a better life.'

Xan smiles back. 'And so do you.'

'So this is it.'

'It's for the best.'

'Please be careful.'

He nods, then hesitates. When he speaks, he makes sure Rachel is looking straight into his eyes. 'You haven't asked me what I did.'

'Do you want me to ask you?'

'I want to be honest with you.'

She nods. 'Tell me then.'

'I hurt someone badly. He was only nineteen. His injuries were life-changing. He's a quadriplegic. I was trying to control a situation, but it went wrong and I live with that every day. I wanted to change my life after prison, to make something of it, but when I close my eyes, it's still him I see at night.'

His nightclub. His responsibility. Telling Rachel rips something open inside him, and he lands back in the past with a thud. He sees the guy with his hand around the neck of a girl, pushing her up against the wall outside the ladies' toilets, screaming in her face, spittle flying. He grabs his shoulders and roughly pulls him away. Xan was a bigger man then, at the gym most days, lifting weights, cardio, the lot. He was proud of his six-pack, his muscular physique. The club had only been open three months but was already thriving. He was busy proving his teachers and family wrong. He'd left school at sixteen with four underwhelming GCSEs, but he wasn't stupid. Not until that night.

The young man fights back, drunk and leery. Xan drags him up the stairs to the exit. He doesn't know exactly how it happens, only that Jake Thompson gets into his face one too many times, a gob of spit hitting him in the eye. The suddenness of it and the visceral memory of his father's sneering face close to his that it provokes causes a reflexive response. He knees the young man in the groin and throws a punch, and Jake torpedoes down the concrete stairs. If Xan closes his eyes, he can see him lying crumpled at the bottom, the pulsing dance-floor lights making his body appear to move when in fact it's frighteningly still. He can feel his own heart pounding, sweat running down his forehead into his eyes.

And then the main lights come on, flooding the place. His security guys push past him, shouting. A young man's potential erased. Xan's too. He lost his business, lost Natalie, lost his freedom.

Rachel observes him silently.

'Say something.'

'I don't believe you'd do anything out of malice or cruelty. It was a mistake, and you've paid the price.'

He nods and hooks his jacket over his shoulder. 'You may find out other things about me, but I want you to know, I fell in love with you, I'm still in love with you, and that *is* real. It was just bad timing.' He kisses her and walks away.

Telling her was the right thing to do, but he wishes now that he hadn't, because she's going to go home and think about this and it's going to colour her memories of him.

He will do what she asks, even though he is pretty sure it's a mistake.

*

The flats loom up in the gathering dusk. Over by the bins, a fox is gnawing at something disgusting, oblivious to Xan's presence. This place is shit, but it's all he has. He's relying on a nineteen-year-old thief to keep him off the streets.

He hears footsteps behind him and turns his head, sees a figure in a baseball cap, long army-style coat and brown boots. As it comes closer, he realises it's Caroline Gordon.

'What do you want?'

'That's not very friendly. I want to know why you haven't sealed the deal. When we last met, you assured me it was going well. You said you were so close.'

'You can't force these things.'

Caroline puts her hands on her hips. 'You were talking for a long time. Neither of you looked happy. In fact, it looked suspiciously like goodbye.'

'You've been following me.'

'I'm simply looking after my investment. I've paid you to sleep with the woman, not have a deep and meaningful relationship that goes nowhere.'

'I tried.'

'And what? She's just not into you? I'm sorry, but that's rubbish. You just haven't been able to tip her over the edge. Try again.'

'I'm not doing this any more, Caroline,' he says wearily. If things go as planned tomorrow, he won't have to. The thought of what he has to do upsets him. It goes against the grain.

'Cute kids, Blake and Tessie.'

'What?'

'Shame if they end up in the care system. I've heard the life chances of kids like that seldom recover.'

'Leave them alone.'

He glances up at Kam's flat. The lights are on in the kitchen and Blake's bedroom. Lately, Xan has been helping with Tessie's homework, playing computer games with Blake, cooking for all three of them, lounging on the sofa with Blake slumped against his shoulder, asleep, Tessie mucking around with her older brother and laughing that big fat laugh of hers, Kam doing his best to keep his sister from skipping school, or hanging out with kids who'll get her into trouble.

'Or what?' Caroline says. 'Kam's record makes interesting reading. When he was at school, he was excluded for thieving. He went to a young offenders' institution for a year when he was fifteen for dealing drugs. Most recently he did eighteen months for theft and criminal damage. You, however, had a clean slate before the punch that landed you in prison. Stealing from a charity event to raise money to help people like you is out of character. It's what I'd expect from Kam. So I looked at why you might have taken the rap for him. He's been raising his siblings since his waste-of-space mother walked out, and by all accounts she isn't about to walk back in. If he gets into trouble, they'll be removed from his care. That's why you played the hero. I can talk to Rob Parker and tell him what really happened, then it will all have been for nothing. So it isn't over until I say it's over.'

Footsteps clip across the car park as a woman in a quilted coat hurries to the entrance to the flats. Caroline waits for her to disappear into the ill-lit concrete stairwell.

'I told her the truth,' Xan says. 'That I'd been inside; that I worked for Stir.'

'Are you kidding me?'

'No. I felt she deserved an explanation.'

'I hope you didn't tell her what you were inside for?'

'I did.'

'For fuck's sake,' she explodes. 'No wonder she isn't interested. Beating up a nineteen-year-old so violently you left him with life-changing injuries is not something you put on your Tinder profile.'

'How do you know about that?'

Caroline meets his furious gaze with a hint of derision. 'I've worked for Begin Again. I can log into the client database on my computer. You did ten years for GBH. What's his name again?'

He doesn't reply.

'Jake Thompson,' she supplies.' A promising young student, according to the *Manchester Echo*. Thanks to you, he is consigned to a lifetime of having his arse wiped by carers.'

'Fuck you,' he says, walking away.

'You're pathetic,' she calls out.

He stops at the entrance, turns to her. 'Maybe I am. But Rachel saw something in me worth saving.'

'She didn't, Xan. You were just her toy. She'll have already moved on, forgotten you.' She tilts her head. 'You look very confident. You're plotting something, aren't you?'

'I'm going now. I don't want to hear from you again.'

'No you're not. You're going to talk to me or it's not only Kam who's going to be in trouble. Rachel is going to know exactly how much I paid you to get into her knickers.'

He thinks about what Rachel wants him to do. His final throw of the dice. She has faith in him, but he doesn't have the same faith in himself.

Chapter 53

RACHEL

'What time should I expect your protégé?' Anthony asks.

We're in our bedroom, a room with a view of the green. It has high ceilings and tall sash windows with old-fashioned shutters. I'm sitting at my dressing table, an antique with billowing curves that stands between the windows.

'Half past seven.'

'And who exactly is he? You weren't clear.'

'Wasn't I?' I was carried away by the impulse when I called Anthony from the gardens of St Paul's Cathedral yesterday evening. That was before Sean told me what he'd done. Now I'm worried I may have made a mistake. 'He's just a colleague. I'm afraid I don't know much about him, but he seems very nice, and he's ambitious.' I focus on putting in a pair of diamond and emerald earrings. 'It's not a problem, is it?'

Anthony leans over me, one hand on my shoulder, and picks up my hairbrush. He starts brushing my hair and I watch in the mirror, rigid. It's a few years since he's done this. It's a habit we fell out of. I used to enjoy the sensuality, but now it causes a nauseating tension throughout my

285

body. I reach up and still his hand. He puts the brush down and walks away.

'What's going on with you?' he asks.

I glance at him over my shoulder. 'What do you mean?'

My dress is lying on the bed. Teal satin with a V-neck and a calf-length A-line skirt. I bought it last summer to wear at the wedding of one of Anthony's godchildren. Hazel said to dress up to the nines. I'm not sure exactly what that means to her, but this is what it means to me. Simple, understated elegance. Anthony picks it up distractedly, then lays it down again and smooths it out.

'You've been distant for the last few weeks.'

'Have I?'

'Yes, you have.'

I turn back to the mirror and uncap a lipstick. 'Well perhaps it's because you hit me.'

'I apologised and I meant it. It's time you got over it, Rachel. Life is too short to be angry at people you love.'

So it's my fault. I don't reply. I apply the lipstick and hope he'll take the hint and go away.

'What's his surname? This Sean character. You never told me.'

'Didn't I?' I go into a mild panic, my mind snatching and rejecting names from the ether.

'No, you didn't.'

'Joliffe,' I say, knowing he won't bother googling it. It's the surname of someone in the accounts department at Asset Plus, but Anthony won't have heard of him. 'Sean Joliffe.'

To reach the chest of drawers, I have to pass close to him. He tries to take my hand and I pretend I don't notice.

286

There's a frisson in the air. I wish he'd respect my privacy. I awkwardly get into my knickers under my gown, then turn away from him to strip and put on my bra.

'I don't understand why you chose tonight,' Anthony says, 'when you knew you were going to be out.'

A flush climbs my skin as I hook my bra and twist it round. I sigh, to sound exasperated. 'I thought it would be better for the two of you if it was a boys' thing. You know, not with me overseeing you like a playdate. Maybe it was the wrong thing to do, but it's done now.'

It feels as though all the oxygen is being sucked out of the room. It's strange, because we've had a good day. Caroline hasn't been in, at least not until the afternoon, and then really just to get ready to go out again. Earlier, Anthony and I went for a walk in Richmond Park. We hadn't done that for ages. It's so beautiful at this time of year. The trees are filling out with green and the grass is lush. Once we found ourselves within a few metres of a family of deer amongst the ferns. The older female stopped munching and looked at me, her huge eyes framed with long, long lashes. We had a cup of tea on the terrace at Pembroke Lodge, gazing out at the view over the Thames Valley. I was on my best behaviour, listening to him, complimenting him, being respectful. Only there was an element of pity there. I wanted to make him believe I was in awe of him. Pandering to the male ego. But he noticed the distance between us. He seems abnormally sensitive at the moment.

You will be in my house in a few hours. It was an impulse, and having slept on it, I'm not sure it was a wise decision, given what you shared about your past. I try not to think about you and Anthony in the same room, because when

I do, my heart starts to race. Anyway, it's happening, good idea or not. I couldn't stop you coming even if I wanted to, because I don't have your contact details.

Anthony hovers as I struggle with the tiny satin-covered buttons at the front of the dress. I'm a bag of nerves.

'Here. Let me help.'

I submit as he slowly fastens them, his long fingers treating the satin like my skin. I suppress an urge to scream. I want to be intimate with you, not him. I remind myself it's over. We drew a line under our relationship last night, for good reasons. You are an ex-con who did a ten-year stretch for causing grievous bodily harm.

'Thanks.' I check my appearance in the mirror. Anthony is behind me. There's an expression on his face that makes me shudder inwardly.

'Caroline said something interesting to me earlier,' he says.

'Oh?' I catch his eye in the mirror.

'She said she saw you on the Underground talking to a man.'

I frown, feigning bewilderment, though my fight-or-flight instinct has gone into overdrive. 'I can't imagine when. I don't talk to strangers on the Tube. Perhaps he was asking me for directions?'

'That's not how she described it.'

I go to the wardrobe and find the gold high-heeled shoes I bought specially to wear with this dress, scooping them up by their straps so they swing from my fingers. 'I can't help how Caroline interprets what she sees, but I'm telling you, I don't remember a conversation with anyone, so if it happened, it can't have been particularly interesting.'

288

'Oh, but it must have been. She saw the pair of you get off the train together. She said you were obviously good friends. Surely you remember that?' His voice is cool, very calm, but I know Anthony. He's charming, until he isn't. 'Who is he, Rachel? Is it Joliffe?'

I feign outrage. 'Absolutely not. There is no one.'

'Are you calling my daughter a liar?'

I've walked into a minefield. I can continue to lie, or I can tell the truth, or at least part of it. I swallow hard. 'No. I'm sorry. She did see me. The guy was someone I'd met ages ago on a training course. We bumped into each other once.'

'Why get off the train?'

My mouth is dry. 'I suppose,' I say, choosing the lesser of two evils, 'it was because we were enjoying our conversation. It was his stop, and it was an impulse. It was a very short-lived flirtation. I haven't been happy since... well, since that night Caroline attacked her boyfriend. You shocked me so badly when you lost your temper.'

'Do you never take responsibility?'

'When it's warranted.' My hackles rise. 'Have you asked yourself why Caroline's telling tales? She's deliberately causing trouble between us because she bears a grudge against me. This daddy–daughter thing is a little too much sometimes. Yes, I spoke to this man, and yes, we were flirting. But between the pair of you, you've been pushing me away. Nothing is going to be resolved until Caroline moves out. The bad atmosphere she creates is corrosive. Or do you think I should be the one to go? Is that it? Do you want it to be just you and your perfect daughter?'

'Have you finished?' Anthony is white around the lips. Twin patches of colour flare on his cheekbones.

'Open your eyes, Anthony. You've created a monster.'

When I stalk past him to get to the door, he grabs me.

'Apologise.'

I glare at him, shaking. 'Not until she does.'

He has my arm and he's hurting me, his fingers pressing into tense muscle. His eyes are strange; there's a flare of madness in them. In that moment, with Anthony looming over me, his eyes like flint, I want you. I wish we hadn't agreed it was over. I know with a knife-sharp clarity that I'll never be happy again.

'Get off me.'

He doesn't move, and I struggle like a trapped animal, panic overwhelming me. I shriek at him, 'I wish that heart attack had killed you.'

'Bitch.' He slaps me so hard my head hits the wall, and I crumple to the floor. He strides out of the room, his feet pounding the staircase.

It takes me a few minutes to pull myself together, but eventually I get to my feet and wander unsteadily into the bathroom. I splash my face with cold water and take a long, hard look in the mirror. The imprint of Anthony's hand is livid against my cheek and my make-up is a mess, mascara smudged, tear streaks through the blusher on my cheeks. I pull a reusable cotton pad out of its glass jar, squeeze make-up remover on and slowly clean myself up, then start again from scratch.

Chapter 54

Pulling a fine cashmere shawl out of the cupboard, I arrange it loosely round my neck and make my way downstairs, carrying a small wheelie case containing the bare minimum I'll need for an overnight stay. Pyjamas, jeans and a long-sleeved tee, trainers, underwear, hairbrush, make-up remover, toothbrush and paste.

I have no intention of saying goodbye to Anthony, but my handbag is in the kitchen and unfortunately so is he. The French windows are wide open. A warm wind is gusting, bringing with it the smell of impending rain, causing the pages of the newspaper on the table to flutter and curtain hooks to rattle in their rings.

'I shouldn't have done that,' he says stiffly. 'And I apologise. But you provoked me.'

'It's the second time, Anthony.'

'Are you going to leave me? I don't want you to go. I love you.'

I can't say it back. I am considering leaving, but it's not a conversation for now. I just want to keep things calm. 'I'm sorry for what I said about the heart attack, I know it must have hurt you, but it didn't warrant attacking me.'

'Rachel . . .'

'I'm going to be late.'

'You're not telling me you're still going to that party?

We need to talk about this. Cancel your friend. He can come another time.'

'I'm fine. Let's not change any arrangements.'

I touch the developing bruise on the back of my head. It's tender, but the skin hasn't been broken. He's anxious now, but I don't care. I need to get away from him, from this house, from everything. I'm glad I agreed to stay the night at Hazel's.

'I think it would do us both good to have some space to reflect,' I say.

Anthony doesn't argue. He seems beaten. 'What do you want me to say to him? Do you want me to offer him a job? I will if it means we can move on from this.'

'It doesn't work like that, Anthony. And you certainly don't need to offer him a job. All Sean wants is advice and possibly an introduction, if you think he'd suit the industry.' I feel bad telling bare-faced lies and can't look at him. Instead I check the contents of my handbag, making sure I have keys, phone, lipstick. 'I'm off.'

He moves towards me, but I back away. I don't want to be touched.

'I'll see you in the morning. I'll be back early.'

'Take your raincoat,' he says. 'It's starting to rain.'

Chapter 55

ANTHONY

Desolation descends like a swarm of flies on a corpse. They've both changed. He was fully formed when he met her and she had barely got going. He has grown old and she has grown up. He should have walked away, but he loved her. Loves her.

Even before Caroline told him about seeing Rachel on the Tube, he had suspected someone was trying to take her away from him. It's the reason he agreed to see this Sean in the first place. Because it might be him. The idea of further adjustments to his will to preclude her from remarrying drifts through his mind, but he dismisses it. That would be the height of vanity and unforgivably petty. He feels nothing but contempt for people who use inheritance to manipulate their family members.

He has hit her twice now. The disease is turning him into a monster. A beleaguered monster seeing betrayal at every turn. He cannot silence the thoughts. They torment him day and night.

He mentioned this to his oncologist, attempting to laugh it off, but the man took him seriously, told him that in some cases cancer can alter the sufferer's mental state, lead to delusions and paranoia. He should have told Rachel he was dying as soon as he found out. The cancer and its possible side effects are no excuse, but when she gets back tomorrow he'll attempt to explain all this to her and hope she understands, because he needs her. Caroline as well.

The house is empty and echoing. He finds it unbearable to be alone these days with no distraction, nothing to stop him dwelling on the malignant cells clustering in his lungs, their diaspora spreading through his body.

Dying focuses the mind. He's considered his life and the choices he's made. Like anyone, he has regrets. Smoking heavily from the age of thirteen until he was in his mid thirties and Mia put her foot down is top of the list, of course, but he also regrets the hurt he caused her and Caroline, although given his time again he'd still have chosen Rachel. He isn't angry. He isn't stupid; he knows his own flaws well enough. He understands that he's forfeited the right to reach the end with her at his side. She may be there in body, if he's lucky, but not in spirit. That is a devastating thought. He wishes Caroline had kept her mouth shut. She is going to be angry with him. She made him promise he wouldn't tell Rachel what she'd said, and he didn't mean to, but he was riled and a red mist had descended.

Caroline is his problem. He's messed up badly. He shouldn't have knee-jerked after that nasty episode. It isn't like him. He's come to realise that cutting her out of his will is bound to be interpreted as spite, not the act of a father who cares, and will do more harm than good. If Caroline inherits a sufficiently large amount, then at least the two women he loves will be able to part company amicably, and more to the point, not hating him. Thankfully, there's still time to put that right. Caroline has to be persuaded to change her ways, but not by withdrawing support. Tim will know what to do. Anthony likes the idea of a trust that doesn't pay out until she's in her mid thirties. It'll give her a chance to test herself. He'll call him before his visitor arrives; that way it's done. He picks up his phone and finds Tim's number.

Chapter 56

RACHEL

Hazel opens the door in a figure-hugging blue sequinned dress.

'Yikes. Come in! Sorry about the weather.'

She takes my wet raincoat from me, leads me upstairs and shows me into a room that doubles as a home office. There's a pull-out sofa bed, already made up in pretty rose-print bed linen that matches the curtains, an IKEA set-up of desk and shelves, and framed botanical prints of roses adorning the walls. I put down my case. Hazel shows me the bathroom, which is fresh and white with pops of pale green in the towels and indoor plants ranged on the windowsill. She hangs the raincoat over the glass shower door and leaves me to freshen up. I wince when I brush my hair. Thank God the red mark from where Anthony hit me has faded from my cheek.

Downstairs, I follow the sound of female chatter into a shiny kitchen with white cupboards, sparkling grey worktops, white tiled flooring and a small army of spots overhead. Beyond that, bifold doors look onto a patio where pink roses hang heads weighed down by the rain. The journey has helped me compose myself, to compartmentalise what happened – that's what we're supposed to do to get by, isn't it? – stuff it in a box and close the lid. I could have done with an extra half-hour, because I'm still a little shaky.

Three women are sitting round the kitchen island, long legs crossed, feet in strappy shoes with stratospheric heels. Hazel introduces me to Lauren, Cynthia and Zandra, and I immediately forget which is which. They're drinking colourful cocktails and picking at plates of finger food. I take in what they're wearing – black tube, hot-pink dress with a plunging diamanté-encrusted neckline, royal-blue shift with a square neckline and long sleeves, all barely skimming bottoms – and turn apologetically to Hazel.

'This dress is all wrong. I feel like someone's mum.'

'Don't be silly, you look wonderful. We're all chilled here. Once you've had one of Zandra's cocktails, you won't give it another thought.'

'My speciality,' Zandra says with a smirk, and I make a mental note: Zandra, royal blue.

'Is there something I can eat? I can't drink on an empty stomach.'

Hazel reaches for a plate of sliced-up pitta bread and a hummus dip. 'You need to catch up.'

I sense I'm being judged and have already slipped at the first hurdle. I climb onto a stool, accept the cocktail. I might as well drown my sorrows.

'Good, yeah?' Zandra says.

'Incredible.'

'It's your bog-standard sex on the beach. Vodka, peach schnapps, orange and cranberry juice – with an extra twist. A slosh of Calvados. Careful, they go down pretty easy.'

'Shall we raise a toast to the birthday girl, now we're all here?' Black Dress says, picking up her glass. 'To Hazel, the best friend ever.'

Hazel keeps the drinks coming, and I keep accepting them, and at first it helps. I can persuade myself I'm having fun, although it's hard to connect with the other women when I'm still reeling from the blow Anthony dealt me. The compartmentalising isn't working.

It hasn't taken me long to unpick the dynamic between Hazel and her friends. They've known each other since primary school, have seen each other through the mad ups and downs of adolescence. Zandra is the ringleader, the one they all rely on to make the fun decisions. As she gets drunker, her humour verges on cruel. While they all suffer to an extent, Hazel is the butt of the jokes. Zandra bigs her up then pulls her down. *I'm only joking. You know I love you.* Lauren is the people-pleaser. She keeps asking me if I'm okay, keeps apologising for talking about people I don't know. Cynthia is the attention-seeker. I notice that she constantly draws the focus back to herself, either by interrupting or by laughing loudly when it strays.

If there's an odd one out, it's Hazel. It feels as though she's part of the gang because she's there, not because she's a natural fit. Perhaps it's because she isn't on the path to marriage and motherhood yet, when two of them are married with small children – Zandra and Black Dress, who I now know is Lauren – and Cynthia is engaged. I can empathise. It's hard in your thirties not to have children when all your friends do, or are about to. You need to work harder, and they still drift away. My friends were Anthony's friends

298

first, and are at least twenty years older than me; I haven't kept up with anyone from my pre-Anthony days.

For the first time I understand why Hazel makes such an effort with me. It's because she sees an ally. I suspect I am insurance against a time when, unless she meets someone, she ceases to have much in common with the women she's grown up with. That time is fast approaching, if it's not here already. I notice most of the conversation is about the past rather than the future, and I feel sorry for Hazel. For myself too, because you are in my past and I'm not sure what kind of future I have with a man for whom I'm struggling to hold onto any affection.

Chapter 57

ANTHONY

'Sean.' Anthony holds out a hand in welcome. Talking to Tim has given him some peace of mind. He'll give Rachel the benefit of the doubt and believe, at least for the short time the man is here, that she isn't having an affair. He has no choice if he's going to repair the damage done this evening and ensure his last months aren't spent entirely alone. The feud between Rachel and Caroline is exhausting him. His wife says his daughter is a leech, his daughter that his wife is unfaithful. What has he done to deserve this? He has more than enough love for both of them. Why can't they just get along?

'Thank you for seeing me, sir.'

'Call me Anthony.'

Anthony leads his visitor into the kitchen. Beyond the doors to the garden, the light is fading and the rain has darkened the old stone patio.

'Drink?'

'Whisky if you have it.'

Anthony moves to the cupboard, finds a glass, puts it on the table. If it's all perfectly innocent, then actually he's rather pleased Sean is here. It'll stop him moping, and it's nice to know that even after what's happened in the last six months, he still commands respect. This man wanting his advice proves that, doesn't it?

His hands tremble as he pours, spilling a little. He finds that peculiarly humiliating, but Sean either doesn't notice or is too polite to bring it up. Anthony pushes the glass over to him and discreetly mops the spillage. He should invite him into his study, but he doesn't have the energy. He sits down.

'You don't want one yourself?' Sean asks.

'I don't drink.'

'Good of you to keep a supply for visitors then. You don't get tempted?'

'Not in the least.'

'This is a beautiful house.'

'I like it.' Anthony can't help noticing that Sean is attractive. Well built, thick hair, good bone structure. He's taller than Anthony, with broader shoulders, and carries himself well. Despite his resolve, Anthony feels the need to put him in his place. He quells it because this is not a pissing contest. At least not officially. 'My wife tells me you want to get into the recruitment business.' He briefly wonders why he didn't say *Rachel*.

'I work in strategic planning, but I need a change. I'd rather be involved in something where people are the commodity, not units of currency. It's been interesting and an education, but it's no longer what I want. I got talking to Rachel a couple of weeks ago, and she suggested I meet you.'

'That was kind of her,' Anthony answers drily.

'It was.' Sean appears oblivious to the irony.

301

'How old are you?'

'Thirty-seven.'

'Old for a career change.'

'I don't think so. It's all about the portfolio career these days. No one thinks they have to stay where they aren't fulfilled.'

'We call that commitment,' Anthony says.

'Oh, don't get me wrong. I have enormous respect for people like you who achieve success in their area, but unless you have a strong vocation, you're a scientist or a medic, and even then... well, attention spans are somewhat different now, don't you think? We millennials like to shake it up.'

Anthony sighs, thinking of Caroline, wishing she would shake it up and forget about acting. He has good instincts about people, it's the reason he's survived, and instinct tells him something about this man is off. But then again, it could be because, despite a huge mental effort not to be, he's predisposed to hate him.

'I want to learn more about the industry,' Sean says. 'I've researched companies I'd ideally like to work for, and I know how they function, but I'd like to hear your thoughts. You'll know the individuals. I'm aiming high, but I want to be sure I'm channelling my energies in the right direction.' He smiles. 'Perhaps you could put me in touch with some people. It's all about the contacts, isn't it?'

There is a look in his eye that makes the hairs on the back of Anthony's neck prickle. It doesn't feel like respect. There's a hint of mockery there. It gives him an injection of adrenaline. This feels adversarial, a space he has always relished occupying.

302

'I'll tell you what I can, but I'm afraid I can't recommend you to anyone. I don't know you. Recruitment is what I do, so I have to be careful. My reputation, you understand?' He enjoys the look that crosses Sean's face at the put-down. He understands all right. Rachel couldn't like him, though, could she? He's an arrogant prick.

But so am I, he thinks. The self-knowledge that comes with one's dying days can be an uncomfortable reckoning.

It feels as though Sean is waiting for something, testing the water; maybe checking out the competition. That he's here for career advice Anthony simply does not believe. This is not the kind of man who would think he needed advice. If it's Anthony's address book he's after, he can take a flying leap.

'Remind me how you know my wife.'

'Through a friend,' Sean says.

'Which friend?'

'Hazel Gifford. They work together.'

That was not what Rachel said. Rachel said they were colleagues. They obviously didn't get their stories straight. How careless. 'I didn't think Hazel had a boyfriend.'

Sean laughs. 'I don't want to be ungentlemanly, but Hazel isn't my type. She's just a mate. I met her for an after-work drink and Rachel was there.'

'Which pub?' As far as he knows, Rachel and Hazel and their cohort always go to the same one.

'I honestly don't remember,' Sean says.

'Try.'

Chapter 58

RACHEL

I am on the sofa. I have reached my capacity and stopped drinking. The music is loud and bouncy, the beat making the house skip in its foundations. I've had enough and I want to go home. All I can think of is you.

I've been over and over our last conversation. The way you let me know who and what you were without saying a word, just that quiet but firm *Yup*, the intense connection I felt. Remembering the way we kissed hurts physically. It's unfinished business of the most acute kind, creating a breathlessness deep inside me, an ache in my diaphragm. You are going to take a lot of getting over.

I remember my first love, when I was seventeen. After I'd been dumped I thought I would die from the pain of it. It took months to recover. Partings have never been that traumatic since. Until now.

You are different. I'm not sure why, but I know it's true. I will never forget you. At least I can be proud of the way I behaved. I have nothing to be ashamed of.

Zandra throws herself down on the sofa beside me.

'Not being funny, but you've gotta make an effort. You're

upsetting Hazel. Lighten up and have some fun, yeah?'
She's slurring her words.

'I'm sorry, I didn't realise.'

'Sitting there all prim looking like you think we're a
bunch of slappers is a bit of a downer. Know what I mean?'

'I don't think you're slappers. I wasn't thinking about
you at all.'

'Ooh. Listen to you. Are we not good enough for you?
Just 'cos your hubby's worth millions and you live in a fancy
house doesn't make you better than us.'

'I never ... That's not what I think.'

'Hey,' Hazel says, shimmying over, her hands held out.
'Dance with me.'

Relieved to be rescued, I do as I'm told. The music has a
heavy beat and I feel even more of a square for not knowing
what it is. Is it house? Garage? Grime? I haven't the faintest
idea. I need another drink if I'm going to get through this.
I dance my way into the kitchen, followed by Hazel, who
bumps into the door frame and giggles.

She pours generous measures of rum into two glasses,
opens the fridge and takes out a can of cola, tugs the ring
pull and shares its contents between us.

'Cheers!' she says.

'Happy birthday.' The cold and the sugar hit are welcome,
the alcohol assault less so. It makes me reel. My brain-to-
mouth connection is loosening. I try very hard to focus.

'You are enjoying yourself, aren't you?' Hazel says.

'Great party. Your friends.' I waggle my hands to help
me express what I think she wants to hear. 'Lovely.' I laugh
out loud.

'I know, but you're my best friend.'

I nervously slurp back my drink, and cough as the fizz hits my throat.

'Am I *your* best friend?' Hazel asks.

'Oh. You're certainly one of them.'

'Are you all right?'

'Course.'

She puts an arm around my waist. 'Sometimes, at work, you withdraw. It's been happening a lot recently. I've wanted to check in on you, but you do this cold-front thing. It's like, *don't come near me.*'

Tears sting the back of my eyes. It must show, because Hazel hugs me, and I try to laugh it off but I start to cry.

'Is it Anthony?'

'Can't do anything right. Don't know what I'm still doing there.'

'He's making himself feel better at your expense, Rachel. Believe me. It's nothing to do with you. You haven't done anything wrong.'

'I'm not perfect,' I say, wiping my eyes on a napkin. 'I've done things I'm not proud of.'

Hazel shrugs. 'Haven't we all? Life would be very boring if we all behaved ourselves. Come on, I'm making you a strong coffee.'

The coffee helps, but I desperately want the night to end. It isn't even nine o'clock. There's a limo picking us up at half past nine to take us to a karaoke bar in Epsom. I used to love karaoke. Maybe I could learn to love it again. All I've eaten is crisps, cherry tomatoes stuffed with mozzarella, and a couple of thin slices of pitta bread with hummus. I need food desperately, and not just because I'm an emotional wreck.

I follow Hazel back into the living room, willing myself to zone out. I am drunker than I've been in a long time, worried I'm going to throw up, thinking maybe I ought to, having maudlin thoughts about you and Anthony: the unsuitable stranger I want with every fibre of my being and the husband I promised to love and to honour till death do us part. The husband who hit me. But then you've also been violent, haven't you? Perhaps if we'd stayed together you would've eventually hit me too. Perhaps I'm just that kind of woman.

Oh God, I'm so pissed. I hold on to the mantelpiece. Lauren and Cynthia are dancing, their movements perfectly synchronised, as if they've done this a million times before. Hazel is being subjected to some kind of pep talk by Zandra. Nasty woman. I catch Hazel's eye and she looks away. Now what have I done wrong? I'm being good, dancing and drinking and generally not being myself, when my heart is breaking, when all I want is to sneak upstairs and hide in the bedroom until it's over.

'Someone's phone's ringing,' Lauren shouts. 'Whose bag is that under the table?'

Chapter 59

ANTHONY

'Which pub?' Anthony repeats.

Sean doesn't respond for a moment. He drinks some of the whisky, then sets his glass down and folds his arms across his chest. It's clear he's registered his host's distrust. 'Like I said, I don't remember.' He drums his fingers lightly on the table. 'Your wife is a beautiful woman.'

'I think perhaps it's time you left.' Anthony stands up.

'You've had a rough year, I understand, what with the heart attack and your directors losing faith in you. And the cryptocurrency crash. That was a bad call.'

Rachel has been busy. Anthony's shocked. She's the last person he'd expect to talk out of turn. 'You'll understand, as you get older, that life is a series of ups and downs, successes and failures. You learn to weather that in business, and to develop a thick skin. Success is a pat on the back, but failure is valuable learning. I have no regrets.'

'Don't you? Rachel's young. She still has so much to do, to experience. You're holding her back.' Sean tilts his head, scrutinising Anthony. 'You don't look well. Perhaps you should sit down.'

'I'm fine.' He sits down anyway. He feels grey with

exhaustion. Is this the man Caroline saw Rachel with? He seems so crass and obvious. 'What is it you're after? Because it's certainly not a job.'

'You're right. It isn't a job. Rachel and I are together. I met her on my commute to work. I'm surprised you didn't feel the change in her. Though I suppose sex has been the last thing on your mind lately, what with your dicky heart.'

Anthony stands up again so abruptly his head swims. 'Get out.'

'She's betrayed you, Anthony. You owe her nothing.'

'And she'll get nothing. And neither will you. If you're in this for the money, I'm afraid you're going to be disappointed. There's a prenup.'

To his surprise, Sean laughs. It's the final straw. Anthony's phone is on the table. He lunges for it, stabs at his contacts, his recent calls. His vision mists. He should get rid of this man and cool off, but he is beside himself. Rachel's phone rings out, then goes to voicemail. He listens to the recorded message, then hisses, 'What have you done?' He slams the phone down and turns on Sean. 'And as for you . . .'

'What're you going to do, Anthony? Punch me? It's hardly my fault your wife doesn't want you any more.'

Anthony lunges at the man, so full of hate he can't stop himself. Sean avoids his fist easily and drives him backwards, his hands tight around his neck, before he lets him go with a shove. Dizzy and sluggish, his body is no longer his to control, his arms and legs dancing, his torso beyond heavy, and he's on a downward trajectory, unstoppable.

Chapter 60

RACHEL

'Mine,' I say. I tucked my bag under the table when things started getting rowdy. Didn't want any teetering heels getting caught in the strap.

The ringing has stopped. I weave across the room and crouch down, reach for the bag and fish out my phone. There's a ping as a voicemail message comes in. I open it, pinching my lips together, bracing myself because it's bound to be Anthony calling about you. There's noise in the background, a muffled expletive, then Anthony's voice, urgent and angry.

'What have you done?' Then nothing. As if someone wrenched the phone out of his hand and switched it off.

I get to my feet, clutching the sofa arm for support, my head spinning. The four friends are dancing, giggling and waggling their arms in the air, their bright, shiny dresses a kaleidoscope of colour as they writhe and shimmy to the beat. I can't stay here. I have to get home. I need to know what's gone wrong. Please God let Anthony be all right.

I flounder out of the room and shut myself in the downstairs loo, where I grip the basin and stare at my reflection in the mirror above it. I'm okay, or I will be if I can force some of the alcohol out of me. I crouch over the loo, shoving my fingers into the back of my mouth. My body heaves as I retch and vomit up the contents of my stomach. It's nothing I haven't done before. Someone knocks.

'Rachel? It's just me. Are you all right?'

'Fine.'

I pull myself up and rinse out my mouth, dry my face on the hand towel and open the door. Hazel backs away and Lauren wanders out of the sitting room, her eyes widening. I must look as awful as I feel. I ignore them and fetch my bag and phone.

'What are you doing?' Hazel says as I shove past her to get to the door. 'You can't leave.'

'I'm sorry. I've got to go.'

Lauren flattens her palm against the door. 'Don't be ridiculous. You can't drive in that state. Whatever it is can wait.'

I can barely speak. I shake my head and pull her out of the way, and we get into an unseemly struggle that somehow leaves Lauren spread-eagled on the floor.

'For Christ's sake, Rachel,' Hazel says. 'This is ridiculous. Come back in.'

I totter down the path, splashing through the puddles. My feet are soaked by the time I get to the car. Hazel and Lauren follow me outside. They pound on the window, make rotating signals with their hands to get me to open it, but I switch the power on and move off. For a few seconds they stay with me, still banging, water coursing through their hair, faces desperate. It's like a scene from a zombie movie, and I almost laugh as I drive away. Then I suffer the ignominy of having to circle the cul-de-sac at the end before passing the house again. Lauren and Hazel are still there, arms by their sides, appalled expressions on their faces. Zandra and Cynthia are standing in the doorway, keeping dry. I drive past them and out onto the open road.

'Rachel?'

I open my eyes to a light that blinds me. Where am I?

Chapter 61

CAROLINE

Caroline is grinning when her phone vibrates, relaxed and a little pissed. The seven other people around the table haven't even noticed. They're howling with laughter at an anecdote their host has told. She mutters, 'Just popping to the toilet,' and slips away, only answering once the door has closed behind her.

'There's a problem.'

'Tell me?'

'Your dad's dead. He went batshit crazy and attacked me. I pushed him too hard.'

She leans against the wall. Speechless.

'I'm sorry.'

'You're sorry!' she explodes. 'No one was meant to get hurt. My father—'

'He tried to punch me, I lashed out. I was trying to get him off me, not kill him.'

'Oh, he was so much bigger than you. Christ.'

'Don't, Caroline. This has destroyed me.' His voice cracks.

'Stop it!' He cannot break down and neither can she. She needs to deal with the situation one step at a time. 'Where are you now?'

'Still at the house.'

'What have you touched?'

'My glass, the chair, the table. The doorbell.'

'You didn't use the toilet?'

'No.'

'Wash up the glass and put it away. Smudge the doorbell, don't clean it. I'll use it in the morning. Wait a couple of hours and leave through the back gate. I'll bolt it when I come in. No one will notice you on the river path. Kew's practically a graveyard after eleven.'

She cuts him off and deletes the call record. In the silence that follows, a sense of shock descends on her. She stares into the mirror at her own face, trying to see her father. How can he be gone? It's not her fault. She was clear what she wanted. He was not meant to die. He was meant to be convinced beyond a doubt that Rachel had betrayed him. She had set it up so perfectly, going to him with a story about seeing Rachel on the train with a man, struggling a little to prove she wasn't doing it out of spite but out of concern for him. She couldn't show him the photograph, but it didn't matter. Her father took her word for it. She saw the devastation in his eyes; and worse, an acceptance. As though he believed he deserved it. A tear wells, and she rips off a few sheets of loo roll and presses them against her eyes. Not now. Later she'll cry. When she's alone in her bedroom. She'll cram a pillow against her mouth and cry until her throat hurts.

Right now, she's stuck in the depths of the country, with people she doesn't much like, whose dinner party she only agreed to attend because she needed to be as far from Kew as possible. And now she's going to have to go back in there and pretend nothing's wrong. She dabs her eyes again, straightens her shoulders and takes a deep breath, then unbolts the door and returns to the dining room.

Her hostess glances up as she sits down. 'Everything okay?'

She realises she's been away from the table long enough to raise eyebrows. 'Yes. Everything's fine. Just needed some time out.' She offers up a rueful smile. 'I'm an introvert really.'

'Oh gosh, I know exactly what you mean.'

She parks what's happened and throws herself into the conversation. They're not all actors here, but some of them are, and up until the moment she got that call, she had been in her element. Now all she wants is to go home, but she can't, because everything has to be normal. She needs to cover herself, and that means not telling anyone what she told her father last night. The photograph might prove useful at some point, but the rest? No. She'll only use that if she absolutely has to. There mustn't be any suggestion that she manipulated events. She must remember all these things. She cannot afford to slip up.

Later, crawling with relief into bed at one in the morning, almost catatonic with the effort to appear bright and beautiful and amusing, she cannot go to sleep. She lies on her back, listening to the silence, missing the sound of traffic trundling to and from Kew Bridge. An owl hoots, which is lovely, but the sound soon begins to grate and she pulls her pillow over her head. What is she going to do? There will be money, but she doesn't want to think about that. Money is not what this is about. Freeing her father from that bitch Rachel was the aim, then making sure no one else

315

got their claws into him. He was a fool, but many intelligent men are when it comes to women. And now he's dead.

The rain has stopped when the alarm on her phone wakes her at seven. She gets up and opens the curtains onto a beautiful morning, the grass gleaming with moisture, the sun shining over distant fields. She feels dreadful: hung-over and shattered and with barely enough energy to pull on her clothes. Her hostess's children are squabbling downstairs. She goes down to join them, ignores the brats and helps herself to coffee, then makes desultory conversation for ten minutes before making her excuses and departing.

Once she's driven away, she opens her mouth and lets out a long howl of fury and despair. Then she takes four deep, calming breathes and sets her sat nav for home.

The house is eerily silent. Even if she hadn't known her father was dead, she would have picked up on the absence of life. She places her bag at her feet, then braces herself and walks into the kitchen. She crouches beside his body and lays her hand on his shoulder. He is like stone. She starts to cry as she leans over and presses her lips against his forehead. It's an unpleasant sensation, but she strokes his hair and kisses him again.

'I'm sorry, Daddy.'

The police arrive within three minutes of her call, which surprises her. She was expecting an ambulance. She moves aside to let them in, but it's only when the two officers don't immediately step forward and take charge that she senses something else is going on.

'Is Mr Gordon at home?' one of them asks.

She doesn't know how to respond, so she simply stares at them. They stare back at her, equally confused, because she's still crying.

'What's your name, madam?'

She wipes her tears on her sleeve and sniffs. 'Sorry, I'm Caroline Gordon. Anthony Gordon's daughter. I live here. I'm the one who called the emergency services about my father.'

They glance at each other. 'May we come in?'

'Of course. Look, I'm sorry. I don't know what's going on, but my father is dead. I've been away for the night. I've only just come in and found him. I thought that was why you were here.'

'We're here because your mother's been involved in an accident.'

Caroline's heart almost stops beating. 'What?'

'The hospital tried to get hold of Mr Gordon on the phone, but he didn't pick up.' The officer looks pained. 'Obviously now we know why.'

'Is Mum okay? Did you try getting in touch with Dave?'

'She's alive, but she's critical. She's in Kingston Hospital, in ICU.'

Caroline's brain scrambles to make sense of this. 'But ... but what's she doing there? She lives in Shropshire.' She closes her eyes for a second as it hits her. 'Ah. You don't mean my mum. You mean Rachel. My stepmother.'

'Rachel Gordon. Yes.' The officer seems relieved to have cleared that up. 'Would you like to take me to your father?'

'Um. Yes. Of course.'

She leads them into the kitchen and hovers near the table, practically clinging to the back of a chair while they check for vital signs, even though it's obvious life has been extinguished. The officer who's been doing the talking radios it in, establishes that an ambulance crew is already on its way, then suggests they wait in another room. Caroline shows them into the sitting room, where they decline her offer of a hot drink.

'I'm sorry,' she says. 'I can't seem to take it in.'

'Please don't worry. We understand.'

'What happened to Rachel?'

The officer hesitates. 'A road traffic accident.'

'Was anyone else hurt?'

'No one else was involved. We believe Mrs Gordon may have swerved to avoid an animal. The force of the impact and the way the car ended up on its side indicates she was travelling at speed, but we'll need to wait for the crash-scene investigators before we can confirm that.'

Caroline steeples her fingers against her face and breathes into her hands. What a complete clusterfuck. 'Will she live?' She hopes she doesn't.

'You'll have to speak to the medical staff about that.'

It's only when they've gone, and the ambulance has taken her father away, that Caroline remembers to bolt the back gate.

Chapter 62

It's afternoon by the time Caroline gets to the hospital. She needn't have gone – everyone would have understood – but she's twitching with energy and has to do something. She tells the nurse on duty she's there for Rachel Gordon and takes a seat.

'Miss Gordon?'

She looks up. A man in scrubs is standing a couple of feet from her.

'Yes.'

'I'm Mr Wilson. I've just come from operating on your mother.'

'Stepmother. How is she?'

'Mrs Gordon has been put in an induced coma. We've incised her skull to release the pressure from a swelling on her brain. All we can do now is wait.'

'Is she going to live?'

'I can't give you any guarantees, but we're hopeful.'

'Will the injuries affect her brain?'

'Again, we can only wait and see.'

Caroline finds her way to the canteen and sits down with a coffee and a chicken and avocado wrap, which she manages to munch her way through half of despite her mental anguish. It simply doesn't feel possible that her world has changed so profoundly. It should be Rachel in the mortuary, not her father.

Her phone rings. She doesn't recognise the number and only takes the call because it might be the police.

'Caroline. Where are you?' His voice is reedy. Stress and shock, she assumes.

'At the hospital, with Rachel.'

'Oh, okay. Are you identifying the body with her?'

She is so tired. 'No. Sorry. Rachel was involved in a car crash. She's in a coma.' She explains briefly.

'Shit.'

'Whose phone are you using?'

'No one's. I bought it just now. What are you doing there? Playing the devoted stepdaughter?'

'I have to at least pretend to care.'

She gets up and heads back to ICU carrying her coffee.

She pushes against the door to the ward with her elbow. 'We can't see each other for a while. We can meet when everything settles down.'

A man is standing beside Rachel's bed. Caroline steps back quickly and lets the door close again.

'For fuck's sake.'

'What is it?'

'I have to go.'

July 2024

Chapter 63

RACHEL

Two days later, the article about my plans for the shares is in the papers and online, alongside a photograph of me and Anthony that I like. It was taken at a garden party, on a summer's day, outside a house in a picturesque village. There are pale pink roses, matching my pale pink jacket, rambling against an old sandstone wall. It was taken a couple of years before his heart attack. We are both smiling, healthy and happy, Anthony lean and tanned in an open-necked white shirt and chinos. Predictably, there are plenty of negative comments online. Some say that I'm giving the money away in a cynical bid to change public perception, others are downright nasty and obscene. I've been expecting the backlash, and I don't give a shit what the trolls think. Giving that money away is a step in the right direction, an admission that I've made mistakes. And yes, I can't deny it, a salve to my conscience.

The doorbell rings. I open the door to find DS Jones standing there. I thought she was done with me.

'This is Constable Sterne,' she says indicating the uniformed police officer standing beside her.

I nod a greeting as I show them in. Sterne is tall and

bulky, with a broad forehead, thin lips and wide-spaced eyes that don't warm as they meet mine.

Jones puts a brown envelope on the kitchen table and slides out some photographs printed on sheets of A4 paper. She passes one to me. It shows a woman standing beside a bronze statue. She has her hands on her hips and is grinning. She has red hair and is wearing cut-off jeans and a white T-shirt. Jones passes me another picture. It's of the same woman, but this time she's with a man, again in front of the statue. I guess he's her boyfriend, from the way his arm is around her.

'Who are they?' I ask.

'Just a couple of tourists. They were on their honeymoon; the photographs were taken outside St Paul's Cathedral on their last day in London.'

'Are they supposed to mean something to me?'

'Look at the background.'

I scan the first photograph again, this time narrowing my eyes and focusing on the occupants of the semicircle of benches behind the statue.

Then one particular bench and the couple sitting on it.

Light fingers dance up my spine. The woman is me and I'm wearing the same jacket I was wearing in the photograph I gave the journalist. The man is undoubtedly Sean. I glance up at DS Jones.

'And?' she says, eyebrows raised.

I point to each in turn. 'That's me. That's Sean.'

'Now we're getting somewhere. Can you spot the difference between the two photographs?'

I check one and then the other. 'I'm not on the bench in this one.'

'Could that be because you took it?'

I hand them back to her. 'It's possible. If they asked me to, I would have done.' Of all the accumulating memories that have been coming back, this isn't one of them. It isn't so surprising, given I was wrapped up in Sean. I expect I was on autopilot and didn't give the couple another thought.

'The couple, Ellie and Gabe, got in touch when they saw your interview online yesterday. They recognised you – your jacket is quite distinctive – and Caroline Gordon has identified your friend as the man she saw with you on the Tube. I have no doubt that if I show this to the staff at Stir, they'll identify him as Alexander Stratton, whose whereabouts are still unknown.'

I nod. This ties in with my memories.

'I presume you met him at the charity event for the Begin Again programme?'

'No, I didn't meet him there. He told me later that he'd been working that night, that he'd seen me. All I remember is that I met him on my commute into work. I had no idea he worked for the charity. He didn't tell me who he was. We didn't exchange those kinds of details.'

'Convenient.'

I rub my forehead. 'He knew I was married and I made it clear I didn't want an affair, so we agreed to just meet on the train and talk. We enjoyed each other's company.' Just for a second, I feel Sean beside me, his shoulder against mine and the ridges of the train floor under my bottom. He said something about catching me when I fell. *I wanted to be your prince.* My eyes well. Somehow I know I'll never see him again.

'But you're above ground here.' She fans the photographs out.

I blink. 'We were saying goodbye.'

'Is that all, Rachel? We know that you made a phone call to Anthony just before the couple approached you. What was that about?'

'I wanted to help Sean get his job back. He hadn't stolen anything. He was protecting someone. A friend.'

'What friend?'

I hesitate. If what I've recalled is accurate, Sean told me he protected Kam and his siblings, and after he lost his job, their roles were switched and Kam protected him. In spite of everything, in the end they were the closest thing to a family he had. I know what will happen. Kam will be arrested and the kids taken into care. Sean was genuinely scared of that happening. He felt strongly enough to put himself at risk. If I can do nothing else for him, I can at least do this.

'I don't remember his name.'

She rolls her eyes. 'Let's hope it comes back to you. What was your husband's response?'

This is going to sound bad, but there's no help for it. I have to tell the truth. 'I wanted to get Sean in front of him, so I lied. I told him I had a colleague who wanted to move into recruitment and needed advice. Anthony agreed to see him.'

She smiles. I've just confirmed what my mother said about me. Liar. She won't believe anything I say now.

'Where is Sean?'

'I don't know. The last I saw of him, he was running away from me at the hospital.'

326

'There is a locate and trace out on Mr Stratton. He is currently a wanted individual. What I can tell you is that he hasn't left the country, unless he did so under an assumed name. He hasn't used his email or his mobile phone. He hasn't spent money on a card or withdrawn cash. Either he has other means of support or he's dead. What did the two of you plan that evening, Rachel? Because I don't believe your sob story. Sending a man round to your house while you were out to ask for his job back? It doesn't ring true.'

'It *is* true.'

'Did you see him again? Maybe to finalise your plans?'

I hesitate for long enough for Jones to raise her eyebrows in query. 'If you need your memory jogged...' she says drily. 'My colleague here had the bright idea of showing the photograph round some of the pubs local to you. Stratton was seen in the Cricketers on the night Anthony died. A hundred yards from your door.' She pauses, watching my face. To me it feels as though it's turned to stone, muscles and skin calcifying. 'He was with a woman matching your description.'

I draw a deep breath. 'Yes.'

'Yes what?'

'That was me.'

'I'll ask you one more time. What were you planning?'

June 2023

Chapter 64

'Take your raincoat,' Anthony says. 'It's starting to rain.'

I jump in my car and turn on the engine. Anthony closes the front door, and I slump, resting my head against my crossed forearms. This is the end. Hitting me the first time was bad enough, but to do it again, and this time with more deliberation, was unforgivable. I as good as told him I wished he was dead; telling him it's over won't be as bad as that. He knows it's coming; I saw it in his eyes. Perhaps subconsciously it's what he wants. I let out a small sob and choke it back. I don't want to arrive at Hazel's with mascara running down my face.

I glance at the clock on the dashboard. You'll be here in half an hour. Maybe I could park on the other side of the green, where Anthony won't see the car, and hang around till you arrive. I imagine surprising you, being swung into your arms, before driving off into the sunset, or in this case, the gathering storm. But that's stupid, because I don't know you very well, or you me. We've ended it and it was the right thing to do. I'll be okay. Desire fades. I look back at the house. So does love, apparently.

I move my foot to the accelerator and only then realise that in the emotional fallout I forgot I was going to wear flats and change into heels when I got there. I look out at the weather and decide it's not worth the risk. I'll go back into the house and pick up my trainers. No need for a conversation, the shoes are near the door. I can be in and out without him even knowing.

My timing is unfortunate. Anthony appears in the hall just as I open the door. He's shocked to see me, hopeful even, but I'm too angry to speak. I slip off my heels and put the trainers on under his gaze, then leave, holding the raincoat over my head to protect my blow-dried hair. That's when I see your familiar figure striding towards the Cricketers, and my heart almost explodes with joy. You catch sight of me and miss your step, but you keep moving. I glance at the car waiting for me at the kerb. I really ought to go.

I don't blame you for wanting some Dutch courage before you meet Anthony, but I hope you don't overdo it. He won't be impressed if he smells alcohol on you. I should speak to you. I can warn you that Anthony is in a funny mood. Five minutes won't make any difference to Hazel, but it might to you. I throw my gold party shoes into the car and run down the street, pushing my way through the doors into the fug of the pub. You turn from the bar as if you knew I'd follow you.

'What are you doing?' you ask, looking round nervously.

I'm breathless and overwrought. 'I just wanted . . . Anthony . . . I'm sorry. I can't . . .' I lose the power of speech. I didn't mean to do this. My cheek still stings. I move over to an empty table and drop down into a chair. You take the glass the barman hands you and come over.

'What's happened?'

I shake my head mutely. I should have done my crying at home, not bottled it up and screwed on the lid to spare my make-up. A stupid lack of foresight. But then I didn't expect to see you, didn't expect to be undone by the sympathy and outrage in your eyes.

Your expression darkens as you frown. 'Did he hurt you?'

I can't even look at you. I look down at the tabletop instead, at a tear as it drops onto the varnished surface and spreads.

'Shit,' you say.

'I don't think you should see him. He's suspicious.'

'I'll fucking kill him.'

'No.'

'Rachel, you can't expect me to just leave it. He needs to be told.'

'I agree, but not by you. I'll deal with him myself after tonight.' I sniff. 'I'm sorry I let you down.'

You sit back, and I read relief on your face. You didn't really want to do this, did you? You just wanted to please me.

'It probably wouldn't have done any good anyway,' you say.

'I should go.' I stand up reluctantly.

'I'm just going to drink this and wind down a bit.'

'Will I see you again?'

You jump up and hug me hard, then you kiss me for a long time.

'I don't think so. Wrong place, wrong time.'

July 2024

Chapter 65

Jones listens without interrupting. Sterne looks rapt. The flashbacks, the recent flood of memory; none of it is complete, but the jigsaw is at that stage where there are only a few pieces left, and my mind is rapidly slotting them into place. It all points to one thing. This is my fault. What I said to the surgeon after I woke from my coma must be true. I killed Anthony. Not directly. It wasn't me who pressed my fingers into his neck, but I as good as did it by allowing Sean to see that Anthony had hit me, even if I didn't say it in words, effectively lighting the touch-paper.

And then Jones tells me she'd like me to come down to the police station for a formal interview.

I call Tim and tell him what's happened. He says he'll meet me within the hour and makes me promise not to say another word in the meantime. I wait, contemplating the freight train my confession has put in motion. My mother will bemoan my fate to her friends, but secretly she will feel vindicated. After all these years, she has finally won. The daughter she was so jealous of is going to wither away in prison.

Tim arrives looking flustered and hot, sweat beading on his forehead against an unhealthy pallor. I want to tell him he should take better care of himself, but it isn't the right time and I'm not the right woman. We are given five minutes to confer in a corner of the foyer.

'What do I do?' I whisper.

He rubs his fingers up and down the vertical lines between his brows. 'Try not to incriminate yourself further. Answer "no comment" to leading questions. There might be mitigation. No one knows what was said between you and Stratton at the pub; it's all speculation.'

'I don't want to play games. If I encouraged him to assault Anthony, I'd rather plead guilty and get it over with.'

'What exactly do you think you're confessing to, Rachel?'

'Not to murder: to being part of the chain of events that led to Anthony's death.' I outline briefly what I've admitted to DS Jones, explaining, with some qualms, the part Anthony played.

His silence speaks volumes. He doesn't know where to look. He doesn't know if it's a lie, but he has to take my word for it.

'It was the second time,' I blurt out. 'I'm sorry, Tim. I know how fond you were of him.'

He glances past me. 'We can talk about this later.'

DS Jones is back. We follow her into an interview room. Tim takes off his jacket and hangs it over the back of his chair. The chairs are narrow and hard, and I feel sorry for him having to perch his bulk on one. Constable Sterne brings plastic beakers of water and places them in front of us. DS Jones switches on the recorder and lists those present.

'Did you arrange for Alexander Stratton to kill your husband?' she asks. She adds, glancing at Tim, 'The man you knew as Sean.'

'I didn't.'

'But you let him know Anthony had assaulted you. You got him worked up. Was it even true? From what I've learned about your husband, he wasn't the type.'

'They often aren't, though, are they?'

She acknowledges this truth with a tightened mouth. 'Do you have anyone to corroborate your story?'

'No.'

'You knew, because Stratton told you, that he had a criminal record for GBH. You saw an opportunity.'

'No. I was upset and shaken by what had happened, but I did not ask Sean to hurt Anthony.'

'I'm not saying you did, directly. But you've shown yourself to be manipulative, haven't you?'

'Detective Jones,' Tim interrupts. 'This is not appropriate.'

'I'm sorry you don't think so, Mr Vaughan, but a beautiful young woman leaning over the desk of an extremely wealthy man and telling him she fancies him seems to me to prove the opposite. Rachel knows how to play men.'

'It didn't feel that way at the time. It just happened.'

'Did it really? Bottom line, twelve years after you married your wealthy lover, you persuaded him to cut his daughter out of his will. Shortly after that, he was brutally killed by a man we now know you were on familiar terms with, while you were conveniently at the house of a friend.'

'You're twisting things.'

'My client is right, Detective,' Tim says. 'This is all speculation. You can't prove anything without interviewing Alexander Stratton himself.'

'Of course, and we're doing our best to locate him, but chances are he's been silenced.'

'Not by me,' I say.

Tim grunts irritably. 'If you don't have any actual evidence against my client, you have no right to keep her here.'

'Mrs Gordon was seen talking to the suspect in the hours before her husband died. She has admitted having a relationship with him. She has admitted arranging for Alexander Stratton, a man who did time for a violent attack, to visit her husband when he was alone at home. She has admitted hinting to him that her husband had struck her. Perhaps she didn't get her hands dirty, but at the very least she has given misleading and false information to the police. Rachel Gordon,' she says, turning to me, 'I am charging you with perverting the course of justice in a murder investigation.'

'No! That's not right.'

'Rachel.' Tim's tone is grim. 'You mustn't interrupt.'

'Thank you, Mr Vaughan,' DS Jones says, and recites the remainder of the caution.

Chapter 66

I go through the motions: identification, fingerprints, hand-over of my bag and its contents – my phone, my keys, my Kindle, the leather holder I keep my cards in. The officer indicates that I should pull them out so that he can list them in my presence. My hands are shaking, my palms sweaty.

To my relief, and DS Jones's obvious irritation, Tim manages to persuade the custody sergeant that I'm harm-less and fragile and don't pose any sort of danger. With bail set at one hundred thousand pounds, I'm allowed to leave the police station with him.

'I don't understand,' I say. 'Why haven't I been charged with arranging a hit on Anthony? Why perverting the course of justice?'

'It's a holding charge. They still don't have enough evi-dence to charge you with the greater crime, so this gives them the opportunity to continue investigating. I imagine DS Jones wanted you in custody because it doesn't suit her to have you poking around.'

'So what happens next?'

'The date for a trial will be set in five weeks' time. The average wait is longer since the pandemic, so I can't see it coming to trial before this time next year. Unfortunately that's in DS Jones's favour, because it gives her time to dig up more leads to pursue.' He glances at me as we leave the building and, with a deep sigh, taps my arm. The gesture is avuncular, but somehow final. 'On the practical side, I'm afraid probate will be delayed until the end of the trial. If in the meantime DS Jones uncovers the evidence the CPS requires and you're found guilty of arranging Anthony's murder, you won't inherit and the estate will go to Caroline.'

I look him in the eye. 'I'm innocent.'

He nods, and I wait a beat before I go on.

'So I could be left with nothing to pay my legal fees?'

'Do you have anything of your own?'

'I suppose my pension and ISAs will still belong to me?' The idea of being stripped of everything hasn't occurred to me up until now. It's terrifying.

'I'll talk to Peter Marlow; get him to make sure your independent assets are ring-fenced. In the meantime, I'm going to pass your case on to a friend of mine, Hamish Cathcart. He's an excellent solicitor. I don't think—'

'Wait. Hang on. Pass my case to someone else? I don't understand.'

I've never seen him look so uncomfortable.

'I'm sorry, my dear. My involvement ends here. Hamish is very good at what he does. You can't do better. If you're innocent, he will prove it.'

I ignore the *if*. 'You promised Anthony you'd look after me. Are you telling me you lied to him?'

'No. I meant it at the time, because we were talking about the prospect of his death from natural causes.'

'I thought you were a man of principle.'

'It's *because* I'm a man of principle that I can't help you.'

'So you have doubts about my innocence?'

He hesitates. 'Let's just say I'm not one hundred per cent convinced that you're telling the whole truth.'

That takes a moment to sink in. I shouldn't have backed him into a corner. He's feeling betrayed and angry and probably sick to his stomach. 'Can you give me any advice?'

He thinks for a moment. 'Find out what's happened to Alexander Stratton. He holds all the answers.'

I mumble a goodbye, walk down towards to the Thames and head along the river path. The heat dries the tears on my skin.

It's stupid that this is what has made me cry. Tim was always Anthony's friend, not a close friend of mine. So why does it mean so much that's he's withdrawing support? I walk until I get to Richmond Bridge, then cross over and go down to the terraces. It's busy with tourists, and there are a lot of children. One runs towards me now, a ribbon attached to a Spider-Man birthday balloon grasped in his hand. The balloon bobs along behind him. He's not looking where he's going, and I have to sidestep him. A young man yells at him to look where he's going, and just for a second we lock eyes. There is no recognition on his part, but I take a sharp breath. Fine features, black curls tied back. Cheekbones to die for.

The badge on his waiter's uniform read *Kam*. I see Sean's face, his lips moving. *I saw the situation Kam was in.*

I spin round and run after them just as they turn up the cobbled path towards George Street. 'Kam! Wait!'

Chapter 67

Kam turns, still holding his brother's hand. He looks bemused, which is hardly surprising, because the only other time he's seen me, I was in evening dress, my hair up, sparkling diamonds around my neck, on my fingers and dangling from my ear lobes. A girl loiters close by. She's about fourteen years old and dressed in skinny jeans with frayed rips in the knees, ridiculously stacked trainers and a cropped tee.

'I'm a friend of Alexander Stratton's,' I pant. 'Xan. My name's Rachel Gordon.' The little boy stares up at me, his hand still in his brother's. The girl gives me a cursory glance before her eyes shift to the screen of her phone. 'Could I talk to you?'

'What about?'

'About Xan.'

He hesitates, then turns to the girl. 'Can you take Blake into Smith's? Buy him a comic. It's his birthday,' he explains to me.

'I can see that. Happy birthday, Blake.'

There's a long pause, mostly while I try to fathom what there is to interest six-year-olds round here, then Kam says, looking embarrassed. 'He wanted to see where Ted Lasso lives.'

I laugh, and Kam breaks into a grin, easing the tension.

He gives the boy a shove towards his sister. She rolls her eyes, then grabs her brother's hand and clomps up to the street with him skipping along beside her.

Kam yells after them, 'And don't let him out of your sight.'

She turns and flicks him the finger, then lets go of Blake's hand, puts an arm around his narrow shoulders and pulls him against her. Even with her surliness, it makes me wish I had a sibling.

Kam shoves his hands in his pockets and leans against the wall beside the cinema, smile gone. 'What about Xan?'

'Have you seen him lately?'

'I haven't seen him in over a year.'

'He was staying with you, wasn't he?'

'How do you know that?'

'Because he told me. Did he tell you he was going away?'

'How do I know you're his friend, not just some woman he's pissed off?'

'You don't. All I can say is that I cared about him and he cared about me. I'm worried.'

'Took you long enough.'

I grimace. 'I lost my memory.'

Kam glances up the lane, in the direction his siblings took. 'He needed to stay under the radar for a while. Then he didn't come back one evening. I don't know why. His stuff's still in the flat.'

'What? Everything?'

'Not his wallet, phone and that. Just his duffel bag.'

'When was this?'

He puffs out a breath. 'I've gotta think. I'd been on a job. Hang on.' He palms his phone and starts scrolling, his brow furrowed. 'June the twenty-sixth. It was a Monday.'

345

I try to remember what I was doing then. I don't do anything as sensible as keeping my diary on my phone, but I can check my emails. I search for the date while Kam shifts impatiently, and discover a message from Trainline. I bought a ticket to York that morning. I was at my mother's house.

'You didn't wonder where he was? If he was all right?'

'I don't know nothing about it. I thought he'd done a runner. I don't ask questions. None of us do.'

By us, I assume he means former prisoners. 'Is there anything else you can tell me?'

'I don't know you, lady.'

Fair enough. 'I was married to the CEO of the Begin Again programme. Anthony Gordon. You're involved with them. You must know that my husband died.'

'Oh yeah. I read something about that.'

Of course he knows. He's being disingenuous. Not only was it covered in the press, the charity's clients and staff will have been written to. 'Then you'll also know he was deliberately killed.'

Kam nods but doesn't make any sympathetic noises.

'The police think I arranged it, or at the very least lied to protect Xan. They think he was my husband's killer.'

'Xan's done nothing wrong.'

'I don't believe it either. I think something bad's happened to him.'

Kam rubs the back of his neck. I sense him weakening. I don't say a word for fear of alienating him further.

'He got a call once, while he was staying with me. From a woman.'

'Who was it?'

346

He hesitates, then shrugs. 'Your husband's daughter. She wanted Xan to meet her.'

'When was this?'

'Dunno. He'd been staying here a few weeks . . . a month maybe.'

Around the time of the crash. I might have sent him to see Anthony, but this could imply that Caroline was pulling the strings. Did she pay Sean to kill Anthony and then disappear? I can't believe it. For all her faults, she genuinely adored her father.

It's not looking good. If Sean is guilty, then nothing changes. I'll still go to trial.

I thank Kam, and he says, 'Whatever,' pushes himself away from the wall and strides off. Then he stops, seems to think, and comes back. He cups a hand around the back of his neck and stands awkwardly. 'He was cool, yeah. A good bloke. He saved me and the kids, and if something's happened to him, I want to see whoever done it go to prison.'

'I understand,' I say, with a lump in my throat. 'I'll do my best.'

'Give me your contact details.'

I do as he asks, and take his.

'I don't want to go to court again,' he says. 'But I'll testify against that bitch if it's her. No other reason. Call me if you need me.'

347

Chapter 68

The more I think about it, the bigger this revelation is. It frames Caroline strongly as a liar and manipulator. It doesn't make me look innocent, unfortunately, just stupid, but at the very least it undermines her testimony. If it can be shown that what happened was all part of a plan, then Detective Jones will see I'm as much Caroline's victim as Anthony was. It proves that her seeing me with Sean on the train wasn't a coincidence. She was keeping an eye on her investment. She and Sean knew each other. She and Dominic knew each other. And I have been a gullible fool.

The question now is, who do I tell? I can't tell Tim, because he's washed his hands of me. I have Hamish Cathcart's business card, but when I call his office, I'm told he's in court all day. I could contact Jones, but I'd rather take advice first. I do not want to put a foot wrong. There's too much at stake.

I tap the table with my fingernails, then get up and wander into the garden. My eye is caught by the empty bird feeder and the leaf-clogged stone birdbath, and I feel a pang of guilt. I haven't refilled the feeder since Anthony's death. It was always his thing. I go to the larder and find the bag of seed, the top clamped shut with a yellow plastic clip.

I refill the feeder at the kitchen table, then hang it again and go back for a scrubbing brush to flick the sodden leaves out of the birdbath with. The garden has worn an air of neglect since Anthony died, roses not pruned, dead stems not cut back, and for the first time in I don't know how long, I feel like doing something about it. It's adrenaline, I expect. I fetch a jug of fresh water to top up the birdbath. It's a good place to start and I resolve not to let it slide again. I'll bring birds back to the garden.

But who will feed them if I go to prison?

I mustn't let my mind go there. I pour the water in, watching it swirl around the stone base, then go back for more. It slops over the edge and trickles down the path, coming to rest in an unevenly shaped dip. I frown. A weathered stone rabbit, mottled with lichen, used to squat there, in the shadow of the dark-leafed viburnum. I stand very still, listening to the distant hum of an aeroplane building and fading. Could someone have come in here and stolen the rabbit? Garden statuary is valuable. This one is a clever reproduction, but an opportunist thief wouldn't know that.

I open the back gate and peer out into the alleyway. It's long and narrow, and mainly used to store bins by the owners of the cottages, which have access through their back gates. We sometimes use it as a quick route to the river, but it's not that pleasant and often smells foxy, so mostly we take the long way round. No one else comes down here, apart from the occasional drunk wandering off the path to relieve himself, or a curious passer-by. There's no street-light because it's private land, but security lights regularly flick on and off when cats and foxes pass through. It has its moments, though. In springtime, a decades-old wisteria arches over from one of the gardens, and from late

May until the end of summer roses tumble through ram-shackle trellising. I can smell them now.

I'm about to go back inside when my eye is caught by something lying on the ground, partially covered by grass and foliage. It's only a pencil, but it's embossed in gold, and something about it tweaks my subconscious. I pick it up and read the name. Blake Jackson. My brain takes a second to accept this extraordinary coincidence. I've seen Blake today. I've spoken to his big brother. Could they have come here, left this as some kind of message? What would be the point? To scare me? An *I know where you live* kind of thing? Unlikely. I revolve the pencil in my fingers, my eyes closed. Where have I seen this? Slowly an image forms. Another memory, as clear as day.

I'm sitting on the floor of the train, and you are beside me. You take the copy of the *Metro* I've been holding and fold it over on the crossword page, then you slip a pencil from your pocket. This is the first piece of evidence that you were here. Did you drop it as you made your escape? Did you panic? I'm not sure what this means in terms of my case, but you knew Caroline. You came to this house. Anthony died. You vanished.

Chapter 69

Somewhere in the kitchen, my mobile starts ringing. I run inside. When I see it's Hazel, I'm surprised. It's been nearly a year. I put the pencil down on the side and answer it.

'Hey. I thought you'd blocked me.'

'Sorry. I was pissed off.'

'I did apologise. Didn't you get my message?'

'Yes, but I'd begun to think you were trying to distance yourself anyway, so I made it easy for you. I'm sorry you've been having such a tough time. I haven't been much of a friend.'

'I don't blame you.' I wrinkle my nose, tearful. I've been lonely since I chucked Dominic out. 'I'm pleased you've had a change of heart.'

'Yeah, well. It's been long enough. And I wanted to see how you were. If you needed anything. Company at the weekend maybe. We could go to the cinema.'

'I'd ... um ... I'd like that.'

'What's the matter?'

'Nothing.'

'You sound odd. Have I called at a bad time?'

Why am I so wobbly that one note of sympathy and I turn into a snivelling wreck? 'It's complicated.'

'Everything about you is complicated, Rachel. Do you have anyone with you? Someone you can talk to?'

'No. I'm on my own.'

'You must miss Anthony. Grief is tough.'

'It's not that,' I say, although it partly is. 'I've been charged. There's going to be a trial.'

'Oh my God.'

'Not with murder,' I add hastily. 'Perverting the course of justice. But everyone thinks I had something to do with it.'

'I don't. Not that my opinion is worth anything.'

'Thank you.' I don't deserve it. 'It might be all right, though.' I tell her about today's discoveries. The unexpected serendipity of it. That Sean and Caroline knew each other through the Begin Again programme; that he's been here.

'And Sean is . . . ?'

'The guy on the Tube.'

'Oh, yes. I remember you telling me about that. So . . . ?'

Clamping my phone to my ear with my shoulder, I pour myself a glass of water. 'I have a witness who's agreed to testify that they were in the room when Sean took a phone call from her. Whatever's happened to me has happened because Caroline planned it. I think she was behind Anthony's death, but she wanted the evidence to point to me.'

Hazel sounds sceptical. 'Do you really think so? There would've been so many unknowables, wouldn't there? Things Caroline couldn't control. If she did put this guy in front of you, there was no guarantee you'd fall for him. And why would she get her father killed? I remember you telling me they had a loving relationship.'

'They did.'

'Would her dislike of you outweigh her love for him?'

My nose is running. I grab the nearest thing, a tea towel, and blow it. 'She's always hated me.'

Even Hazel can hear how weak and childish that sounds. She responds like she's my big sister.

'Okay, so Caroline called the ex-convict she met through work. Big deal. Caroline's young and single. If he's handsome, charming and dangerous, she might have been attracted to him. It doesn't mean there was a plot. It might just have been sex.'

'Are you sticking up for her?' I'm incredulous, and too weary to be polite.

'No, of course not. I'm just trying to be rational. It feels like you're making these things fit round a narrative that suits you. It's understandable, but it doesn't make it real.'

The tears are pressing up again. I want her off the phone because this is overwhelming, it's swallowing me whole, and if I don't walk away, I'm going to break down.

'I'm sorry, I have to be somewhere. Could we . . .' I stop and swallow back the impending flood, 'talk tomorrow?'

'I'm worried about you.'

'Sorry. Got to go.'

I hang up and slump back in the chair. Then I blow out a breath, get up, tip my water into the sink and refill the glass with red wine.

I glance at the pencil. There might be DNA on it, but if it's been out in the elements for as long as I think it has, it's probably been destroyed. There could be another reason for Kam's little brother's property having ended up in the alleyway. Kam is a thief. Maybe he stalked me after the charity dinner. That kind of thing does happen. I remember the unprovoked look of contempt he gave me; like I was

353

some shallow rich bitch. But he told me about that phone call, didn't he? He didn't have to do that. I'm not waiting for my new solicitor to get back to me to report this. This morning I was charged with perverting the course of justice. It's only a matter of time before I'm charged with arranging a murder. It's vital that DS Jones knows there was previous contact between Caroline and Sean.

Her number goes straight to voicemail. Why is no one answering their phones today?

'It's Rachel Gordon. Please give me a call back. It's urgent.'

If Caroline has any sense, she'll have deleted the record of her call, but a good technical guy should be able to get it back if he knows where to look.

Evening is drawing in when the doorbell rings. I'm listening to the news on the radio and I don't get up. I don't want to see or speak to anyone else today. A mudslide has swamped a village in China, and in the UK, the Met Office are advising people in the south not to travel unless strictly necessary because a low-pressure system is sweeping in from the west bringing with it heavy rain. The bell rings again, and I still ignore it. The third ring is followed by someone who sounds remarkably like Hazel calling my name through the letter box. Blake Jackson's pencil is still lying on the kitchen table. I tear a freezer bag off the roll, drop the pencil in it and shove it in the freezer behind the frozen peas.

Chapter 70

Hazel is wearing my raincoat and holding my wheelie case. In the hazy twilight, street-lights pick out the raindrops. They fall almost vertically, pounding down, splashing the road, skipping off the tarmac. There'll be accidents. As if to confirm it, somewhere in the distance sirens wail. I take the case from her and move it to the bottom of the stairs.

'I was worried about you,' Hazel says in explanation.

I can hear her nerves in her voice. We both know it isn't normal behaviour to drive thirty miles in terrible weather when there's no need. Look where it got me. She slips off the coat and wipes her feet on the mat.

I deliberately block the way to the kitchen. This is going to be a short visit. 'You shouldn't have come. It's getting bad out there.'

'I couldn't settle after I put the phone down. There was something in your tone ... I thought you might do something stupid. And then you didn't pick up when I tried to call you. I was anxious.'

'I'm fine.' Do I sound fine? I can't tell these days, but I'm beginning to realise that I don't see myself how others see me.

'But also ...' Red blotches appear like a rash on her throat, 'I think I may have done something unhelpful.'

My heart sinks. 'Go on.'

It comes out in a rush. 'Caroline cornered me at the funeral. She asked me to spy on you for her.'

I remember seeing them talking, and being surprised by it. 'Why did you listen to her? She was vile to you.'

'Yeah, I know, but she apologised. She said she hadn't been herself and that there were two sides to the story. She seemed genuine.'

'So she actually said that? Spy on Rachel?'

'I mean, not in so many words. She just said she was concerned, and that because you hated her so much, she didn't feel she could talk to you.' Hazel breathes out slowly. 'She . . . uh . . . she asked me to tell her if you said or did anything that particularly worried me.'

I stare at her in disbelief. 'And did you?'

'Yes, but only once, when you came with Dominic that time. I told her everything, but she didn't seem that interested.'

I'll bet she didn't. Dominic would have got there first.

'After that, well, I couldn't face you. That's the main reason I didn't reply to your message. That and not liking him.'

'And now?'

She takes a deep breath. 'After I spoke to you earlier today, I rang her and told her about our conversation.'

'For God's sake.' The day just gets better and better.

'I was genuinely worried about you.' Hazel grimaces. 'She laughed like she didn't give a shit. She said she couldn't do anything about it because she was out of London. She made me feel nervous, so I started jabbering on about you saying you had proof connecting her to Sean. As soon as I put the phone down, I knew I'd done the wrong thing. That's when I tried to call you back. When you didn't answer, I panicked. I needed to warn you, so I came.'

Her smile is anxious, but I don't smile back. I'm livid. So Caroline knows I have proof that could incriminate her. That isn't good. I glance at my watch. 'How long ago did you have this conversation?'

'Not sure. About an hour and a half?' Hazel looks like she's about to cry. 'I am really sorry. Truly. I thought I could trust her.'

'Well, you wouldn't be the first.'

'I can stay if you don't feel safe.'

'I can look after myself. If I'm worried, I'll call the police, but I think I'll be fine. Caroline and I know where we stand with each other.'

I move round her and open the door. Outside, the road is awash, the gutters full. I can't believe how enormous the raindrops are. On the road to the bridge, the traffic is moving slowly, drivers straining forward, trying to see through the rain and the refracted lights.

'Where are you parked?'

'Across the green.'

She looks so pathetic, I hand her the raincoat. 'Take this. I can get it back another time.'

She hesitates, then thunder rolls and she puts it on, doing the zipper up and lifting the hood over her head. 'I didn't mean to hurt you. You made it clear you didn't want me in your life, that I was just a work friend, but Caroline seemed to really care about me.'

'That's what she's good at.'

Hazel steps into the street, a small, sad figure. She shakes her head. 'That's not the point, Rachel, and you know it.'

As I close the door and walk back down the hall, something changes in the atmosphere, raising the hairs on the back of my neck. I'm not sure what I heard. I hold my breath and listen, but there's nothing now except the driving rain.

I've been horrible to Hazel and I wish I could put it right. But that still doesn't excuse her. Thoughts of eating push their tendrils through my mind, and my fingertips tingle. There isn't much in the house, but there is Deliveroo. I scroll on my phone, salivating as I go through the options. I shouldn't do this, but things have got so bad, surely I deserve it? Just the once, to quash the cravings, then I'll be good. No one will know. Only me, and I can always get rid of it. I can't control everything; sometimes I just have to let go. My mother shakes her head slowly and rolls her eyes, but I don't care about her, or what she thinks.

I'm just about to click on Five Guys when the front door opens, and my heart misses a beat.

Chapter 71

Caroline. Shit. Did she see Hazel leaving? No, it's been ten minutes. She'll have missed her. Keys jangle as they fall into the bowl. I make a mental note to ensure she doesn't take them away with her. Her boots hit the hall floor with a thud. The zipper of her black padded coat – she calls it her shoot coat, and I know it cost over six hundred pounds because Anthony paid for it – hisses down, and her socked feet are silent on the tiled floor. She comes in and acknowledges me with a nod.

'A bit late for a visit, isn't it?'

'It's only nine o'clock. There're a few more of my things I need to pick up.'

'So you're not here because Hazel called you?'

'I have no idea what you're talking about.'

'You knew Sean, and I can prove it, so stop lying and tell me the truth.'

'Rachel, you can't work with Begin Again or Stir without occasionally bumping into the clients. I met all of them.'

'You knew he had been dismissed, so you took advantage and offered him money to get close to me.'

She picks up a magazine and flicks through it while I glare at her.

'You can't deny it,' I say.

'All right. Keep your hair on. I was hoping he'd prise you

359

away from Anthony. But it was you who decided to get him together with my father that evening. It had nothing to do with me.'

'It had everything to do with you.' I raise my voice and she flinches, then gathers herself, fixing a rueful smile on her face.

'I didn't come here to quarrel with you, Rachel. I came to apologise and explain.'

'Right.'

'I mean it. You've had a shit time, and I haven't helped. I . . . um . . . This is difficult for me. There's been no love lost between us, and I accept I'm partly to blame.' She draws a long breath. I wait, fascinated to see where this is going. 'I still think I was justified in hating you for splitting my parents up. I know what Dad was like. There were flirtations, maybe even the odd fling. The difference is he dropped Mum for you. I didn't understand why it was serious that time, so I blamed you when of course it was just as much his fault. And don't you dare tell me I was being unreasonable.' She tilts her head, forcing me to look at her. 'I was a child. I loved my parents, and the thought of them not being together was unbearable.'

'You weren't being unreasonable,' I say quietly.

'Thank you.'

'Tell me about Alexander Stratton.'

She sighs. 'It won't help you, but okay. I'd helped organise a couple of Stir events and had seen him around. He was confident and he came across as unbroken by the system, but he also needed money, so he was perfect.'

'Perfect for what?'

'To lure you into betraying my father. But you know that

360

much. I told him I could guarantee him enough to get his life back on track.'

'How easy was he to convince?'

'Not easy at all.' She sniffs. 'He's a decent bloke and he didn't mean you any harm, but he was desperate and I came along at the right time.'

'How did you get the money to pay him?'

'From Dad. I told him I needed it for singing coaching. I got the first tranche out of him, and would have got it all except you started accusing him of ruining me by funding my lifestyle.'

'I'd had enough of you causing tension between us.'

Caroline grimaces. 'I know. I know. In your shoes I'd have done the same thing. I've come to terms with it.'

'So what exactly happened here that evening? I can't believe Sean deliberately killed Anthony.'

'He didn't mean to, but he's hot-headed. They got into a row over you.'

I nod, acknowledging the possibility. Sean was angry when I left him at the pub.

'There was some pushing and shoving. When I heard what had happened, I had to think quickly. I knew with a bit of digging I could be connected to him, so I persuaded him he had to disappear.'

'Persuaded,' I say, my voice sceptical.

'He didn't want to go back to prison.'

'Were you sleeping with him?'

'No, I was not! And I'm not in a relationship with Dominic either, by the way.'

'Forgive me if I don't believe you.'

'You can believe what you choose. Dominic and I had

an affair years ago, but I'd lost touch with him. When Mum told me the name of the psychiatrist she'd arranged to give me counselling, I couldn't believe it.'

'Why didn't you refuse to see him?'

'Why do you think? I was curious. He's much worse than Xan, by the way. Xan was genuinely fond of you, despite the silly games you played. Dominic's an unscrupulous chancer. I saw the way you looked at him that morning and I knew what he was up to.'

'And you didn't think to warn me?'

She shrugs. 'I was in a bad place. Xan hadn't succeeded with you, and I resented you for that, so after Dad died, I let Dominic throw his hat into the ring with the rich widow while I went home with Mum and Dave. It was a way of hurting you because you'd hurt me. And then the job in Canada came up and that was so wonderful and all-engrossing I parked the rest of the shit in my life.'

'Very sensible,' I say drily. 'And hoped I would get blamed.'

'Everything is so fucked up,' she says. She smiles sadly as she looks around. 'This place means the world to me. I don't think you realise that. I was born here, and everything I went through as a child and teenager happened here. I can't bear the thought of losing it.'

It is beautiful, lived-in, a real home. Perhaps I haven't appreciated its meaning to my stepdaughter. 'You didn't give me a chance to see things through your eyes,' I say. 'You rejected me from the beginning. I was very young; I had no idea what raising a stepdaughter meant.'

'That was Dad's fault.'

I smile for the first time. 'You're partly right. He gave me credit for more maturity than I possessed. You suffered, and I'm sorry. I really am. But this is important. If you know where Xan is, please tell me. According to DS Jones, he hasn't used his cards or his phone since the end of June last year. If he killed Anthony, I want him caught as much as the police do. But I want to talk to him first.' I need to look him in the eye when I ask for the truth. 'I promise I'll do my best to keep you out of it.'

Caroline thinks for a moment, and then says, 'Yeah. All right. I owe you that at least.'

Chapter 72

'Xan has been on the run since Dad's death,' Caroline says. 'I've had no contact with him until now.'

'So you know where he is?'

She closes her eyes for a second, and takes a deep breath. 'He's in Shropshire. Dave and Mum took him in. I can take you to him if you like.'

'I don't believe you.' Yet a tiny part of me clings to the hope that it's true, that Sean is alive and well and all this can be unravelled. 'You're not as good an actress as you think you are.'

She shrugs. 'I deserve that after everything I've done to you. But it's true.'

'Dave wouldn't harbour a criminal.'

'He would if it was his son.'

I laugh out loud; it's so patently ridiculous. 'Xan is not Dave's son.'

'Dave is originally from Manchester. He had a son by his seventeen-year-old girlfriend when he was eighteen. He stuck around for a couple of years, but it was never going to work, and eventually he left the area and lost contact. When Xan went to prison, his mother tracked Dave down and Dave started visiting. Guilt. It was Dave who got him on to the Begin Again programme.'

'Anthony would have told me.'

'Dad didn't know.'

I narrow my eyes. 'Why haven't you handed him in to the police? Surely it's in your interest that he tells them I was involved. It's exactly the kind of information DS Jones is desperate for.'

'Because he's refused to implicate you. Sweet, don't you think? But a little stupid. If I betray him, he's sworn that the only thing he will admit to is taking money off me to seduce you.'

Could that be true? Perhaps he did care about me in the end. Perhaps I haven't been quite as much of a fool as I'd begun to think.

'I can take you to him tonight if you like,' Caroline says.

'Tonight?' I glance at the windows and the raindrops coursing down them. 'Shouldn't we wait until morning?'

'That's the thing. He'll be gone. He has contacts from prison. He's got a new identity. He's going abroad. He'll disappear.'

I don't want to believe her, but there is some logic in what she says. Sean has no choice if he doesn't want to go back inside.

'Let me do this,' she presses. 'I owe you. At the very least you can say goodbye.'

'The Met Office said not to take unnecessary journeys.' But I know I'll go; I can't afford not to.

'I'll drive carefully. I've driven in worse. You should see the storms in Canada; they make this look like a breezy day.'

'How do I know you're telling the truth?'

'Call Dave and ask him.' She picks up her phone and finds his number, taps it and listens. 'Dave. Hi. No, nothing's wrong. Could you have a word with Rachel?' She smiles and hands the phone to me. I say a tentative hello.

'Rachel,' Dave says. 'How can I help?'

'This is a really odd question, but is Alexander Stratton staying with you?'

There's a long pause. 'Caroline told you that?'

'Is he there?'

'He's staying here, yes.' His voice is stiff with restraint. 'But he's not here now. He's out for a run.'

'At this time of night?'

'Less likely to be seen.'

I glance at Caroline. She's watching me. 'Is he your son?'

A deep sigh. 'Yes. For my sins. I'm sorry, Rachel. You've had a tough time and you deserve an explanation. Next time I see you . . .' His voice tails off. He sounds strained, distant. It's odd, because he's such a warm and relaxed person normally. He's choosing his words carefully.

'Caroline has offered to drive me up to your place tonight. To speak to Xan.'

'That's extremely kind of her. We'll be in bed, but Caroline has a key. I'll let Xan know.'

Caroline grabs the phone out of my hand. 'Thanks for being so good about this, Dave. I think it's the right thing to do. We'll try not to wake you.'

I'm surprised at Dave, but I don't have my own children, so how would I know what lengths I'd go to to protect them? For the first time, I allow myself to hope. But hope is a dangerous state. It fills you up like a glass of water until your emotions spill over and you lose control. Hope makes you peculiarly vulnerable.

Chapter 73

We make a dash for the Bentley. Why agree to something when my judgement is off, when a niggling voice tells me I could be walking into a trap? Why do I go along with it, opening the passenger door and sliding onto the tan leather seat, when chances are Caroline is putting on the performance of a lifetime?

This is the first time I've sat in this car since before Anthony died. A flowery perfume lingers in the air, overlaid by the biscuity odour of damp clothes. My nose twitches, but once we set off, I no longer notice it. Caroline taps the touch screen and the radio comes on, removing the need for conversation. There's a feeling of grim intent in the air.

Could Xan really be Dave's son? It just seems so unlikely. DS Jones would call it convenient and roll her eyes. And why wouldn't Dave have shared that information with Anthony? Was he ashamed of Xan? That doesn't sound like Dave at all. It belatedly occurs to me that I should let someone know where I'm going. I'll message Tim. As we turn off the roundabout onto the M4, I slip my hand into my bag, expecting to find my phone, but it isn't there. I check my pockets. Nothing.

'Shit, I forgot my phone.'

Caroline flicks me a glance. 'We're not going back for it.'

Anxiety awakens a tic under my right eye. I press against it with my fingers. I can't swear to it, but I am pretty sure I put my phone in my bag before we left. Caroline could have removed it and I wouldn't have noticed. The suspicion adds to my feelings of unease.

Despite the sheeting rain, Caroline drives fast. Tension stiffens my joints. We don't make conversation and there's a knife-edge to the atmosphere. At the petrol station, I manage to find the wherewithal to offer to pay, and she takes my debit card as if there's no question.

'Do you want a sandwich or anything?'

I nod.

She replaces the nozzle and runs to the shop. She's left the key fob in the car and my eyes drift towards it. I could drive away, leave her here. The thought makes my lungs constrict. These are the exact same weather conditions that I crashed in last time. Worse if anything, because this storm has a name.

I can see her paying at the till. I'm scared. I'm sure now that I put my phone in my bag and that she removed it when I wasn't looking. And then I'm panicking, thinking I've been duped, that something bad is going to happen to me, that Caroline isn't taking me to see Sean, she's taking me to my death. Swallowing back nausea, I shift myself across towards the driver's seat, but the pocket of my coat catches on the handbrake, and by the time I've unhooked it, she is striding across the uncovered part of the forecourt holding her bag over her head. I move back into my own seat, and she jumps in and passes me a sandwich, water and my debit card. I don't know whether she saw.

'Don't look so worried!' She gives a theatrical little

laugh. 'Nothing bad's going to happen to you. You're going to see Sean.'

'Why?'

She darts me a look before her eyes go back to the road. 'What do you mean?'

'I can't work out what's in it for you.'

'I just want to prove once and for all that I haven't done anything bad. I was only trying to help Dave by helping his son, because he's been so good to me. Maybe it was a mistake to get involved, but it's done now.'

I watch the rain laying horizontal tracks along the window as I eat. I want to stay alert, but after a while, a full stomach and exhaustion trump fear, and my eyelids grow heavy.

In my dream, it's Anthony in the driver's seat. He turns his head and smiles. 'Tell her, Rachel,' he says. 'You know secrets can eat you from the inside.' Then he bares his teeth, and there's blood on them.

I wake with a start. 'Where are we?'

'Two minutes away.' Caroline sounds tired. It's still raining. Trees bend like dancers in the wind.

I straighten up, rolling the stiffness out of my shoulders and neck, and brush crumbs off my lap. I feel like crying. It was only a dream, but it brought everything to the surface. What Tim told me about Anthony's change of heart. Who I want to be as a person.

I steal a look at Caroline's profile, so like her father's, with her straight nose and high forehead. Neither of us says another word.

She turns into a driveway and pulls up. With the engine

switched off, the sound of the rain on the roof almost drowns out her voice. 'Ready?'

The house is smaller than I expected, with a slate-tiled roof and two pitched dormer windows. There's a porch above the door and a greenhouse attached to the side. Over to the right, an elderly Land Rover is parked in a yard surrounded by outbuildings. This was once a working farm. These days a local farmer grazes his sheep on the land and Dave just grows enough for their needs.

Uncertain, I get out. The wind whips me as I run under the porch, splashing across puddles that are rapidly fusing into a shallow lake. Caroline unlocks the front door, precedes me inside and switches on the lights. We're standing on a stone floor covered by a tired Persian rug. The hall is murky, the eco bulbs not doing a very good job. She dumps her bag down on the antique storage bench beside the door. There are two empty dog baskets at the far end, and it is deathly quiet. Why is there no barking? Paddy and Katie are supposed to be guard dogs as well as pets. I still retain a vestige of hope that this is real, that I haven't been incredibly stupid, but it's almost one in the morning, and unless they sleep in Dave and Mia's bedroom, which knowing Mia I doubt, they should be scrabbling across the stone floor to greet us.

The door opens behind us, and we both turn.

Chapter 74

Dominic steps inside, dripping wet in a heavy-duty raincoat and walking boots. I look behind him, thinking he must have been walking the dogs, which would be strange at this hour but not impossible. He is alone. His eyes meet mine, but there is literally no connection.

'Where are the dogs?' I ask.

'With Mike,' Caroline says. 'Dave and Mum have gone to Edinburgh. Dave's got an exhibition.'

'I don't understand. When I spoke to him, he implied he was here.' When neither of them responds, realisation dawns. That was Dominic. 'You should have stuck at the acting.' And I should have listened to my gut.

Dominic gives me a disingenuous smile and shrugs modestly.

Caroline, I notice, hasn't taken off her coat. She's approached Dominic and is murmuring something into his ear. Hoping her car fob is in her bag, I grab it off the bench and make a run for the door. Dominic is beside me in a flash. He grasps my arm so hard I cry out.

'Get off me!'

He pushes me down to the floor, and while Caroline struggles to restrain me, he pulls something out of his pocket.

I kick out, my feet bunching up the rug, raising dust and

dog hairs. Caroline's hand is on the back of my head. I'm forcibly doubled over, my hands yanked roughly behind my back. Dominic breathes heavily as he binds my wrists with rope. Between the two of them, they hoist me to my feet and manhandle me outside, marching me across the flooded yard to the Land Rover. Dominic heaves me onto the back seat and Caroline gets in beside me. When I attempt to deal her a blow with my head, she slams my face against the window and holds me there with her body weight. My mouth and nose are pressed against the glass and I can barely breathe.

The window mists up. I wipe it with my cheek and shoulder. A few yards away, Dominic opens the boot of the Bentley, hefts something cumbersome out and loads it over his shoulder. He is a fit man, but whatever it is, its weight causes him to stumble. I wipe the mist away again. He rights himself. The burden he's carrying looks very much like a body, and it's swathed in my raincoat. I suppress a sob of horror. Hazel. It must have been her perfume I smelled earlier.

'Is she dead?' My voice wavers. Of course she's dead. 'How could you?'

'It was an accident.' Caroline gives me a look that chills me to the bone. 'She came out of the house in your raincoat. I thought she was you.'

'You meant to kill me.'

'I didn't want to kill anyone. It just happened.'

She shifts her weight and I fall backwards on the seat like an upturned beetle. Then she climbs out and runs round to open the back door of the Land Rover.

I roll my body and get up on my knees, almost falling

into the footwell in the process. Dominic lumbers over and dumps Hazel in the boot, then jumps into the driver's seat. Caroline climbs in beside me again and we both lurch backwards as he mashes the car into gear. I knock the side of my head against his headrest, and feel myself toppling until I'm wedged between the seats. Dominic swears and shoves me back with his left hand. I end up lolling drunkenly against Caroline. She recoils, but I snatch at the opportunity.

Dry-mouthed, I keep my voice to a murmur, hoping Dominic can't hear. 'I need to tell you something,'

'What?'

She sounds stressed. This is hell for her too. Perhaps there is a chance. The old Land Rover is noisy, and with the storm, Dominic's focus is necessarily fixed on what he can see in the headlights as we bump across the rough ground.

I speak quickly. 'Anthony told Tim he was having second thoughts about the change to his will. They had agreed to meet the week after he died. Whatever it is Dominic's making you do, you don't have to. You can have the lot.'

'Just like that?'

'Yes,' I say, taking in the set of Dominic's shoulders. 'I'll sign everything over to you. You can have it in writing tonight if you like. Just stop what you're doing. The two of us should be able to restrain him.'

I look up and catch Dominic's eyes in the rear-view mirror. He's heard.

'Things have gone much too far for that, I'm afraid,' Caroline says.

We turn onto a track so uneven the car rocks from side to side. My face is wet and snotty, which makes it itch, but I can't even reach to rub it with my shoulder.

Dominic is straining forward. Wrapped around the steering wheel, his knuckles are chalk white. I'm jolted and bruised by the time we come to a shaky stop.

'Can't you get any closer?' Caroline says irritably. 'This is too far to walk with them.'

'The car'll get stuck in the mud,' Dominic says. 'I had a look earlier. We'd never get it out again.'

Caroline swears. He ignores her and goes round to the boot while she drags me out. Dominic stomps ahead, a dark figure hunched against the storm, Hazel's body slumped over his shoulder. I kick Caroline so hard she loses her grip, then I run, heading back up the hill. I only manage a few yards before I trip on the rutted earth. Without my arms to break my fall, I hit the ground so hard my head bounces, and I black out.

Chapter 75

'Get a bloody move on!' Dominic roars and the horror of what is happening engulfs me again.

'I'm trying, for fuck's sake. She's too heavy. Put Hazel in the boat and come back for Rachel.'

'Jesus.'

The mud sucks at my limbs and clothes as I get to my knees and fall forward again. Moments later, Dominic is there, trying to catch his breath as he hooks his arms under mine and hauls me up, forcing me to walk down the hill towards a black lake pitted with raindrops. This is the man I was going to spend my life with. This is the man I thought loved and supported me. It's a pity I realised what he was too late.

'Dominic.' Rain pours down my face. A lock of hair is trapped in the corner of my mouth and I have no way of removing it. 'Dominic, please. She isn't worth killing for. You're ruining your life. Can't you see that?'

'Shut the fuck up,' Caroline says from behind me.

I keep walking even though my bones feel like jelly; it's either that or refuse to move and be killed right here in the mud. The instinct to live up until the last possible moment trumps all others.

Thirty yards away, a rowing boat is moored to a wooden jetty. It looks like a painting. Even in my terror I can appreciate its vulnerable beauty: the night, the howling wind, the bowing trees and the whipped-up water.

'What about Xan? What happened to him?'

Dominic picks his way down a steep path, the heavy oil-skin coat buffeting, dragging me after him like he's pulling a recalcitrant horse, Caroline grabbing my other arm every time I slip. My boots, jeans and coat are waterlogged. I skid in the mud and land on my bottom. Caroline screams in my face as they pull me up, long black rat's tails glued to her cheeks, so stressed I fear she's about to explode. This was evidently not the plan.

They are going to kill me. I jerk away from them and try to run for a second time – the triumph of hope over experience – but Dominic comes after me, spins me round and punches me hard in the face. A universe of stars revolves before my eyes as I reel. Between them they half drag, half carry me to the boat, and I sink to my knees through sheer exhaustion.

'You wanted to see Xan?' Caroline screams into my face, spittle flying. 'I'll take you to see him.'

Chapter 76

Dominic tumbles me into the boat, where I land on Hazel's body. I cry out in revulsion and shuffle up onto a seat. Hazel's eyes are open and blank. Caroline clambers in and sits facing me. Dominic pushes us out into the water, then jumps in and grabs the oars. He pulls awkwardly, then settles into a rhythm. I peer through the darkness at Caroline. She's trembling almost as much as I am. Wet and cold, frightened and traumatised; this is not the outcome she envisaged. The oars cut the water with a splash that barely registers.

'Why are you doing this?'

'I wouldn't have had to if Hazel had kept her mouth shut. You've connected me to Xan and you would have told the police.'

'How do you know I haven't already?'

'Because DS Jones called me when I was on the way to yours. We had a long conversation about Dad. She wanted to reassure me that it wasn't her choice that you'd been granted bail, and that she was still investigating Dad's death. If she'd heard from you, I think we'd have been talking about something very different, don't you?' She waits, and when I don't answer, she goes on. 'You've taken everything from me, Rachel. From the day you met my father, you've been stealing my life, and you went on stealing it even after he died. You're not taking my free-dom too.'

'I pity you.'

I turn my face away from her and huddle into my sod-den coat, trying not to imagine what lies ahead. Close to my feet is a coiled stretch of rope and some weights; the kind with handholds used to anchor down marquees and gazebos. We have some in Kew, kept in a cupboard in the utility room for garden parties because there aren't enough soft areas to stick pegs into. I wonder if these are the same ones, but they can't be. This whole escapade has an air of panic about it, as if the pair are responding to each develop-ment as it hits them, like diving into waves and hoping you aren't churned so hard you hit a rock. No, Dominic must have got hold of them from one of the outbuildings and brought them down here. Hence the wet coat and boots when we arrived. I imagine he's wondering how the hell he got to this point.

He rows us out to the middle of the lake, where he and Caroline tie the weights to Hazel's legs and roll her over-board. Her body goes in with barely a splash. For a moment the raincoat balloons with air, then it too disappears.

It's my turn. Dominic tugs my boots off and attempts to bind my ankles. When I kick out, Caroline slaps my face. She straddles me while he finishes his knots then attaches the remaining weights with more nylon rope.

'Don't do this,' I urge him, my voice cracking. 'You haven't killed anyone yet. She's done this to you. You're as much her victim as I am.'

His eyes are almost black, his mouth a thin line.

'That's not quite true,' Caroline says. 'He was the reason

Dad died. He pushed him too hard and he fell and cracked his head.'

'I don't understand.' I scramble to catch up. 'You were there? Sean was never there at all?' His lack of response tells me I'm right. 'You didn't mean to kill him, though, did you?' I say desperately. 'If you kill me now, that's murder.'

Dominic's eyes are bloodshot, his lips cracked. Thunder rolls and crashes as he speaks into my ear. 'He wasn't dead. I finished him off. Suffocated him.'

'Why?' My mouth hangs open.

'Why the fuck do you think? He could identify me.'

'Come on,' Caroline shouts.

'It's all over now,' Dominic says, again so quietly that only I can hear. 'I'm fucked whatever I do.'

He struggles to get up, as clumsy as a walrus out of the water, and takes hold of my legs while Caroline rolls me to the side of the boat, which rocks dangerously.

I try to tell her what Dominic said, but she hits me so hard the pain empties my mind of all its words. My scream is loud enough to disturb a pair of ducks. They explode from under their shelter of reeds and take off across the lake in a flurry of panic. Dominic hauls up the weights and lets them drop into the water.

I wedge my feet against the side, yelling with pain when the rope jerks my ankles, burning them. His hands go under my arms and round my shins. He's going to tip me forward. I brace.

Behind me, Caroline has her hands on either side of the boat, trying to steady it. Her efforts are wasted. I feel Dominic work at the knot on my wrists, and then he whispers something that sounds like 'Now fuck off,' though maybe I'm imagining it; maybe he simply says, 'Fuck you,' before he releases me, pushing me backwards into the swollen water, where the weights quickly drag me to the bottom.

As I stare through the opaque gloom of the lake, I see you. What's left of you. I remember you now. You are tall, you have beautiful brown eyes and you smell of the morning. Coffee and soap and toothpaste. I don't know what you look like without your clothes, but I know what your forearms are like, I know your ankles, and the triangle of chest below your throat. I know the feel of your skin under my fingertips, and I know your smile, the way your eyes crinkle. I know one of your ears sticks out more than the other, I know your hairline is just beginning to recede at the temples. I know you wanted me and cared about me. I know where you came from, or at least as much as you told me on that last day, but what I didn't know until this moment was where you went.

I'm so sorry. So very sorry.

June 2023

Chapter 77

CAROLINE

Rachel has gone to see her mother. Caroline wonders what DS Jones said to precipitate this unusual filial behaviour. She was sure mother and daughter were estranged. But actually, who cares? Rachel won't be back until tomorrow. It's a miracle. Her shoulders have felt as though they've been up round her ears lately, aching with tension. She can't bear the house when that woman is in it. It was bad enough when her father was alive, but since he died, it's been torture. And there's no respite, because even if Rachel's out, Caroline is permanently on edge, listening for her key in the door. No doubt Rachel feels the same about her.

Caroline came downstairs just as the detective was leaving – she'd been waiting – and Jones acknowledged her with a smile of satisfaction, so she must have gleaned something to her liking. With any luck there will be an end to this soon. She's feeling good.

She'll invite Dominic round this evening. He'll have calmed down by now, and she's forgiven him for what happened. It was an accident after all. They can get a Deliveroo, get pissed. Fuck each other's brains out like they used to.

She calls him, sitting at the kitchen table on the chair her father favoured.

'Dominic,' she breathes when he picks up.

'Good to hear from you, Caroline.'

'Do you really mean that?'

You can never tell with him. That's how he keeps her interest. There's an edge of insecurity to all their interactions. She sits up straighter, adjusts her posture, as though he can see her. She can already feel his hot breath on her neck, his fingers in her hair.

'Weirdly, I do.'

'Are you busy? Do you want to come over here?'

He hesitates. She remembers their last conversation. She hung up on him at the hospital.

'Don't you think it's too soon?'

'Come in the back way. I'll unbolt the gate. No one need know.'

She briefly wonders, while she's showering, whether his pleasure at hearing from her has more to do with her father's legacy than her own charms, and dismisses the thought. They've quarrelled violently in the past, and yet they've always found each other again. They are meant to be.

Later, she leaves him in bed sleeping and comes downstairs. It's only ten o'clock and she's restless. She pours herself a glass of water and drinks it standing at the sink. She tries to hang on to the ecstasy of being with him again, of being forgiven, but her insecurity is already gnawing at the edges. The fact that he's staying the night is a good sign, isn't it? He's never stayed over here before; there simply hasn't been the opportunity. They've used his flat, and in the morning she's always had that niggling feeling that he's relieved when she leaves, that she's been shooed out like she's overstayed her welcome. She wrinkles her nose. This is a new her, since her father's death. She has to at least pretend to be confident. That's the only way to hang on to men like Dominic. Pretend you don't really care one way or the other.

A movement in the dark garden makes her take a swift breath. A fox? No, something a lot bigger than that. There's someone out there. When Dominic arrived, she rushed out, and he moved towards her, and it started there, the kissing and tearing at clothes. They forgot to bolt the gate. She moves quickly and switches the lights out, then grabs a small knife from the magnetic strip on the wall and holds it behind her back. She checks the French windows are locked and peers into the darkness, almost jumping out of her skin when a figure steps forward and walks up to the glass.

Chapter 78

It's Xan. Caroline quickly conceals the knife in her sleeve and unlocks the door. She blocks it, not letting him in. 'Get the fuck out of here, or I'll call the police.'

'I want to talk to you.'

'There's nothing to say.'

'You're trying to pin this on me and Rachel. You know perfectly well your father's death had nothing to do with me. You told me not to come here that night. You made it clear what would happen to Kam and the kids if I didn't do what you said.'

'You still had a choice. Just because I requested that you stay away doesn't mean you did.'

'Well, that's true at least.'

She frowns. 'I don't understand.'

'I *was* here, Caroline. I assumed you'd told me not to keep my appointment in case I dropped you in it. Either that, or you just wanted rid of me because I'd failed with Rachel. And you're right, I did have a choice and I was still in two minds, so I went. I had a drink in the pub first. Rachel saw me and followed me in. She was in a state because your father had just hit her.'

'That's a lie. My father would never hit a woman.'

'You can believe what you like. It helped me make my mind up. I decided I would talk to Anthony, but it would

386

be a very different conversation. I didn't want his charity; I wanted to tell him what I thought of him. But your friend got there before me. I saw Anthony let him in, then I went round the back. I'd already googled the place, so I knew about the alleyway. Your gate wasn't locked.'

She's surprised she doesn't feel shock, or even anger. Physically things are happening: her breath shortening and audible, her fingers tingling. Is this panic? She looks into his face; Xan is unafraid, brave in his righteousness, keen to show her how clever he is. Well, let him. 'Go on.'

'I saw what happened. Rachel needs to know she isn't guilty of anything.'

'It's not going to help you, though, is it? If she regains her memories, she'll still think you were responsible for Anthony's death. She won't believe your story about a mystery visitor.'

He shakes his head. 'I don't care. I'm not abandoning her. I've been in prison. I can look after myself. If she gets done for this, she won't survive it. That's why she needs to be told that she isn't guilty of anything, because I didn't keep my appointment with your father. I know she must think I did, and that it's her fault.'

'What a hero.'

'I've never claimed that.' He smiles. How can he smile at a time like this? It's infuriating.

'You won't get any thanks. Rachel never loved you. She and Dad were going through a rocky patch, so I expect you made her feel better about herself. She has very low self-esteem, you know. She's a recovering bulimic.' She can see she's shocked him. 'She didn't tell you that? Not as close as you thought, then.'

387

He glares at her. 'I want to know the name of the man Anthony let in.'

Caroline contemplates him. She understands two things. One: there's no point trying to elicit sympathy by sobbing prettily. Unlike most men, Xan is immune to her charms. And two: he's not stupid.

She thinks about Dominic asleep upstairs, oblivious to the danger they're in. Should she scream? Maybe not yet. 'So you're going to tell the court you watched my father die and didn't do anything about it? I can't see that going down well.'

He just looks at her. She used to fancy him. She hates his face now.

'I'm not proud of myself,' he says finally. 'I saw him go down, and when he didn't get up, I left. Call it an ex-convict's instinct: don't get involved. And to tell you the truth, part of me was glad he was getting his comeuppance. I was even sorry it wasn't me meting out the punishment, but now I wish I had intervened. I didn't want him to die.'

'None of this will hold water.'

'I'll take my chances. You can't sustain this, Caroline; sooner or later your lies are going to catch up with you. Whoever it is, give him up.'

She almost glances at the ceiling. 'I'm not going to do that.'

'And I'm not going to let Rachel be blamed. Her memories could come back at any time, and I want to make sure the police have this information before that happens. I don't want to be accused of feeding her a story.'

Caroline sighs. 'All she'll remember is that she sent you to the house when she knew Dad would be alone.'

'I'll take that chance.'

'If it's more money you want, I can get it for you.'

He laughs bitterly. 'I regret every penny I've ever taken from you. I certainly don't want any more. I'm going to the police. Even if they don't believe me, they'll take a harder look at you.'

'It won't get you anywhere without evidence. You have a criminal record for violence, you were dropped from the charity for thieving, you tried to get back at my father by seducing his wife. You're a nasty piece of work. They'll enjoy taking you down.'

'You're forgetting. You phoned me.'

That was a stupid mistake.

'There was a witness, and it'll be on both our phones.'

Caroline remembers with an inner shudder the knife piercing Dominic's flesh. She also remembers the immediate kick she got from it, before reality hit home. She could so easily have killed him. It was only luck that made him veer at the last moment so the blade missed a major artery. She finds it hard to cope when men refuse to do what she wants, but she likes the rage. She should probably see a therapist.

'Can't we come to some arrangement?' She smiles softly at Xan, lowering her lashes.

'No, Caroline. We cannot. You have until nine o'clock tomorrow morning to change your statement, then I'm going to walk into the police station and ask to see the investigating officer. It's up to you.'

He turns his back on her and walks towards the garden gate. She strokes her thumb along the knife blade. She does not want to go to prison. She does not want to lose the chance to spend her inheritance – the silver lining to her daddy's death. She does not want to give up the successful acting career she knows she's destined to have. She certainly doesn't want to be famous for all the wrong reasons.

She moves swiftly, grasping him by the shoulder as he lifts the latch. As he turns to shake her off, she plunges the knife into his stomach. He grunts, then sinks to the ground, clutching the wound. He looks surprised.

'Surely prison taught you not to turn your back on an enemy,' she says as blood spurts through his fingers and flows onto his jeans.

She pulls the knife out and stabs again, her eyes locked onto his. She is Rosamund Pike in *Gone Girl*, she is Sharon Stone in *Basic Instinct*, she is Bridget Fonda in *Single White Female*. Forensic officers have been here already; the case is closed. She'll clean up thoroughly, but they won't be back. She doubts anyone is going to miss him.

When it's over, she goes back inside and washes her hands, interested to see that they're trembling. Her whole body is shuddering. It isn't an unpleasant sensation. She deletes the record of the call from both their phones and, to be safe, removes the SIM card from his and destroys it with the hand blender.

She runs upstairs. Dominic is still sound asleep. She kisses his naked shoulder, then shakes him awake.

'What?' He looks at her blearily.

'Something's happened. Get dressed.'

If he wants her and her father's money, he's going to have to earn it.

July 2024

Chapter 79

RACHEL

Above me the boat moves away, oars dipping under the water, a shadow swallowed by the darkness. At first I think I'm imagining it, but as I struggle, the rope around my wrists unexpectedly loosens. It takes a fraction of a second to free my hands.

Lungs bursting, I bend, swimming myself down to my feet, trying not to panic as my fingers work at the knot attaching the weights. It was tied in haste, the pair of them anxious to be out of there, and it succumbs to my busy fingers. The weights fall away and I kick up like a mermaid, my ankles still bound together, and break water with a gasp. I catch my breath, then pull my knees up to my chest and grab hold of my feet. The final knot is tighter, but I know I'm going to survive, and that I have time, as long as I'm not seen. Caroline has her back to me, and Dominic seems not to have noticed me bobbing around in the water.

It occurs to me, now that I'm able to think beyond the immediate danger, that he deliberately sabotaged Caroline's plan, giving me a slim chance of survival. Not a murderous *fuck you* then, but a less lethal *now fuck off*. A chance. Does he have a conscience after all? More likely he wants to raise the possibility of leniency in his sentencing if they get caught. He knows it's the end and he's a strategist.

Dominic and Caroline drag the boat onto the shore, dark figures in a haze of rain. I doubt Caroline will take the time to check I haven't surfaced, because time is running out if she wants to get back into London in time to pretend this never happened. As they run clumsily up the muddy slope towards the Land Rover, I take a deep breath and start swimming. It's slow going, the far bank taking its sweet time to solidify. Above the noise I can hear the protesting rev of the Land Rover's engine. The wheels must have sunk into the mud. With any luck it'll keep them occupied while I swim to the bank and climb out.

The rain gets in my eyes, half blinding me, and my arms tire quickly. Every few seconds I need to rest, rolling onto my back and floating, eyes and mouth closed tight as the rain batters my face. I tell myself this isn't the sea; there's no tide to fight. If I just keep going, arms pulling, legs pushing in a steady breaststroke, I'll make it. And then I'm there and gasping as I crawl out, clinging to grass and reeds.

I lie on the bank for a long time, heaving, my cheek in the sludge. Once my legs feel up to it, I get up and force them to carry me. Rainwater pours down the back of my neck, waves of shivering assault my body, my clothes feel like they're lined with lead. I have a vague idea of the shape and extent of Dave and Mia's land, simply because I'm nosy enough to have googled the house, so I'm confident that if I keep walking, I'll hit a road.

Thunder rolls across the sky. In the white glow from the fork of lightning that follows seconds later, I make out the silhouette of a solitary farmhouse. I turn myself towards it and stump across a meadow, liquid dirt sucking at my bare feet. I clamber over a gate into a field and pick my way over soggy tilled ground until I reach a country lane. Not far now. There must be a gate onto the property somewhere close by.

I keep walking. I'm so cold. It's the dead of night, and without street-lights it's almost impenetrably dark. I can barely make out the shape of the lane as there are no road markings, and I weave like a drunk, off balance and disorientated. It doesn't help that my ears are full of water.

There are headlights in the distance. I don't think it can be them, but I'm taking no chances. I squat down in the ditch and hold my breath. The car stops suddenly, skidding on the wet tarmac. It isn't the Bentley. It's a black Audi. Dominic's car. The passenger door opens and Caroline gets out.

'I didn't see anything,' Dominic yells. 'Get in. We need to move.'

She ignores him and comes towards me, tilting her head, then she smiles. 'I told you,' she shouts back. 'She's here. Give me a hand.'

I lurch up and stumble away. I'm exhausted, cold and dizzy and I can barely keep upright, my feet hitting the ground like mallets. Dominic catches me easily.

'I gave you a chance. I can't do any more for you,' he hisses.

Caroline is pulling me by my coat, her hands slick with moisture. I've used up every ounce of energy getting here; there's nothing left to fight with. My legs are like jelly, my muscles refusing to obey commands shrieked by my brain.

My legs won't kick, my hands won't curl into fists. My whole body is flailing, unable to process the emergency.

My father once said, when I asked him why he didn't fight his corner with my mother, that sometimes it's better to lean in to your nemesis. I was disgusted at his response, and defeated by it. Now I understand what he meant. Fighting hurts. Giving in is soporific.

We reach the car, and I know I mustn't get into it. It sparks something in me. I cling to the door frame until Caroline gives a shout of impatience and whacks my head against it. The pain is unbelievable, and my body goes slack, my hands loosening.

As they shove me onto the back seat, the world pulses with a light that washes everything in blue. Dominic steps back. Caroline covers my mouth with her hand.

'Don't say a fucking word.'

I don't need to and she knows it. I can hear it in her voice.

Chapter 80

When I wake, sluggish, dopey and sticky-eyed, I'm in a hospital bed. Last night slowly comes back to me. First the police station, where I handed over my sodden clothes and submitted to inspection by a forensics officer. She photographed me, then took samples from my torn fingernails, my skin and my hair before allowing me to shower. The rest of it, what went before, what I saw beneath the surface of the lake, I'm not ready to think about. I had a lucky escape and that's enough for now.

In the small hours of the morning, Dave had got an alert on his phone that there were intruders on his land. The police were slow to arrive because the unit was dealing with a gang stealing machinery from a farm a few miles away. Rural crime is a problem in the area. Dominic thought he'd overridden the sensor, but all he'd done was pause it for half an hour, by which time Caroline and I were about to arrive.

'Looks like you've had a rough night.'

My eyes flicker open. Standing at the end of my bed is DS Helen Jones, neat as a pin, a reusable cup of coffee in her hand. The smell of its contents gives me a headrush.

She places a clear plastic bag containing my belongings on the end of the bed, pulls over a chair and sits down. 'Are you up to talking? The sooner we get your statement, the better.'

I shuffle upright, pulling the pillow behind my back. 'Dominic Parrish killed Anthony. He told me last night.'

'I know. We've had a confession. He's saying it was an accident.'

That's not what he told me. Do I report what he actually said? That he'd finished my husband off? With everything that was going on – the panic, the storm and Caroline a whirlwind of desperate fury – I was in no state to make sound judgements and could have misheard or misconstrued. And then there is the unavoidable truth that I would be dead had he not given me a slim chance of survival. Quid pro quo. By not speaking up now, I'll have paid my debt in full. But then I think about Anthony alone in the house, not as fit as he used to be, hoodwinked by his daughter and her lover. Yes, I'd wanted to leave him, but what he had become doesn't cancel out what he was before that: a good husband who loved me, built me up, gave me confidence.

'He's lying.'

I have a fit of coughing. Jones pours water from a plastic jug into my glass and hands it to me. She picks up her notebook and pen and I tell her what I know. That Dominic hadn't gone meaning to kill, that he had gone at Caroline's behest to trick Anthony into believing I was unfaithful. Caroline so badly wanted her father to ditch me; her hatred of me had become an obsession. Dominic had killed him after the scuffle that had left Anthony unconscious, because he couldn't take the risk.

Jones looks up. 'Was there a witness?'

'Only Xan, unfortunately.'

She has gone bright red. 'The signs of asphyxia are non-

398

specific, so it's possible they were missed, especially since Mr Gordon had been half strangled; but I'll follow that up.'

I don't say it because I know she's thinking it, but in that case it's a pity Anthony was cremated. 'Did you find Xan and Hazel?'

'Yes. The divers went in at dawn. I'm very sorry about your friend.'

'Me too.' Hazel wanted to help me even after I pushed her away. I'll never forgive myself. There is no crime in wanting to be someone's friend. 'Has Caroline been charged?'

'She has. For the murders of Alexander Stratton and Hazel Gifford, and for your attempted murder. She's pleading self-defence for Stratton, accusing him of stalking her since she met him when she was working with the Begin Again programme, and manslaughter for Gifford. She says it was raining so hard she failed to see her crossing the road. As far as you're concerned, she's maintaining that she was being controlled by Dominic.'

'Will she get away with it?'

'I doubt it. There's no evidence of Stratton stalking her. But you never know with juries. And she's a good actor.'

'She told me Xan was Dave's son.'

'That was rubbish.'

'I thought so.'

'So why did you get in the car with her?' DS Jones's eyebrows rise. 'Surely you realised it was a trap?'

'I wanted it to be true.'

'It very nearly got you killed.'

'Dominic loosened the rope around my wrists before he pushed me in. He was giving me a chance.'

'Or he was panicking and fumbled it.'

399

'I don't think so.'

Jones frowns. 'You were in love with him at one point.'

'That's over now. I just wanted you to know that at the end he tried to do the right thing.'

'And if we hadn't turned up when we did, do you think he'd have given you another chance?'

I allow myself a moment to picture Dominic when I met him that day in Richmond, his soaking T-shirt flat against his muscular chest; his wet hair and gorgeous smile as he grasped his thighs and caught his breath.

'No.'

Jones nods and stands up. We both know that Dominic will swear he would have done. 'I'll leave you to get some rest. I'll be driving back to London once I've seen the Chief Constable. If you need anything further, you have my number.'

'So it's really over?'

She hesitates. 'If you mean will the investigation into you be dropped? Yes. And the charge of perverting the course of justice has been withdrawn. Your trial won't go ahead. Your lawyer has been informed. He knows where you are. I expect he'll contact you shortly.'

SOME TIME LATER

Chapter 81

I sit in the front room while a smartly dressed estate agent who is trying and failing to conceal his excitement at the opportunity to market this house and earn a whopping commission works his way through the last fourteen years of my life with a laser tape measure and a Dictaphone. Another man takes photographs. I'm rattling round this place and I'm not sad to be leaving. My hair has grown out, my bones have mended, my mind is calmer and I've gone up a jeans size and haven't let it drive me crazy. My relationship with food is improving. I walk or jog every day and find being outside highly beneficial. I don't have a job, but I'm working towards a therapist's qualification and expect to start seeing my first clients under supervision in a year's time. It'll fit in with my future plans as well as giving meaning to my life. If I do an inventory of myself, physically and mentally, overall I'm pleased with my progress.

Caroline wasn't granted bail because the prosecution convinced the court there was a risk she might hurt someone else. Namely me. In their turn, Dominic's legal team persuaded them he was a victim of Caroline's manipulative behaviour, proved by his last-minute change of heart when he attempted to save me, so he is currently out on bail. I have no idea where he is, and despite that act of compassion, I don't want to know.

I visit Caroline every couple of weeks. I won't abandon her. It isn't out of pity; it's because she is her father's daughter and I want to do something for my husband. She gave permission the first time out of boredom. It wasn't much fun. The prison was loud, intimidating and upsetting. I left with my head clanging from the noise, the combined odours of institutional food, stale sweat and disinfectant clinging to the inside of my nostrils and the taste of the air on my tongue. I've become accustomed to it. Caroline settled surprisingly quickly and behaves herself. About one month in, she began teaching presentation skills to prisoners coming up for release. Apparently they love her there.

I see Anthony in my stepdaughter. She possesses his dry sense of humour and firm grasp of situations, and now that she's been given boundaries, she's found focus. She will always be self-serving and verging on narcissistic, but since I've come to accept that she was born and nurtured that way, it's been easier to understand how those personality traits could also make her vulnerable. As with her dad, it must hurt like hell when things go wrong. I liaise with Mia so that our visits don't clash. Our relationship has become warmer because she's come to trust my word. She knows I won't desert her daughter. She is one of the few people with whom I can talk honestly about Anthony.

Caroline's trial begins tomorrow and is expected to last six weeks. Given Sean's criminal record – I've tried my best, but I can't think of him as Xan or Alexander – it is not inconceivable that her plea of self-defence will be believed, but after the trial, I will go to the press with my story and at least attempt to make people understand that he was not a bad person, or a violent one.

On the charge of my attempted murder, Caroline is citing a period of undiagnosed paranoia and psychosis after the death of the father she was emotionally reliant on. On the charge of killing Hazel Gifford, she is pleading manslaughter again. With the rain pelting against the windscreen, wipers flying, she simply didn't see her run out into the road swathed in my old raincoat. She's pleading not guilty to perverting the cause of justice, although Dominic has used her coercion of him in his own defence. Coward that he is, he is putting the entire blame on her. *She made me do it.* Pathetic. I don't know who to believe and the jury may not either, so when it comes to the crunch, it'll be down to the most convincing actor.

The thing that makes me angriest is that they took Anthony's last months from him. I could have made them good months; loving months. He could have been surrounded by the women he was closest too: me, his daughter, Mia. I wouldn't have kept anyone away from him. If he'd told me what was happening, I'd have ended the relationship with Sean, taken compassionate leave and remained at his side until the end. Caroline stole that good death from her father, stole from me the opportunity to make him feel loved as his life ended. Instead he died a horrible, angry death at the hands of a stranger and believing I was responsible. I was barely given the chance to grieve.

I know he would have wanted me to support his daughter. I'm not being a martyr. Well, perhaps a little. But I am genuinely happy to do it. I'm even hoping that if she is convicted, she isn't sent too far away. I've surprised myself

405

by keeping everything crossed that this won't be the case. I even put off selling this house until now because I didn't want to make a decision before I knew where she would end up.

I am paying her legal fees. A chunk of the IFR shares worth five and a half million has been donated by the newly set-up Anthony Gordon Trust to the Begin Again programme and Stir. The remaining chunk, valued at one point eight million, is being put to use in Caroline's defence. People think I'm mad, but despite everything, it's what I want. I didn't try hard enough with her when she was still young enough to influence, and I blamed my failure to connect on her. This is one small way I can atone for that. Anthony should shoulder some of the blame. He allowed me to be the bad one. He never encouraged Caroline to take her ire out on him. He wanted to be 'popular Dad'.

The agent is standing in the doorway looking embarrassed. He's caught the client enjoying a private reverie, momentarily lost to the world. My face is naked.

'Sorry,' I say. 'I was miles away.'

I assume he knows about me. You'd have to be living under a rock in the middle of the ocean not to have seen the stories that flooded the media in the aftermath of that nightmare. *Lake of Horrors.*

'We're all done,' he says. 'I'll draw up the particulars and send them to you to check. We should be able to get them online for Monday. There's already a lot of interest. This is a very desirable area.'

My mother rang this morning, asking for money. She says I owe her for my education, my room and board and all

406

the trouble she had from me. She says I'm rich. She's never asked before, and I guess that's because she knew she wouldn't be able to wheedle Anthony. They disliked each other from the start, my mother baffled and annoyed that he didn't respond to her flirting, Anthony feeling a deep distaste for the way she behaved when the attention in the room was not on her.

I'll pay her something, because she did feed, clothe and educate me. It's like any other invoice. There's no emotion attached these days. When I was little, I thought my parents were perfect. My mother was as beautiful as any princess in a Disney movie, my father strong and handsome and kind. I was a pretty little girl, and at first Mum was proud of this, showing me off, dressing me up, brushing my hair, making me perfect. But once I was four, that changed. I felt her jealousy, even if I didn't understand it or know what to call it, and it broke my heart.

Dad adored me, but his outward displays of affection grew few and far between because he was a coward. Mum tutted at my weight, talked about it in front of me, pinched my chub and fed me doughnuts and milkshakes. I didn't realise until much later that she needed to damage me. That was around the time I was eleven, and girls at school were talking about anorexia and bulimia, throwing the words around like they were projects, something to boast knowledge of. I know this girl . . .

Bulimia was how I survived my adolescence; men were how I survived my early adulthood. Each time I fell quickly and I fell hard. To be wanted was the ultimate validation. But they never stuck around. Perhaps they understood what they were there for and didn't want to be propping up this young woman's self-esteem, pretty though I was. With Anthony, all that fell away. Of course there were relapses – with food, not men – but by and large I had it under control. Until he hit me. And then there was Sean. Right place, right time.

Sean may have been manipulated by Caroline, he may have embarked on our friendship for any number of reasons, but I truly believe he cared about me. It's hard to call it love, even though it felt that way at the time, because we were virtual strangers, but it was powerful, and in the end we wanted to help each other even though there was risk for each of us, and if that isn't love, what is?

Sean. You left my life as suddenly as you came into it, but I won't forget you. If it hadn't been for Caroline, I'd never have met you, never have fallen for you. I regret the damage it's caused, I deeply regret that Hazel got caught up in it and lost her life, but despite everything, I don't blame you for deceiving me, because I know at the end you were true.

The police told me what happened to you, but they don't know why you turned up in the garden that fateful night, because Caroline keeps insisting you came to hurt her and she is the only one who knows.

I sometimes cringe when I think about the rules I laid down, the silly games I played. What was I thinking? I should have taken an earlier train. I shouldn't have played with fire.

I don't avoid the District Line; there is nothing quite like the London Underground for getting you around the city. I still sometimes think I glimpse your reflection in the darkened glass as the train speeds through tunnels. It never fails to jerk something inside me awake.

As for those future plans, I know what I want for myself, and I have the money, time and love to devote to it. I have an appointment at the clinic on Monday. You told me, didn't you? You said, if you want a baby, you can have a baby. I have given myself permission.

Acknowledgements

My first thank you goes to London Transport. The tube has carried me around London since I was old enough to travel independently, which, in the 1970s, was a fair bit younger than would be considered safe now. It's carried me to school, shops, jobs, friends and boyfriends. I've sat on the Circle Line with my heart breaking because I've been dumped, I've sat on the Northern Line giggling and drunk with friends after a night out. I've used it to get to work, to dates, to the theatre, to some of the best and worst moments of my life. I've fallen in love on it and said goodbye on it. I've traveled the Piccadilly Line euphoric after my first visit to a literary agent and again to Corvus Books. It's about time I gave it a starring role in a thriller.

At AM Heath, I'd like to thank my amazing agent Rebecca Ritchie for being such a support and source of advice, Oli Munson who read *The Commuter* and gave me lots more work to do, and their invaluable colleague Harmony Leung.

I feel so lucky to be published by Corvus. Thank you to Sarah Hodgson for being a fantastic editor, whose patience with my complicated plots and ability to steer me into taking my novels to the next level, gives me confidence and makes me want to do better and work harder, and to

Felice McKeown, Kirsty Doole and Dave Woodhouse for their hard work in Sales, Publicity and Marketing. To Jane Selley for the copyedit and Mayura Uthayakumaran for the proofreading. Thank you for your patience.

To Anthony Fowler and John Goodchild for their tips on inheritance and financial matters, of which I'm alarmingly ignorant. To Graham Bartlett who advised me on police procedure. To Liz McAulay for my gorgeous publicity photos. To Derek Collett for helping me find the snags in the very first draft.

To the reviewers, bloggers and kind readers who go online to share their love of books. I am so grateful to you for getting my books seen. It's a tough world, and there are lots of amazing titles coming out every week, so your belief in my work and generous words are such a boon.

And lastly to my family and my friends, writers and otherwise, for all your love and support. I genuinely couldn't do this without you.

MORE GRIPPING THRILLERS FROM
EMMA CURTIS

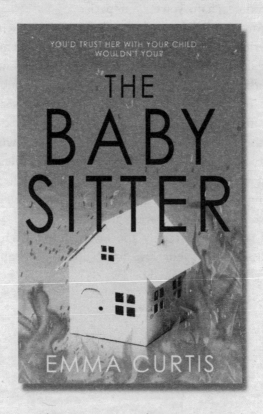

Three women. Three secrets.

But only one of them is
capable of murder...

'EMMA CURTIS IS A GENIUS'
ANDREA MARA